HUDSON HOUSE VICTORIAN

MYSTERIES

www.hudsonhousemysteries.com

"For all of us there is a twilight zone between history and memory; between the past as a generalized record which is open to relatively dispassionate inspection and the past as a remembered part of, or background to, one's own life."

—Eric J. Hobsbawn
The Age of Empire

کس کو سنائیں حالِ دلِ زار اے ادا!
آوارگی میں ہم نے زمانے کی سیر کی

Who will hear the sadness of my heart,
Ada? In wandering life's journey took us
near and far.

—Umrao Jan Ada, Lucknow courtesan
from a novel of the same name
by Mirza Muhammad Hadi Rusva
trans. from Urdu by David Matthews

SHADOWS
OF
EMPIRE

ALAN MCKEE

Proof reading: Margaret Ferris

Photographs of British India with permission of
www.harappa.com

ISBN
978-0-9813524-2-8

Great gate of the Hoosienabad bazaar, Lucknow, circa 1870

Jane Booth's Diary, which plays such a large
part in this history.

Chapter 1
Lucknow—before and during the seige

I begin these pages in the shadow of the gallows. I write them to prove that I am not guilty of any crimes whatever, in spite of what my accusers say. If I am caught, I know that any British court will almost certainly condemn me to death. But the truth behind the events must be known, and I am now more certain than ever of that truth. I have delved ever deeper into the mysterious crimes of which I am accused and have learned that they are rooted in my childhood, which I spent in my birthplace, Lucknow, court city of the kingdom of Oudh in Northern India. So, I must begin there.

More than any other place I have ever seen, Lucknow with its golden minarets and gleaming stuccoed buildings, polished to look like the whitest marble, brought the *Arabian Nights* to life. Lucknow was a place of dreams made real. Courtyards with magical buildings and luxuriant lawns where peacocks wandered, uttering their piercing cries, were reminiscent of Persian paintings and ceramics. Deer roamed in the parks which lay around the *Nawab's* palaces, and even the bungalows of the East India Company where we lived stood near gardens and fruit trees that would have been envied by the builders of Versailles. The scent of exotic blossoms was everywhere and even stole into the little gothic church the Company had built for us near the Residency. Acres and acres of mango, orange, pomegranate, nectarine and date palm grew all around us. Less evident to my childish senses was the rich cultural life that also grew in the city's unique environment of security and the royal patronage of the astonishingly wealthy *Nawabs*. In Lucknow, literature, music and dance flourished and created a civilized, sybaritic way of life known throughout India as *Lahknavi*. Lucknow was arguably the most refined and beautiful city on the subcontinent, perhaps the world.

In many ways, the city of Lucknow was a tangible symbol of the fabulous cultural and financial wealth the Honourable Company stole from India. Perhaps that is why some later saw war-torn Lucknow as a symbol of the deterioration of our eastern empire. To the puritanical Dalhousie, the Governor General of India who presided over the illegal and fradulent rape of Oudh, Lucknow was a place of rampant immorality that needed to be taken over by us, the British.

I once believed these lies we told ourselves. Now, to my own peril, sorrow and delight, I have learned how false Oudh's keepers were and how great was the kingdom's art and culture. How sad that only traces of Lucknow's exotic beauty remain. The city was washed in innocent blood in a war that left the entire subcontinent and the British empire forever changed. Oudh saw the greatest atrocities of the Mutiny. The road out of Lucknow leads directly to the city of grisly death, Cawnpore, where innocent women and children were hacked to pieces by the vile minions of Azimullah Khan and Nana Sahib.

After the war, some Europeans thought Lucknow a "strange jumble of vulgarity and bad taste." But it had been severely damaged in the fighting and deliberately despoiled by our troops after they retook it. Fortunately, I saw its beauty as a child and in my thoughts it remains unstained. To this day, in my mind's eye, I see it is as I saw it in childhood: a place of enchantment, wonder and the flower of a unique and beautiful civilization.

This enchanted place of my early years is the city that a member of the Bengal Lancers entered in secret on a warm moonless night just after the first siege of Lucknow had been lifted by General Colin Campbell. As soon as Campbell left to escort the women and children of Lucknow to safety, the rebels had regrouped. By then, I was on an East Indiaman bound for England and was unaware that my parents lay dead at Cawnpore.

As my ship rolled and pitched through the troughs of the sea, the lancer slipped between the campfires of the rebels as silently as one of the great striped cats of Bengal. The moist, heavy darkness conspired with the lancer's need for stealth. The seasoned veteran of countless conflicts on the subcontinent, he cautiously penetrated the private parks of the now empty homes and palaces, and made his way toward the building that had been the centre of the famous siege of Lucknow, the East India Company's Residency, sitting at the top of its hill, turned into a fortress by the vision and strategic cunning of Henry Lawrence.

Unlike many of Campbell's army who later sacked the city when they permanently recaptured Lucknow in March, the lone lancer did not come for revenge or the fabulous wealth in gems and gold that many wealthy Indians and Anglo-Indians had hidden among the gardens, the golden minarets and in the secret chambers of the curious buildings. Material wealth was the furthest thing from his mind. The prize he sought was a painting of Major General William Sleeman, a British hero who had helped tame the savage sub-continent, who had even warned of the possibility of the Mutiny years before it occurred. The truth is that the fighting in Oudh was nothing more or less than the inevitable outcome of our own policies.

The lancer crept through the heavy darkness of the old city, redolent of rotting offal and human blood, avoiding the watch fires of the rebels who had returned after Campbell's force left. Moving with the almost noiseless tread of a jungle predator, he made his way down the road of the Hazratganj. This major thorough-fare came from the southeast and was a very elegant street even by European standards, above a mile in length, with bazaars at each end, and the *chowk*, the city's major market, in the centre. The *chowk* had a lofty gateway at each end, which presented a Grecian front on one side and a Moorish one on the other.

Usually, the Hazratganj and especially the *chowk* were all colour and motion: heaps of precious metals normally lay near the market entrances and were sold with the dust of the street still coating the ingots. Open stalls offered colourful embroidered shirts. In elegant shops, smartly dressed women sold opium, *bhang* and tobacco. Goldsmiths flourished alongside condiments, shoes, hookahs, paper kites, enamel and silver jewelry and dealers in precious stones and fine fabrics. The air was redolent of spices, and scent, particularly fresh jasmine. The pretty courtesans of Lucknow called down witty verses to customers from their high carved wooden balconies, but the most famous beauties were silent and simply waited. A carnival atmosphere was the norm. *Tablas* were usually playing, accompanying the courte-sans who sang to guests in their *kothas*, but on the night the lancer stole through the ancient city, an uneasy stillness rested on the shops and houses. The balconies were empty. Nothing was heard except the lancer's light footsteps and the occasional rustling of feathers when some of the thousands of jade-green parakeets, nesting among the magical buildings, stirred in their sleep.

View of the Qaiser Bagh, Lucknow, looking North, showing
Sundit Ali Shah's Mausoleum

The lancer watched over his shoulder as he
crossed the empty street and progressed to the *Qaiser
Bagh*, the most magical place in the magical city, a
walled enclosure that housed a complex of courtyards
with many free-standing buildings set in landscaped
gardens, including the former dwelling of the last king
of Oudh, Wajid Ali Shah. Within this complex, bizarre
trompe l'oeleil effects added to the ghostliness of the
strangely unquiet silence. Doorways that suggested a
large solid building turned out to be nothing but open-
ings cut in a façade. There were inviting gazebos that
had no entrance. There were extraordinary buildings
and gardens, and some would say, pointless, structures
such as the fabulous two storey pigeon house with its
Corinthian columns and a triangular pediment designed
in the style of the Parthenon.

I remember myself, as a little boy, standing in
front of this amazing aviary, watching the prized birds of
the *Nawabs* flutter in and out.

Unbeknownst to me, in those days, the *Qaiser*

Bagh was home to even more exotic creatures: some of the most beautiful and cultivated courtesans of Lucknow lived on the grounds of the *Qaiser Bagh*, in apartments more luxurious than the most fanciful descriptions in the *Arabian Nights*. Among these women were some of the greatest poets, musicians and dancers to be found anywhere in Asia. These courtesans were the standard bearers of *Lakhnavi* culture: influential, rich and respected; as different from the other prostitutes of the city as emeralds from mud. They were known as the *deradwar tuwaif*, the most talented, the most carefully trained, the most beautiful entertainers in the world.

On the night of the lancer's personal mission to Lucknow, the Residency had already been an overcrowded refuge, bursting with women, children, loyal *sepoys* and Englishmen, but now the building was empty and scarred, ghostly, and like most of Lucknow between the acts of the great battle, there was a tension in its silence, an expectant quality about its emptiness, waiting for yet more horrors and blood. The shot marked stones silently cried out against the terrible things that had been and were yet to come, things never to be forgotten by anyone then living within the empire.

After prying open the latch of the French doors on the side of the building, the lancer stepped into the Resident's library and walked across the thick, Chinese carpet and out into the great hall. Once in the hall, his footsteps echoed hollowly on the stone. Though the building was dark, he went to his goal without hesitation. On a wall above the main staircase he found what he sought: George Duncan Beechey's portrait of William Sleeman, the man who was believed to have destroyed forever, the Indian cult of murder, the *Thuggee*. This criminal cult killed tens of thousands of people over several centuries in the service of their patron goddess, *Kali*. Never was brutal death so effectively worshiped as by this ghastly cult. But William Sleeman tracked them with a methodical doggedness previously unknown to the subcontinent. Yet, I maintain, and you shall see, that it was an example of the *hubris* of the British to think we could, in the space of a decade, uproot a centuries-old society that had grown out of beliefs predating recorded history.

The lancer opened his clasp knife in the dark and in a few deft strokes, the sound of which seemed to roar through the nearly denuded halls, he cut the painted canvas from its frame. It had hung on the wall of the Residency all through the siege and was, incredibly, unharmed. The lancer intended to preserve the work and its spirit without relying entirely on Providence. He rolled it up and tied it carefully into a compact tube. In the dim light, however, he did not notice that on the back of the canvas were faint charcoal marks, which, in fact, were words written in *Ramasee*, the strange secret tongue of the *Thuggee*.

With his treasure, the daring lancer retraced his steps through the city and once again slipped past the sentries and campfires of the rebels.

A short time later, General Campbell would return to finish his work in Lucknow, driving out the rebels and retaking the city.

After this dark night, my narrative must progress to England. I pray that you who read these pages, especially you, Mary, will realize that I have no reason to lie about what has happened. I will relate the true events as if they had befallen someone else, to make my words as impersonal as possible.

Sweet Mary, it was a great blow to me to find that you had tried me in the court of public opinion and found me guilty in spite of all our close ties. As it is, I must hope that you and those who have known me will credit the honesty of my account and acknowledge the truth of my assertion that the British needlessly destroyed much of Lucknow's beauty, simply because it was a beauty that admitted of excesses, a beauty that invited intoxication.

The outright theft of some of Lucknow's greatest art treasures, such as the Glass Tiger, which stood in the *Bara Imambara*, is only one example of the outstanding prizes the British have stolen from the Indian people. If there is blame to bestow regarding the horrors of the Mutiny, was not the greed of the Honourable Company the beginning of the catatrophe? I think so. As atrocious as were the crimes of Nana Sahib—and especially Azimullah Khan, who worked hard to infect Nana with his venemous hatred of us — I think we must admit to our own responsibility for the horrors. The British have raped and pillaged India while pretending friendship and protection. Of course, there have been some British men who were genuine heroes and came to serve India. Of the even greater heroism of British women in India, I shall have much more to say later. But for every one of these heroes and heroines, there were ten other British civilians and officers who sought to despoil India and its native people.

That is the real truth behind the horrors of the Mutiny, and I am in a better position to know than most. That is another reason why I write this history. The truth must survive even if I do not.

May God have mercy on those innocents who died in the *bibighar* and are commemorated at the Memorial Well, on those who died in the fighting and on anyone who has been touched by these events.

—Henry Booth near the Regent's Canal, London, 1874

Chapter 1
Oxford, Trinity Term, 1874

Trinity term in Oxford is often confounded by new students with a lengthy boating party on the Isis, accompanied by a bottomless lunch hamper packed with *foie gras*, strawberries and champagne. But Henry Booth knew better. As he looked out from the cloister quadrangle toward the New Building of Magdalen College where the latest crop of freshmen would be housed, it was easy to sympathize with a superficial view of the ancient city. Whilst Oxford's ancient stones, ancient cornices, ancient mouldings, ancient windows and buildings gave a venerable accent of history to the wooded walks and gardens, the sky was an especially brilliant blue, with just the sort of clouds to mislead new students into thinking that Oxford was actually Heaven, a place where one could float forever in a punt. What new student or even senior fellow could be displeased with anything in Oxford on such a day, unless he shared the current prejudice against Georgian architecture and so was put off by his first view of the New Building residences at Magdalen. But woe to new students who were seduced by the beauty and intellectual grandeur of the city and continued a sybaritic existence through the entire term. When exams came at the end of the school year, the habitual boaters would find the Isis grown suddenly very deep, dark and swirling over their heads. At Oxford colleges, the final exams make up the entire mark and there is no second chance.

As a senior student familiar with the subcontinent, Henry had been asked by his tutor in Greats to pay a call on a new fellow recently come from India and to help prepare him for the mad sprint which final exams entail. And if a warning was wanted, Henry was just the man to deliver it earnestly. He worked hard at whatever he did. Perhaps too hard. In some ways he was a young man who wasn't as young as his years and, considering his history, with some reason. He was a good student and a good athlete. He fenced, boxed and rowed as well as any man of his year, but he had few friends and usually prefered his own company. His subjects were British history and law, in which he was hoping to take a First. But his greatest love was music, and though he excelled at the keyboard, he could not credit struggling along with a wife and children on the money a musician, even a successful one, could make. Perhaps, he would go back to Asia. He hadn't made up his mind. His Uncle in Calcutta had offered him a place with his export firm, one of many such firms that had filled the vacuum created by the dissolution of the East India Company.

In 1858, when the Mutiny was ended, the horrors of the conflict forced Parliament to confront the Honourable Company's gross abuses, and India was placed under direct government control, without, however, offering any compensation to the people of the subcontinent. It was an administrative solution that meant more to British bureaucrats than to the people of India. The plunder of the subcontinent continued unabated and offered great opportunities to English merchants like Henry's uncle.

Henry crossed the rectangular fields lying between the Cloister and the New Building with a brisk powerful stride, feeling the sun on his back through his college gown. His lean, athletic body moved easily and his jet black hair caught highlights of the sun. His face was sharp and well-defined; his nose straight, chin strong and set forward. His eyes were a startling shade of amber brown and were set off by his tanned face. The memory came to him of a particularly warm day at Lucknow when he had been crossing the lawn around his family's bungalow. That day he had the awareness of feeling, for the first time, the sensation of the sun's heat on his back. He must have been about five. This wasn't long before he'd been sent back to England to live with the Suttons, his mother's relations. For the most part, India, other than Lucknow, was a hazy blur of images to him, except for his mother and the ill-treatment she received at his father's hands.

Both of his parents died during the Mutiny in the siege at Cawnpore. His mother had, in all probability, been dismembered in the dreadful *bibighar* and thrown into the grisly well along with the other women and children. As he reviewed these facts yet again, his jaw knotted and relaxed several times. As he had so many times before, Henry pushed back the pictures he'd seen in the *London Illustrated News*, which he'd found in the Sutton's parlour one afternoon. But he literally had never been able to forget the words of a Highland subaltern who had visited the *bibighar* just weeks after the atrocities and sent an account back to the newspaper, later to be published as part of his personal record of the Mutiny, *A True Record of the Mutiny by a Highland Subaltern*. The dreadful words rang in Henry's mind as clearly as if he'd just read them:

The small yard where the bibighar, "house of women," stood had a blighted tree at its centre. Somehow, this tree had on its branches, not leaves, but tiny rags of clothing torn from the murdered women and children. It seemed to me a horrible trophy of innocent death. These rags called attention to themselves by fluttering in the slight breeze. Something about that slight movement seemed more horrible than all the slaughter I had seen in any of the fighting. When I stepped inside the small house I saw great splashes of blood everywhere. The desperate clinging of feminine arms had left bloody imprints on the pillars of the veranda. Clearly, the women had clung to the building while they pleaded with their butchers. But worse was yet to come: in the yard outside was a well, around which grew prickly plants in abundance. These plants now held great quantities of human hair—hair which had been torn or

The Well and Memorial at Cawnpore

cut from the heads of the women and children. I shall
not say what had been thrown into the well.

Henry's mother had beautiful golden hair. It's quantity and brilliant colour had never failed to delight his childish senses. Each time Henry began to think of the *bibighar* where his mother had died, some impersonal voice in his mind droned out the subaltern's words as if they had been carefully committed to memory, though Henry had only read the words once, when he was seven years old. Charles Sutton, his mother's cousin had torn the newspaper from the boy's hand, but it was too late. The words were with him forever. Once the recitation began, all Henry could do was wait until it had passed, or take heavy physical exercise to stop it. Stopping the dreadful words was actually part of the reason he had started fencing and boxing in his first year at Oxford. He had always been an avid oarsman. He began to jog across to the New Building. No new fellow would hear Henry's earnest admonitions about the depths of the Isis, a river he knew well, and regard them lightly.

Henry heard his own footsteps echoing in the arched open portico of the building. Then, he raced up the three staircases to the top floor and found the room number he had been given. In spite of his sprint up the steep flights of stairs, he was not even breathing hard when he stood in front of the door and knocked.

"Come in," a rather clipped voice answered.

Henry opened the door and stuck his head inside.

"I'm looking for Harry Clayton," he said.

A slender young man with unusually dark skin and very black hair stood up quickly.

"Oh, sorry. I thought it was the scout. He just left me."

"Henry Booth," Henry said reaching out his hand to the new man. "Final year. I'm here to help, if I can. Answer questions about the College and University. Help you get settled in—and warn you about exams."

"Thank you. Again, I apologize for just calling out and not opening the door myself."

"Not at all."

As Henry's eyes traveled around the room, they were caught by a photograph of the Holiwell Monument in Calcutta.

" Henry said. "I see you brought some of India with you."

"Oh, then you know Calcutta?"

"Not really. I spent just a couple of weeks there before the Mutiny. My parents were stationed in Lucknow and then Cawnpore."

"Oh, heavens," Harry said.

There was an embarrassed silence for a moment, then Henry spoke. "Look, I can see you're not finished unpacking. Why don't you carry on and I'll come back after evensong, about six-thirty. By then, you'll probably have questions. We can go down together to the dining hall. I know I hate eating alone in a strange place."

"Thank you. That's very good of you."

"Not at all," Henry said moving toward the door.

Harry opened it for him and saw him out.

"Thanks again. I shall see you later."

Henry was feeling unsettled after seeing Harry Clayton's photograph of Calcutta. It seemed that the best thing to do was drink in the sights and sounds of Oxford in the beautiful weather and wipe out all thought of India. He was sorry that he had offered to come back and visit Clayton again. He shrugged it off, walked back to the cloisters and came out onto the High Street near the Tower. He walked west and turned eventually into his favourite Oxford street, New College Lane, which ran behind the Sheldonian Theatre. If one walked up this street and then looked back, even in 1870, one had no way of knowing that it was not the fourteenth century. At the Broad, he turned toward Banbury Road and eventually circled back and strolled along Addison's Walk next to the river. Even with the thoughts that had been stirred up by the picture of Calcutta, it was impossible to be out of sorts in Oxford on a day like this. The city was fairly empty. The term had not started and the weather was perfect.

He wandered and dreamed his way through the afternoon in a city whose paths, gardens, woods and quadrangles had touched countless generations of men his age.

"Perhaps," he thought, "if I do well enough, I could teach here." The idea of living permanently in the "city of spires" appealed to the young man, especially after having his bad memories of India stirred by the photograph. Why should he go back to India just to make money with his mother's brother, after whom he'd been named? There were more important things in life than acquiring material possessions.

The stately Christ Church College, which he was passing at that moment, was a long way from the fantastic buildings of Lucknow, but for that very reason, it appealed to Henry that afternoon. Oxford's traditions and future seemed as solid as the ancient stones from which the city was built, the antithesis of the fragile arabesques of Lucknow's stucco structures.

He managed to dream the day away until he heard the bells which told him it was time to fulfill his promise and return to dine with Clayton in Magdalen's Hall. He usually ate in his own chambers but since term had not yet started, the commotion of the Hall would not be too insupportable. Slowly, he traced his way back to the New Building of his own college, approaching it from behind, after crossing the River Cherwell. The lawns and foliage exuded a wonderful freshness and he found it impossible to be annoyed with the new student, who would rob him of the delicious solitude of the late afternoon and early evening. He wondered, idly, if the new fellow knew that the college was called, "maudlin" and not Mag-da-len. If he had come recently from India, he might not know. Charles would be sure to mention it. Clayton would feel a fool if he made such a mistake about his own college. It was just that sort of *faux pas* that Henry was supposed to help the new man avoid.

He soon found himself facing the door to Clayton's chambers. At his knock, the door was opened so quickly, Henry almost felt as if the other man must have been waiting just inside. The chambers had been transformed in the intervening hours. The room now bore the unmistakable flavour of India. There were curios of all kinds from the sub-continent scattered around the room: an ivory inlaid sandalwood carving of a rajah's elephant, a large brass tray with a wooden pedestal that made it a table. Allah's name was inscribed in the centre of the tray's incised surface. There were more pictures from Calcutta and other places in India Henry did not recognize. Before he could respond to Clayton's greeting or cross the threshold, he suddenly felt all the blood leave his head and upper body. A wave of shock passed through him, for there, on the brass tray was a picture of a beautiful middle-aged woman who looked just as his own mother would have looked, had she survived the Mutiny. It was like seeing one of his own memories that had been strangely transformed by passing years which had never taken place.

"I say, Booth, are you all right?" he heard Clayton ask.

"You're white as a sheet. Can I get you a brandy?"

"Thank you, Clayton," he croaked. His eyes were fixed on the photograph.

A few moments later when the other man turned back with a restorative in his hand, Henry was feeling more collected.

"Pardon me, Clayton, but I must ask where you got that photograph."

Jane Booth,
Henry's Mother

"Oh, that's my mother. It was taken before she and my father left for Turkey. I was raised by *ayahs* in India while my parents were traveling most of the time. Why?"

Henry tossed off his drink before answering. As the alcohol finished bracing him, he said, "It bears a startling resemblance to my own mother. A truly astonishing resemblance. Though, of course, it is only surmise since my mother didn't live to reach the age of the woman in that picture."

"Oh, I am sorry, Booth."

"No. It was just pure astonishment for a moment. You see, my mother died at Cawnpore. We believe in the *bibighar*."

"How dreadful." Clayton darted toward the photograph and put it face down on the brass tray.

"No, please, don't let my personal history disarrange your room."

"Really, it's all right. I can't even imagine how you must have felt just now."

"It was an extraordinary moment," Henry agreed. "I hope you'll excuse me."

"Absolutely nothing to excuse, really. Perfectly understandable. Do you feel like dining, or perhaps you'd prefer to be alone?"

"No. Let's go to the hall. The stir might be good for me."

So the two fellows adjourned to the hall.

When they entered the enormous room Clayton exclaimed, "What a magnificent place to dine."

"It is really quite grand, I agree. It was begun in fourteen seventy-four and probably completed in the same decade."

The two young men sat down at the long refectory table with a small scattering of other students. They ordered and then Henry continued his introduction to the history of Magdalen's dining hall.

"The so-called linen fold paneling behind the high table over there was put in during the first half of the sixteenth century. There is an old tradition, probably mythical, that it came from Reading Abbey after the Dissolution. The only thing known with certainty is that it was bought in London, shipped up the Thames to Henley and brought overland to Oxford."

"I hope not all the rooms here have so much history. I feel I should know the provenance of my own college. By itself, it sounds to be a full term's work."

"We are privileged to be in one of the most historic schools in one of the most historic cities in Great Britain," Booth answered a little sharply, "I'm afraid you'll find yourself continually surrounded with art and architecture of historical note."

"Yes, I suppose that is true," Clayton answered somewhat unenthusiastically.

There was a long silence as their plates were put on the table. For an Oxford dining Hall, the meal was very informal. There was no prayer led from the High

Table. In fact, there was no faculty at the High Table at all. The Hall was only open as a courtesy to students like Henry and Clayton, who, for whatever reason, had to come up before term started.

After eating in silence for some time, Henry finally asked, "How did your family happen to be out in India?"

Clayton looked uncomfortable, then replied, "The usual sort of thing, I suppose. Father had a large domestic business in Calcutta dealing in carpets and other Asian antiquities. My mother was one of those women who came out, hoping to catch a Company husband. But she met my father and, in spite of the, ah, differences..."

"Please, Clayton," Henry said interrupting the other man. "I am not a bigot. And I know how it is among some of the *sahibs* in India about mixed marriages. Relieve yourself on that point. I have never subscribed to censoring that sort of thing."

"Thank you," Clayton said with genuine gratitude.

It was from this moment, when Henry saw the honest warmth and appreciation in the younger man's face that he started to like him.

"Damn rotten business," Henry thought. Charles Sutton, his mother's cousin, who had raised Henry as one of his own family, had always told him that the assumed superiority of the white race was insupportable in an empire that stretched across the globe. In spite of being a rather prim man of generally conservative beliefs, Sutton had taught Henry that merit alone should be the measure of how a man was treated by his fellows. For a well-to-do High Church Dean, Sutton was unusually liberal in his views.

It was Sutton, his wife and daughter who had

met Henry on the India docks in London. Henry got off the tall-masted east Indiaman a dazed boy, after months at sea. London looked terribly dark. The wind felt bitter cold and smelled foul to the boy. But Amelia Sutton, the Dean's wife, who had little of the stiffness usually associated with a woman in her position, made Henry forget the strangeness of England when she greeted him with a tender kiss on the forehead. She was a warm, auburn haired person, slim and athletic.

When the deaths of Henry's mother and father at Cawnpore were finally confirmed and the boy was told, it was Amelia Sutton who had sat next to his bed all night, rubbing his back whilst he sobbed uncontrollably. She had been truly a second mother to him. She even offered to take the orphaned boy to one of the many prayer meetings that had been held throughout England to raise money and offer sympathy to relatives of the victims. For when the deaths in the *bibighar* were reported, the entire nation went into shock, disbelief and outrage.

Amelia Sutton had given the boy a mother's love at one of the most difficult times of his life. So it is no wonder that Henry eventually fell in love with her daughter who shared many personal characteristics with her mother. Under the watchful eyes of the Suttons, Henry's childish infatuation with Mary Sutton had ripened to deep affection. As the pair grew older, they developed a degree of intimacy with each other usually not given to young couples. They regarded their attachment as quite a settled thing and were as familiar with each other as a brother and sister. Henry had no experiences with other young women, eschewing the many prostitutes in Oxford. Mary, of course, knew nothing of any men outside the family circle. Such a relationship has its strengths and weaknesses. Mary was the primary reason that Henry and both the older Suttons balked at the idea of the young couple returning to India. The dreadful deaths in the *bibighar* were still with them all. More than a decade later, it was difficult for the Sutton's to forget the sleepless nights and the fervent prayers for Henry's mother, Amelia's cousin, and his father. The pain and manner of the loss had branded the entire family. They were wary of the eastern empire, in spite of the great wealth that would almost certainly follow from Henry's taking up a position as the heir apparent in his uncle's firm in Calcutta. Charles and Amelia Sutton were in favour of commercial success, but they were not at all sure they wanted their daughter to go to the subcontinent. If Henry really took first class honours, everyone in the family would be pleased. Then, he and Mary could easily settle into a less resplendent but honourable academic life in England. With Charles Sutton's connections, Henry would almost certainly have the chance to teach at Oxford, perhaps even at his own college. With all this, it was odd that Henry couldn't entirely give up the idea of returning to India. His memories of Lucknow and his mother tugged at him, though he thought his own feelings on the matter an odd freak, a contrariness in himself that went against his love of Oxford, the Suttons and England. Mary had already told him she would go anywhere with him, and was quite curious to see the exotic eastern colony. There was a fascination about the tiger hunts and the strange culture of the natives. She was probably less averse to the idea of going out to India than anyone else in the family. She had told Henry that she might teach a Sunday school there, and help bring the Christian Word to the children of the Queen's new subjects, children whose parents had raised them in idolatry and without the light of Christ. She liked the idea of being of use, and in many ways, felt she could do more in India than in England.

Like her mother, Mary was delicately formed, with finely made features and a slim figure, but had a strong constitution and had been encouraged not to spare herself in the service of others. Just because her father was well-off, she had not been coddled and spoiled. In her most adventurous moments, Mary hoped that Henry would decide for India. She could see herself riding on an elephant with Henry at her side. At other times, a distinguished life in Oxford seemed the best use of Henry's gifts. Being a faculty wife would be almost like living in her parents' home. Instead of distinguished churchmen, there would distinguished scholars and students.

Mary's disposition was fairly placid, though she could be very fiery on matters of principle. Her father had trained her always to do her best and be content with what that effort and Providence brought her. And that was how she looked at her future with Henry. She saw other young women struggling to find good husbands. None of them would ever know their spouses as she knew Henry. She felt that God had given her a great gift in Henry, a stalwart man who had for her the familiarity and reliability of a brother without having lost the dash of a lover.

Henry and the new fellow stayed quite late at table, talking about India. In spite of everything, the subcontinent had a strange attraction for Henry, and for Harry Clayton, it was home. Harry found the English summer chilly and damp. Henry could remember how strange he had found England when he first came and he commiserated with the other man. They walked through the college in the twilight, smoking their after dinner cigars. Clayton was of a strongly scientific bent and seemed well up on the plants, animals and insects of his home. Henry could see the new fellow was of a studious nature and likely to do the college credit. It was too bad that his Indian blood manifested in small bones and short stature, which would probably prevent him from making any mark in athletics.

"I believe," Clayton said, "that the use made of plants and animals to cure illness in India will one day be studied by our own medical men here in England. I should like to be part of the discoveries which will be made."

"So you would go back to India?" Henry asked.

"I expect so. My father's business seems to run it-self, though he does travel a great deal with my mother. He makes no demands on me other than to be honour-able in whatever I do. Since I am interested in the flora and fauna of the subcontinent, it would seem to be the right place for me."

"And you won't mind the *sahibs*? Their attitudes, I mean?"

"I cannot adapt my interests because of fools," Clayton answered. "Indian people are just as able as anyone else. I have heard many army men say that the Sikhs were the greatest fighters in the world. Were it not for superior fire power, we might have lost the Sikh wars. Certainly, there are also great scholars there, as well, some British and some native. Some of the re-search I should like to do could only be done in the in the jungles there."

"Good for you, Clayton, that you know your own mind so well. I confess to being much more di-vided in my views about India. I suppose I shall let it be decided for me by the class of honours I take, here. If I turn out to be a poor scholar, I shall go to India and make money."

"I wonder if your uncle knows my father?" Clayton said abruptly. "They're both in a good way of business in Calcutta. It seems likely, even though my father is a Moslem and a native. Though I have no idea when or even if my parents will come back from Turkey."

"Forgive me for saying so, Clayton, but I think you are too self-conscious about your mixed parentage. This is England, not India."

"And the English are not bigoted?"

"Some are, certainly. But the values of the empire rest solidly on all the Queen's subjects being equal before the law. And in England, those laws are obeyed to the letter. Don't forget, I am reading history and law."

The two men smoked in silence and then Henry said, "It sounds as if you haven't seen your parents for some time."

"Not for three or four years. And then, they only made a brief stop in Calcutta. They had only a few hours between ships. Then, they were going to Russia to buy gems which my father will resell. We've never really spent time together as a family. I suppose you and I are both different species of orphan."

"I shall be writing to my uncle soon," Henry said. "I shall ask him if he knows your father."

"I'll be interested in his reply," the other man said.

"Well, it's getting late," Henry said. "I think I should do some swotting. You will find that the longer you're here, the less time you have for anything but work."

"Thanks for the evening, Booth. I do feel more at home, now, Clayton said. The two men shook hand and went back to their rooms.

Once alone, Henry almost wanted to follow Clayton to his room and see the photograph of the stranger who looked so much like his own mother, but the moment passed and he went back to his own chambers directly.

Contrary to his plans and expectations, Henry couldn't settle down to work. He kept thinking of the woman whose photograph he'd seen in Clayton's room. On Henry's own desk was an oval photographic portrait of his mother taken in Calcutta just before Henry came to England. The frame of the little portrait of Jane Booth was inset with pretty coloured stones, like a tiny mosaic. A photograph of Henry had also been taken the same day and had remained with his mother.

Henry got up and looked out of his window. There were practically no lights illuminating the rooms facing the quad, but a wonderful moon hung low in the sky like a silver lantern, which for no good reason made him again think of Lucknow. In his mind, he traveled through the ancient city, picturing some of his favourite places there. He tried to remember a night in Lucknow when he might have seen this particularly silvery light and a moon like this one. Suddenly, he recalled an evening when he had sat out of doors very late with his mother. There had been a huge, low moon that night. It had looked like an enormous disk of polished silver. In his memory, the moons of India were much larger than in England. He had watched the moon with his mother from the screened gazebo. It had been very hot and his father had returned home late in the evening. Several times, his father had called out to his mother from the house, asking her to come inside. Finally, he came out to where they sat in the yard behind the bungalow. He grabbed his wife's arm and jerked her to her feet.

"Bitch," he spat the word at her. It was the first time Henry had heard the word directed at a woman. He remembered his father looming over him and his

mother as she was pulled into house. At first, she resisted but then two sharp sounds cracked sharply in the
heavy night air, two slaps on his mother's cheek.

"Brute," his mother's tearful voice had answered
as her husband continued to tow her inside.

Henry dared not say anything. Once, when he
had tried to interfere in a scene between his parents, his
father strapped him so hard, he could not sit for a week.
By the time Henry left India, his parent's fights had become a chief item of gossip among the other Company
families who lived near the Residency.

Returning abruptly to the present, Henry spun
on his heel to look at his mother's picture. The silvery
light erased some of the small differences of age between
his mother and Clayton's, so the resemblance seemed
even greater. Though his mother was dead, and all
relatives accounted for, perhaps there was some family
connection of which he was ignorant, some close but
forgotten family member who lived in Turkey. Yet, he
had always been told that the Suttons were his mother's
only living relations.

For another hour he struggled fruitlessly with
medieval law. Then, he pushed his books aside and
began writing to his uncle to make enquiries about the
Claytons, particularly Mrs. Clayton.

Chapter 2
Oxford and London:
Michaelmas and HilaryTerms, 1874

Henry spent the summer in Oxford studying and rowing, taking as much time on the river as he could afford. The first week of Michaelmas term finally came and promised well for the year. Henry won a university-wide single-stick tournament and the papers he wrote were well-received by his tutors. It began to look as though at least one First would be within his grasp by year end. Mary told him that her father was already talking about canvassing his friends to find an opening for Henry at the University and a house for them nearby after they were married. Mary was hoping for a lovely June wedding after he graduated. It was all perfect, yet the more settled things became, the more Henry thought of India and his Uncle. After Clayton came to cheer him on during the singlestick tournament, he dined with the new fellow three or four times and they continued talking of India. Henry had a chance to study the photograph of Clayton's mother and had half convinced himself that she was not really so like his own mother, after all. Then, Henry finally received his uncle's reply to the questions he'd asked about the Claytons. The reply came in the form of a package.

Hilary term was well advanced and everything out of doors was brilliantly green, though the foliage was not yet in its full glory when Henry got the small parcel wrapped in coarse brown paper and tied with the tarred twine that his uncle used for shipping.

Being something more than a letter and coming from such a long way, Bannister, the scout, hadn't wanted to leave it in Henry's empty room. So Henry picked it up at the Scout's cubby. When he looked at the package, he was intrigued. He recognized his uncle's hand, but couldn't begin to imagine what he would have sent. He took it back to his chambers, unwrapped it, and was mystified when there was nothing but several sheets of pasteboard wrapped in the paper. His uncle was a hard headed man of business, and the idea of a false package sent at great expense to his nephew, was not in his line at all. Henry was disappointed at not getting any answers to his questions about the Claytons. He told himself that he owed the new fellow a visit to see how he was getting on, though he knew he wanted to look once more at the photograph of Mrs. Clayton to see if perhaps the whole business was a mare's nest.

It was a warm afternoon and by the time Henry ascended to the third floor of the New Building, the air was stifling. It seemed unlikely that Clayton would stay in his top floor rooms on such a day. Yet, when Henry knocked, Clayton opened the door quickly.

"Booth," Clayton said in a friendly, welcoming tone.

"I hope I am not disturbing you, Clayton. I was just thinking you probably weren't in since you are right under the leads, which must be nearly on the verge of melting on an afternoon like this."

"I like the heat. This isn't hot, in any case. Please, come in. How are you getting on? I haven't seen you since you won the tournament."

"Things are going well. I just received an honours mark on my latest paper. I only hope I can keep it up to the end."

"I haven't a doubt of it."

"And how are you getting on? How do you like the college?"

"Very well. And I have something to show you. Here, look."

Henry's eyes swept the room and found the photograph in the same place atop the brass tray. The brilliant spring sunshine was falling directly on the picture.

As he furtively glanced at the photograph, Henry almost felt a catch in his breath as he confirmed the astonishing likeness to his own mother.

"How unfortunate," he thought "that some employee of uncle Henry's has sent me the wrong package."

As he stood blinking into the sun in Clayton's room, Henry felt he would give anything to have the questions he had asked his uncle, answered.

"Here, I finally got some of my specimens unpacked," Clayton said proudly.

Henry looked up, pulling himself away from his own thoughts.

The strong sunlight was illuminating a huge, cunningly made glass shelved case with numerous compartments in it. In each were specimens of exotic creatures from the subcontinent. To Henry's surprise, they were alive.

"What an extraordinary cabinet, Clayton."

"Thank you, I designed it myself."

"And the specimens also look remarkable. I am surprised they are alive."

"Well, they are mostly creatures who go into a dormant state and so are able to make the trip without much food. The one danger is cold. If they get too cold, they will die. But I'm pleased to say that I didn't lose a single one on the long voyage. I had a cabin near the engine room, which was actually hot. And this south window should keep them happy. I specifically asked for a south window and since nobody else wanted the direct sunlight, I got it."

"Remarkable," Henry said with honest admiration. You should make a presentation on these creatures to the college. This fellow, what is he?"

"Ah, believe it or not, he is a type of toad. He comes from the south coast of India just above the Andaman Islands."

"His skin certainly is beautifully coloured," Henry said looking at the bright scarlets, blues and greens that mottled the creature's strange skin.

"And deadly poisonous," Clayton answered. "Any predator who tried to make a meal of him would be dead in moments. His skin contains one of the deadliest natural toxins known. I believe this toxin will be used in future medications. It causes numbness before death. Perhaps it could be useful in the operating theatre."

"Fascinating."

Henry left Clayton about an hour later after getting an informal presentation on the creatures in the glass cabinet, he had been impressed by the knowledgeable way the new fellow discussed his specimens. The new man would certainly make a creditable Magdelan fellow. But Henry had been particularly moved by the photograph of Clayton's mother. In the full sunlight, with no tricks of shadow, it was less a resemblance that Henry saw, than it was a duplicate of his own mother, aged by about a decade, her face showing only minor alterations: a few crow's feet, cheeks slightly thinner. He walked quickly back to his own rooms, determined to write to his uncle again. He would ask his questions even more forcefully and press his uncle on the meaning of the pasteboard package.

But Henry's surprises for the day were not over. When he opened his door, the scene that greeted him was chaos. All the things in his room had been thrown about. His dresser drawers were emptied, as was the wardrobe. Even his bed had been torn apart. Naturally, the young man was furious at the breach of his privacy, but once he got over the shock he wondered who, in all of Oxford, would have even thought of doing such a thing?

He went out to look for Bannister. The little cockney prided himself on knowing every movement of every living thing in his domain. He found him reading a London paper in his little snuggery.

"Mr. Booth," the wiry little man said when he saw Henry. "What can I do for you?"

"Bannister, I must ask you to come to my room, immediately. Something has happened."

With his twenty-five years as a scout, Bannister had seen everything there was to see in student rooms, from women to animals, yet, he could not conceal his astonishment at the disorder in Henry's room.

"Good gracious, sir. Anything taken? Have you examined your valuables? Anything taken, sir?"

"I don't think so. I don't keep money here. I can't imagine what someone would have been looking for."

"If it is a prank, it is an affront to us all," the

scout said.

It took upwards of an hour for Henry to restore order to his room. As he worked, he tried to make sense out of the reason for the disorder. Why? Was it just a clumsy attempt at robbery? Why would anyone have thought there would be something valuable to take? How had they opened the door? By the time he was done restoring his rooms, a longing for some cool, fresh air lured him out of doors once more. But once in the quad, he loitered near the entrance to his staircase. The vandal might return, if he did, Henry didn't want to miss the chance to confront the villain. He stayed around his door for several hours and finally gave it up as a bad job. For all he knew, someone could be watching from one of the windows.

He decided to stroll up Addison's Walk where the river and the trees would make for deliciously cool shadows and where he could walk off his anger against the unknown perpetrator of the outrage in his rooms.

He had just crossed the Cherwell and was entering a more wooded and private part of the Walk, when he noticed an odd looking man who kept pace with him some hundred yards behind. The man appeared to take no notice of him. He was dressed like a common sailor and his skin had the sun darkened complexion of the sort that a sea faring man would have. He looked utterly out of place on a college walk. Given the already outlandish events of the day, Henry was suspicious of the stranger. When Henry slowed his paces, so did the sailor. The man's face was wizened and narrow, dried out and wore a furtive expression.

Finally, Henry decided to confront the stranger. There could be no harm in asking if he could direct him to his destination. He turned and walked back toward the sailor. The man's face registered surprise at Henry's manoeuvre. The walk was now sheltered by low hanging branches and a good thicket of trees.

"I was wondering, sir, since you don't look familiar to the college, if I could be of assistance. I am a fellow at the college."

The man stood as still as a statue. Henry wondered if he was going to bolt, if he did, Henry promised himself he would catch the man. Instead, the sailor began walking quickly toward Henry. The cover on this part of the walk was dense, making it very sequestered. There were no other pedestrians. Now Henry began to wonder if the man would try to assault him. As he drew close to the sailor, Henry was amazed when the man reached into his coat and drew out a package that was wrapped in coarse brown paper and tied with twine. The sailor thrust it at Henry.

"What?" the young man asked.

"Explained inside," the man said, "Take it," and, thrusting the package with an insistent gesture at the younger man turned and walked quickly in the other direction. Henry only had time to notice a peculiar odor on the man's clothing before he turned off the walk and into the trees and was gone. For a moment, Henry was too surprised to do anything. What was more strange, the package looked like an exact duplicate of the one he'd already received from his uncle. It was addressed to him in his uncle's hand. Henry was astonished. The furtive manner of the other man made Henry glance quickly around the Walk, before walking briskly back to his own rooms with the package clasped tightly under his arm.

Once inside, Henry carefully put the package down on his desk, took out the pasteboard, paper and twine from the other package and reassembled it. The two packages were identical, indistinguishable from each other. It seemed unlikely that they should so closely resemble one another by accident, but if it was deliberate, Henry could not imagine the purpose for his uncle's curious ploy. He carefully untied the twine and unwrapped the new package. Inside, he found a stained, leather and cloth bound volume and a letter addressed to him in his uncle's hand.

"Dear Nephew,
The enclosed diary belonged to your mother. She wanted you to have it. I hope it does not bring you trouble. Keep it safe for her sake. I am sorry to pass on such a heavy burden to you, Henry. God bless and keep you. Your Uncle, Henry."

Just as Henry finished reading the letter, there was a knock at the door. Bannister stood in the hallway looking at Henry sheepishly. "Sir, the President of the College requests your immediate presence in his office."

"Is this regarding the outrage in my room? Have you caught someone already?"

"I'm sorry, sir. I really couldn't say. The President summoned me and sent me here. That is all I know."

After the outrage, Henry didn't want to leave the diary behind, yet he didn't want to take it with him either.

"Tell the President I shall be along directly."

"I'm sorry, sir, but he told me to bring you myself, directly to his office."

"I regret to say Bannister, I must have a few minutes to myself."

"And that is what the President said I was not to give you, sir."

Red-faced and angry at the scout, Henry went downstairs with him. When they reached the quad, Henry bolted and sprinted across the green to the New Building. He ran up the stairs and knocked on Clayton's door.

"Oh, I say Booth, is something wrong?"

"My room was broken into this morning. Would keep this for me for a few hours? Some place safe."

"Certainly, I've got just the place."

He took the diary and carried it over to his glass case full of specimens. In one of the compartments was a brownish speckled mass. It moved when Clayton put his hand inside the compartment. When the creature raised its head, Henry could see it was some sort of viper.

"Good lord, Clayton, what is it?"

"It is a swamp adder, the most poisonous snake in India. One bite and a man would be dead in less than half a minute."

"But you just put your hand in there."

"It's all right. She knows my scent. But any stranger who tried to take your book would be bitten immediately and dead very quickly."

"Astonishing, Clayton. What a horribly effective guard."

At this point, Bannister came up the stairs, breathing hard.

"That was not at all cricket, sir," the scout said to Henry in a tone of remonstrance.

"Sorry, Bannister, but I really had no choice. I'll go with you now."

"Very good, sir."

The scout and Henry walked back across the lawn to the President's lodging which adjoined the cloister quad and which had been built quite recently. Henry had very little to do with the President, few students did except on formal, ceremonial occasions. He had always struck Henry as rather supercilious in his behaviour and when the scout knocked on his door, the President did nothing to lessen that impression.

"Come," was heard after a few moments.

Bannister pushed open the door.

"Ah, Bannister. Did you find him?"

Bannister pushed the door open further so that the President could see Henry.

"You may go, Bannister. Come in Booth. I don't really know what to make of you, Booth. You've done well here up until now. So what is all this about meeting strange people on college grounds and accusing college people of breaking into your rooms?"

"That is exactly what happened, sir. Someone did break into my room, but I never insisted it was someone belonging to the college."

"And what about this sailor you met on the Walk? What was the meaning of that? And where is the package he gave you?"

"I have never seen the man before in my life, sir. He was acting as a courier for my Uncle."

"And the package, where is it?"

"Some place where it cannot be disturbed by anyone."

"I must have this package, Mr. Booth."

"It is a very private thing, sir, my dead mother's diary."

"I must insist, Mr. Booth. If you do not cooperate, the consequences for you could be dire."

"Why, I should like to know, sir, am I being treated like a criminal?"

"You astonish me, Mr. Booth. How dare you speak to me that way?"

"My mother's diary is a private thing, sir. I will not release it to anyone, at least until I have read it."

"Then you are no longer a fellow at this college, Booth."

"What?"

"You heard me, Mr. Booth."

"Sir, I protest this summary expulsion. I..

"If you fly in the face of my authority, Mr. Booth, I have no choice but to expel you. Now, once more, will you bring me the diary?"

"No sir, I shall not. I shall be contacting the Chancellor's office, sir. Your behaviour is grossly unjust."

"I am astonished, sir," the president said as he looked down at his desk and began writing as if Henry were not in the room, "that you have done so well at Magdelen until now. Usually, your sort breaks out early on. Good day."

Shocked, disbelieving and furious all at once, Henry left the President's office. Making a scene would do nothing but put him more in the wrong. He would write immediately to his step-father, Charles Sutton and see what could be done about the President's behaviour.

He returned to his rooms intending to write immediately, but in just a quarter hour, Bannister was again at his door.

"I am sorry Mr. Booth, but the President says you have been expelled for nearly criminal behaviour and I am to help you pack and leave the college."

"Bannister, you have known me for years. What is going on?"

"I'm sorry, sir. I only know what the President told me. It would be my place, sir, if I didn't follow his instructions. I have a family, sir, and I need my place at the college."

"Of course, Bannister, I wouldn't think of getting you into trouble."

"May I help you pack, sir?"

Two hours later, two years of Oxford life had been packed and sent to the train station. Henry could not even write to the Suttons before leaving, but he did

Mary Sutton

send a telegram, announcing his arrival in London.

At the last minute, he thought of the diary which had, for the moment, cost him his place at Magdalen. As he walked over to Clayton's rooms the catastrophe seemed like a bad dream. He knocked on the door twice and was surprised to find it ajar. He pushed it open and called out, "Clayton, I say, Clayton. Are you about?"

There was no answer. He stepped just far enough into the room to see the diary inside the glass case. It's guardian seemed to sense his presence and lifted its diamond shaped head. The diary was certainly safe, Henry thought. Should he wait for Clayton? The last train for London would be leaving soon and if he missed it, a whole other day would have to pass before he could talk with his step-father and start to take steps to regain his place at the college. If necessary, he felt sure he could wire Clayton and ask him to send the diary to London.

He took one more quick look around the college for Clayton, and then put his portmanteau into a cab and rode to the train station. By evening, Henry was standing on the platform at the new Paddington station beneath one of the curving skylights, which arched above the tracks and admitted the murky spring twilight.

As his portmanteau was handed out to him, Henry inquired after his other things.

"Booth, from Oxford, sir?" the porter asked, reading the luggage tag.

"That's right."

"There were no other things, sir."

"But I sent a carriage laden with clothes, books all manner of personal effects. The driver was to put it on the train."

"All I can speak for sir is that it never got onto the train."

Wilfred Smythe-White

Henry, angry and baffled, turned away and began to make his way across the station's huge, open hall. Even with the intervening period of the train trip, Henry was still in shock over his expulsion—even if it was only temporary. And now, all his Oxford things had vanished. He vacillated between rage at the supercilious President and complete astonishment that he should find himself in such a situation. Yet he knew he could not blame the President for his missing things. He pushed his way through the crowd, making for the cab rank outside. He was reaching for the door handle when he felt a numbing blow fall on his arm, just above the hand that carried the portmanteau. A moment later, a tall Indian man had seized the portmanteau while a smaller Indian swung a cane at the same arm, and broke Henry's grip. Henry parried the next blow with his umbrella and jumped on the instep of the larger man, who let out a howl of pain. Even so, Henry could not retain his grip on the portmanteau. He saw the two men fleeing with it until they melted away into the evening crowds around the station entrance. Henry threw himself into a hansom and called out the Sutton's address to the driver.

The *contretemps* at the cab rank was one more astonishing event added to the already astonishing day. Tomorrow, he told himself, he would try to trace the thieves and the driver in Oxford, but he was thoroughly done up after the latest incident in what had been one of the strangest days of his life.

By the time he arrived at the pillared and porticoed home of the Suttons on Gower Mews near London University, Henry was in a state which he judged calm enough to meet his family. The shiny black door with the brass doorknocker was instantly flung open as he emerged from the cab. Mary stood in the doorway, smiling at him. It was only when he saw her sweet face welcoming him that he realized how alone he had felt with his trouble.

Henry Booth

"Are you well, Henry?" Mary asked.

"Yes, Mary. I am well," he answered as he kissed her cheek chastely, while she put her arms around him and pressed her figure against him.

"I've missed you so much, Henry. But why..."

"I have been sent down from Oxford, Mary, under the most outrageous circumstances. I very much need to speak with Mr. Sutton."

Before Henry could say another word, a man stepped into the hallway from the library. He was tall, sandy-haired, his features somewhat soft and undefined giving him a very youthful look in spite of the fact that Wilfred Smythe-White stood between the generations of the Sutton family, being some ten years older than Mary and Henry and a decade younger than Charles Sutton. He was a cousin of Charles Sutton's and a minister who had gone out to India and then returned to Britain several years ago. His avocation was doing good works for Indian immigrants who came to England after the Mutiny. He had apparently made good use of his knowledge of the languages and culture of the subcontinent to aid new-comers to Britain. He particularly struggled against any unjust hostility directed toward immigrants from the sub-continent. He earned a modest living writing columns on British issues of interest to residents of the subcontinent. He also helped bring deserving Indian natives to settle in Great Britain. He had been back in England for about five years and had rapidly gained Charles Sutton's complete confidence as a scholar and as a Christian.

Henry had never liked Smythe-White. He had the feeling that secretly the man coveted Mary and, what was worse, Mary sometimes seemed to be interested in his religious homilies. She even went to hear him speak in church, occasionally. She was impressed by his good works and, Henry had to admit, Smythe-White was no fool and a definite cut above the usual divines who promulgated the causes of some remote tribe on the edge of the empire, without having any first-hand experience of their culture or language. Smythe-White could speak Arabic, Hindi, Urdu and even a smattering of Persian. He had a doctorate in divinity and, Henry had to admit, he did something tangible for the people he patronized, raising money and helping them get settled in Britain. He offered no overt rivalry to Henry, but the younger man felt it as an undercurrent whenever Smythe-White was around, which was often since he was a distant family connection and Charles Sutton's ecclesiastical protege.

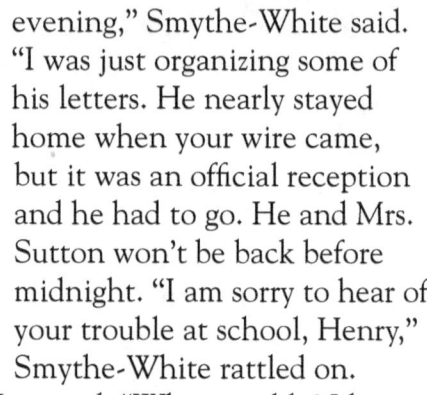

Dean Sutton

At times it would shock Henry how Charles could swallow the obvious way in which Smythe-White would try to ingratiate himself with his wealthy cousin.

"The Dean is out for the evening," Smythe-White said. "I was just organizing some of his letters. He nearly stayed home when your wire came, but it was an official reception and he had to go. He and Mrs. Sutton won't be back before midnight. "I am sorry to hear of your trouble at school, Henry," Smythe-White rattled on.

"Oh, Henry," Mary said. "What trouble? I have heard nothing. Tell me what is wrong."

Talking about the events at Oxford was the last thing in the world he wanted to do in front of Smythe-White.

"I think I should discuss it with Mr. Sutton, first, Mary," he replied testily.

The reassurance that Mary and the familiar house gave him, made Henry realize just how upset he had been all day. He was aware for the first time that he was ferociously hungry. He hadn't eaten since morning, just before meeting the sailor on Addison's Walk. It seemed like weeks ago to the young man. He had already decided that he would not alarm Mary by telling her anything of the scuffle at the station, but he did think it dreadful the way the criminal element seemed to be getting the upper hand in London, and even in Oxford.

Henry ate while Mary gossiped with him and then played some new songs for him on the pianoforte in the parlour. She played adequately but with little feeling, but Henry never gave any sign that he minded her inadequacy, though, he was quite sensitive to the mechanical quality of her playing and it often pained him. He thought "The dear girl can see that I am not quite myself, of course," Henry said to himself, so she is exerting herself to be amusing and cheerful. Her efforts were gradually repaid. Henry felt himself sinking deeper and deeper into the settee.

Mary eventually left the pianoforte, after Gibbons had come in response to Smythe-White's ring and been dismissed. Once they were alone, Mary came over and leaned on Henry's shoulder. Her delicious lips were only inches away from his, but he had vowed to Charles and Amelia Sutton that there was to be no love making of any sort as long as Henry lived with the family. Henry agreed fully that it would be underhanded to take advantage of the dear girl when so many tempting opportunities were presented by their situation. As she leaned even closer to him he said, "Don't worry about Oxford, dearest. It will not affect our plans."

Then, Smythe-White suddenly stuck his head into the room, "Are you hungry, Henry? We had dinner hours ago, but Gibbons can find something, I am sure," and without waiting for an answer pulled the bell.

"It is as though he is the one who lives here and I the visitor,"Henry thought. "A truly considerate man would leave the room so Mary and I could be alone." Now it looked as though they would be stuck with him for the evening, but to Henry's surprise Smythe-White stepped into the room and held out his hand to Henry and said, "I am certain this will all blow over, Henry. I must get back to my work. I just came out to greet you." And with that, Smythe-White disappeared back into the library. A short time later, Henry could hear the front door open and close as Smythe-White left the house.

Then followed an indeterminate time of silence as the two young lovers sat, very close together, on the settee. The moments of exquisite torture grew longer as they felt and resisted their attraction. Outside, the sun had set. Mary was nearly on Henry's lap when they heard the door to the room open. The young people sprang apart as Charles Sutton's austere presence came into the room.

Charles had never scolded either Mary or Henry. He had taught them both what he expected and had trusted them fully. His quiet, poised manner had always compelled their admiration and good behaviour. He was tall, his movements very deliberate and yet graceful. His hair was a sandy gray as were his oddly military mustachios. His features were sharp and straight beneath a prominent forehead. His face was marked by the habit of reflection and the advantage of good breeding. Mary knew it was time for her to withdraw, which she did.

"Good night, Father," she said kissing Sutton on the cheek. "Good night, my dear."

Charles closed the parlour door and sat down.

"Now, what incomprehensible thing has transpired at Oxford, Henry?"

Henry had long since arranged his thoughts for this interview with his stepfather. If anyone could get to the bottom of the President's behaviour, it would be Charles Sutton. He traveled in a rarified circle of senior government and Church officials. More than once, the Archbishop of Canterbury had been in the Sutton's house.

Henry presented the day's odd sequence of events, omitting nothing. When he finished speaking, Charles Sutton said, "Well, you have had a remarkable day, Henry. We can make no mistake about that. I shall see what I can learn about the whole affair at Oxford. I trust your account was complete?"

"Absolutely, sir."

"Well, I believe it is all some freakish misunderstanding that has taken place between you and the President. I think he only wanted to see the diary to establish the true connection between you and the man you were seen with on college grounds. It is the only possible reason for his interest."

"Then why expel me, sir?"

"Well, I believe the President got a little too warm with you. The idea of a student defying his authority made him over reach himself and he didn't quite know how to withdraw gracefully. We are all capable of such things, and men in high places are often tempted to be imperious. You said he was the kind of man who took his dignity very seriously."

"Yes, sir. That is true. I find him very supercilious."

"Yes, well, I understand. I think all of this will dissipate tomorrow, after he gets the wire I shall send."

"I do hope you are right, sir. But what about the disorder in my room?"

"That sounds like a rather nasty student prank to me. Let us not enlarge our troubles. First, let us get you back on good terms with the college. Heaven knows that the Lord gives us enough work to do, without our anticipating it."

"Yes, sir."

"Now, sleep well, Henry. And try to put this unpleasant business out of your mind, until I can pay a few calls tomorrow and send a wire to the President."

"Thank you, sir. I knew I could count on your support."

"You are a good, man, Henry, and have proven your quality many times to me. I only wish you took your religion a little more seriously."

"I'm sorry you find me lacking, sir."

"That is between you and your Saviour. I have nothing to complain of as long as you keep His laws, which I know you do."

Thank you, again, sir. Good night."

"Good night, Henry. Things will look much simpler in the morning."

Unfortunately, Charles Sutton couldn't have been more wrong.

Chapter 3

A Young Girl's Fears

Naturally, Henry was in an agony of suspense while he waited for the President's reply to Charles Sutton's wire, but it did not prevent him from enjoying Mary's company during several excursions around London.

A trip to the Regent's Park with its zoological garden, on a magnificent June day gave the young people the opportunity to be alone and take in a rare London afternoon of fresh air and sunshine. They both enjoyed animals, and recently, the zoological gardens had received a tiger from Bengal. This was the creature Mary most wanted to see. She vaguely felt that seeing the creature was a way of testing her own likely response to India. In her mind, Henry's trouble at school brought the subcontinent closer as a possibility for their future life. She didn't fully understand what had happened, but she knew that Henry or her father would tell her when they were ready and when they could say something definite. In the meantime, she was curious to see if the tiger's size and ferocity would frighten her at all. She had also resolved to ask Wilfred more about life on the subcontinent, but she would not do it in front of Henry. She knew it would annoy her lover.

As they rode north to the Park in the family carriage which Charles Sutton had graciously lent them for the afternoon, Henry studied the face of his betrothed. He once again admired her finely formed features, and her large gray eyes beneath a broad handsome brow which tapered down to a strong, well-formed chin. Her nose was straight and her eyes large and thoughtful. Her figure was a little above medium height, slender without seeming slight. She had a very feminine, deferential way of carrying herself which always made Henry feel even taller than his six feet and two inches. He searched her countenance for any change in feature or expression since he had last seen her several months ago. He was glad to find none, just a few freckles across the bridge of her nose.

There were, of course, two Bengal tigers. The obvious power of the beasts' rippling muscles and their growls of displeasure made Mary nervous enough to cling tightly to Henry's arm.

"Goodness," she thought, "what would I do if I met creatures like these in the wild?" She was not pleased with her own nervous reaction. "I must conquer this sort of nervous fear if we are to live on the subcontinent," she told herself and slowly released her hold on Henry's arm and stepped closer to the cage. She also felt it her duty to go to the recently opened snake house. Those alien creatures with their biblical connotations made Mary particularly uneasy and she usually avoided their cages. But she knew that India was filled with snakes and she must overcome her unease if they should have to go. A simple English garden snake could make her jump in fright when she saw one in their yard at home. What would she do if a cobra or a gigantic python came near her?

"It is of the last importance," she told herself, "that I learn to distinguish the venomous from the non-venomous. If we have to go, Henry will have no time for a nervous wife. Nor will I be of use to anyone as an active Christian, either, if I cannot make myself easy with these ubiquitous creatures. The natives will think me a foolish *memsahib* and will have no respect for me. And if they do not respect me, they will surely cheat us. Who knows what wild places Henry might have to go as his usncle's agent?"

Her vision of the subcontinent was strongly coloured by the horrors that Henry's parents had suffered and the published diaries which many of the victims of Cawnpore and Lucknow sieges had written. Mary only hoped that she would live in Calcutta most of the time. The life there would be considerably more civilized than in any of the upcountry outposts.

Whilst they walked through the English sunshine in Regents Park, Mary thought of the accounts of the brave women who had withstood the dreadful siege at Lucknow and protected their children, often doing the work of men, living daily with the prospect of savage death or worse from the natives. Could she measure up to the trials of India as those women had—as a Christian woman should? Would she be frightened of the natives—of everything? She must not be. It was a Christian duty to overcome her fears.

"Dear Mary," Henry said, " you were so gay when we started out and now you are so thoughtful. Is something wrong?"

"I confess, Henry, I was looking at these animals from India and wondering if I am strong enough for the vicissitudes of the subcontinent."

"Don't worry, dear girl. Your father will take

care of the President of my college. He will smooth him down. I still believe we shall live in Oxford."

"When I look at these creatures, I do think I would be happier there, Henry, dear."

"Of course, Mary. It is second sons, adventurers, civil servants or politicians who go out to India by choice. Who would not prefer the very English beauty of Oxford and its venerable buildings?" Yet, even as he spoke, a prospect of the groves of Lucknow seen from the top of the Dilkusha chateau rose in his mind; for a moment he could smell the delicious scents and see the colours of the blossoming fruit trees under a twilit sky of exquisite indigo. It was as if his own memory defied him to disavow the place of his birth.

"What a curious old thing I am," Henry said to himself, "to feel drawn back there by some childhood memories. It really wouldn't do for Mary. She has the heart of a lioness, but she is too refined and delicate for India. Her skin is so soft and white. She would burn up under an Indian sun." He took her arm and led her out of the snake house.

For their next outing, the couple planned a picnic lunch to Greenwich. Mrs. Vesey, the cook, made wonderful, delicately flavoured sandwiches. There was a light moselle wine and Mary wore a pretty green dress which showed her perfect, unlaced figure to very great advantage. Henry thought the shape of her torso between her waist and hips, as seen from the back, particularly charming.

As he watched her walk slightly ahead of him, Henry felt that their wedding day couldn't come soon enough. What would he ever do without her? Risking her in India seemed suddenly ridiculous, no matter what happened in Oxford. There were other schools which needed lecturers. Then, once again, as if to contradict himself, at the same moment, Henry's memory showed him a huge oriental moon rising over the gleaming white *Rumi Darwaza*, an ornate sixty foot triumphal arch, the most beautiful purely ornamental structure in Lucknow, which housed a maze in its upper storeys. This time, however, Henry turned away from the past immediately. It was just the barest glimpse he saw of the glowing city, as it reflected moonlight from its white stucco buildings, fashioned from the calcareous deposits of ancient lake beds.

"It must be the strain of waiting for this business at Oxford to be resolved that makes me so contrary, turning to the past when I should be looking ahead," Henry thought to himself. Perhaps there would be an answering letter tomorrow.

There was a reply. But it was not the answer Henry or Charles Sutton had hoped for. Charles called Henry into his study, which was handsomely paneled with good English walnut and bookcases that reached the ceiling. The thickly covered walls always made voices sound muted in the room. Charles was standing behind his desk when Henry appeared in answer to his summons.

"I am dismayed to say, Henry," he told his adopted son, "that Sir Percival seems indeed a supercilious man and most jealous of his authority. His stand with me is that either you give him the journal he asked for, or your expulsion shall stand. He and he alone has the right to decide who remains a fellow and who does not. He refuses to make any explanation for his actions and tells me, nearly in so many words, not to bother him with personal requests. I am surprised and disappointed, Henry."

This last statement Charles made very slowly, emphasizing each word carefully. Henry knew that it was as close as Charles Sutton ever got to a display of anger.

"As am I, sir."

"I shall write to him once more, this time by letter, telling him that if he continues in his unreasoning obstinacy, I shall write to my friend, the Vice Chancellor of the University. Perhaps the prospect of being questioned by Sir Phillip Vale will be daunting enough to get us a more serviceable reply."

"I have already decided, sir, that no matter what happens, I shall not go to India. I..."

"No, Henry. Decide nothing until this business is resolved. I know it is difficult to remain in such an unjustifiably ambiguous position, but facing it down coolly is a sign of strength and maturity. We are in the right and we shall win through."

"Yes, sir."

Charles mailed his letter and this time the reply was even more startling. It came in the form of a visit by two members of the Metropolitan Police Force's detective branch, operating out of Old Scotland Yard. The door was opened to them by Wilfred Smythe-White, who just happened to be going out.

"Is Mr. Charles Sutton and Mr. Henry Booth at home?" A tall, stolid looking man in plain clothes asked as he held his identification.

After a quick look, Wilfred Smythe-White said, "Mr. Charles Sutton is in his library. If you'll walk in and wait, I shall get him. I cannot answer for Mr. Booth."

"Thank you, sir," the big man said. His partner, a small man with a pointed ratlike face continually glanced around, his quick, darting black eyes looked everywhere at once. The two detectives said nothing as they waited. The big man sunk into complete immobility while his partner kept up his rapid squinting looks, twisting his head this way and that.

Within five minutes, Charles Sutton appeared with Smythe-White walking behind him.

"Good day, gentlemen. What can I do for you?" Charles asked. Smythe-White withdrew.

"We're conducting some routine enquiries, sir, and we would like to talk to you and Mr. Henry Booth, if possible."

"Certainly," Charles replied, and pressed the buzzer that would bring Gibbons.

A few moments later, the butler appeared.

"Please call Mr. Booth, Gibbons, and tell him I want him in the front parlour."

Then, turning back to the detectives he said, "This way, gentlemen," and led them to the front parlour, a large gray room with overstuffed furniture and a pattern of roses on the wallpaper. By the time Henry joined them, he could see that Charles was pale and agitated.

"Is anything wrong, sir?" Henry asked Charles.

"Henry, I have just had the most shocking news. Prepare yourself. The president of your college has been murdered."

"What?" Henry exclaimed. The hair on the back of his neck was tingling.

"How do you do, Mr. Booth?" the big stolid looking policeman said. " I am detective superintendent Lane."

"How do you do?" Henry answered mechanically. "How terrible. It is difficult even to associate Oxford with murder. There can be no mistake—that it was murder?"

"No sir. When was the last time you saw the President, sir?"

"Friday. At five o'clock."

"And what was your meeting about, sir?"

"He wanted to see some private family papers that had just been sent to me from India. I did not wish to release them and he expelled me."

"And that is the misunderstanding you refer to in your wire to the President, Mr. Sutton?"

"Yes."

Amelia Sutton

"And, Mr. Booth, what time would you say it was when you left the President's office?

"It couldn't have been past five-thirty."

"So you came at five and stayed no more than a half hour?"

"Yes."

"Was your meeting cordial?"

"Well, hardly. I am a third year student at Magdalen. The President told me I must hand over private family papers or be expelled."

"So you were upset, sir?"

"Naturally."

"Did you and the President have hard words?"

"Well," Henry began, but then Charles Sutton broke in, "Gentlemen, I think we should continue this in the presence of my solicitor, Sir Joshua Franks."

"That is your right, sir. But if there is nothing to hide..."

"There is nothing to hide, gentlemen. Mr. Booth was here in London by the time you say the murder took place. But I do not want him to answer any more questions until our solicitor is available."

"Then, shall we say tomorrow, sir, some time in the late afternoon in Scotland Yard? You have my card."

"Fine, gentleman. I'm sure Sir Joshua will make himself available. I shall write to him directly. Incidentally, how can you be certain the President was murdered?"

"He was strangled and his neck was broken."

Charles shuddered. "Good heavens. How horrible."

"It was certainly a brutal crime. And the criminal must have been a large, strong man," the smaller detective said, looking appraisingly at Henry.

"Very good, sir, we'll expect both of you and your solicitor tomorrow afternoon at the Yard," the blonde policeman said as he and his partner stood to leave. Then, Gibbons led them both out into the hall.

Once Henry and Charles were alone, they each looked at the other with perplexity.

"This is dreadful, sir," Henry said.

"It certainly is a very shocking incident, Henry. Why should anyone want to murder the President of an Oxford college?"

"Unless," Henry said, "it was some mad student with a grudge. A large, strong student," Henry said, looking down at his own powerful hands.

"Yes. I am afraid I can't blame the police for coming here first. The disorder in your room, the argument with the President, your expulsion— and only your family to vouch for your presence here. Thinking of all this is why I felt we should consult Sir Joshua without delay."

"But sir, you don't think..."

"Of course not, Henry. But if you look at the circumstances from a policeman's point of view, they do point strongly in your direction."

"How ghastly, sir. We mustn't tell Mary. I don't want to alarm her."

"Nor shall I tell Amelia. I believe that the fewer people who know about this, the better. Certainly, we shall do nothing until after we have seen Sir Joshua."

"Shall you write, then?" Henry asked.

"No. Get your umbrella."

In less than ten minutes, Henry and Charles were in the barouche and clattering across the west end on their way to Lincoln's Inn and the chambers of the famous solicitor. They had no idea that Wilfred Smythe-White had heard the entire interview with the police from the adjoining library where he was working.

The chambers of the famous lawyer comprised two rooms, one very large, high-ceilinged and with a fireplace and a row of windows that looked out on New Square, Lincoln's Inn. Looking diagonally across the square, the large anteroom had a prospect of the greenery of the Fields. Neoclassical images were painted on the walls and ceilings, adaptations of pagan contests: Heracles strangling Antaeus by holding him up in the air, Achilles slaying Hector, Perseus facing the Minotaur, undaunted. Victory was the theme everywhere one looked in this large comfortable room. When Charles sent in his card, Sir Joshua stepped out in a very few minutes.

Sir Joshua's large, bluff appearance was always so reassuring, Charles thought. The lawyer's white hair was perfectly coiffed and his broad pink face and large features were genial. He looked more an elegant man about town than what he was, one of the sharpest legal minds in the country. His face was good-natured and open, the antithesis of Mr. Voles, the lawyer whose character Mr. Dickens had forever stamped on the popular imagination.

"Good to see you, Charles. How are you, Henry? How is Oxford? Ah, I see by your face that I have asked an indelicate question. Let's go inside. No interruptions, Mr. Yellowlees," he called to the stern looking clerk, whose dour face and red hair could only mean the man was Scots.

Charles rapidly recounted what the police had said about the murder, and Henry added the strange incidents leading up to his expulsion. The lawyer listened, said nothing and wrote rapidly.

When Sir Joshua felt satisfied he was in full possession of the facts he said, "Really, gentlemen, I don't believe there is anything the police can do. I can see why they hypothesize that you may be involved, but it is a long way from that to presenting a criminal case. We shall go to their interview, of course. I shall answer any questions that aren't straightforward. I don't know what we can do about Henry's expulsion. Oxford has its own legal system that is not answerable to anything but its own officials and the Almighty, Himself. Let me write a few letters and see what I can do. Though, I am a Cambridge man myself. In the meantime, Henry, you might want to apply to London University to make certain your degree is completed."

"I suppose it would be wise, in case..." Henry said.

"I think so, Henry," Charles Sutton said.

"Well, I shall look on the bright side: if I don't go back Oxford, I shall be able to spend more time with Mary."

"Now that really is a bright prospect," Sir Joshua said.

"Yes, naturally, though, I should be disappointed at not receiving my degree at Oxford."

"Of course," Sir Joshua said. "I still hope to

reverse the President's actions," Sir Joshua said. "I just think it wise to be certain of your degree."

There was a pause in the conversation and then Sir Joshua spoke again, "So we'll meet tomorrow at, say, two o'clock in Old Scotland Yard and dispose of the police?"

Henry nodded.

Charles said. "Thank you for your time, Sir Joshua, and your sound advice."

"My pleasure, gentlemen."

The subject of concern having been discussed exhaustively, Henry and Charles rode home without mentioning it again. Instead, Henry raised something else that had been in his thoughts.

"Sir, what sort of work is Mr. Smythe-White doing for you, sir? Perhaps I could obviate the need for his presence in the house and take over from him. I should be happy to be of use to you, sir."

"Ah, Henry, you still feel some antipathy for Wilfred, don't you? I am sorry, for really, I believe he is a good man. And you don't speak Urdu and right now, he is translating some letters written by native converts to Christianity."

"To what end, sir?"

"I am interested in the whole process of conversion, what takes place in such a person's mind and spirit when they are swept up into Christ's kingdom. I thought it might be more evident in converts from another culture. Smythe-White's many friends among the east Indian population in London have been providing me with some rare insights. Hardly your kind of thing, eh Henry."

"No, sir, I must confess, it is not."

Instead of taking Henry's answer badly Charles said, "Mary will be the making of you, Henry. Once you are together in the married state, her Christian goodness can't fail to touch your heart and spirit."

"It just seems to me, sir, that other religions also have valuable teachings."

"As curiosities of philosophy, perhaps. But only Christ is the Son of the one true God and our Church is His true representative on earth."

Henry knew that Charles did not view him as quite Christian enough for Mary, but the Dean knew he could not turn back the clock and undo the years during which his daughter's preference had been formed.

After the Dean's remark, Henry and Charles rode in silence. They had never been close, but Charles was not a man for intimacy. He had taken Henry into his home as a family and religious obligation, and later had come to respect the boy for his diligence and accomplishments. Charles was just, he was thoughtful and lived the precepts of his faith, spending many long hours in the service of his religion.

"It must be," Henry thought," that it is with Amelia where his heart resides, and only with her."

Henry knew he was very different from Charles. His nature was warm and he enjoyed things that involved intimate contact with others. Amelia was like that, as well. Mary was less so. Still, he thought, as they rode home, "she is a dear thing and will be happy when she hears that I may be staying in London for the rest of the year."

The following day, the interview with the police took place as planned, and Henry was shocked to realize that the authorities completely discounted his and Charles' assertions about his whereabouts at the time when the murder was presumed to have taken place. The idea that anyone could disbelieve a clergyman with a social position like that of Charles Sutton, staggered him.

Sir Joshua smilingly pushed aside the scandalous attitude of the police and basically said to the minions of the law, "Prove your assertions, otherwise do not bother my clients with your theories."

It seemed that nothing could make the solicitor lose his good humour.

Sergeant Abdul Salim Sadat as a
young man, fighting the Thuggee
undercover with William Sleeman

Chapter 4

Sergeant Abdul

Once the police interview was over and he had explained everything to Mary, Henry felt confident that he was at the end of his bizarre adventures. He was settling down to his lectures in London and getting used to home life once again when he remembered the diary that still lay in Oxford in his friend's chambers. He wanted to read it now, more than ever. His Uncle Henry had suggested that it might bring him trouble. Considering what had happened since it first appeared, it seemed prudent to read it closely.

Mary was out with her mother, starting to purchase her trousseau, Smythe-White and Charles were working in the library. Why not go to Oxford and get the diary? He could wire Clayton from Paddington to make certain he would find him in his chambers.

It would be nice to get away from the city for the day and see the greenery of Oxford once again. So by the time the shadow of Magdalen Tower had crossed the High Street, Henry was knocking at Clayton's door.

"Ah, Booth, here you are. Yes, of course I got your wire. How are you?"

"Rather busy with the new school and all that."

"So you're not coming back?"

"I am still waiting to hear, but it is getting late in the term and London seems a good university. It is nice to be with my family again, too. Oh, I say, where is your cabinet?"

"We've had yet more excitement here," Clayton answered. "I suppose you heard about the President? Incredible! Killed in his own apartment by person or persons unknown. Oxford is still reeling from it. However, crime is trickling down to lowly undergraduates. Day before yesterday someone forced their way into my rooms and began tearing my things apart. In the process, they knocked over my cabinet."

"Oh, gracious. Your specimens."

"Pretty well in order. I'm just glad that whoever it was had the good sense to avoid the adder. I could have come home and found a corpse on the floor. As it was, I found your book on the floor with the adder coiled around it. I just hope they catch whoever is committing these absurd burglaries. It's very unsettling for everyone."

"Yes, of course," Henry answered, as he looked over at the photograph of Clayton's mother. Each time he saw the picture, he was startled by it.

"Now, Booth, I don't want to be a rude beast, but I have a lecture. I was going to leave your book with the porter and pin a note on my door. Oh, incidentally, here is a single-stick that belongs to you. Your scout told me you must have overlooked it the day you packed up."

"Oh, excellent. That is a good stick, ironwood, heavy and hard as metal. No, I shall let myself out. Of course. I understand. I won't keep you. You must come up to London sometime soon, Clayton."

"After term is over."

"Definitely, after term is over."

As he walked back through the familiar streets of the college town, Henry felt some sadness that he might not be returning. He had looked forward to facing life with an Oxford degree.

Instead of going up the High Street, he turned up New College Lane and admired the theatre and the ancient stone wall that ran behind it. Students were everywhere, rushing around on bicycles in their gowns.

"Well," he said to himself, "I have Mary instead of Oxford." His work would sort itself out.

The warm, soft air made him sleepy and he dozed in his compartment, going back to London. As he crossed the waiting room of Paddington, he remembered the last time he was here during the evening rush. If any of those villains were still at large, he would make short work of them, he thought, as he hefted his ironwood stick and got off the train.

In less than thirty seconds from the time he had the thought, he was assaulted again, in the same place where all the crowds rushed in and out of the station. This time however, the outcome was very different. Henry took the blows on his guard. The first man who lunged at him was turned away with a single overhanded blow of the stick. The crack of the heavy dense wood hitting bone and the man's cry could both be heard above the din of the crowd. When a second man tried to hit him in the head with a cane, Henry was ready for him and when the villain saw that, he ran. Both of the men were Indians. Henry couldn't remember what the other attackers had looked like.

He was about to get into a taxi when a small, inoffensive-looking Indian man plucked at his sleeve.

"Young, sir," the man said in his clipped English, "You are injured. I am a surgeon. Allow me to help you and dress your wound," and he presented his card.

"Gratis, sir, gratis," the man went on. "Those countrymen of mine do our race no service when they behave in such an uncivilized way. Allow me to erase some of their infamy and show you that not all of us with dark skins are evil."

Henry lightly touched his forehead and was shocked to see a surprising quantity of blood on his fingers. His hat had been knocked off by the first attacker. The wound must have been caused by the second.

"Please, young sir, take this clean cloth and hold it against your head," the little man said and he reached into a black leather bag he carried and handed Henry an immaculately white cloth.

"I think I am starting to feel a little faint," Henry said. "But I hardly felt the blow."

"Such is the body's skill, young sir. It gives us strength and energy for urgent needs and afterwards when the danger is past, we feel our wounds. Allow me to take you to my surgery. It is not far." And the small man led Henry to a waiting cab.

Henry must have dozed in the taxi. He remembered glancing at the card. It read: "Sergeant Abdul Salim Sadat, qualified medical surgeon, loyal attendant to Her Majesty's troops during the siege of Lucknow." Then he must have dozed off again and the next thing he knew the Indian was helping him out of the cab.

"I must have fallen asleep," Henry said.

"I woke you several times. With a concussion, you must stay awake. Do not let yourself fall asleep. You may not wake if you do. Do you understand, young sir."

"Yes, doctor— Lucknow, where was it— I mean, did I read it? I certainly sound a fool. What I meant to say sir was, do you know Lucknow?"

"Very well, young sir. I received many honours there. Come, come," he added pulling Henry into a dark doorway in a grimy old brick building.

The next thing Henry remembered was a stinging pain on his forehead.

"Ouch. What are you doing to me?"

"I am merely washing the wound, young sir, before I put on a bandage."

"The stinging has stopped," Henry said. "In fact, that side of my face seems to be getting a little numb."

"Do not worry, young sir. It is a medicine from India that can help stop pain"

"It does feel much better."

"Yes, but you must not go to sleep, young sir. I would like you to sit here for a time to make certain you can stay awake before I send you off in a cab. It is of the last importance, young sir, that you do not fall asleep. I must go into the next room for a few minutes. Please stay awake." With that final adjuration, the little man vanished and Henry promptly fell into a pleasant, semi-conscious condition.

Yet, when he had slept for a few moments, he had fleeting images of the most delightful dream, a beautiful, golden skinned girl had appeared to him, like one of the *houris* out of the *Arabian Nights*. He would enjoy seeing her again. The doctor re-appeared.

"How are you young sir?"

"All right, doctor."

"I am just a surgeon, young sir."

"Then, what shall I call you?"

"Sergeant will do."

"That's right, you said you were a Sergeant. At Lucknow, you said."

"That is correct."

"My parents were there. Then they went to Cawnpore."

"Ah, that name is a reproach to all of India, to all of us."

"Oh heavens," Henry exclaimed. "Where is

the diary?"

"This book, young sir?" Sergeant Abdul held out the thick, badly tattered leather and cloth bound book to Henry.

"One of your assailants tried to pull this away from you, young sir. He must have thought it valuable. Were I you, I should put it into a bank vault very soon."

But Henry had dozed off, once again.

"Oh, dear, oh, dear," the Indian man said. "I must use something to keep you awake." He turned to some shelves filled with pigeon holes and from one of these drew out some powder. He took some of this powder and began rubbing Henry's gums with it.

"Was I asleep long?" Henry asked, a few moments later."

"No. Young sir, not long. I have given you something to help keep you awake. I will give you some to take home with you."

"I do feel more alert, Sergeant."

"This powder has been used for thousands of years in India. It will help keep you awake."

"I have a friend, Sergeant, who would be very pleased to meet and talk with you. He is very interested in the native medicines of India."

"Then he is more intelligent than most," the diminutive man said as he packed some powder into a small glass stoppered bottle. "If you feel sleepy again, rub some of this powder on your gums. You must stay awake until this time tomorrow."

"Yes, sir. Thank you, sir. Please, allow me to pay you something for your trouble."

"No, young sir, my countrymen assaulted you, I must clear their debt."

"Then you believe you are your brother's keeper?" Henry asked.

"We are all responsible for each other. I shall walk out with you. It is only two streets to a drinking establishment where you will find a cab."

As they walked along, Sergeant Abdul continued, "You will have to cross the river. You are on the Surrey side, now. We are not far from Lambeth Palace. This is Abbey Street."

"Thank you again, Sergeant," Henry said as they trudged up the badly lit street.

The low, squat buildings appeared to be brick but with the fog and dirt, it was impossible to tell. A heavy fog had settled in with the darkness and was getting thicker by the minute. The wet, dirty streets seemed a thousand miles away from Oxford's green quads and elegant spires where he had spent the afternoon.

As Henry got into a growler, Sergeant Abdul said, "Remember, young sir, put that book into a vault or you may not see the last of those devils. And no sleeping until tomorrow. Use the medicine to stay awake."

"Thank you, again, Sergeant," Henry said as he waved and then clattered off across the Thames.

He may have dozed in the cab. He wasn't sure, but it seemed only moments before he was seated in front of the Sutton's familiar door in Gower Mews. The moment Henry entered the house, the whole family seemed to converge on him in the front hall.

Amelia and Mary were the first ones by his side.

"Where have you been, Henry?" Amelia said. "With this fog settling in we were becoming concerned."

"Goodness, Henry, what has happened to you?" Mary exclaimed. You are injured."

"What was the cause of your wound, Henry? And who bandaged it so neatly?" Amelia added.

"Ladies," Charles interjected as he came into the front hall, "give the man a chance to explain himself instead of rushing at him from all directions."

"Thank you, Charles, it is rather a tale."

So with his family gathered around in the parlour, Henry recounted the events of day.

When he had finished, Charles asked, "Are you certain that this little Indian surgeon wasn't in with the others?"

"What would be his aim, sir?"

"Henry," Mary said, "Perhaps you shouldn't take any more of the medicine he gave you."

"Why ever not, Mary? I tell you its effects were most beneficial."

"But I have heard that there are dangerous herbs that at first seem effective but can also be quite destructive, like opium."

"That is true, Henry," Amelia said.

"Good heavens, I tell you, he was the most harmless, no, helpful little man I have ever met," Henry replied to them all.

"But they were all Blacks," Amelia said.

"That may be," Charles put in, sharply, "But Christians really cannot judge people by the colour of the skin God gave them. That is wrong."

"Thank you, sir," Henry said. "He also told me he had been at the Lucknow siege. It sounded as if he had been decorated. He had a rank of Sergeant, I believe."

"If he treated the soldiers in the siege, he would certainly know his trade," Charles said.

There was a knock at the door and Wilfred Smythe-White stuck his head into the parlour.

"I have quite finished that last lot...gracious, what happened to you, Henry?"

"Some black roughs at the station attacked him," Mary answered. "Can you believe that London can be so dangerous? We might as well be in India."

"Were they thieves? Did they take anything from you?" Smythe-White asked.

"No. They got nothing from me but a thrashing. And then an Indian surgeon patched me up," Henry went on, "Actually, I just realized Smythe-White, you knew Lucknow before the siege. There couldn't have been too many native surgeons on the post. Did you know a little chap named," and he paused while he drew out the card and read, "Sergeant Abdul Salim Sadat."

"A tiny chap, with very fine hands and woolly hair?" Symthe-White cried.

"The very one," Henry answered.

Smythe-White came in and sat down as he said, "He was quite famous at Lucknow."

"Famous or infamous?" Amelia asked.

"Oh, famous. Some English people swore he was the best doctor in the city. He used to attend Sleeman when he was Resident at Lucknow."

"Really?" Charles said. "Not many men more famous in India than *Thuggee* Sleeman was in those days."

"The little Sergeant was thick as thieves with Sleeman. He had odd ways of doctoring, but they seemed to work," Smythe-White said.

"Extraordinary," Charles said.

"There," Henry said, "so the doctoring he did for me is not to be feared on any account."

"I am relieved, Henry," Mary said. "But perhaps you could show Wilfred that powder he gave you."

Henry somewhat reluctantly passed over the stoppered bottle to Smythe-White, who removed the stopper and sniffed at the powder inside, dabbed some on his finger and put it on his tongue.

"A refined form of betel nut," Smythe-White said. "It is a stimulant, a mild one. Indians use it for everything. Perfectly safe if not taken in the huge doses the natives use."

"Thank you, Wilfred," Mary said passing the bottle back to Henry.

For his part, Henry did not care for all this informality between Smythe-White and Mary. It must have started since the beginning of term.

"He did seem to think that the others might come after me again," Henry said to draw back Mary's attention from Smythe-White.

"Why, Henry?" Mary asked. "Why should they?"

"He said one of them was trying to steal the diary," Henry said.

"What diary was that, Henry?" Smythe-White asked.

"My mother's diary. My uncle in Calcutta sent it to me only a few weeks ago. I went down to Oxford today to get it. I was on my way home from Paddington when these roughs appeared."

"Your mother's diary," Smythe-White repeated.

"Yes, one she kept at Lucknow before I came home and they went to Cawnpore."

Smythe-White got up suddenly. "Excuse me. I have much still to do this evening, Charles," Smythe-White said. "I shall be in early tomorrow. Good night, everyone. Take care of yourself, Henry, though you've had some of the best doctoring on the subcontinent," he said as he slipped out and closed the door.

"Oh, I am glad that Wilfred was here, this evening," Mary said after the door had closed.

Amelia nodded her head and said, "It is fortu-nate to know someone so knowledgeable about practical things."

nate to know someone so knowledgeable about practical things."

Henry wanted to say something to the contrary, but knew it would simply sound ill-mannered and so said nothing about Smythe-White.

"Are you going to put the book in a bank, Henry?" Mary asked.

"It is hard to credit the idea that these fellows were after my mother's personal thoughts. Why should they be...yet..."

"Yes, Henry, what is it?" Charles asked.

"Well, come to think of it, all these odd things seem to have started happening after I received the diary from Uncle Henry. In the letter that came with it, Uncle Henry said something odd about hoping the diary didn't bring me trouble. And, and," Henry went on, getting excited as he stood up, "Dr. Tripp also asked me for it, if you remember. Let's not forget that was the starting point of all my trouble with him. A very curious starting point, too. I really begin to think that in some obscure way there's something about my mother's diary that has stirred all this up, though I can't imagine how or why."

"Let us not be carried off on the wings of our own imaginations," the Dean said. "I still think the only reason the President wanted to see it, Henry," Charles said, "was that he wanted to know who the strange man was on college grounds. I think he planned to use the diary to cross question you."

"I am not so sure," Henry said in a thoughtful tone. "It is just as well that Sergeant Abdul told me to sit up all night. I shall read the diary and guard it. Until I can get to the bottom of all this, I shall put the book in your bank's vault if I may, Charles."

"Certainly, Henry."

"Are you hungry, Henry?" Amelia asked.

"No, thank you, Mother, just tired. I think I shall have to take more of this powder to stay awake all night."

"I shall stay with you, Henry, dear," Mary said.

"No, Mary, really. I don't want you to lose a night's sleep."

"And why not? If you are not well. Who else should watch over you and make sure you don't sleep?"

"All right, dear girl. Perhaps some tea?" Henry said.

"The very thing," Mary said reaching for the bell pull.

"No, Mary, don't make Gibbons put on his jacket to come to us. I shall go downstairs and make the tea," Amelia said.

Charles patted his wife's hand affectionately and said, "Mother, if our parishioners knew how constantly you consult the comfort of others, even our servants, they would want to make you Dean."

"Nonsense," Amelia said, looking pleased.

"I shall help, Mother," Mary said, standing up.

"And I," Charles said, rising, "shall go to bed."

A few moments later, Henry found himself alone in the parlour. He stood up and walked over to one of the windows. It was a wet, miserable night out and it had not improved in the time he had been home. Rain dashed against the glass and in the distance, he could hear carriage wheels splashing through puddles. The wind whistled sharply against the house; there was even a slight chill in the parlour.

"How curious life is," Henry mused, thinking of the little surgeon. "He might have known my parents, yet we meet by chance on the other side of the world. I wonder how he and his countrymen feel in London on a night such as this?"

"I really must begin to read my mother's diary. Charles was probably right about it having nothing to do with the bizarre events that have overtaken me recently."

Even so, the thought of knowing his mother better was a great attraction. What kind of thoughts had she deemed important enough to write down? Had she done any writing in the *bibighar* itself? Conditions were said to have been dreadful. There had not been enough room in the little house for all the women and children to lie down at the same time. Could she have written under those conditions?

The sounds of the storm were almost mesmerizing. He felt his eyes closing. Then, just as he was on the verge of sleep, Mary returned, carrying the tea tray.

"Henry, come and have some nice hot tea. What a night for the middle of June. It could be September or even October."

"Thank you, my dear girl. Where is Mother?"

"She thought we would enjoy our tea more without her and has gone to her room."

"Mr. Sutton's comments about her were just. She always thinks of others, first," Henry said.

The two sat on the settee, Mary put milk in their cups and then poured the steaming liquid. "I hope you know she is much more selfless than I," Mary said as she stifled a yawn.

"Dear girl," Henry said. "You don't have to sit up with me, really. I can stay awake on my own. I have the Sergeant's powder, too."

"I am all right. The tea will refresh me, I am certain," Mary answered. But a short time later, Henry was watching Mary sleep.

"Her face looks so young and fresh," he thought. "I wonder what she sees in her dreams?"

thinking of the beautiful harem girl he had dreamed about at the Sergeant's surgery, feeling a little guilty.

He felt his eyes start to close, shook himself and reached for the little stoppered bottle next to the tea tray. He put the powder on his index finger and rubbed it into his gums as Sergeant Abdul had shown him. This was followed by a pleasant tingling sensation and a slight feeling of greater wakefulness, but a short time later, Henry, too was asleep with his mother's diary underneath him on the settee.

The candles guttered and in her sleep, Mary's hand reached out for Henry, but did not find him. How long the stillness rested on them in the darkened room, neither Henry or Mary knew. But, suddenly, the dog's baying came crashing into Henry's sleep. All seemed confusion for a moment. The wind was blowing into the parlour, one of the french doors was banging to and fro in the wind and Archibald, the blood hound who lived below stairs, was giving blood curdling cries as he tugged on the lead Gibbons was holding. Henry could feel some of the cold rain whipping into the room. He just managed to get some candles lit when Gibbons and the dog rushed to the open door and closed it. The dog was obviously anxious to give chase.

"Sir, Miss, are you all right?"

"Mary," Henry asked the sleepy girl, "Are you all right, dearest?"

"I am well, Henry," Mary said as she sat up. "I must have fallen asleep. A fine way to look after you, Henry."

"Sir," Gibbons interjected, "there has been an intruder. Look," and he held a candelabra close to the floor. Imprinted on the thick carpet near the door was a very large muddy footprint. Archibald, sniffed at it and then clearly wanted to go through the french doors to the yard outside.

"Shall I let him go, sir?" Gibbons asked Henry.

"Certainly, Gibbons."

The hundred-odd pound dog bolted through the french doors the moment Gibbons had opened them.

"If there is anyone still near the house, he will regret it, now," Gibbons said with satisfaction, as he looked out into the darkness.

"What on earth is going on, here?" a tousled Charles Sutton asked from the doorway as he stepped into the parlour.

In as few words as possible, Henry told him and showed him the muddy foot footprint.

"I really think," the Dean said, "we must call the police."

"There will be no rest for any of us tonight, if we do, sir," Gibbons said.

Yes, that's true," the Dean agreed. "But after the suspicious way they have treated Henry, I don't want to give them any excuse for saying that we are not good citizens. I'm afraid I shall have to ask you to bring them, Gibbons."

"Yes, sir, I understand. I shall just slip on some trousers and get my brolly."

Some time in the small hours, the family once again received Inspector Lane in the parlour. The big stolid man looked sleepy and irritable, yet held his tongue through much of the description of the outrage. Finally, after listening and after examining the footprint minutely and being introduced to Archibald at his place in the story, he said, "I'd like all the men in the house to bring one of their right shoes to this room."

"What are you suggesting, Inspector?" the Dean asked with some asperity.

"Sir, I have been trained to do things a certain

way, in a certain order. I am sure that a scholar like you can appreciate method, sir. The first thing I must do is be certain that no one inside the house could be involved."

"That is preposterous, sir," Amelia said.

"Amelia," Charles said, "We must let the detective inspector do his work in the manner he thinks correct. No one here has anything to hide."

"Why, he has already as good as accused Henry of murdering the President of his college."

"It is all right, Mother," Henry said. "We all want to clear this up and go to bed. I am sure the detective inspector would rather not be from home on a dirty night like this."

"Quite right, sir. Let's get to it, everyone, if you please. Robbins, will you go downstairs with the servants and help them get things organized. I'll go upstairs with the family. The women of the house can go back to sleep."

Robbins was a uniformed policemen with gigantic mustachios, who was assisting the detective. He was quiet and had good manners. Henry thought him an improvement over the little rat-faced detective who had come the last visit.

By the time all the men reconvened in the parlour, detective Lane was able to line up seven mens' shoes in a row on the floor.

"Most of these," the large rumpled detective said, "are of average size and would definitely not fit this print. But four of them look fairly close. Let us see."

So saying, the big man knelt on the carpet and moved all the smaller shoes to one side. Of the four remaining shoes, two, based on their quality, must belong to family members. The other two could belong to servants. One by one, the detective placed each of the shoes within the impression made by the intruder. Shoes one and two were far too small. Number three was a perfect fit and four was too long. The detective put the perfect fit back into the impression.

"Whose shoe is that?" he asked.

"I think you must know, sir," said Henry, his face turning a dusky red "that it is my shoe. I also think that it is what you expected when you began this charade."

"Quite right," the big detective said, heaving himself to his feet.

"Ridiculous," Mary said. "To what end would Henry to do this? Answer me that. I had fallen asleep on the settee only inches away from him. I could have woken at any time."

"Well," said the policeman slowly, "if there had been a break-in while Mr. Booth was asleep, it would lend weight to the idea that someone else was causing all the trouble, would it not?"

"You mean the murder in Oxford," Charles Sutton said.

"That, and the attack at the station. We have not found a single witness to corroborate Mr. Booth's story."

"Oh, really, sir," Amelia said, not even trying to hide the disgust in her voice.

"What you should be doing instead of badgering my son is to be out in the rain with the dog tracking down the person or people who did this."

"You may be right, madame. But I may also be right. I did not say we would let things remain as they are. I think the truth will come out, and soon enough."

"Your meaning is clear, sir," Henry said. "You think I am a criminal."

"No sir, not a criminal, simply a young man who lost his head with a college President."

"Must I call upon Sir Joshua, again?" Charles Sutton said to the policeman in his frostiest tone.

"No, sir. Not yet. We shall look further into this and you will hear from us again. Goodnight."

"Astonishing," Mary said when the sound of the front door closing had reached them.

"Not really, my dear," Charles Sutton said. "That was a very dramatic demonstration that the detective gave us with the shoes."

"But, Charles," Amelia said. "To come into a respectable home with insinuations like that. Really. I should like you to write to our Member about it."

But Charles Sutton's face had settled into a polite mask. "Let us all go to bed. Henry, I shall want to talk to you in the morning. I shall have something to ask you."

"Yes, sir."

Once again, Mary and Henry were left standing alone in the parlour.

"Oh, Henry, what is all of this? Suddenly, for no reason, one misfortune after another is befalling us. Even my father sounds as if he wants to cross question you."

"I am sure Mr. Sutton and I can resolve any problem between us. He has been very supportive since all this started."

"But it is all so frightening and confusing, Henry, dear. Our lives used to look so settled to me."

"Don't worry, Mary. I shall sort things out with the Dean in the morning."

But the following morning, Mary heard raised voices in her Father's library. Henry and her Father were quarrelling.

"I must absolutely insist, Henry," she heard her father say.

"But even I have not yet read it, sir."

"Even more reason, then, Henry."

"If you do insist, sir, I shall give it to you. But I think you are being most unjust, compelling me to give you the private thoughts of my late mother before I have looked at the diary, myself."

"This household is being threatened and it is my responsibility to find out why and what I can do to stop it."

"It is a very bitter draught to drink, sir. I begin to feel that I am being suspected of something right in my own home. Here it is."

Some time later, Mary, sitting in the dining room, heard the door of her father's library slam and Henry's angry tread on the stairs.

"Oh, dear," Mary said out loud. She sat for some time waiting to see what would happen next, but all was quiet. Mary poured some tea and took some toast from the warming rack. She felt confident that whatever strange bedevilment the diary had brought into the house, would soon be dispersed by her father.

After finishing her solitary breakfast, she went and stood for some moments at the library door. All was quiet but as she turned away she heard her father mutter in a tone of horror, "Good Heavens, woman, how could you do it?"

Mary knocked, and called, "Papa, may I come in?"

"Not now, Mary, go and see, Henry." And then there was silence for a moment, then, more softly almost to himself, he muttered, "Poor devil."

"Father," what is wrong," she called through the door.

"Mary, I shall see you later. Not now," he said more sharply to his daughter than he had ever done.

"Good heavens," Mary wondered. Why was Henry, 'a poor devil.' What a dreadful thing for her father to say. She had never heard him say anything like that about anyone. What did it mean? And why was Papa so out of sorts?" For a moment, she felt strangely lonely in her own home, then she ran lightly up the stairs and knocked on Henry's door.

"Henry? May I come in for a moment?"

The door swung open and Mary flung her arms around Henry's neck. She could see that his face was still red with anger.

"Why did you and papa have to quarrel, Henry? It is so dreadfully unsettling. Mama is in her room with a headache, which I am sure has the same cause."

"He is reading my mother's journal before I do. It is grossly unfair."

"But Henry, does it really matter that much?"

"It does to me. I am very out of sorts. I'll see you later."

Some half an hour later, which she spent in her room, Mary came downstairs to find most of her family, including Wilfred Smythe-White in the hall outside her father's study. He was speaking to Henry.

"We agreed on a time to meet that has passed a half hour since. It is so unlike him"

When Henry saw her he asked, "Where is the Dean? He does not answer my knock."

Smythe-White said, "We had an appointment to meet and read over some letters together half an hour ago. I tried his door but it was locked.

"How curious," Amelia said, knocking on her husband's door. "Charles," she called. All was silent within.

"I think I should get the key from Gibbons," Henry said, walking toward the buzzer. He has duplicates for every room in the house."

"Ah, I did not know," Smythe-White said.

"Don't make him come up, Henry. I gave him the afternoon off," Amelia said. "He is probably reading in his pantry."

While Henry went downstairs in search of Gibbons and his keys, Amelia again knocked on the library. "Charles," she called.

A short time later Henry was back with a massive iron ring of keys, fluttering with several dozen pieces of paper upon which was noted the room to which each key belonged.

"Pantry, garden, ah, here it is, library," Henry said. As he bent over to put the key in the lock, he noticed some fresh scratches on the brass plate of the door, as if someone had tried to force it. He said nothing but turned the ornate iron key in the lock.

"Charles," he called as he stepped inside. Smythe-White was immediately behind him. When they caught a glimpse of the figure sprawled across the desk, Smythe-White slammed the door shut against the women. They could hear the surprised exclamations through the door, but not for a split second did it distract them from the form of Charles Sutton who lay sprawled across his desk with open, staring eyes and a huge purple welt around his throat.

"Good God," Smythe-White exclaimed. "What has happened?"

"Oh, Lord," Henry said as he approached the still figure. "It looks as though he has been done to death like the President of my school."

"Look," Smythe-White said. "He was writing something," and peered over the dead man's shoulder. There was one word on the paper, "Henry."

"Henry," Amelia's angry voice echoed the name

on the paper in front of the dead man, "open the door this minute."

"We can hardly hide this from them," Henry said.

"But we don't want them actually to see it," Smythe-White said.

"But where's the diary?" Henry asked out loud.

"Your mother's diary, the one you mentioned last night?" Smythe-White asked.

"Yes," Henry answered. "Ah, here it is. Strange, it was dropped on the floor."

"How do you know he was reading it?"

"Because he asked me for it," Henry replied with some asperity.

"Henry, what are you doing? Why have you shut us out?" Mary called from the other side of the door.

"We had better call the police," Smythe-White said But I'm afraid it could be terribly hard on you, Henry."

"What do you mean?"

"Gibbons told me you'd been arguing with Charles this morning. He is sure to say the same to the police when they come. If Charles died the same way your college president did, they will assume that you did it. They already believe you are implicated in the Oxford killing, do they not?"

"How did you know?"

"Charles told me about your examination at Old Scotland Yard. Perhaps you'd better be away from here until some of this settles down. I can meet you later tonight and tell you what has happened here."

"That seems rather cowardly," Henry said, visibly shaken.

"Look, old man, you can always turn yourself in later, accompanied by Sir Joshua."

"I suppose it would be better to see them with a lawyer. Charles thought so."

Smythe-White put his hand on the diary. "Are you sure you want to take this dangerous thing with you?"

"More than ever" said Henry. He turned and leapt into the window. "They mustn't see Charles like that." Henry said with one last look at the figure on the desk.

"You may depend on me," Smythe-White said.

And with that assurance, the young man sprang out the window, holding his stick and the diary, clearing the window sill in one leap like someone running hurdles.

Wilfred Smythe-White watched from the library window as Henry jogged across the back lawn, opened a little gate in the low iron fence and disappeared down the tradesmens' lane, which ran behind the house.

"Poor devil, indeed" Smythe-White muttered.

Chapter 5

Sergeant Abdul takes charge

"Young sir, young sir," dimly Henry heard a voice behind him in the street. The cries were punctuated by the sound of running feet. Lost in his own thoughts about Charles, Amelia, his own mother and Mary, it took Henry some moments to realize that the voice was familiar. He looked over his shoulder and saw sergeant Abdul running after him, holding his hat on with one hand and clutching a much larger hat in the other. Henry stopped and waited for the little man. He was surprised at how glad he felt to see the Sergeant.

"Sergeant Abdul," Henry called and waited for the small brown man to catch him up. With the eye of a trained athlete, Henry noted the Sergeant's graceful, fluid movements as he pumped his short legs. This, in spite of the fact, Henry noted as the other man drew near, that the sergeant must be fifty if he was a day. He could see now that his black hair was heavily streaked with gray, though his face was smooth and unwrinkled.

"What are you doing here, sergeant?" Henry asked as the small man drew abreast of him.

"Your hat, young sir. You left it at my surgery."

"But how did you find me?"

"The hatter. His name is inside and he told me you are his only customer with such a broad brow. I am glad to see you are feeling better, young sir. At least in body if not in mind."

"Why, what do you mean, Sergeant?"

"You are wearing the same shirt you had on yesterday. It is rumpled and looks slept in. I see you running away from your own house, frowning deeply. I conclude that your mind is disturbed, though your body is in good working order."

Henry blinked owlishly at the sergeant and then started walking. Sergeant Abdul fell into step with him.

"You know, it's odd, Sergeant. Even with the terrible events of the last few days, I find your company soothing. I can't understand why—unless—he said stopping suddenly.

"Did you know my parents at Lucknow? Have I met you before?"

"Your mother was a beautiful woman and an unusual lady, young sir, especially among the other *memsahibs*. No one could forget her who met her. But you and I never met in Lucknow."

Henry continued walking as he said, "I keep thinking, perhaps irrationally, that all these strange events are connected with the past. I must read the diary."

"You have not read it, yet, young sir?"

"I've had no time."

Suddenly Henry turned to face the diminutive Indian and burst out, "Look, I've got to trust you, sergeant. There's no one else. I must tell you that I think it possible the police are looking for me, or soon will be."

"Why would they seek you?"

"Because my step father was murdered today just after he and I had a quarrel. The police already think I killed my college president in Oxford. And the way both men died was the same, I believe."

Henry felt transfixed by the sharpness of the glance the Sergeant fired at him. It was several long seconds before he asked, "And what was that way of dying, young sir—what was noteworthy about it?"

"My college president was strangled and his neck was broken. My step..."

"Never mind," the Sergeant said, suddenly stepping to the curb to hail a passing cab.

"Say no more of this now, until I tell you it is safe to do so."

Henry was shocked at the tone of command in the little man's voice. It was as though he had suddenly become someone else. As he got into the four wheeler, Henry wondered if he was making a great mistake in trusting the Indian, but he really felt he had no choice.

"Seven-two-five Abbey Street, quickly driver. And then you will wait for us."

The Sergeant's brown face might have been carved out of some close-grained wood, and he said not one word as the cab plunged through the traffic toward the London Bridge and the other side of the river. All of the man's mildness seemed gone. He seemed hard as flint.

Once Henry realized that he would get nothing more out of the Sergeant, he tried to sort out his own thoughts, which seemed to whirl as blindingly as London cinders caught in the wind. Yet, through the clouds of fear, confusion, puzzlement and memory he could see his mother's face in his mind more clearly than at any time he could remember. It reassured him. He was glad that Sergeant Abdul had known and liked her.

When they arrived at the Sergeant's surgery, Abdul got out and said to Henry:

"Wait here. I shall just be a moment." And before Henry could ask any questions, Sergeant Abdul had entered the surgery.

Once he was alone, Henry had an impulse to get out of the cab and run away, but he couldn't think where to go. Where, he wondered would the Sergeant take him? What had galvanized the little man so, just before hailing the cab? Henry tried to think back on their conversation but in another moment, he was astonished to see Abdul, black bag in hand, with a tiny veiled woman on his arm. She was carrying two large but apparently lightweight embroidered bags with shoulder straps on them.

As he handed the woman into the hansom, Sergeant Abdul said, "My niece, Umrao Devi. This, my dear, is Mr. Henry Booth, whom you met in a semi-conscious state the other day." He helped her rearrange the bags and then got in himself.

"I hope you are feeling better, sir," a wonderfully low musical voice said. She brought a curious exotic fragrance into the hansom, like flowers mixed with spice.

"Then, the *houri* was not a dream," Henry said. Then, feeling somewhat embarrassed by the epithet he'd used he said, "I mean, I saw a very handsome woman when I was in the surgery, dozing. I thought she was a dream."

"Thank you, Mr. Booth, but our dreams are usually much more beautiful than life. I was there. I tried to talk to keep you awake as my Uncle directed. I was not very effective."

Henry felt there was something truly fascinating about the voice coming from behind the veil. He wanted to reach over and pull the fabric away. His memory of the face he'd seen when drifting in and out of consciousness was vague and imperfect.

"Twenty-five Upper Swandam Lane," Sergeant Abdul called to the driver as the hansom began to move.

"Where are we going, Sergeant?"

"To a place where I hope we shall be safe." Then the little man closed his eyes and crossed his arms, signalling that the subject was at an end.

Henry rode in silence for a while wondering how to start a conversation with the woman who sat next to him. Finally, the aroma she exuded, suggested something rather obvious to him.

"That is a wonderful scent you are wearing, Miss."

"Thank you, Mr. Booth. It pleases me that you like it."

"Very much. I don't recall anything quite like it, but it does remind me of India, somehow. But, recently everything seems to remind me of India."

"The base for it is jasmine," the wonderful voice said. "That's why it reminds you of the garden at the Residency. Many jasmine trees grew nearby. But I mix other herbs and spices with it."

"The Residency," Henry said. "Then, you,..."

"Yes, I was also born in Lucknow, Mr. Booth. Though, hardly in the Residency or even near it. But I have performed there several times ."

"Performed?"

"I am a singer and dancer, Mr. Booth."

"I thought there was something unusual about your voice. That is, it ah, has a very musical quality."

"I am not accustomed to such compliments from a young Englishman, sir."

The implication that he was flattering her made him blush.

"It really was my honest opinion, Miss. I hope I haven't given offence."

Her laughter was so silvery and unexpected that

it took a moment for him to recognize it as laughter.

"What woman, if she is honest, was ever offended by a compliment from a handsome young man?" she asked. "Especially, a compliment honestly meant."

Henry was quite at a loss to know what to say in reply. A moment later he was even more surprised when the veiled woman took one of his hands in hers and spread it out, palm upward, on her knee. She seemed to be looking at his hand very intently. She traced some of the lines in his hand with her delicate, gloved finger.

"You are a good man, Mr. Booth. I hope all will end well for you."

"Is that a sample of Indian fortune-telling?" he asked, smiling.

He heard her wonderful laugh again, then she said, "No. I am just looking through one of the windows of your soul. Your palm tells me some things about you, and your eyes, as well, but it is not fortune telling."

"What do my hand and eyes tell you?"

"That you are honest and want to be good to others. You want to take care of others, especially women—like an English knight. Many Englishmen pretend to feel this way, but you really do."

Henry believed the girl was sincere, but he could also see that everything she was saying could be said about almost anyone.

But even as he had the thought, she said, "You have a women who watches you from far, far away. You miss her. However, she is with you all the time. That is why you want to take care of women. You wish you could take care of her."

"My mother. She is dead, but Sergeant Abdul must have told you."

"No. He has said nothing about you, except that you were born in Lucknow near the Residency."

Henry suddenly wondered, who were these people he was riding with, really? He knew nothing about them, yet he somehow trusted the little Sergeant. Was the girl lying, or could she really divine something about him by looking at his palm. The idea was absurd, yet, there was something about her that seemed inconsistent with lying.

She let go of Henry's hand and lifted her outer veil, but her lower face remained covered with a piece of diaphanous fabric. Her almond-shaped eyes were brown but so dark that they seemed almost entirely black, it gave them a curious opaque quality. Her dark eyebrows were perfectly shaped, tapering delicately toward the sharp planes of her temples, but were strong over her eyes, yet, still suiting perfectly the finely carved bridge of her nose. The expression of the eyes was strong and deep, passionate, almost fierce. He couldn't help but compare their expression with Mary's meek eyes. He felt her gaze enter his own and then she picked up his hand again. This time, however, she made no attempt to look closely at it.

"I won't tell you falsehoods about yourself, Henry Booth. But you know nothing about me or where I have been or come from, or why I am here. Once you know, you may not care even to talk with me again." Then she once again released his hand and looked away from him.

"I think that very unlikely," Henry said. "I confess to finding you quite remarkable, though I must say, I have forgotten your name, Miss."

"Remarkable, but you forget my name?" she said. "Perhaps it is you who are not sincere with me, Henry Booth," her silvery laugh once again pealed in the narrow confines of the four-wheeler.

"No, I, really, please tell me your name, again. It

was something between a cat's purr and growl. That is all I can remember. But I shan't forget, again."

"I made you forget it," she said. " I pushed it out of your mind with my beauty and the things I said about you. But this is your last chance. So remember. I am called Umrao."

Henry suddenly realized the girl was flirting with him, teasing him, something he and Mary had never done with each other, for flirtation requires that a lover not be fully known. There must be some mystery we can fill with our own dreams.

"Umrao," he repeated.

"Umrao," she echoed.

Then he blushed deeply, feeling suddenly ashamed of his attraction to the Indian girl who seemed able to make him forget Mary and nearly everything else so easily.

The four wheeler began to slow. The streets through which they now passed were grimy, narrow lanes on the north side of the river to the east of London Bridge. They were following the Regent's Canal. The hansom finally stopped in front of a what seemed to be a mere gap between two buildings, with a steep flight of stairs leading down into the darkness. The dreadful aspect of the place put Henry on his guard and he clutched his stick tightly.

"Don't worry, Mr. Booth," Sergeant Abdul said. "For us, this is the safest place in London."

"But for the lady?" Henry asked, looking down the staircase which vanished into the gloom. Again, on the ancient steps whose treads were worn hollow with age and use, Henry heard Umrao's silvery laugh.

"Do not be concerned for me." She took his arm as they plunged into darkness. "I have my knight protector with me," she said.

He couldn't tell if she was laughing at him or not.

At the bottom of the staircase, by the flickering light of a profoundly begrimed oil lamp, Sergeant Abdul found the door latch and lifted it. They made their way into a low room, whose air was thick and heavy with brown opium smoke. Here and there a few flames flickered in the murky gloom, not lamps but stoves used to cook the drug.

Henry could dimly make out rows of wooden berths, like those aboard the poorest ship. The patches of illumination from the stoves allowed him to see people in all manner of grotesque poses: bent shoulders, heads thrown back and occasionally, dark lustreless eyes turned on the newcomers for a moment. The glowing pipes made little red circles in the gloom, first waxing bright then growing dim as the drug was burnt up and inhaled. Some of the inmates muttered to themselves or their neighbours in sounds that were barely intelligible as words, each monotonous voice wrapped in its own dreams, paying little attention to what was being said by anyone else.

To Henry, the darkness, punctuated with the red lights and the gibberish of the wasting minds seemed hideous, a vision of Hell. Yet, Umrao walked along beside him with an easy stride, as though she were passing through a park, garden, shop or any usual place. No one stopped or questioned them. Evidently the Sergeant was known here. What could it mean that he was known in such a low haunt? Perhaps, in spite of the good impression he had formed of the Sergeant and his niece they had some sinister purpose in bringing him here.

Sergeant Abdul led the way up a flight of wide creaking steps at the back of the opium den, climbed to the top and knocked on the door. It was opened by a grotesquely twisted silhouette. As Henry and Umrao drew close to the doorway, they could see a monkeyish sort of man who was bent nearly double and who walked on two crutches. Whether he was brown, yellow or white, Henry couldn't tell, so puckered with exposure and hardship was he. His wild tangle of beard and hair hid much of his face which, because of the way he was bent, was always looking down at the floor.

"Ah, my good doctor," the strange creature said when he saw Abdul. "I have been hoping you would come. My sleep is absolutely shattered."

"I warned you that the reaction was bound to set in."

"But if I do not use it, the pain is too great."

"I know, I know," Abdul replied. "I have a favour to ask of you, Smith."

"Anything for you, doctor. You have given me more ease than any man alive."

As Henry listened to this dialogue, his fears and questions were answered. Obviously, the little surgeon came here out of mercy, providing medical help for the poor broken man who owned the establishment.

Abdul and Smith dropped their voices for a few moments and then their host said, "Of course, doctor. You may stay as long as you wish. There are other places I can go. My two lascars down below will look after customers."

"Thank you, Smith. Now, let's go into the other room and I shall have a look at you."

The two men left Henry and Umrao in semidarkness.

"Have you been here before, Umrao?"

"No. Abdul has many patients who rely on him all over London. I have not seen a tenth part of them, I am sure."

"Do you know why he has brought us here?"

"I know only what he told me when he came to the surgery. He said we were all in danger and had to go to some place where we would be safe."

"So you know no more than I."

"No."

"Henry," she said touching his arm lightly in a solicitous way. "Do not worry. You may rely on Sergeant Abdul. Believe me. I know."

Henry noted her calm assurance and fearlessness. He could feel her strength and fortitude. It was the first time in his life he had the opportunity to admire courage in a living woman.

"You are very brave," he said.

"There is no bravery or fear," she said, "only the will of Allah. If we know His will is all, we cannot be brave or frightened."

Her words resonated strongly in his mind. He felt that, as with the harmonics of a musical note, they had meanings on several levels, not all of which did he hear consciously or understand.

"Where did you learn that—those words?" he asked.

"In my heart," she said. "I wrote it. It is a translation of a verse form called a *ghazal* in my country."

"What is a *ghazal?*"

"Literally, in Urdu it means, 'talking to women.' In your language, I believe you would call it a couplet. But it has taken on other meanings having to do with our poetry. When I sing, the words are often *ghazals* I have written."

"You are a remarkable women, Umrao. I hope I may hear you sing sometime."

"Ah, if you knew all of me, you would wish to know nothing of me."

"Is that another *ghazal*?"

"It is the truth," she answered.

Their *tête-à-tête* was broken up by the sound of the old door scraping across the swollen boards of the floor. Sergeant Abdul reappeared without their host.

"We have the use of this apartment as long as we need it," he told the young people. " Umrao, there is another room in there where you will sleep. I shall bring the blankets for us all," and he turned and went back to the other room and reappeared with his arms full of blankets.

Without saying another word, Umrao slipped away from Henry into the other room. A few moments later the two men were stretched out on the floor on the mouldy wool Abdul had put down.

After a few minutes of silence Henry said, "Sergeant, what is happening? Why are we here? Do you know who committed the murders? Can you help me bring them to the police and prove my own innocence? So many things have happened that I don't understand. Can you tell me anything?"

"Some things I can tell you. Not all, I do not think. Tomorrow, when I am rested I shall tell you what I believe is happening, Henry. You will learn more when you read your mother's diary, I believe. You like Umrao, I think?"

"She is extraordinary, Sergeant. I've never met any woman like her."

"Nor will you again. She is one of the last of her kind. If you have curious dreams, tonight, Henry, it will be the opium fumes coming up through the floor. Good night."

But Henry was far from sleep. He felt restless, worried and exhilarated all at the same time.

"Good Lord," he thought. "Here I am, hiding

from the authorities in one of the lowest dens in London." His family would know only what Smythe-White would tell them... "Oh, no," Henry muttered, sitting up suddenly. He had completely forgotten about meeting Smythe-White at Nelson's Column. He would have to find some safe way to contact him tomorrow. He must know what was happening at Gower Mews.

Looking around the grim, crumbling room, he felt a million miles from the Suttons. The Suttons? Charles was dead! He could scarcely believe it, but there was no way he could forget the dead, staring eyes, entirely devoid of the qualities he associated with the Dean. How could anyone believe in life after death when they had seen such a face on such a religious man?

He looked once more around the room to draw his mind away from the horrid picture of Charles' face. There was a moon reflecting off the murky waters of the canal just outside the window. It made strange moving patterns of light on part of the ceiling and walls. He wondered if Umrao were asleep in the next room. He would have liked to go in and talk to her. It amazed him that he could even think of sitting on a strange woman's bed to visit with her. He had never had such a thought in his life about Mary nor anyone else. Then he allowed himself to think of the exotic girl he had just met. Through the entire day and evening, no matter what had happened, she had been absolutely steady, he thought. She seemed afraid of nothing.

"An extraordinary girl in every way," he said to himself.

He recalled his first impression of her, when he had been injured, a vision of an oriental fairy creature. She did seem like a being from the *Arabian Nights*, filled with music, poetry and words that resonated strongly in his thoughts. He wondered if she would remove her veil tomorrow and let him see her full face.

At his side lay his mother's diary. He put his hand on it. Perhaps, somehow, the key to all the inexplicable events that had befallen him did lie in this text from beyond his mother's grave. After all the bizarre occurrences that had completely changed the current and direction of his life, anything seemed possible. Tomorrow, he hoped, would be a day of discovery, unlocking the mysteries that seemed to have closed around him, and perhaps also the day he would see Umrao's face. A *ghazal*, how did it go? "There is no bravery or fear, only the will of Allah." Something like that.

The fumes that Sergeant Abdul had warned Henry about seeped into his fading awareness and soon he saw Umrao step out of his mother's diary, wearing nothing but a diaphanous garment that flowed and billowed around her as she danced to a melody of strangely constructed music played on an instrument completely unfamiliar to him. Her voice joined the instrument and drum in a plaintive, weeping key that seemed more sorrowful than anything he had ever heard. As her voice receded, her billowing garment filled the horizon and became clouds the colour of brown opium smoke. These grew darker and darker until they were black, then suddenly, like a magic lantern show, projected on the clouds was Mary's white, frightened face, as he had seen it at the zoological gardens. Next to her he saw Smythe-White whisper something and the two began to snicker. Then all went dark as the snickering continued and the scene switched again to a horrible image of poor Charles' staring eyes and bruised neck as he lay across the desk in his library. The black clouds thickened once more and he felt there was menace he could not escape. It pursued him, reached out for him. He ran, first through the bungalow on the Residency grounds, through the gardens outside and then, somehow, he found himself at the Cawnpore Memorial Well, which he gazed at in horror and disbelief. An angel made of stone stood on the top of the well. It was suddenly lifted up from underneath and toppled off to one side, where it lay broken in pieces. Out of the well came his mother, looking like the photograph in Harry Clayton's room. As Henry stood and looked at her, he felt a thrill pass through him like an electric shock, but there was also the horror of her sudden reappearance from the most ghastly grave in all the world. Gradually that horror gripped him more and more, everything grew darker and darker until, mercifully, there was only oblivion.

When he woke, drenched in cold, nervous per-spiration, the strange watery patterns of the moonlight were still flickering over the walls and ceiling. If any-thing, they seemed even brighter than before. He picked up his Mother's diary, carried it over to the window where some faint light spilled onto the sill and began to read.

Chapter 6
The Journal of Jane Booth

First Reading

Entry: March 20, 1856

"Why anyone should want to record a life such as mine is hard to comprehend. Even I no longer find my life interesting. Probably, the desire to write is sheer loneliness. I have no one to whom I dare speak. The other ladies of the Residency would first pity me and then scorn me. For, I got what many of them wanted, the great handsome Lieutenant Booth, youngest hero of the Sikh wars. All the women in Calcutta wanted his strong arms around them. Perhaps, if I had a reader I should say to her: It is perhaps shocking to speak of ladies in this way. But it is true. They did all want him. To be swept up by him and look up into his sharp blue eyes was something they all dreamed of, I know. That was the first thing I did wrong, a schoolgirl without a fortune, without rank, fresh from England, and I stole one of the most dashing heros in India. If those women knew how my good fortune has turned to bitterness, they would take great pleasure in rebuking me.

Throughout our courtship, I know people talked of us wherever we went. We would stroll along the Strand and watch the muddy waters of the Hugli lap the white stone embankments. There were balls at the Residency. We were presented to the Governor General and I had a charming and exquisite green parasol trimmed with ostrich feathers which Broderick gave me, committing himself much more quickly than most men would have done. It had a handle and clasp made of inlaid ivory. He had dash and money in those days. He and I were inseparable in those happy times. We even went on two tiger hunts together, as well as a pig sticking. It was great fun being the only woman on these expeditions. I wasn't the least afraid, and all the men treated me with perfect courtesy, yet, I could sense that quite a number of them would have liked to flirt with me had they dared.

Riding in the *howdah* with Broderick atop the elephant which the maharajah lent us was like riding through the sky. The beaters spread out in front of us, like an army of slaves, made me feel as if I were a *sultana*, myself. I wore pajaymas, oriental pants, that were really more modest than a dress for climbing on and off an elephant. I know some of the other Calcutta ladies thought it frightfully dangerous and improper that I accompanied Broderick on these expeditions. We didn't care. We were up in the clouds, invulnerable. I had married the hero of every woman's dream. But in my case the old nursery formula reversed itself: after our first kiss, my hero became a frog, then a vicious drunk and finally a monster. But he was so beautiful when I first met him. He carried a riding crop tucked under his arm. So tall and broad-shouldered in his uniform.

It was my idea that he transfer out of the army

and join the civilian service. There was less chance of my becoming a grass widow, I thought. But, everything has gone horribly wrong. And though it violates everything they tried to drum into us at Mrs. Lofters' about Christian marriage, I regret my union with Broderick more bitterly than anything in my life. I am not even sure I shall have the courage to see my honest thoughts written on the pure white pages of this book.

I just realized: that's why I am writing. I want to confess my wickedness, and I dare not confess to the Vicar, he is such a chatterbox. Only last week I heard him telling Mrs. Snodgrass about poor Emily Finch's overeating. She had told the Vicar's wife that she ate at night. She wakes desiring her husband, but he never touches her. So she gets up and eats. The Vicar was scandalized by her appetite for her husband, so of course, he had to pass it along. By now it has gotten about that Emily is a woman who can't get enough sex. That's what the Residency is like, at least among the Company ladies. I know nothing of the other women, the wives of the European hangers-on and the half-castes. If you tell one person something scandalous, all will soon know it, repeated with the most prurient and shocking construction possible. And as everyone knows, we Company ladies are such good Christians whose morals never lapse.

Sometimes when I am sitting with the other ladies, I want to do something frightful, scream or take my clothes off, anything, to let something unpredictable into our stale lives. I am sure I don't know why I have these feelings. Others must have them, too, but of course we shall never speak of them together. We wouldn't dare. That is rather sad, I think. Sometimes it seems that it would be better to be a half-caste or a native so that I could do as I liked and no one would care.

Even before I came to India, I always wanted to set the rules of society at defiance. I don't know why, but after grandfather lost his money and we had to live modestly, I began to find it extremely vexing to worry about appearances and what other people thought of us. When we had money, it didn't seem to matter if my gloves weren't perfectly white, but once we were poor it was quite another matter.

Papa began ignoring me then, because he had to spend so much time worrying about money, I believe. Mummy stayed in bed all the time when she could no longer donate to her charities.

It seemed to me then and still does that the less money one has, the more important is one's reputation and respectability. What a dreadful principle to fall from the pen of a young woman! But I believe it is true, and in this book I shall allow only truth. I am writing only for myself. This shall not be one of those ladies' diaries which is meant to demonstrate Christian principles or depict myself as a heroine, written in private but intended for publication. So much of what is professed in public seems so false to me. Before I came out to India, I found an old dusty book in the attics, *Dr. Watts Edifying Verse*, it was called. Heavens, how I despised the sentiments in that book. They were what I shall call "public sentiments," sentiments one is supposed to feel. I want to write about only my private sentiments, the sentiments I really have, the things that are really in my heart, no matter how others might judge them. How else can I know what will truly make me happy and serene, or discover God's purpose for me? I seem always to want something essential from life and end up with something ephemeral and empty.

At any rate, now, I find myself on the other side of the world in the most priggish society imaginable in, with a brute for a husband, who either beats me or wants to rut with me constantly. It is no wonder I became pregnant so soon.

But of course, that is what I am supposed to do. Yes, the hero actually slaps me with his great beefy palms and then expects that I shall always let him have his way with me. He throws a box of Chantilly lace in my face and wants me to put it on so he can admire me! Not all men are such brutes, I feel sure.

It is as though by trying to avoid convention and the rules of society, I have unwittingly made their bonds much tighter and more painful. Should I do things differently if I had them to do over again? I don't know. What sort of life could one lead that would permit escape from the banality of "correct" views? Would one have to be a native?

Eventually, I was able to convince Broderick to transfer to the civilian service. In those days he would have done anything for me. We would have more money as civilians, too. And Broderick might have made a very good thing out of it. Some men have come out to India in the civilian service for the Company, made good business connections and ended up wealthy. Not Broderick. He hated the Company's civilian service and started to drink almost as soon as he moved into his office in the Residency building. I thought it was a lovely office with windows looking down the hill, but he despised it, and things just went from bad to worse. Since that time, he has blamed all of his troubles on me, and perhaps it is true. He is a physical man with little patience for anything but action. When he is not in motion he is like a chained animal, and then he treats me like the beast that he is.

Oh my Dear Lord! I read over what I have written and I sound to myself like a tiresome harridan, already old and bitter and filled with nothing but com-plaints—but I am not! Surely, I can find something happier to put into these pages than bitter regrets. I am only twenty-two! There must be something else that will sweeten my life, besides my dear little boy. He is always glad to see me and asks nothing better than to be close to me. I shall keep him by me, always, until he is grown. Then, of course, I shall lose him to someone. I hope that he will be kinder to her than his father is to me—and I hope he will trouble to discover the most genuine thoughts and feelings of her inmost soul."

Thuggee, the ancient cult of murder

Chapter 7

The Goddess of Destruction

The sun was rising over the Thames as Henry read the first mention of himself in his mother's journal. He had never heard anyone, let alone a well-bred woman, chafe this way against the duties and expectations of society. Certainly, Mary and Amelia never did. He wondered, for the first time, if they ever did in their private thoughts. He tried to imagine asking this question of Mary or Amelia and was unable to conceive it. In his own life, Henry had felt little conflict in obeying the demands of what was expected of him, at least until very recently, when he felt the demands were unjust. Jane Booth began to interest him as a person, not merely because she was his mother.

He was curious to see what conclusions she would draw about life before her existence was taken from her in the terrible *bibighar*. The crimes of the mutineers who killed her seemed that much greater to him as he felt the living force of his mother's soul, reflected by the pages of her journal. It was a curious sensation to experience the inner life of this passionate woman, whom he had only known in his childhood memories, and to see her apart from himself and possessing her own character, a character lacking in self-regulation, perhaps. A character that was so different from everyone else in the Sutton family.

But how her personal musings could relate to the strange incidents taking place in his own life nearly twenty years later was still an impenetrable mystery to him. He certainly remembered his father's brutishness. His parent's combative family life, and especially his father's behaviour, would have been frowned upon by the Resident and other Company men and would not have improved his chances for advancement. If not for his fame as a hero of the Sikh wars, his domestic behaviour could have caused him to lose his place in the Civilian service. Apparently, he just couldn't stop himself from drinking. Perhaps, like his wife, he was bitter and disappointed with the life in which he found himself. He had been a hero in the army, but perhaps behind a desk, Lieutenant Booth felt as discontented as his wife. Henry would never know. The only feeling his father had ever elicited from him was fear.

"Henry," a voice seemed to call from far away, but when the young man turned around, he saw Sergeant Abdul standing fully dressed.

"Sergeant, I didn't hear you stir."

"Do you want to talk about what has happened, Henry, what is happening to you?"

"Yes, sir, most definitely."

"Then I shall wake Umrao. I would like her to know, as well, what we are facing.

The little man walked to the door and knocked. There was no answer. He knocked again harder and louder. This time a sleepy voice said, "Yes, yes, yes. I will come, only do please stop knocking. Can someone please get some tea?"

Her voice sounded huskier to Henry than it had the day before.

The Sergeant paced slowly back and forth, finally he said, "Waiting for a woman at her toilet is like waiting for the monsoon, she will always come at the least convenient moment."

Henry looked out over the canal's murky water and said nothing. He was surprised to find himself waiting so anxiously just to see Umrao again. It was almost as if he was waiting to find out if she seemed as remarkable in day light as she had the night before in twilight.

Finally, her door opened, and her costume staggered him. She wore long rose-coloured silken pants that were very tight around her hips and thighs, loose below the knees and tight at the ankles. To Henry's fascinated eye, they revealed as much as they covered. Her upper body was clothed with a long, colourful, snugly fitting jacket. Her bosom was perfectly formed and in perfect proportion to her rounded arms and shoulders. She was drawing a long, diaphanous shawl around her shoulders which was like a cloud of blue silk. In the flowing shawl she looked smaller and more delicate, even more like a fairy creature out of the *Arabian Nights*, and out of his own dream the night before. For the first time, he saw her hair unbound. It was thick and blue black, gathered with a golden clasp into a single heavy lock that flowed down one side of her body almost to her knees. Her golden skin was glowing from the repose of sleep. She gave off a delicate scent slightly different from the one of the day before. She exuded the charm of her sex in a way that Henry had never before experienced. He had to admit that she was the most purely female creature he had ever beheld. He felt her attractions in a profoundly physical way. It bothered and surprised him. For the first time since Mary Sutton had taken his childish hand on the East India Docks as they faced the sooty London wind together, he questioned the nature of his feelings for her. If he could feel this way about Umrao, what did it mean about his attachment to Mary? For the first time in his life, he felt uncertain that he could stifle the animal aspect of his nature.

Mary's feminine delicacy had always helped him damp his own ardor. But Umrao deliberately called these feelings from him, he could sense it. She enjoyed waking his animal self. She smiled at him, as though reading his thoughts. To Henry's disappointment, she still wore her veil.

"You like my costume, Henry?" she asked.

Henry blushed deeply. "Yes, Umrao, very much."

"Ah, that's good. You remember my name," she added archly.

"Now that you are here," the Sergeant said, "we can start. Henry, you have been touched by two murders that have taken place recently. If you are ever to be left in peace, we must know who is responsible for these killings and bring evidence to the authorities, yes?"

"Yes, sir. Absolutely. You may be sure I am in full accord with you. You seem to have some idea of the identity of these killers.

"I would call it a strong indication, young sir." The little man walked away from Henry and began pacing again. He was frowning.

"Have you ever heard, young sir, of the *Thuggee?*"

"*Thuggee?*" Umrao repeated the name with a sharp intake of breath. It was obvious to Henry that she had heard the name or term before and did not regard it

116

as a good omen.

The Sergeant barked some words to his niece that Henry could not understand. Neither her face nor her body gave Henry any idea of what the words meant. Her expression was completely blank.

"I've asked my niece not to interrupt any more," Sergeant Abdul said. But Henry felt something more had been said, but he held his tongue.

"Who or what is *Thuggee?*" Henry asked.

The Sergeant crossed and re-crossed the room a few more times before answering. Finally, he stopped in front of Henry and looked at him intently.

"*Thuggee* were or are an organization of killers who believe they have a divine right to commit murder."

"What?" Henry said. "What do you mean by a divine right?"

"Do you know, young sir, who is *Kali?*"

"No."

"Ah. *Kali* is one of the Hindu pantheon, one of the gods and goddesses that make up an aspect of the Hindu faith. Do you follow my point?"

"Like Our Lord Jesus Christ."

"Something like, yes. *Kali* is an aspect of the Divine Mind. She is the aspect that destroys. She causes death, disaster, anything that is an affliction for the world, anything that causes dissolution. Do you understand?"

"An aspect of God, like the Holy Ghost, but negative."

"Ah ha, young sir," the Sergeant said doing a small skip, "that is very well put, very. I must remember it."

"All right," Henry said a little impatiently as he followed the Sergeant's movements with his eyes, glancing every so often at Umrao. "*Kali* is a destructive aspect of God."

"Yes, yes, that's it," the little man cried excitedly. "You have stated it perfectly, young sir."

"And..." Henry said.

"The *Thuggee* believe that *Kali* has given them the divine right, no, the duty of killing people in Her name," Abdul said.

"How could they believe such nonsense?" Henry asked.

"You believe that because Jesus allowed himself to be crucified and rose from the dead that you shall be able to live forever, do you not, young sir?"

"Yes. Well, we'll enjoy Eternal Life."

"And is this belief rational? Is it based on anythng other than belief in a story that took place many, many years ago?"

"I suppose not," Henry admitted.

"It is the same with the *Thuggee*. The story they believe in runs thus, young sir:

Once upon a time the world was infested with a monstrous demon named Rukt Bijdana, who devoured mankind as fast as they were created. So gigantic was his stature that the deepest parts of the ocean reached no higher than his waist. *Kali* cut this monster in twain with her resistless sword but from every drop of blood that fell to the ground there sprang a new demon. For some time she went on destroying them, till the hellish brood multiplied to endless numbers. So she created two men and gave each a rumal or handkerchief and commanded them to strangle the demons. Then she said that the men should keep the handkerchief and destroy all men who were not of their kindred. About the period of the commencement of the *kali yuga*, Bhowani or *Kali* cooperated with these men and their descendents so far as to relieve them the trouble of interring the dead bodies by devouring them herself. But one day a young *Thug* watched her while she ate and saw a body hanging out of her mouth. *Kali* did not like being seen thus and so she refused to eat anymore of their victims. But the *Thuggee* still believe that the murders they commit is a divine right and duty."

"That sounds like a fairy tale out of a nursery book," Henry said derisively.

"No more so than baby Jesus performing miracles or the man Jesus the Christ rising from the dead, turning water into wine, young sir. Do you follow my point, young sir?"

"Yes, I suppose so."

"Good."

"So there are a lot of these people who have these homicidal beliefs? Why does that concern us? Wait—are you trying to tell me that my college President and Charles were killed by these, *Thuggee?*"

"Thugs, young sir. *Thuggee* refers to the whole sect."

"Good God. And how many are there in this gang?"

"My friend, the last Resident of Lucknow, William Sleeman, prosecuted and convicted hundreds of them in India. He uncovered networks of *Thug* families that stretched all across India."

"Hundreds?"

The Sergeant's face was very solemn as he shook his head affirmatively.

"And you think there are more? And that they're here in England? How horrible. How many more?"

"My late friend, mentor and patient, Major General Sleeman believed for a long time that with the help of the great *Thuggee* chief Ferangee, he had caught them all. Alas, knowing India as I do, I did not believe in such complete success. The *Thuggee* have been committing murders in India for at least three-hundred years."

"Three hundred years? That's impossible. How could a single gang commit hundreds..."

"Not hundreds, young sir," the Sergeant said wagging his finger from side to side under Henry's gaze. "Major General Sleeman believed that their victims were upward of forty-thousand. But who can say, the numbers were so enormous."

"One million murders, or a mere forty thousand, in either case, this is the most incredible tale I have ever heard, Sergeant. How could such a gang ever have existed anywhere? It sounds utterly impossible."

"It sounds impossible as we stand on the soil of the practical British Island, young sir, where there is a Peeler on every corner. But India has mysteries that will never be plumbed by the mind of mankind, I do believe so, young sir. I told Major General Sleeman he could not so quickly destroy the cult of *Kali*'s followers.

Only in his very last years in India did he begin to believe me, though. Alas, that the greatest of all policeman is no more."

"But how are you so sure that it is them, here, now?"

"The way the crimes were commited, young sir. Not merely strangled but also neck broken. This is *Thuggee*. This is the way their *rumals* and nooses kill. They can throw them over the head of a victim even from a distance. The murder in your home, for instance, if the window were open, the *Thug* may never ever have entered your home."

"Incredible," Henry said, "No wonder, neither Smythe-White or myself could imagine how anyone got

120

into Charles' room. And the window was partially open when I lifted it to jump out and leave the house. I remember, now."

"I give you my promise, young sir. It is *Thuggee*."

"So the British government believes they're all caught, but they are not? " Henry said. "Good God. What can we do? How can we convince— Wait—," Henry said, suddenly pausing in mid-sentence. "Wait, why should they come here, now, if they have been in India for centuries. And why should they kill these two particular people? They must have a strong reason to come all this way to a place where they do not know the lay of the land as well."

"That is another reason that makes me think this is *Thuggee*. When a Hindu crosses the Ocean, he loses his caste forever, his position in Hindu society. *Thuggee* is a sect that subsumes both Hindu and Moslem beliefs. Only a Hindu who was a *Thug* would cross the ocean without fear of losing caste, trusting in *Kali*. *Thuggee* is the only religious group in India that contains both Hindus and Moslems as brothers. That has always struck me with the strongest blow of irony. But you are right. I believe they do have a special reason. "

Without saying another word, Sergeant Abdul turned away and went to the window where Henry had been reading. earlier.

"This, young sir, is the reason." He stooped down and picked up Jane Booth's diary from the windowsill where Henry had left it.

"What can you possibly mean, Sergeant?" Henry said, looking at small man incredulously. Then his frown turned to a thoughtful inward turned gaze. "It does make sense in a way. All the trouble started with the arrival of the Journal. But what possible connection could there be between my mother and this cult of murder?"

"I can only tell you what I guess at, young sir. I am not entirely certain of my ground here, at all. I am not, after all, the great Major General Sleeman. I am only his friend who studied his greatness, and treated his minor illnesses."

"And what is the connection? I still do not understand?"

"I cannot give you a precise answer, young sir. How much of this journal have you read?"

"Only a few pages, but I don't see.."

"Somewhere in this book there is a clue to a great fortune, I believe," Abdul said, "a fortune that the *Thuggee* believe belongs to them."

"What makes you think that?" Henry asked.

"This," Sergeant Abdul said drawing out a paper from the inner pocket of his waistcoat.

It appeared to Henry to be some words in a different language which used an alphabet other than the Roman.

"I still cannot see the connection between this, whatever it is, and my mother's journal."

"This paper bears words that were left in the residency and then taken from Lucknow at the time it was recaptured. I cannot read it all. It is written in the secret tongue of the *Thuggee*, Ramasee, which is a language derived from ancient Persian. But I do know that the word 'treasure' is written here. The great Sleeman could read Ramasee. I cannot. Major General Sleeman also believed that there was a list of names of prominent people who have been secretly in league with the *Thuggee*. Some in India, some here. I know that some of the great Indian banking families helped finance *Thuggee* operations. This was known long ago. But we always believed there were more. And, Major General Sleeman believed that there was at least one Englishman who had actually participated in the gruesome rites of *Thuggee*. My guess, and it is only a guess, is that a great cache of wealth was brought back here to England where it now resides, exactly where I do not know. Perhaps, somewhere, hidden in your mother's journal is more information about the *Thuggee* treasure and the Englishman or men who joined the cult of murderers. The strongest reasons I have for believing as I do are the events that have overtaken you since you had this diary in your possession."

"But how did you find out about this treasure and these collaborators, if the *Thuggee* are so secretive?" Henry asked.

"Unbeknownst to himself, the son of a friend brought the information I have on this paper to England from Lucknow. It was written on the back of a painting of my friend Major General Sleeman. This man recovered the painting from the Residency and brought it to England. When the *Thuggee* saw Lucknow was about to fall to the English again, I believe they wrote this note to any of their brethren who might survive the war."

"But if the painting was in the Residency, how were the *Thuggee* able to write on it?"

"When Major General Sleeman prosecuted the *Thuggee* in India, there were many minor officials among them. I always suspected Major General's *khitmutghar*, Lal Rao of being a member of *Thuggee*, but the Major General would not believe me."

"It is all so extraordinary. Secret writing, hidden messages and a cult of murderers hundreds of years old. How could my mother be connected with all this?"

"Instead of answering you myself, young sir, I believe your mother's own words will answer you. I believe she knew a man who knew about these things and that he told her things in a way that she would not realize the significance of his words."

"But who was this man? And why would he tell my mother?" Henry asked.

"I would prefer, young sir, that you get the answer to that directly from your mother's journal. Much of what I am saying is surmise. Let us see if her words bear me out."

"But if she did not know..."

"Please, young sir, continue reading the journal. Now, I have patients to attend. I shall leave you and Umrao here where you will be safe."

"But what about you? If anything happens to you, we shall be lost."

"Among these narrow, ugly streets, I have many friends. I shall be watched over. Besides, I, too, am a single stick expert, young sir."

"And what about me?" Umrao asked. "I also have work to do, as you know. How long must I stay here and wait, Uncle?" She turned suddenly and looked at Henry. "Not, Henry, that I do not like to be with you."

"Until," Sergeant Abdul said, "the danger is passed. I know you chafe to finish your business, Umrao, but you will have to be patient. We must protect Henry, and we must stop the *Thuggee* from hiding the names of their British helper or helpers and getting the vast wealth which I believe this cache of treasure represents. It was my pledge to Major General Sleeman to fight the *Thuggee* until my last breath. Now that I definitely know they are active in England, I must do what I can. Now, I shall go out and see my patients and be back this evening."

"Wait, Sergeant, I must get a message to my family. I was supposed to meet a cousin last night after we found poor Charles. I forgot all about it until I was going to sleep."

"I will take a message to them, young sir."

"I would hope also to get an answer from them as well."

"Then I shall wait for an answer."

Henry wrote, "Smythe-White, forgive my missing you last night. I am in danger from more than the police and am in hiding. Please give a message to Sergeant Abdul, telling me how Mary and Amelia are and, generally, what the state of the household is after the events of yesterday. What did the police say and do when they came to investigate Charles death? You might also contact Sir Joshua and tell him the current state of things and explain that as soon as it is safe, I shall go to him to get his help in clearing my name with the authorities. I have the most astonishing things to tell all of you."

He folded the paper and gave it to Sergeant Abdul, who slipped it into his waistcoat pocket.

"Your note does not tell anyone where you are?" he asked Henry.

"No."

"That is well. I think it better if no one knows for the present time." Then the little man picked up his battered black bag, put his stethoscope into his hat, pulled the door shut and Henry found himself alone with Umrao. He didn't know what to say, so he said the first thing that came into his head.

"Umrao, must you wear that veil over your face?"

"In Lucknow, ladies always remain covered in public. But I am not a lady so I shall take off my veil in front of you." She reached up and unfastened the veil on each side of her face and removed it.

Henry was not disappointed by what he saw. Her face was triangular with high cheekbones and a straight nose, which flared into delicately chiseled nostrils. In one nostril, she wore a very fine golden ring. It was barbaric, yet, it suited the sharp boldness of her chiseled features and enhanced her beauty. With her dark eyes, generous lips and small chin she looked something like a beautiful child carved in ancient yellow ivory. He felt she was ancient, young, simple and wise; able to contain all these contradictions at once. It was not what he had expected, but while he found her appearance less beautiful than he'd anticipated it exerted a kind of fascination that was entirely unlooked for. She was more mysterious than anyone he'd ever met. Everything about her seemed remarkable and surprising.

"Umrao, Umrao," he said softly.

"You see, you are in love with me already, are you not, Henry?"

He turned scarlet and was silent for some moments. Then he spoke, "In a way, I suppose I must admit that I am. I am astonished and chagrined by the feelings you make me feel."

"It is as it should be. I made you fall in love with me."

"No. No one can do that."

"Yes, that is my trade. That is what you don't know about me, Henry. I am a courtesan. Love, music and poetry are my arts. The courtesans of Lucknow were known throughout Asia to be the most desirable women in the world."

"That is why you said to me last night that line of poetry, what was it? 'Ah, if you knew all of me, you would wish to know nothing of me.' But somehow, I cannot believe you have ever sold yourself to any man."

"I have not, yet. I have not had my formal deflowering ceremony that would have initiated me into the profession. Something happened just before I completed my education and so I have not yet been introduced to my first client. If I had, my name would bear the suffix 'Jaan' after it. I would be Umrao Jaan Hasan. But I am not. And now that I have come to this cold island of yours where all courtesans are merely sexual toys and are universally and hypocritically despised, I don't know if I wish to be anything other than a singer and dancer. Certainly I would never be a courtesan here, in this cruel island. It is very strange to see my art through British eyes."

Henry was quiet for a long time. Finally, he spoke: "Why do you say, 'hypocritically' despised?"

"Because the men who go to them do not despise them, only the hypocritical English society. If men do truly despise the women they make love to, they must despise themselves."

"And in Lucknow the people do not feel any contempt for the courtesans?"

"There are some from the lower classes who do not have the refinement to appreciate the *deredar tuwaif*, but the cultured people, the *Nawabs*, never lacked in respect for us."

"So you credit the English with spoiling a refined culture—the musicians, poets and courtesans along with the *Nawabs*??"

"Certainly. When the British took Lucknow away from the *Nawabs*, they wanted to punish the courtesans for supporting the *Nawabs*. They looted many *kothas*. Now, the British are trying to destroy the culture of Lucknow courtesans, altogether. They kidnap talented and beautiful artists and take them to British cantonments where any refinement is impossible. Women who were once respected across Asia are now debased and degraded as sexual slaves for British troops. Ah, I see," she said. "I have shocked you. Now you think me less beautiful. There was a slight catch in her voice. She sounded genuinely saddened at his reaction.

"No, no, " Henry said quickly. "I am only trying to understand. There are no prostitutes in England
who are poets and dancers. It is an altogether foreign
idea. Please don't be hurt by what I have said—or didn't
say. You are not less beautiful. Not at all. Only, you
say things that are so—extraordinary— and different
from any thing I have ever heard a woman say. You talk
openly about things... I hardly know what to think—or
feel. There was another long silence before he continued, "And—you said that you had made me fall in love
with you—and you have not said that you have any
affection for me in return."

"I like you very much Henry, but, courtesans
must be ruthless. You must always remember that about
me. I am not a tame little British girl. I do not submit
to men. I have been trained to make them submit to me
and do what I want them to. In Lucknow, the society
was ruled by men—except in the *kotha*.

There, we have the right to be ourselves, make
money and own property. The *Nawabs* supported our
freedom. The British want to take it away. They want to
take everything, to swallow Oudh and all of India."

"But none of this has anything to do with
whether or not you care for someone." he said, biting
his lips in vexation. "Certainly nothing you've said has
anything to do with how you feel about me. Yet, by
your own account, you make me say things I have never
before said in my life," he ended looking away from her.
He heard her push open the door to the other room.

"Do not feel sad or angry at what I have said. I
did not say my heart was altogether empty of you," she
said. "I must go into my room now and practice."

And she slipped through the door into the room
where she had slept the night before. All Henry could

think of were the words, "I did not say my heart was altogether empty of you." And she stepped into the other room.

"How can this be happening?" Henry said out loud. "My entire life is in ruins and I am deserting Mary in my thoughts. Umrao has bewitched me."

Ever since being expelled from college, his life had begun to seem more and more dream-like, no, not dream-like, it certainly seemed real enough, but so different from what it had been that he didn't recognize himself. He shook his head and went over to pick up his Mother's diary. His only refuge from the present seemed to be in the past. That, too, seemed bizarre.

Chapter 8
The Journal of Jane Booth

Second Reading

Entry: April 30, 1856

"I wonder if I should really carry on with this? I find myself and the other "memsahibs" so inexpressibly boring so much of the time. So I shall write about my little boy, Henry. He really is a charming little fellow. His hair is so dark and his eyes such a beautiful amber colour, I suppose he will grow up to be beautiful like his father was. I hope he does not grow up to be a drunkard, as well. Not that Lieutenant Booth is a drunkard in the way most people would understand the term. He never looks drunk. He never falls. He never loses any physical control, whatever, but he becomes mean, irritable and small-minded. I hope my perfect little boy will never be such a man. Lord Jesus, how I hope You, my God, will make it so.

Broderick and I had another Residency couple over for dinner last night, Michael and Helen Ferguson. Broderick had too much to drink at dinner, I could see.

Our guests didn't even notice. But what did Broderick do to assert himself and his superiority over his colleague? He asked Ferguson to "help" him carry a dresser out from the storage shed in our compound.

Of course, we do have servants for that sort of thing so I said, "Broderick, what an idea. Of course you don't need Michael to help you."

"Just a trifle, really Michael," Broderick said, ignoring me completely. "It's back in the kitchen."

Then I knew what he was going to do. Michael is about eighteen stone. He is quite fat, does not take any exercise and spends all day at a desk. He is apparently quite brilliant with figures and knows how to squeeze the last drop of money from the *zamindars* and their lords. But Broderick rides every day and is obsessed with staying in training. In our kitchen we had a massive mahogany chest that was used for kitchen things. Broderick had once mentioned in an off-handed way something about using it in the storage shed for some of my clothes, which are, actually, overflowing my own chest in our bedroom. Men are so stupid. Michael must have known by the time he reached the outer door with the chest that he could barely lift his end. Broderick, of course, was not even breathing deeply. No matter. With Broderick at the light end, poor, foolish Michael allowed himself to be put down on the heavy end of the chest so that most of the weight was on him. Then, he staggered out the door. I was truly afraid he would trip and fall and hurt himself. He didn't, but he was gasping and perspiring by the time they returned.

Helen and I stood in the parlour and watched the whole absurd play. .

"I'm sorry, Helen, really I am," I said. "Michael should have refused."

"And Broderick really should be a little kinder," she replied.

And then she tried to injure me by saying, "To other people and to you. It doesn't help your standing with the Resident, you know. Your fights are getting to be the talk of the station."

I realized the truth of her assertion, but wasn't about to admit it. When he was drinking, Broderick really did enjoy hurting people, and I already knew our rows were talked about. Fortunately, little Henry is always asleep by the time Broderick is drinking, otherwise, I should start to worry about him being hurt. Horrible! Imagine fearing that a father will hurt his own son, not for instruction, but in anger, in a moment of anger and loss of self-control.

Anyway, I said I wanted to write about my little darling and here I am once more talking about the beast that Broderick has become. Men are supposed to be our lords and masters, but not through physical force. We women are supposed to be the soul of our race, and really, we should never have to suffer blows from anyone, especially from our protectors. If a man strikes us with his superior strength are we supposed to accept it silently, as part of fulfilling our marriage vows? If that is the Christian thing to do, then I am not a Christian! I shall break out at it! I shall be defiant! If all I can do is shake my fists at heaven, I suppose I had better talk of something else.

9:00—evening

It is several hours later than when I wrote my last entry. I become enraged because there is nothing I can do about Broderick's behaviour. It is my own impotence that makes me so furious. I believe many of the Residency wives get worse treatment than I do, but their husbands are more careful than Broderick, and their wives are more careful than I am. I cannot help goading Broderick, telling him how much I used to love him, and how little of that love remains. I know it makes him feel even more like a failure, and I know he does feel a failure in his civilian career. If I were a better wife, I should be kinder and not tell him how I feel. But it is so difficult to hide my disappointment in both of us. If we could only both pledge to live for our little boy. That could retrieve much from our quarreling.

September 22, 1856 8:30—evening

I haven't written for some time, even though the drumming rain of the monsoon has driven me nearly mad. Thank God the wet weather will be ending soon. But I am already dreading the heat which will soon be upon us. Those stifling nights when I want to sit outside on the lawn and Broderick wants to drag me up to our hot room and crush me underneath him. It is hard to believe that he was once a gentle and courteous lover. How I miss the touch of a gentle hand! When my little boy comes to me and rubs my back or strokes my hair, which I know he loves, his touch is so gentle, but of course, it is quite different than the way a man would touch me.

September 28, 1856 6:30—evening

Broderick is still at the Residency. He sends word that he must work late tonight. We are so trapped up here on the Residency Hill. The servants tell me the *Chowk* is very lively at night with all manner of entertainments, everything from snake charmers to poetry contests to performances by the courtesans, some of whom, Mrs.

Wells told me, are really highly trained musicians and dancers. Of course it's native music and dance but still, the spectacle would be a reprieve from these long dull evenings.

September 29, 1856
7:30—evening

Broderick is working late again. My choice of entertainments is whist with a few of the ladies or to sit here and simmer in my own discontent. I am such a bad Christian, I shall probably choose to simmer. I am not long-suffering. I do not want to bend to God's will, and that is sinful. But I don't care. There, I've said something truly dreadful, now. If anything terrible befalls I shall have brought it on myself.

When I first came to Calcutta, and danced gaily at so many of the balls there, I could never have believed society in India could be as cramped and narrow as this.

I remember when I was presented to the Company's President at Fort William. The ladies there enjoyed educated conversation, read whatever newly arrived books came from home. A few even engaged in flirtations with some of the young officers. I had my handsome and adoring Broderick, then. Then, he would not have been parted from me for a single evening. Now, look at me. I have read how the natives keep their women in seclusion, but are any of the English ladies here on the Residency Hill who are any better off? Am I a fiend because I would like some amusement? The vicar's wife implied as much when I made a comment about organizing some outdoor entertainments before the heat comes. Must a Christian woman not be happy in her life?

Even the reading that is available is appallingly dull. Missionary tracts, a few novels from the last century and that is all. And I used to be such a great reader. Yet, I hear it said that Lucknow is supposed to be one of the most amusing places in India. But perhaps that only pertains to men. Women are supposed to sit at home while the men dine and drink and go to the courtesans, and then we are to come to their bed when we are called. I sometimes wonder if men realize that women can think and want to occupy themselves constructively just as they do? I cannot understand why God has arranged things so that we are so often treated like property. I do not believe that Eve was responsible for mankind's fall. Surely the responsibility was equally Adam's.

September 30, 1856—afternoon

I was only today unpacking a trunk of books in the storage shed and found all my George Sand novels. I have not looked at them since I first came out to India. How I loved reading them when I was young. I even paid for their extra weight on the ship. Only today did I remember the dreams that this woman once stirred in me, in the days before I was caught up in my family's desire for me to come out here and "get a husband," so they would no longer have to maintain me.

I sat down on the floor of the hot dusty shed and spent all afternoon re-reading her great novel, *Indiana*. I felt goose flesh when I read the following words from the author's most recent preface to the book:

> *I yielded to an overpowering instinct of outcry and rebellion which God had implanted in me, God who makes nothing that is not of some use, even the most*

insignificant creatures, and who interposes in the
most trivial as well as in great causes.

George Sand is a woman with respect for herself and her sex, and of course that means she is not altogether respectable. But she echoes my own feelings and shows me how to regard myself and respect myself and that is better than the respectability of the Residency.

I am certain that no one here has ever read any of her novels. She is not respectable enough. Yet, I must admit, I don't seem to have the courage of my convictions. If I had a tenth part of the conviction and spiritual strength of this Frenchwoman, I would act, instead of complain.

If only I could write like her. What is that line I found I had written in the margins from another of her novels, *Mauprat*? The words made me shiver even in that hot, stuffy shed as I began to read my way through her novel once more.

She wrote:
> *"We cannot tear out a single page of our life, but*
> *we can throw the whole book in the fire."*

I felt that she had written these words just for me. The next moment I said to myself, "And here I sit, doing nothing with my life. I am a coward. When she was unhappy with a man, she got another one! She treated them just as they treat us."

I cannot even use my darling little boy as an excuse for my inaction. George Sand had two children with her husband before she left him.

At least, I can resolve to start today to re-read all of the George Sand novels I have. Perhaps her words will give me the strength to "throw the whole book in the fire."

October 2, 1856 7:00 —mornimg

I woke today with a true inspiration. Why could I not write something about India that would be of interest to women, and even men, back in England? I have recently heard of another English woman doing this. She had the rather common sounding name of Fanny Parks. If I had money of my own, perhaps I would find some way to get away from Broderick and this place, the oppression of the Honourable Company's Residency.

I remember how I thought India would be an exotic place. I thought it would be quite fascinating. It was fascinating when I lived in Calcutta and Broderick was in love with me. Could I make India a fascinating place to others? Certainly not the Residency Hill. But what about descriptions of the Hazratganj and the *Chowk*? Everyone says Lucknow is an immoral, amusing and wicked city. Surely, there are young women in England who would be interested in this piquancy from the safety and comfort of their own parlours?

November 2, 1856 8:00 —morning

It has been a month since I have written in this book, but I have been in a fever of excitement all that time with my idea of writing about the wicked life of Lucknow. I passed through the days scarcely knowing what I was doing. But last night I was shown the way to put my plan into execution.

Dinner tasted so exceptionally good that I went into the kitchen. I found a new girl there. She was quite nice looking for a native. Her teeth and mouth were not stained from chewing betel nut and she looked very clean. When I told her that I liked her cooking, she was very appreciative.

"Oh, thank you, *memsahib*. The flavour is better because I buy my herbs from my cousin in the *Chowk*. He always gives me the freshest of the fresh."

"But I have not seen you here before," I said.

"No, *memsahib*, my cousin is indisposed, so I came in her place."

"Perhaps you could stay in her place? Stay and cook for us?"

"It would make her angry, *memsahib*."

I've learned enough about natives to know that anything other than an outright refusal is an offer to bargain.

"I could pay you more than I pay her. Six rupees a week."

"Very well, *memsahib*."

"What is your name?" I asked.

"Sita, *memsahib*."

"Very good, Sita. You'll come each day at seven and leave after dinner, yes?"

"Yes, *memsahib*. I shall come."

November 3rd, 1856

When Sita came today, she brought several bottles of spices, which, she explained, she would need if she was going to do her best for us in the kitchen.

"I get more tonight from my cousin's shop for your kitchen. Then, I can make you anything. Best Lucknow food."

It suddenly occurred to me that this new girl could be my guide to the *Chowk* and, more importantly, could give me the excuse I would need for going there without my husband. Overseeing the shopping of a new cook is something that could excuse even one of the Company ladies from venturing into the market. Broderick couldn't become testy about it. I would simply be doing my wifely duties.

"Sita," I said, "I think I should go with you the first time you shop for us."

To my surprise she immediately began to look petulant and said,

"No, *memsahib*. I not work here. You don't trust Sita. You think I rob you."

"No. Sita. No. In fact, I'd like your help. Ah, to show me the best shops in the *Chowk*. It is difficult for me to go there alone. I shall pay you extra to take me with you."

She looked puzzled for a moment and then brightened. "You meet someone?" she asked.

"Meet someone?"

"You have man in city?"

I felt the blood drain from my face. Then I felt myself flush and grow hot.

"How dare you say that, Sita?"

Even though I had nothing to be guilty about then, I still felt culpable for having thoughts of wanting to leave Broderick.

"I only want to serve you better, *memsahib*. Some of the English ladies with old husbands have young men in the city."

"They do?" I asked, too astonished to hide my astonishment.

"Yes, *memsahib*."

"Who? What are their names?"

"Better not to say, *memsahib*."

"Perhaps you're right. But I have no man in the city. I simply want to see the *Chowk*. I've never been there."

"Never?"

"No. I have been in Lucknow over a year and I have never been in the market. I didn't know any white women went down there."

"Oh, yes, *memsahib*. Some to shop. Some for pleasure."

"Not with black men?"

The girl shrugged her slender shoulders. "I do not know, *memsahib*."

A year ago, when I came to Lucknow from Calcutta, the native girl's answers would have shocked me but now they did not. I wasn't the only bored, lonely Englishwoman in the Residency. There were others among my sanctimonious neighbours who were even more desperate.

"Well, I wish to see the market and do some shopping," I said. "You can tell me which are the best stores, can you not, Sita?"

"Oh, yes, *memsahib*, I show you," she said with a very pretty smile.

"My husband will probably be working at the Residency tonight. The *ayah* will be with Henry, so there is no reason we cannot go after dinner. I'll pay you an extra six rupees for the evening."

"Oh, thank you, *memsahib*."

When the usual message arrived from the Residency that Broderick would be working late, I was glad. There was nothing to prevent me from going, except my own cowardice. I confess that when Sita came into the parlour after dinner and told me it was time to go and that she had hired a *palanquin* and bearers for the evening, my heart beat like a wild animal. I almost told the girl I wasn't going to go. Then, my fear made me angry. I wasn't breaking my marriage vows. How debasing to realize how frightened I was, merely to do something on my own, something which Broderick might not like. I had to go. To do otherwise would have been a betrayal of myself.

We set out. The *palanquin* would have been charming with its brightly painted designs, but it was dirty inside and smelled badly. One of the bearers told me proudly that these litters are made on a single street here in Lucknow, Finaswali Lane. I thought, "they are proud of the workmanship but will not even bother to keep it clean."

Once we got off the Hill the flies began swarming around us even more thickly than at home. I always forget how many more flies there are once we climb down the Hill. It is the dirt of the old city that draws them. Thank goodness, Sita was clean or riding in the confined space of the *palanquin* with her would have been dreadful.

In a way, I wish she was not such a good cook and I could have her for my own maid. The woman who combs my hair, rubs my feet and bathes me is not nearly so clean. As we rode down into town, I told myself that I must remember to watch for the picturesque, things that could be made to sound charming and exotic. I would certainly leave out the flies and all the dirty monkeys running around the narrow streets.

Sita continually leaned out of the *palanquin* and waved to acquaintances. I'm certain she was proud to be riding with an Englishwoman instead of walking in the dust. I sat well back in my seat. The covered box we rode in suited me well. I did not wish to be seen.

I cannot be certain how long we bumped and

swung in our conveyance. It was only about three-quarters of a mile to the *chowk*. I do know that by the time Sita told the bearers to stop, I was dusty, and though the sun was nearly down, I was hot. I was not in a wonderful state of mind for exploring. However, I had come to do something and I was determined not to come away from the *chowk* without accomplishing my purpose.

I was astonished by the din on the street as we approached the great arch that led into the market. This part of the city was very dense, the streets narrow, and I believe there was sewage running in the gutters along either side of the streets. We had some shops on the Residency grounds but nothing like the rows of tightly packed stalls and people milling about in the *chowk* itself, and on the old west road which led into it. Everything was a blur of colour. The sweet scent of jasmine was everywhere, but it was mixed in with a range of odours that went from delicious smelling food being cooked to decaying offal. In short, my senses were assailed. For a few moments I was simply stunned by the noise and life around me. Then I heard Sita.

"*Memsahib*, best shops this way. My cousin has his shop over there."

I could see she was smiling, enjoying her holiday with me, no doubt also thinking of the money she was earning for having a pleasant evening.

Suddenly I heard a rapid drum beat over my head. It was the ubiquitous native drum, which is called the *tabla*, Sita told me. Details will be important to readers back in England, I believe. A woman's voice pierced the air with long moaning notes. She sounded almost as if she were in the throes of passion, but I have to admit, her emotional voice and the drumming was quite mesmerizing.

We stood and waited under the balcony and

listened to the song. When the music ended, a woman, whom I judged to be the singer, stepped out onto the ornate balcony over our heads. She had long oiled black hair and her teeth were black with antimony. I thought her most unattractive, though I could see through her gauzy garments that her body was full and very ripe. A few moments later, a white man followed her out into the open air. I started. It was Broderick.

I have wondered many times since that night if Sita stopped the *palanquin* on that particular corner on purpose. I shall never know, but I could clearly see my husband and the woman who talked mockingly, familiarly, even insolently with him. I turned quickly, got out of the *palanquin* and plunged into the crowd. If Sita hadn't been watching me closely, I would have been lost to her in moments.

I surprised myself when I felt my cheeks were wet with tears. I didn't feel jealousy or any kind of romantic feeling, just a strange empty ache which I can best liken to the feeling of having a tooth extracted. Something long familiar was now gone. I allowed Sita to lead me in and out of various shops. I paid no attention to the time. The milling street was like an ocean of noise and colour that stopped my thoughts and any sense of the hour. I was brought back to myself by the sudden sensation of something around my neck. Two large native men, quite drunk were standing before us blocking the way.

"Memsahib," one said with a leer, "I give you the flowers of my heart." He had thrown a garland of flowers around my neck.

Before he could utter another word, a tall, slender man, a native, but dressed in western clothes, came up behind my assailant and grabbed his thick neck between his fingers.

"Begone, dog," he said, "and if you or your friends ever bother this lady again, I shall see that you have the hide flayed from your bones."

I was surprised by the gross familiarity of the men who accosted us. Generally, I have felt altogether safe anywhere in India. Otherwise, I never would have gone to the *Chowk* with Sita. Perhaps the rumours about the natives becoming more arrogant in Oudh were true.

I didn't know who our rescuer was but our assailants seemed to know him and bowed to him repeatedly with their hands pressed together in front of them in that universal Hindu gesture of respect. While he watched them go, fixing them with a cold, penetrating eye, I studied his person. He was of medium height, with very black hair, sharp featured, clean shaven and very light-skinned for a native. His English clothes were impeccable and he wore them with an elegance that would not have been out of place in London. I had not seen anyone like him since leaving Calcutta.

When he turned back to us he said, "So sorry, miss that you and your attendant were bothered by those ruffians. As he said this he raised his hat to us, and then added, "Perhaps I could walk with you until you reach your destination?"

"I—I just came to see the *chowk*, sir," I said, impressed by his manners.

There was something imposing about him which forbade my addressing him like a native.

"Then allow me to walk with you until you have seen what you wish to see. Or perhaps I can guide you, to help you find what you are looking for?"

"It is just that I have lived in the Residency for over a year and have heard a great deal about Lucknow's picturesque *chowk*. I simply wanted to see it."

"Ah, the famous wickedness of Lucknow?" he said with a very charming smile. "May I show it to you and protect you from it at the same time?"

And he introduced himself to us in a very gentlemanly way. His name meant nothing to me, and Sita said nothing about him then, or later.

Needless to say, I was delighted by his offer, and the tone in which it was made. It fell in so exactly with what I required, a guide and protector in one.

"Would you object to visit the home of a very famous courtesan, Madame Booth, one who receives the *Nawab* himself? She has even performed before the Resident. There you would experience the very best of *Lachnavi* culture. The best food, the best music and dance."

Of course, I never would have dared to visit the house of a courtesan by myself or with little Sita, nor is it likely that the opportunity would have arisen, but something about the man made me trust him.

"Is it far from here?" I asked.

"Not far at all, a few steps, really."

He led us through the crowded bazaar and stopped in front of a beautiful house with an ornate double arch which gave access to the front door. On either side of the arch were handsome windows with elaborately carved balconies. My heart beat quite rapidly when I thought of the marvelous start my first article was getting. It felt as if I was beginning a new life. I shall "throw the whole book in the fire," I thought as he led us inside.

Two muscular men in turbans and fierce black mustachios stood in the anteroom, which lay between the outer arch and the actual door to the house. As soon as they saw my guide, they opened the double doors and showed us in. There was a long dark hall, which had wonderful smells of cooking pervading it. Normally, I do not like food odours in a house, but this was both sweet and savoury at the same time.

We came into a large open area—a sort of large room with pillars all around. It was roofed but it also had a balcony or mezzanine running all around it. The ceiling was very high and the floor had many different carpets on it. There were cushions where men in native costume were sitting. A white cloth was placed on the floor at the front of the room. Our guide indicated two cushions for us, and I sat down as comfortably as possible. He slipped away from us and walked behind a curtained doorway.

Sita and I were curiosities in the male enclave, but I supposed that the man who brought us knew the rules of the place. Then, an older native man with a white beard and wearing clean, white loose-fitting pants and shirt came over to me and held out the mouth-piece of the *hukkah* he had been smoking, inviting me to smoke as well. Not wanting to seem ungracious, especially when our guide was not present, I took the mouthpiece he offered. I was surprised to find the smoke so mild. Broderick's cigars or pipes make me choke, but this was much nicer. I inhaled once or twice and handed the mouthpiece back to the man who bowed very politely. Then, just as he turned away I began to feel strangely light-headed. Sita was looking at me, studying me closely. The next moment, the curtain where our guide had gone was parted and a woman in silken pajay-mas and an embroidered vest with gold thread came out onto the white cloth that had been spread on the floor. With her were four musicians: Two had drums, the other a long-necked instrument I did not recognize and the fourth carried a strange instrument with a bow. It had a long neck and many strings on it. Sita said it was called a *sarangi*. After a few minutes of what seemed to be tuning, the music began. And what music!

I had never in my whole life heard or seen anything like it. The drums and the dancer seemed to be racing each other but also taking turns. The dancer's feet made sharp slapping sounds even on the cloth. She wore three rows of bells around each of her ankles so that when she stepped the tiny bells gave off a kind of silvery rattle. I was transported by the colour of her costume, the racing music and the wild but carefully controlled motions of the dancer. Her thick, black, braided hair was worn very long and fastened behind her to her belt. The effect was barbaric but remarkably beautiful. Of course, I realized later that much of my reaction was due to the *hukkah* I had smoked. It must have had *bhang* in it, mixed with the tobacco.

It seemed hours and hours that we sat on the floor, listening and watching the performers. Suddenly, it was all over. Our guide came back and sat down near us.

"Oh, that was wonderful," I said to him. "I've never heard anything like it."

"Nor will you soon," he answered. "Those are some of the best musicians in all of India, the *tabla* players especially. And I must say that Indira danced like one of the *houris* of paradise."

"Indira? Is that the dancer's name?" I heard myself asking from what seemed a great distance. "You know, I am so unaccountably hungry."

"Did you have a *hukkah*?"

"Yes," I said. "Is it all right? That white haired man came over and offered it to me. I didn't want to insult him so I had two inhalations."

"Well, then I am certain you got the most pleasure from the *kathak*. Could you follow the story?"

"No. I felt there was a meaning, but it eluded me. The music would just sweep me up and carry me off. Oh, thank you so much for bringing us here. I shall have a wonderful article to write."

I put my hand up to my mouth when I realized what I had said and giggled.

"Article," our guide asked. "You are writing an article?"

But for a few moments, I could not stop giggling. I felt so foolish but I could not stop. The more worried I became about seeming foolish, the more I giggled. Finally, I was able to recover myself.

"I want to write an article about Lucknow for people in England."

"And that is why you came to the *chowk*?"

"Yes. I hope you are not angry that I didn't tell you."

"No. It is very unusual for an English lady to have such an undertaking. I applaud your project and your courage."

I asked again, "What was the instrument that the other man played in the second piece of music? Not the sitar. The one with a bow. The one with the strings that followed the singer's voice so well?"

"The *sarangi*," our guide said smiling.

"*Sarangi*," I repeated. I felt so wonderfully light and happy. I smiled at the man who brought us and he returned my smile with a lovely smile of his own. He really seemed very nice.

The next thing that happened was that bowls were brought to us. Then steaming plates of food, which the servants scooped into our bowls. I was ravenous, but there were no eating utensils. Then I remembered that often when not at an English table, the natives ate with their hands. In my euphoric frame of mind, I stuck my hand into the warm food. There was no meat, but I have never had such delicious vegetables in my life. I had gravy all over my hands and face, but somehow I didn't care. I felt so wonderfully happy. I smiled at our guide and he made a motion to go on eating, which I did until I was ready to burst. Finally, I could eat no more and leaned back on my cushion. I felt perfectly happy. I was proud of myself. I had the courage to act and now I would write an excellent article, sell it and "throw the whole book in the fire." As I sat there that evening, everything seemed bathed in a warm glowing light. Then, I noticed that Sita was gone. I sat up suddenly.

"Your attendant had to leave," my guide said. "She lives not far from here and felt it was time to go home."

"Oh, heavens," I said getting to my feet awkwardly. "Where is our *palanquin*? How shall I get home? It must be very late. Oh, gracious, what shall I do?"

"Please, dear madame. Do not distress yourself. I shall take you home in my carriage."

"Oh, thank you, sir. You are very kind. You have been very kind all evening."

"It is very easy to be kind in such charming company, Mrs. Booth."

It had been such a long time that a man had spoken to me in such tones. A few tears sprang to my eyes. I am afraid he saw them. He handed me an immaculate white handkerchief. I dabbed at my eyes as he led us out of the house.

Once we were outside, I looked back at the ornate front of the house.

"Is that really a house of ill-repute? I mean, do men come there for..."

I would not have dared ask such a question if the *bhang* hadn't still been working in me.

"Yes," he answered smiling. "Very wicked is it not?" he asked, his smile growing even broader. He really was very nice and gentlemanly.

Just a few steps from the door of the place where we had eaten, he stopped next to a handsome carriage. It was a kind of landau, painted white with a little roof over each seat that could be pulled closed in case of bad weather. The horse was a beautiful dappled Arabian. It was a charming conveyance, much nicer than the foul smelling box Sita and I had come in.

"This is yours?" I asked.

"At your service," he replied, opening the door and handing me up the step.

A native in livery sat just behind the horse on a little seat. Perhaps he is one of the wealthy native bankers, one hears about, I thought.

We walked slowly through the rutted streets and up toward the Residency. The stars were large and bright. I can remember it all so clearly. I feel I shall be able to recall each detail for the rest of my life. What an exhilarating evening!

And just at that point, at the very summit of my happiness, I felt fear.

"Do you know the time, sir?" I asked. It suddenly seemed as if I had been away from the Residency for hours and hours. Without answering me, my guide asked me, "Do you know someone in England who will publish your article?"

"No," I answered, feeling rather foolish. I, I thought I would just send it to some of the periodicals we take."

"I might be able to help you. It can be very difficult to get published if you have no connections with the press. I recently spent an evening with William Howard Russell, the *Times* correspondent. Would you like me to see what I can do?"

"Oh, sir, your kindness overwhelms me."

"I shall write to him. It may take some time since he is usually at the front lines of a war. Of course, I can make no promise. But he is one of the leading journalists in the world."

"Oh, but you are so good just to try, sir."

After this, I returned home fearlessly. I no longer cared what Broderick thought or did. There were other people in the world who would help me and who appreciated me for myself. As it turned out, Broderick was fast asleep with an empty bottle of *arak* next to the sofa where he was snoring. Altogether, it was the most perfect night of my life. Through divine inspiration, I had the courage to set in motion a plan that would enable me to start over again, "to throw the whole book in the fire."

This plan, —which God had implanted in me, 'God who makes nothing that is not of some use'— was already coming to fruition. He was showing me His approval by making my way smooth.

Umrao in dance
costume

Chapter 9
Love, music and mystery

The unhappy but determined woman Henry was meeting in the pages of his mother's journal did not coincide with any memories he had of her. He could remember her beautiful hair, pretty face, and fond touch, but little else. She had always been his father's victim, and then a victim of the evil men who killed her. Mostly, what he remembered were his own feelings about her as a boy, a strange ache in himself, which he usually felt when he thought of her, only now, he realized, it was not she who was the source of these feelings, but himself. He had never been aware before that this feeling was a kind of loneliness, which only departed when Amelia Sutton or Mary was with him. It was all very familiar and yet very strange to him. The longing of the past mixed with the present and made him sharply anxious for Umrao to come out and join him. What a strange, remarkable girl she was. Not strange, but exotic, mysterious, even dangerous because she was so unpredictable. He did believe it when she said that no man would ever be her master. He had never felt so powerfully attracted to anyone, and he had to stay here with her. He had nowhere else to go.

On a practical level, his reading had told him nothing, so far, that might be of use in his present difficulties. There was still no indication of any meaningful connection between the events of the past and present, the connection that Sergeant Abdul had implied might exist. How many hours had passed over Henry's head while he sat reading, he couldn't tell. The London day had been twilight from its first moments. The moon of the previous night had shone more brightly than this nearly invisible sun, veiled in thick curtains of yellow fog.

Henry rose from the wooden box which he'd used as a chair. He was restless in the gloom of the bare, unlit room, and as the day crawled forward, he began to feel more and more impatient. He was anxious to extricate himself from the opprobrium and the dangers that seemed to dog him. He was anxious to clarify his feelings for Mary and Umrao. He wondered if Sergeant Abdul had learned anything useful. He was terribly anxious to see what message the Sergeant would bring from home.

No sound whatsoever had issued from Umrao's room, except a few soft thumping noises. He longed for her company and felt rather foolish for his longing. Then, he felt or remembered that he often felt this way. It seemed to be in him, not in the external situation.

"How odd," he thought.

In his state of suspense, time moved very slowly, so it seemed like many hours later when Umrao's door finally opened.

Henry stood up as Umrao came out of her room. She was wearing a long robe with a hood attached to the back of it. She came over to where he sat, with the ease of an old friend.

"My poor, dear, Henry," she said as she reached down and touched his face gently.

"This is all very hard for you, is it not?" Her gesture and words were very intimate, something Mary or Amelia might say and do.

"It is, Umrao. You cannot know. I chaff at this inactivity, but I don't know what to do."

"But it is only natural, Henry. Until now, everything in your life has been smooth. Now, you feel you have lost everything. Yes?" She moved close to him and hugged his head to her side as one might with a child.

"You are very kind, Umrao."

"It is easy to be kind to you, Henry. I, too, am struggling to keep my balance in this strange land."

He felt her lips brush his. It was done so gently, so artlessly, it might have been a kiss from a child.

Henry felt at a complete loss to know what to do. He wanted very much to take the exotic young woman in his arms, but he did not want to frighten her. He also feared the strength of his own feelings if he released them. The whole situation added to his sense of having lost everything familiar. He was at sea. He didn't know what the boundaries would be with Umrao, if there would be any boundaries. It was the direct opposite to his relationship with Mary, where the Suttons had laid down definite rules for behaviour. And, regardless of his powerful attraction to Umrao, it would be a betrayal of Mary to do anything. So, he did nothing.

"I wonder when Sergeant Abdul will come back," he said.

"Shall I entertain you, Henry?" Umrao asked. "You once said you'd like to hear me sing. Shall I do so, now?"

"Yes, please, Umrao. I am a musician, too. I play the pipe organ and pianoforte."

"I did not know. Some day you will play for me. Wait, I will get my *tambura*."

She was smiling and obviously pleased at his interest. She disappeared into her room for a moment and came out with a very large, long instrument, nearly as long as a bass viol but with a much smaller body and neck. She sat down and lay the instrument across her lap and plucked the strings. A strange whining note rang in the empty room. Then, Umrao began to sing and her voice and instrument made a harmony on the verge of dissonance. The intervals she sang were unearthly and at first he could not decide if they were beautiful or ugly.

She seemed to finish the piece and looked up at him. She read his puzzlement immediately.

"It sounds very strange to you," she said.

"Yes, but I could grow to like it, I think. If I understood it better."

"Yes. Then, I shall try to explain, but I have never taught, only studied. And mostly we study by doing, not by talking. And I know very little about your music. The most important part of my music is the *rag*, which comes from the sanskrit word *raga*, which means colour or passion. It is also linked to the word *ranj*, which means 'to colour.' This I learned, not while studying music but from the *maulvi*, the man who taught me languages and poetry. So, *rag* may be thought of as a way of colouring the mind of a listener with an emotion. Do you understand? No?"

"No, I'm sorry, Umrao. But what exactly is a *rag*? I can understand music but 'colouring the mind.' We have major and minor scales that I would say tend to evoke differing emotions. Is it anything like that?"

"Scale? Ah," she said brightening. "Do, re, mi, fa,—like that? Then, yes, I think. Each *rag* has specific notes. They are called the *swar*. There is also a specific number of notes used in the *rag*, this is *jati*. There is an ascending structure called *arohana* and a descending structure called *avarohana*."

"We have only one type of scale where the ascending and descending structure are different," Henry said.

"In addition to these main characteristics of *rag*, there are some other less important ones. Certain *ragas* are traditionally associated with particular times of the day. They have also have families of male and female *rags*. There are many, many different *rags*," Umrao said. "Different notes in a *rag* have different degrees of significance. Some are more important than others. The important notes are called *vadi* and *sama vadi*. Do you understand?"

"If those special notes are anything like the tonic, dominant and sub-dominant I would understand."

"I don't know those names," Umrao said. "These notes are like the soul, the breath, of the *raga*. Do you understand?"

"I don't know. Your music is like you: fascinating and perplexing."

She laughed her wonderful laugh. "So you do know how to talk to a woman."

Henry blushed at her compliment.

"To other women, perhaps. To you...I am not sure."

"Oh, that is very good, Henry. You make me feel more than special—there is a special English word—unique. No other can be compared. That is correct, is it not?"

"Unique," Henry put in.

"Yes. Unique," Umrao agreed. "Every lover, man or woman, king or courtesan wants that."

"I suppose that is true," Henry said, thoughtfully. "But I really meant what I said. I was not trying to flatter you."

" That is love's great deception," the girl said,

putting her instrument aside and sitting cross-legged in front of him. "It makes each lover believe absolutely in the uniqueness of his or her love. Yet, we are all the same. Especially when we love. Every courtesan knows this deceit that love forces on lovers, and she uses it in her work. Yet, she knows the truth of love: All lovers are alike. It is only in very small details that they are different from one another. But the courtesan pretends to believe love's lie. She sighs convincingly, goes without food, dangles her feet at the edge of a precipice. All these things. But all the while, she knows the truth."

"So courtesans never fall in love themselves—and—and believe the lie?" Henry asked.

"We try not to because it would make us tender-hearted and we would take less money from our customer."

"How cold blooded," Henry said.

"Oh, yes. Courtesans are the most ruthless women you will ever know." She was quiet for a moment, her thought obviously turned inward. Then she turned and pulled her instrument to her. "I am supposed to be teaching you about music, not about the tricks of courtesans."

"I don't like to think of you being so, so cynical and cold. You don't seem at all that way. I don't believe you really are."

"I have certainly been trained in the arts of *nakhra*, deception. And if you didn't believe me innocent, I should have failed my teacher. One of the best ways to deceive someone is to do it openly, tell them you are deceiving them."

"Are you saying that you are deceiving me? No. I don't believe you are a cold, scheming creature, Umrao. Not in your heart."

"Having a heart is a luxury only for the very

strong or privileged —and even then— but let us go back to music, a subject we cannot argue over," she said, smiling. "So, I shall sing to you about the morning. This is a *rag* that is generally played only in the morning. While you listen, think of the sun rising over the Gomti. Remember the animal cries of the jungle at dawn and feel the flash of heat as the sun casts his first look downward over the edge of the world. Think of these things and they may take you more deeply into the music. Usually I would also have a *tabla* player. The *tabla* is a special kind of drum and a very important instrument in our music. It provides the *tal*, the pulse of our music, the other half of our music. So we are missing half the music. But you must listen carefully." And she again struck some notes and began to sing.

This time, Henry felt he could better feel the music and follow the strangely drawn out notes which Umrao sang. Before the end of the song, he felt more able to enter into it. The sound was less foreign. At times, he could dimly sense the refinement of this tradition, its great antiquity, a distillation of the heat, dust, colour and beauty of India. He felt the peculiar magnetism of the subcontinent in the girl and her music in a new and powerful way yet, there was something of his own memories mixed with it.

Though they did nothing that mating men and women usually do as dusk spread over London, he felt very close to Umrao. She did have a gift for creating a sense of intimacy. She relieved that carking sense of unease which, he had realized just recently, only a close connection with a woman seemed to do. Whether or not this was *nakrha*, he preferred not to consider. Like everything else that had happened to him since he had received his mother's diary, Umrao and her music drew him back to India and made his life with the Suttons seem far away, indeed. At times, he was intoxicated with the strangeness of everything; at other times, he was terrified. He could go from one extreme to the other in just moments, especially as he sat listening to her. He did not know how long she sang and played. God alone knows what the drugged inmates below thought had invaded their stuporous dreams, but it was dark outside when she stopped and they both sat together in the silence and darkness of the room for a long time. This profound bond was only broken when Sergeant Abdul pushed open the sticking wooden door.

"Sergeant Abdul," Henry exclaimed.

"You are unharmed, Uncle?" Umrao asked. "I see you limp slightly."

"I did have two men attack me after I left your house Henry. But they were not Indian. They were British men. I felt they could be policemen in ordinary clothes."

"Policemen?" Henry repeated.

"Yes, they may have been watching the house for you, thinking to apprehend you there."

"And they attacked you, Uncle?" Umrao asked.

"As I was leaving the house."

"So you were able to speak with Mary, Sergeant?"

"No, Henry. I spoke with a Mr. Smythe-White. He told me very little. He said he preferred to speak with you. But I fear he may be working with the police. He wanted you to come to the house and would make no appointment to meet elsewhere."

"I cannot guess why that would be," Henry said. "He has only been helpful to me in my difficulties. Perhaps he is just being cautious, though he claimed to know you from Lucknow."

"But the policemen were there," Sergeant Abdul

said. "They were waiting for you, I am certain. Considering the treatment they got from me, there may be even more of them next time. Here is your dinner," and he handed each a greasy roll of newspaper which held some fried eel and potatoes.

Henry watched Umrao pick out the bits of eel.

"Is something wrong with your food, Umrao?" he asked.

"No. This was a living creature. I cannot eat it."

"We are vegetarians, Henry," Abdul explained.

"I did not realize how hungry I was," Henry remarked as he ate. "So I am now cut off from anyone at home."

"I fear so," Abdul said, taking an apple from his pocket and biting into it.

"And did you learn anything from the people who had the painting of Major General Sleeman?" Henry asked.

"I learned that no one in that house could read a single word of Ramasee."

"So the day has been completely unprofitable," Henry remarked in a somewhat bitter tone.

"If that is so, Henry," Umrao said, "I shall not sing for you again."

"No, no, forgive me, Umrao. That is the only good thing about the day."

Then he turned back to Abdul. "Well, what shall we do? It occurred to me today that Smythe-White might be able to read the inscription if no one else could."

"He is a linguist?" the Sergeant asked.

"He knows a number of Indian languages and some Persian, I believe."

"Perhaps, if he knows ancient Persian, he could help us. However, I am not certain we can trust him after he tried to help the police. It is of the last importance that we get this inscription fully translated. I believe it is an essential part of what has been happening to you, Henry."

"I still cannot see the connection," Henry replied.

"Nor can I," Abdul admitted. "But we must follow the threads we have. We can do no more."

"But we are blocked at every turn," Henry cried.

"Do not disturb yourself, so, young sir. A quiet mind is the way to see through walls. That is what I will do now. Make my mind quiet. Go into the other room with Umrao, please."

Henry and Umrao, got up but instead of following Umrao into the other room, Henry turned back to Sergeant Abdul.

"What are you going to do?" Henry asked.

"I shall meditate on emptiness," the Sergeant said.

"What?"

"Please do as I ask. Go to Umrao. Inner silence is what I need now."

After hesitating for a moment, Henry walked across the room and knocked on Umrao's door.

"Come in, Henry."

Two flickering candles lit the darkness of the tiny cubicle. Some beautiful robes had been pinned to the walls. A strongly perfumed smoke was rising from a little brass dish near one wall. Umrao's blanket was folded into a makeshift mattress. A brightly coloured picture of what looked like Arabic calligraphy sat propped against the wall. Umrao had obviously just lit the candles and incense.

"This is beautiful, Umrao. I am amazed to see

what you could do with such an unpromising place."

"A place always reflects the mind that inhabits it."

"But this is quite lovely, artistic, even."

"Have I not told you I am an artist," she said, squatting on the blanket. Henry stood looking down on her.

"Your singing was truly marvelous, Umrao. I'm sorry if I implied..."

"But that is only a single aspect of my art, Henry. Come and sit down," she said, holding out her hand.

He knelt facing her.

"You were worried about whether I liked you. I will show you how much I like you," she said and began to unbind her hair. First, she separated the thick plait and then brushed out each lock. When she was done, she suddenly pulled the robe over her head and threw it aside. She sat, without a trace of embarrassment, perfectly naked in front of him. Her hair cascaded over her shoulders and back to her waist, falling like a combination of cloud and water across her golden skin.

Henry was staggered. He couldn't turn his eyes away from her, yet he felt repulsed by her shamelessness.

"You have done this with many men?" he asked with a trembling voice.

"With no one, Henry. I told you. I had no initiation, no customer. You are the first man I shall know. I have chosen you for myself, not because my *chaudharayan* tells me. It is for myself that I want you. I give myself to you as a gift. For no other reason than I want to lie with you. I am lost in a strange land among cold strangers. I crave the affection I know you feel for me.

Any woman, queen or courtesan, can only give this gift once so, no matter what happens, you will know that you also are unique to me. In the *kotha* it is said that every girl remembers her first lover to her dying day. I have studied the art of love for a long time—from books and from Akhtar Devi who explained many things to me. But you are the first man whose flesh I will touch with my flesh. Do not be afraid."

With the softest touch of her fingers, Umrao began to undress him, kissing his face and hands lightly as she moved around him.

"Umrao, I.."

"I shall take care of us, Henry. Do nothing. Trust me, that is all I ask. Give me the gift I know you want to give me, your heart."

She kissed him lightly on the neck as she opened his collar. At the light touch of her fingers his clothing seemed to fall away from him and then she touched and kissed him in ways he had never even imagined. But as his body responded to her, he felt some lurking fear in himself. Of what, he could not say. He felt he should stop her. He started to get up.

"Umrao, I don't think..."

"No," she said sharply pushing him down. A moment later his breath was taken away as he felt her delicate hands on his genitals. He had not even realized he was naked. He had a momentary glimpse of Mary's white face, just before Umrao mounted him. Still, he pushed against her shoulders, as though he would push her away.

He felt something in himself resisting. He was afraid, he realized. Umrao kissed him deeply and pulled him up into a sitting position so she could wrap both legs around his waist. She held him close to her.

"Don't be afraid, sweet Henry," she said as she

kissed his face with long slow movements of her tongue and lips. Her body began to sway rhythmically, and finally, he could resist no longer.

"Umrao, Umrao, what are you doing to me? This must be wrong." he asked in a voice he did not recognize as his own.

Suddenly, out of the darkness of his own mind came a startlingly clear picture of his mother and he felt a sharp pain in his abdomen, he gasped out his sorrow, crying as Umrao made love to him more urgently than before, faster and faster. The pain of his mother's death which he had only felt as a child, now rose up from some secret place in himself and as Umrao moved her inner and outer muscles in a perfectly synchronized dance, the knot of anguish exploded, mixing pain and ecstatic pleasure in one moment he would remember for the rest of his life.

The next thing he was aware of was Umrao's weight on him, the tent of her magnificent hair, her warmth and quick breath pressed against him and his own voice murmuring, "My sweet, sweet girl, my astonishing beauty."

Umrao kissed the tears that streamed across his face and licked his eyelids. Then it seemed he may have slept for a few moments. He woke suddenly to find himself being swung through the air as Umrao rolled underneath him, changing places with him without any separation of their bodies. Her slender, muscular legs slipped from his waist and wrapped around his thighs, teaching them how she wanted him to move. Her nails dug into his back, causing him an exquisite pain. Her feet touched him as eloquently as her hands had done. First following her and then able to sense them both, Henry found what Umrao had tried to make him discover. Then, he moved with certainty and listened with pleasure to her little whimpering cries, which rose to the crescendo of a long wailing note, a note that trembled through many different pitches, a complete song of ecstasy sung by a gifted singer.

Then, they slept.

Sometime near dawn, Henry felt Umrao coax him out of sleep to make love once more. Both of them were barely conscious and quickly slipped back into oblivion.

Henry woke like one swimming up to the surface of a clear pond. While still immersed in sleep, he could see the waking world become more and more clear as he drew nearer to it. Umrao was not next to him. She had covered him with her coat and he felt a great tenderness toward her for this caring gesture. Then he sat up quickly, remembering all the problems that still faced them in spite of their ecstasy, ecstasy that Henry's wide-awake mind was telling him was immoral from every possible point of view. Quick flashes of Mary's face stared at him.

Of course, now he would have to marry Umrao as soon as their other problems could be solved. Last night had changed everything in his life. After what had happened, marriage was the only possible course— and it was also his own desire.

Would she marry him as an Anglican? he wondered. As he dressed, he was surprised to feel sore muscles. He thought of himself as being in training, but apparently the muscles he had taxed during the night were entirely different from those he used in athletics. As he completed his attire, he remembered, too, that Sergeant Abdul was Umrao's uncle. Surely, he would know what had happened. He resolved to begin the day by proposing to Umrao in front of her uncle, so the Sergeant would know, that in spite of what had happened,

Henry Booth was an honourable man. This resolve braced his courage for facing Umrao and her uncle and with this thought, he grabbed the leather strap on the door and pulled it open.

"Hello, sweet Henry," Umrao said, smiling, as soon as she saw him. She was alone in the room. She had been doing something to the smaller instrument, the one she had called the *sarangi*, cradling it in her lap, but now she got up and came over to Henry and kissed him.

Henry put his arms around her waist. "Dear astonishing, magnificent woman," he said huskily. "As soon as your uncle and I can sort things out we shall be married, of course. I shall tell..."

"Married? What for, Henry?"

"But you can't mean you don't want to?"

"I think we have to know a great deal more about each other, first. Especially what our reasons are for marriage."

"Reasons? After what has happened?"

"Physical love should not be the reason for getting married, Henry. Many other things are more important. Your heart is so beautiful. I felt the sorrow buried in you..."

"But, I thought..."

"You see, we are at cross purposes already. We come from two different cultures. And, Henry, I was raised to be a courtesan."

"But...I want to marry you. You said..."

"Right now you do."

"No. I want to."

"Let us be lovers first, Henry. Let us see what happens. No one can take away what we have already had. Before we can talk about any future, there is something I must tell you about myself, first. Before we can

166

make any kind of decisions. You must know why I came to England."

"You came to stay with your Uncle."

"No. There is more."

"You are not engaged to someone else?"

"No."

"Then what else can possibly matter?"

"I have sworn to kill someone here in England."

"What? Good God. What are you saying, Umrao?"

"A man came to my mother's house and murdered her. I know he was English and I know he has returned to his home somewhere in this forest of stone and dust. So I came here. That is why I was not initiated, and I am now much older than any other girl in the *kotha* who has not been initiated."

"But you can't just decide to kill someone. We have laws and courts, here. Let us capture the brute, then our laws will deal with him."

"No. Look at how the British laws are dealing with you. I must know that my mother, my more than mother, is avenged."

"You do not understand things here," Henry said. "I don't want anything to happen to you."

"No. You do not understand."

"All right. Explain it to me."

"My parents died when I was little, so a cousin sold me to a famous courtesan."

"Sold you?"

"They were starving and knew the life I might have with the courtesan would be far better than anything they could offer. If I had talent for music and dance, they knew I might become wealthy and honoured."

"It still seems a strange thing to wish for a child."

"Not if you are starving. And as I've said, in Lucknow, there was a class of courtesan which was made up of highly trained, dancers, singers and poets. We are known as the *deredar tuwaif*. Many *deredar tuwaifs* lived on the palace grounds at the Qaiserbagh or other royal houses in earlier times. Many were rich. Many slept only with one man. Only the *takaiyas* slept with many. They were prostitutes for the lower classes. The *randis* were for the gentry. Neither *randis* nor *takaiyas* were artists. But, the *deredar tuwaifs*, consorted only with the leaders of society, the *nawabs* and their friends. We were the leading artists in the city, known all over India and Asia. We were the experts in correct social behaviour and in ritual observance. The greatest families of Lucknow sent us their sons to learn how to behave in society."

"So this class of courtesan only sings and dances?" Henry asked, looking pained.

"No, Henry," Umrao said reaching out and taking his hand. "Of course sex is part of our service. But it is often a very small part and with only one man. Sometimes we may become one of his legal wives and live in the *zenana* like any respectable Moslem woman."

"I forgot," Henry said slowly, "that Moslem men may have more than one wife."

He sighed deeply. His face was contracted and puzzled.

"You see, Henry, we have many things to learn and understand."

"Umrao," he said, pulling her close, "there is one thing I have already learned. I want no other woman for my wife but you. It pains me to betray Mary this way, but it is what I feel."

"But you have known no other woman."

"I have been engaged to Mary since we were children."

"But you have never known her body."

"No."

"How much do you really know of her mind?"

He was silent for a moment, obviously struck by what she asked.

"It is very strange you should say that. My mother's journal has made me start to wonder that very thing. Her words made me think for the first time about what women really feel, what their thoughts are, rather than just the polite forms of how we are supposed to treat them."

"Then, as a wife, you don't know this British girl as well as you know me, no matter how many years you lived in her house."

"But all this doesn't matter now," Henry said. "And you never were with anyone before last night. Were you?"

"I told you I was not, but I was trained by my benefactor in the arts of physical love and all the arts of the *deredar tuwaif*. I know how to entice men and make them fall in love with me and give me money. I knew how to give us pleasure last night, because I was trained. Henry, Henry, this is what I am. You cannot make it go away by saying it doesn't matter, because we are in England. I have trained for nearly fifteen years to be what I am."

"You mean last night didn't mean anything to you?" he said huskily, as he studied her face and ended by brushing her cheek with his lips.

"Oh, my poor Henry. Of course it meant something to me. I told you. I chose you for myself. You are a beautiful man with a wonderful, warm heart. What more could I ask for?"

"Then, why shouldn't we get married? What we did last night does make us married, or ought to."

"Henry," she said taking both this hands as she pulled him down to the floor to sit opposite to her, "You are like a blind donkey who smells two piles of oats. Either he eats from this pile or he eats from that pile. One or the other. That is all he knows. Do not force us to be a particular way with each other. We must learn more. Then we will know what is right for us."

"Please, Umrao, I know you are right for me. Will you or will you not accept me?"

She closed her eyes for a moment. Then opened them and spoke.

"I will accept you if you ask me again when we stand in the meadow of the Residency in Lucknow and smell the jasmine in the air." Then she added sadly, "You will be shocked by the ruins. The Residency is just a pile of shattered stones, standing in a meadow dotted with wildflowers."

"I know that the Residency was used as a fortress during the Mutiny."

"Yes."

"What you really mean, is that you want to fulfill your vow of vengeance, first."

"And see you released from difficulties with the laws of your country, and free yourself from the shadow of the *Thuggee*. Yes, I want all those things."

They sat very close to one another. Henry took both her hands in his. Her fabulously long hair was once again bound on top of her head.

"I will ask you there and I will do those other things, as well. I swear it. Will you promise to belong to no other man until we have stood in that meadow together? And then to be mine and mine alone?"

She leaned over to reach his lips and kissed him.

Then she said, "If we go to Lucknow and you ask me again, I promise to be always my true self with you and to have no other man. But you must never try to govern me or impose your will on me. We, the *deradar tuwaif*, are not like the *memsahibs* I have seen. If you try to rule me, I shall hurt you. Do not say 'mine' so often. I belong to no one, except when I choose to give myself. That is the power I learned from Ahktar Devi, the power of a courtesan. If she is wealthy she can choose, when, where and how she will accept a man—unlike a *memsahib*."

Henry shook his head. "Your views turn everything upside down yet, when I look closely at them, I cannot argue with their soundness. Abdul said you were the last of your kind. What did he mean?"

She smiled and then said, "Before the war and when the *Nawabs* truly ruled Oudh, this was the golden time of the *deredwar tuwaif*. We consorted with the *Nawabs* of our free choice and were handsomely paid. Later, many were trained at the *Parakhana*, the school founded by Wajid Ali Shah, the last king of Oudh. I told you before that now, many of the best dancers and singers have been abducted by the British and made slaves of dirty army men who give them diseases. The British do not understand our art. They are coarse and abuse us. But my mother, Ahktar Devi taught me how to use money to gain power, and unlike most other *kothas* in Lucknow, her skill at giving bribes has kept us unmolested. There are few left who speak and write Arabic, Persian, Urdu, and English as I do— know all the ancient verse forms as I do—, who understand the laws and history of *rag* and *tal* as I do. The British have destroyed most of us in one way or another. That is what Abdul meant."

"You certainly speak English very well," Henry said.

"That was more of Ahktar Devi's cleverness. 'You must be able to speak their language as well as they do,' she used to say. 'Only then will they listen to you. You must make them listen since they are the new kings of Oudh.'"

"I agree that the British have been brutal and greedy in India," Henry said.

Umrao did not reply but kissed him lightly.

After her lips left his, Henry asked, "Where is your Uncle, Umrao? When I left him last night he said something about meditating on emptiness. He didn't say anything about going out."

"He must go out every day. Many people wait for him. I don't know where he is. Meditating on emptiness is the most fundamental form of meditation."

"And what is meditation? It seems to have a special meaning the way you and your Uncle use the word."

"It is completely relaxed one-pointedness of mind."

"One pointedness of mind," Henry repeated. "So it is a kind of mental concentration?"

"Yes." she answered sitting down. " When you play music are you not completely relaxed, yet perfectly alert, listening to yourself without any other thoughts intruding? No thoughts, no feelings just listening, as though another were making the music?"

"When I am playing well, that is how it seems, yes."

"That is meditation."

"But meditating on emptiness?"

"It is applying that kind of concentration without having a mental or physical object."

"Now, I don't understand."

"When we were joined last night, did not something happen to you? When you started to cry?"

Henry jumped as though he'd been stung.

"I had forgotten, I..."

"No. Don't tell me about it. Do you remember your thoughts just before that?"

"No. I was just with you. You were everything. My mind thought of nothing."

"Yes. And when the little mind thinks of nothing, greater aspects of ourselves, of life, can become known."

"Did you learn mental science with your other studies?"

"I certainly learned to concentrate deeply. The *Malauvi*, the scholar, who taught me languages and philosophy always emphasized the state of my mind when I was receiving his knowledge. But I learned most about meditation from my Uncle, who was born a Moslem but studied with a Hindu *sadhu*. We are not actually of the same blood family. Like a *deredar tuwaif*, his talent makes his family."

"His talent?"

"His gift for healing. People invite him into their hearts wherever he goes."

"I wish I knew where he is," Henry said.

"He will come."

Henry sat down next to Umrao and tried to kiss her neck while she was tuning the *sarangi*. She giggled but squirmed away from him.

"You are so mysterious in some ways, Umrao." She put her instrument aside and looked Henry in the eyes.

"Now you touch on another great secret of love. I will put my instrument down for a moment and tell it to you, if you wish it."

"How can I resist being taught another one of the great secrets of love? Especially if you are my guide."

"This is not for laughing. Are you listening, sweet Henry?"

"Yes, of course."

"Mystery is the root of romantic love. Without mystery, the plant of romance cannot grow. This is one of the reasons why your love with Mary has never blossomed for you in an erotic way. You know her too well in ordinary ways. You contain all that she is. When you look in her eyes there is no incomprehensible depth there, no secret. But she does not know you. You have more mystery for her than she does for you. Women need less mystery. But for men it is the essence of romantic love. That is the most important reason why you must know me better before we discuss marriage. When the mystery suddenly goes away, as it often can, all feeling can go too, in the flash of an eye. I have seen it happen."

Before Henry could ask his question, Umrao giggled again.

"No, you sweet blind donkey. Not with me. With others."

"You make me feel like a child sometimes, Umrao," Henry said, grinning. "It is disquieting and delightful at the same time. Like being naked with you."

"You are a child, Henry. Losing your mother the way you did has kept your heart very soft and young. That is a wonderful thing, to find a man with a truly soft heart. But you must also be able to protect it."

"I never felt I had to protect myself from Mary."

"She is not a threat, Henry. She is not a woman, yet. She may never be."

"And you?"

She turned to look at him with her wonderful eyes, a deep brown in the direct sunshine coming through window, but nearly black at all other times. Her skin was the colour of honey, he thought as he watched the sun glint from the fine gold ring in her nostril. She looked at him for some time, almost sadly, it seemed to him.

Then she said, "I could break your beautiful heart, Henry. And I do not want to. I want to be most careful with it." And she put her arms around him, held him close and rocked back and forth with him. When she released him she said, "Now I would like to practice my music. Will it bother you if I play in here?"

"Bother me, hardly. But I think I must read some more of my mother's journal or your Uncle will upbraid me when he returns."

Henry got up and sat down near the window and picked up his mother's journal as Umrao sang a sobbing note.

Chapter 10
The Journal of Jane Booth

Third Reading

Entry date: November 10, 1856—morning

"Of course I know that if I succeed, I shall not be the only Residency wife who has left her husband. In times past, I believe one of the Residents was proud of getting a wife to return to her husband. It is ironic that Broderick actually mentioned this old piece of Residency gossip to me after he had been going over some old files in his office. I would never do that. When I leave, I shall be prepared and be certain of where I am going.

November 16, 1856—afternoon

What a charming surprise. I have just received a hand-delivered letter from a livered servant which contains many details of my evening in the *chowk*. It gives me the exact menu of the food we ate. It explains the instruments and music and provides some further details on the "house" where we were visiting. I would never have even thought of these things until I sat down to write. And how would I ever have gotten this information, then? It must have taken him hours to do this. How kind and thoughtful. When I think of him, I must confess, that for a native, he really was quite a good looking man. If he takes this trouble for me, there must be some admiration in it. I should be on my guard if I see him again for any reason.

November 17, 1856—afternoon

Now I know that my friend from the *chowk* is sincerely disinterested in his attentions to me. He has sent an invitation to me and Broderick to be his guests near Cawnpore next weekend! He offers us what he calls distinguished accommodations and a barouche to take us both ways. What a delightful break from our tedious. fly blown existence, here.

8:00—evening

I showed the invitation to Broderick when he got home and he seems delighted to go! Oh, perhaps this outing will be the beginning of a change of heart with me and Broderick. If only it could be so and we could return to the past, the good days in Calcutta. What am I saying? We were both different people, then. I hardly recognize us as the same couple and it is only two years in the past. I could never be reconciled to him now. I've seen him disporting with prostitutes. But Cawnpore would be fun. I've heard it said that the people who attend the Cawnpore races are rather a fast set, but that would be the perspective from the people here. I have no qualms about leaving Henry for the weekend. I have complete faith in our *ayah*. Henry adores her and he will have a vacation from me.

Dec 9, 1856—morning

Only two days until the weekend and Broderick has told me that he cannot go to Cawnpore! He must go to Delhi on Company business. He leaves it to me if I should keep the appointment with our new friend. He says it will be perfectly respectable since I will be with a group of English people. I shall certainly stay at the Residency. Broderick actually urges me to go, saying that I might make some valuable acquaintances for him at Cawnpore. It possesses after all, the second largest European population in India, and the gardens are superb. I may even get to see a play in the grand new theatre with its imposing columns all round.

Perhaps I shall go to the races and be admired by all the young officers. The Residency there is picturesque, too, set right on the Ganges. I imagine the patio would be a delightful place to have drinks. I could watch the wading birds and the pelicans swooping down to the water. Everything looks so lush there. Here we are dry and dusty most of the time, and our wildlife is truly wild. There was recently a report of a wolf carrying off a child just on the other side of the Gomti.

In Lucknow, everything is according to the whim of the fat native king and his degenerate courtiers. Even the Resident has to consult him about the most absurd things. The Resident has been trying to get the king to fix the drains in our bungalow for ever so long. The king insists on doing it and then does nothing and won't let us do anything! Cawnpore is truly British.

On the one hand, there are all those reasons for going, yet something in me hesitates. Perhaps it is because I know how strongly my feelings lead me in the direction of any place that is away from here. Those are my feelings. My thoughts, on the other hand, are these: our Moslem friend is too charming and, I believe, admires me too much to spend a weekend in his company without my husband. Maturely examined, the weekend in Cawnpore could be a situation which might be uncomfortable for me. Of course, I should always be in control. I'm certain he's a perfect gentleman. And I don't want to lose the chance of being introduced to the famous journalist he knows. I suppose Broderick is right. In this, our interests do lie together. This man could be valuable to us both, though of course Broderick knows nothing of my ambitions. I should see what I can do to make certain of my own opportunity and possibly even form some mercantile advantages for Broderick. I mustn't let my timidity stop me, as I almost did when I wanted to see the *chowk*. It would relieve my conscience to think I had actually done something good for Broderick, even while I am plotting to leave him.

Poor man. He should have remained a soldier—an unmarried soldier. Then, he could have had all the native women he wanted. Though how he could kiss someone with blackened teeth, like the woman I saw him with, is beyond my ability to imagine.

I read over the foregoing and dislike myself. I sound so absorbed in my own pleasure. But really, what am I to do? If I stop at home and do nothing, and Broderick and I continue to quarrel, we could find ourselves in the midst of a scandal. He has already behaved abominably toward me. If he should lose control of himself with me and really bruise or hurt me, then what? I should have to go to Dr. Fayrer and he would know about Broderick's brutality. Such an incident would be bad for us both. I shall not go back to my family in England with nothing but a failed marriage to my discredit, and nothing but another mouth to feed. It was their ill-considered economies that sent me to India, in the first place. If that is how they felt about me then, why would they condescend now to look after us? And I must always think of dear little Henry. I must somehow make him secure and unafraid. I do so want to do what is right. I want to be kind, and it seems the kindest thing to do is to prepare the way for myself to be independent and leave with Henry. I must be brave and try to remember the example of George Sand.

Dec 11, 1856—afternoon

It is all arranged. Our friend is to send the carriage for me and I shall leave here tomorrow afternoon. I'll spend the night at the Residency in Cawnpore and our friend will take me and some other English ladies out to the palace where he lives in Bithur and then back in time for the Saturday races at four o'clock.

  Now that I have decided, I must confess I am quite excited about going.

Midnight—Cawnpore

A day of extraordinary events! The road between Lucknow and Cawnpore is abominable. We rocked and swayed, banged and bumped for ten hours. My first great surprise was that my friend had come to escort me, in person. He said that I was under his protection and that there are *dacoits* or bandits along the road. I said I doubted that they would trifle with an Englishwoman and he said that I was still his "precious" responsibility. He was very courtly and kind.

  He had a magnificent lunch packed for us and we stopped in the midst of a delightful grove of mango trees and had our lunch there on a beautiful folding dining set. When I admired the inlay and workmanship of the picnic furniture, he insisted that I take it home with me so that I would remember, "our idyll in the mango grove." And it was an idyll. We had chilled french champagne, smoked salmon and other British delicacies. Where he got them, I cannot imagine, but he certainly took a great deal of trouble for me.

We dined completely alone in the grove, for he sent his servants to watch the nearby road for *dacoits*. I knew when I accepted the invitation, I would be treading on dangerous ground, but I had no idea that danger of any kind could be so pleasant and care-free. In short, he tried to take my hand once I had removed my gloves. Of course, I did not allow it. By then it was obvious that his admiration for me was great.

His manners were otherwise charming and he is quite handsome, slender and graceful. Broderick, I've noticed is getting that red, beefy look that so many British men get in this climate.

My friend accepted my slight remonstrance gracefully and then started to tell me about the country we were passing through: the flora, the fauna and the way the countryside was ruled. I was astonished when he told me that none of the grandees of Lucknow would dare to come out into the country because they were Moslem and seen as oppressors by the entirely Hindu farming and land owning population.

Apparently, the nobles of Oudh must hide in their cities, collecting very large rents from the rustic landowners, called, *zemindars*. Some of them own vast tracts of land and live in castles surrounded by bamboo forests. It was very interesting to listen to him, not so much for what he said, but the way he said it.

My friend made me realize that we English

always speak of India as though it is a very unpleasant place except behind our own walls. He made me see the beauty of the subcontinent. He described the landscape of Kashmir where the people live in brightly painted houseboats on huge lakes, fishing in the same way that they have for thousands of years. It is cool and dry there, and pleasant most of the year. For the first time since I've been here, I was able to see the grandeur and beauty of the land. I think it was because I was not shut up in a city, my behaviour watched and judged by everyone around me.

He told me that the English cannot make India into England, and that we must learn to appreciate the country for itself. He made me realize what a tiny, narrow corner of the subcontinent with which I am acquainted.

The heavy shade of the trees was deep and refreshing. When he led me away from our table to show me a little nearby stream, I did allow him to take my hand to help steady me on the uneven ground. The forest where we walked seemed very wild to me, filled with vines and creepers, but in a short time we stopped next to a very beautiful stream with mossy banks where some mango trees were growing down into the water. We did see some serpents, but he knew all about them and so I was completely unafraid.

By the time we continued on our journey, I was sorry to leave our bower but apparently we had already stayed longer than was wise. After consulting his large gold pocket watch, my friend frowned and said that we must make haste, otherwise we should find the Residency closed against us until morning. Gaining admittance would mean rousing all the guards. He was concerned that arriving in the middle of the night in his carriage would not be good for my reputation.

Nothing of moment happened during the rest of the drive, but it was long after dark when we drew near Cawnpore. It was remarkable how the time passed with him. He talked so well, about so many subjects and he was obviously so interested in me and my plans to change my life. He already knew that I wanted to publish articles about India, but now I confided all my plans and my reasons for wanting to leave Broderick. I am afraid I even shed a few tears when I spoke about Henry. He offered me a fine immaculate handkerchief.

By the time we reached Cawnpore, I felt we really knew one another. In many ways, I feel I know him better after our ride than I knew Broderick after years of marriage. He seemed to have a remarkable ability for giving words to thoughts which I found difficult to express. I felt we were truly friends, and in many ways I believed that he was more deeply interested in me than anyone I had ever known. I am certain he could not have divined my thoughts as he did if his true regard and interest in me was not profound.

My experience with him during the ride was so remarkable that I made haste to note it here as soon as I was shown to my room, so as not to forget any part of it. In spite of feeling tired, I am still wide awake and take advantage of the balcony on my room which overlooks the gardens. I sat outside and watched the moon reflected on the ripples of the Ganges and the wet islands of silt that emerge from the waters at this time of year. My friend had told me that the Ganges was the soul of India and that if I learned to appreciate all of its aspects, at different times of day in different seasons, I should know India.

To sum up: In a single afternoon, the world had become much larger. I eventually fell asleep listening to the lap of the waters, the soft flapping of palm branches, the occasional cry of a water bird and my friend's voice speaking in my thoughts.

Cawnpore, evening

Many things I had looked forward to, took place today. I went to the races with a group of English people and watched the Arabians run. We did not go to my friend's house. Fortunately, the wind was blowing from the right direction and the sandy ground around the track was not thrown into our eyes. I lost a few rupees along with others who betted much more heavily. I was admired by many of the young officers, would-be rakes for whom any grass widow was fair game. I believe my blond hair and very fair skin gives me a great ascendancy over other women here because the men are so used to the dark skins and hair of the natives.

In the evening there was a dinner party on the patio of the Residency. We did have drinks overlooking the Ganges. I did watch the birds swoop and dive for fish, yet, through it all, I thought most of my friend, who was not present. Whether it was because he was a native or for other reasons, I had no way of knowing, and, of course, I could not ask. I was only aware that his voice and face ran through my thoughts all day. And when I listened to the gossip of the Residency couples, I remembered what he said to me about the English in India, "They try to shut out India from the Residences and from their cities, but India is too vast and great for that. One day it will overtake them."

When I looked at us having our drinks and then turned away toward the river and saw the wide water with its great sky, it did seem as if we were ignoring India's grandeur and trying to shut it out.

I wonder how Henry is? I shall see him soon.

I hope he is having a good time with the *ayah*, whose name, I just realized, I have forgotten for the moment.

Sunday Morning

Though the church here is quite grand by the standards of the one back in Lucknow, I did not at all enjoy being there today. I felt restless and wondered if I should see my friend today. We all live our lives in such darkness, never experiencing what we imagine the future will hold. It is as though things always seem one way from a distance and by the time they are near, have changed into something else. Sometimes they are improved, but in my experience, they are more often worse.

　　　　The day, which was overcast and comfortably cool in the morning, turned detestably hot and I have spent most of it lying in a stupor in my airy room. If I am still, it is almost bearable with *tattis* up over the windows. The breeze from the Ganges helped and it will be even stronger by evening, I am told.

Sunday Evening

I have been dancing at the evening party. It was cool enough and the breezes from the river were delightful on the patio. It even prevented the flies from biting. The Resident, of course, had all the best regimental musicians play for us. They really were an excellent ensemble and I believe that apart from my journey here with my friend, the fine music was the high point of my sojourn. I really have no idea if I shall see him again before I leave. I don't even know if I shall see him at all. He said he would help me to get my article published, but I have not written anything, yet. And I do not have any kind of appointment with him at all. Perhaps, he just found me another boring *memsahib*, with all the same prejudices of other English people whom he dislikes.

He is good at hiding his disapproval of us, but I can feel it in him, though I know he is well received here in European society—and that society here is much above what it is in Lucknow.

A rather comic footnote to my stay here: the pelicans are quite tame and sit on the fence of the patio and beg for food. Some people do feed them and I imagine that is why the birds come back. When I went down to breakfast this morning they were lined up in a row like a group of gray coated bankers waiting for morning scraps.

Tomorrow morning, I depart. Back to my old, empty life. I have received a message that the barouche will be sent for me, but I have no idea if he will be in it. I wish I knew.

Lucknow, Monday Evening, after my return
from Cawnpore

The barouche came, but with no one inside. I was astonished at how disappointed I felt. The same driver and footman were in charge of the conveyance, but no one else.

"Well," I thought, "I am certain he has more important things to do than ride back and forth between Cawnpore and Lucknow with me."

I wondered if he would still help me get my writing published. I thought that I must get to work on my article once I am home. It would be too horribly embarrassing if he did contact me offering to forward my work to Mr. Russell and I had nothing to give him. But perhaps after our long conversation, he does not find me so interesting anymore. I thought him rather inconsistent in his concern for me after what he had said about bandits on the road. I moped in the jolting carriage until we were quite outside of Cawnpore. Then, in a lonely place on the road, we began to slow. I did feel some alarm and wondered what was going to happen next. I couldn't believe his servants would try to harm me in any way. Before the carriage stopped entirely the door opened and he got in and spoke.

"Good day, Mrs. Booth, I thought this was a good way to avoid gossip."

I was so glad to see him, I hardly knew what to say. I suppose I was quiet for a long time. He finally asked, "Would you rather ride alone?"

"Oh, no. I was just so surprised. I confess I was actually terribly disappointed when you weren't in the carriage."

"I didn't think I should expose you to the opprobrium of the other *memsahibs* who would surely comment on the intimacy of our ride together in each direction."

"That is very considerate," I said, "I would not want to be the object of gossip, but it never even occurred to me. Do you think it is improper?"

"They would certainly think so."

"But it is important what you think of me—to me," I said offering my ungloved hand. He pressed it briefly in a very unassuming way.

"I do not think I could find it in my heart to censure you for anything, Mrs. Booth."

I wasn't quite sure what to make of his reply, so I let the matter rest. I had thought of our previous conversation with so much interest in the intervening days that I was now at a complete loss to understand the feeling of constraint which I think we both suffered under. Even nature was against us. We stopped at the same place for lunch, only this time there were swarms of biting flies. By the time he left me at my own door and unpacked the picnic furniture he had promised, I felt quite out of sorts with both of us. I felt cross with him, without knowing why. I felt disappointed, but I could not say what he had done to disappoint me.

We parted like strangers, and only two days earlier, he had seemed my best friend in the world. I could so little comprehend any of it that I resolved to put my perplexities out of my mind and spend the day with my little boy, who was so delighted to see me. He rushed into my skirts and flung himself against me. No matter how much he likes his *ayah*, he still adores me. He reached up to touch my hair when I bent over to him. Something in that moment of his childish enthusiasm for me resonated deeply within me, though in what way was obscure, as though his gesture had a second meaning which I had missed.

8:00 —evening

Broderick must be with his native whore tonight, though he has not even bothered to make an excuse this time. My spirits feel horribly depressed. I feel very lonely. I do not even find Sita in the house tonight. I should try to begin my article, but to do that I should have to look at the paper of information my friend drew up for me and then I should start to think about our disappointing ride home.

10:00—evening

I have just received a note from him! He asks me to meet him in the *chowk* tomorrow night. He seems to know where Broderick is spending his evenings and assumes I shall be able to get away. Suddenly, all my disappointment and low spirits are gone. How quixotic I am. I do not understand myself at all. He wants me to come to the same house where I had dinner on my last visit to the *chowk*. He will send a common *palanquin* to me and will put a *burqa* inside for me to wear over my clothes when I get out in the *chowk*. He is so careful to protect my position.

December 16— morning

Oh my God, my God, what have I done? Do I dare write it down? I must tell someone, surely I can find the courage to say it to myself.

I got into the *palanquin* when it arrived and put on the *burqa* as he had directed me in his letter. I did not need to say anything to the bearers. They stopped at the house in the *chowk* and I was handed out by one of the men who guard the door.

He led me down a different hallway from the one I had used to enter the large common room on my last visit. This time we climbed a flight of curving stairs up to another floor and entered another part of the building. The front of the house had looked rather small, but now, it seemed to contain a large warren of rooms, but where one would have expected to see windows, there were only blank walls. This lack of prospect made the dark halls seem like those of a prison. My usher held a flickering oil lamp to light the way. By this time, I doubted I could find my way back to the entrance door even if my rising sense of panic had overwhelmed me.

Finally, the man opened a door and we entered a magnificently appointed apartment. It was furnished in barbaric splendour with tiger skins and thick cushions everywhere. A low, beautiful table inlaid with brass and mother of pearl was lit by a brass lantern overhead whose pierced shade cast mysterious shadows around the fabric covered walls of the room as the lamp revolved slowly. The effect was like an extremely luxurious tent. There was a beautiful *hukkah* within easy reach of the table.

My friend wore an elegant dark suit and helped me off with my *burqua*. Then I sat down on one of the low cushions and without either of us saying a word, I took the *hukkah* from him when he offered it to me.

The mild smoke had a different taste from what I'd had on my last visit. My friend was smiling at me. His eyes were filled with tenderness and I felt all the interest and concern from him that I had on our ride to Cawnpore. We spoke about my trip to Cawnpore, and I felt myself drifting away into a kind of wonderful dream. It was as if I was watching myself from a distance.

There was so much I wanted to ask him but instead, without offering a word of protest, I let him slowly and delicately unfasten my buttons and laces. It was amazing to realize what was happening, and to see myself simply watch him undress me, without any resistance or comment whatever.

When I lay completely naked on the cushions before him, he looked at me very carefully, much more carefully than Broderick has ever looked at me. His attitude was one of a connoisseur admiring a treasure. He told me I was the most beautiful woman he had ever seen and that he would like to keep me like a Moslem woman, nearly naked, hidden in a *zanana* away from the sight of any other man but himself.

The thought of being admired in this jealous,

exclusive way by him made the fire in my belly burn even more strongly. I am ashamed to admit that my body actually ached for his touch. I felt a lust no decent woman should feel. And I had these feelings even while my mind was amazed and horrified by my desire. How could I, a married Christian white woman, feel this and allow this, I kept wondering? The uncontrolled lust of native men was the secret terror of every white woman I'd met in India. But my own lust was infinitely more shocking to me.

The more my mind disapproved, the more I wanted him. He began to tease me with very light strokes, scarcely making contact with my skin, but each feather touch reached into my soul in a way that Broderick never had. I could feel the kindness and affection this man felt for me in his fingers, his lips, any time he touched me.

He stayed close to me even after he had possessed me, and kissed my eyelids and face very tenderly. For me, who had been living with Broderick's insensitive, violent batterings and sudden departures, this lingering tenderness afterwards was like a long forgotten dream, recalled from the earliest days of my marriage.

At the same time, my mind was thinking that if anyone ever found out that I had allowed a black man to possess me, I should be regarded as disgusting, and immoral, far worse than the ignorant native whores with whom Broderick consorted. I had the advantages of my religion, my race and my education, yet I had trampled those advantages into the mud.

While my body felt wonderful and my heart was melted by what had occurred, part of me still could not believe what had happened. I fell asleep in his arms, wrapped in wonderfully soft cloth.

When I woke, I at first thought I was alone,

but when I turned my head, I saw the woman who had danced during my first visit to the house. She sat next to me very quietly, and I could see that without the face paint, which she'd worn on the stage, she was no longer in the prime of her beauty. Still, she was very lovely and had a truly regal dignity about her. Next to her sat a lovely little girl who radiated the same calmness as the older woman. It was a surprise to see a child here. We looked at each other for what seemed a long time. The most striking thing about both of them was their poise. I don't think I have ever seen human beings sit so perfectly still—even the child. I felt a calm and repose in them I had never before seen in anyone.

Their calm was in sharp contrast to my own state of mind. I was angry at myself, fearful and I felt abandoned by my friend. Finally, the older woman spoke.

"Thank you for returning to my house, Mrs. Booth. You are always welcome here."

She put her hands together and bowed slightly. I felt her sincere gratitude, and I believed that she was telling me her home would always be a refuge whenever I wanted it. It was very odd the way her words made me feel calm and safe. I could not remember when I had felt such a sense of protection and safety. Certainly not since being married to Broderick. Yet, I still felt embarrassed about being in such a place and I said so.

She smiled and said, "If you knew how many respectable English ladies and Moslem ladies pay me for the protection and safety of my walls, you would not feel so. Some of the first in the land. I cannot give you names. That would be a breach of confidence, but all the rooms on this floor are set aside only for such as yourself. None of my girls come to this floor. Only people meeting their lovers. Would you care to wash yourself or have attendants do it?" She asked.

"I—I think I should like to be alone while I bathe, thank you."

"All you need is in that room," and she pointed toward a door that was half hidden behind a curtain.

"Shall I—will you be here when I am done?" I found myself asking.

She leaned over and hugged me, pressing her cheek to mine.

"You are a good girl. I shall wait for you and we shall talk. You will not mind if my little attendant stays with us?"

"No, she is lovely to look upon."

The child put her hands together and bowed to me in acknowledgement of my compliment.

"Excuse me," I said, "what is your name?" I thought it was Akhtar Devi but someone called you 'Indira.' Which should I call you?"

"Indira is more informal. It is a stage name which I use when I dance. You may call me whatever you choose."

I stood up, keeping the cloth around me, and walked through the door she had indicated. A large pool of warm, fragrant water was sunk into the floor of the room. Once alone in the water, I was possessed by the strong feeling that I had crossed a threshold and that my life would never be the same. I did not know how it would change. I knew that I had committed a terrible crime by the standards of my own people, but I also felt there was something new and good beyond the darkness. No other Englishwomen would see any possiblity of good in my situation. Only minutes before, I, too, could only see disaster. But I felt that the woman in the next room would help me. I felt this in spite of the fact, or perhaps because, she was obviously a courtesan, I felt that she understood my situation and could help me find what might be salvaged from what I had done. Her presence gave me enormous comfort and may have even prevented me from committing the horrible sin of taking my own life. When that realization occurred to me, I wondered if that was why my friend had asked her to sit by me until I woke."

Chapter 11
An old serpent in Rotherhite

Henry put down the journal. He was shocked, amazed and fascinated, all at once, by his mother's immoral behaviour. He thought of his night with Umrao. She certainly had strong physical desires. In spite of that, he had felt that he was the one who was lustful and had committed a misdeed with her, not that she was guilty in any way. Yet, when he thought of his mother in the situation with the native man, he felt it was very wrong. And it made his relations with Umrao seem wrong, too. No matter what his father's behaviour, Henry felt repelled by what his mother had done. Was it easier to accept Umrao's behaviour because she was a courtesan, and a woman of a different race? Or had he simply put the blame for their sinfulness on himself? Men were, after all, more inclined to amourous adventures. Mary seemed to have no feelings like those of his mother or Umrao. What did that mean? Wasn't that the way women were supposed to be—exemplars of purity? Yet, the bond that had been forged with Umrao during the night of their physical love was something he could not imagine sundering for any reason. Mary's tepid kisses had been erased by the passion he'd shared with Umrao. Would Mary have changed if they had gotten married and had intimate relations? He felt deeply perplexed by what he had read and done in the last twenty-four hours. He and his mother had both violated all the values taught by the Suttons and the Church itself.

Was their lustfulness some sort of link between mother and son? And if that were so, were all his troubles the working of a providential retribution?

Henry's perplexities were interrupted by the sound of the door opening and a moment later Sergeant Abdul stepped into the room. He walked with a decided limp.

"Are you injured, Sergeant?" Henry asked.

"Only slightly, young sir. Part of the day's work."

"What do you mean, Sergeant?"

"Well, I had determined that we must put ourselves ahead of the *Thugs* by knowing exactly what their purpose is in coming to England. So, I reasoned that it was of the last importance to get the inscription from the painting translated. With this in mind, I went to the heir of Major General Sleeman to see if he could understand Ramasee, and also to check the inscription against what was written on the back of the painting."

"And?" Henry said, impatiently.

"The heir thought me a deranged little foreigner, I am certain. It was only that I had very intimate knowledge of the Major General that prevented him from having me put out of his house at once. Not only did he not understand Ramasee, but he was reluctant to let me even see the painting, fearing that in some way I would diminish his relative's great achievement. 'Major General Sleeman destroyed the *Thuggee* forever. That is all over and done with,' he said. 'So why should I let you see something written in their cursed tongue?' That is the thrust of what he said. I pointed out that the inscription must have been written before the *Thuggee* were destroyed and that there had recently been two *Thug* style killings in England. It was reasonable, I argued, to think that the one might shed light on the other. It was only when I detailed the manner of the killings and named the two highly respectable men who were victims that he gave way and allowed a servant to take me to the painting and remove it from the wall so I could see the back."

"And?"

"Here," the Sergeant held out a piece of paper with curious symbols on it.

"Good heavens. What does it mean?"

"I don't know."

"So then we are at a dead end."

"No, young sir. I am not finished. On my way back here, I was attacked by two Thugs."

"That is why you are limping. Come and sit down, Sergeant, on our makeshift chair."

"Thank you. To make it short, it was the stick against the noose and the noose lost."

"You beat them off, sir?"

"Yes. And I saw that I was being watched by another man, an Englishman. That is my most important news."

"Why, Sergeant."

"Because it means that we are not only dealing with the *Thuggee*. Someone else is involved as well."

"Good heavens, so things become even more difficult to unravel."

"Perhaps. Umrao is in her room?"

"Yes."

The little man got up and knocked on the door and said something to her in their own language. A moment later the door opened.

"I was just explaining to Henry, Umrao, that I begin to suspect something more than *Thuggee* is behind our present difficulties. There was an Englishman who followed me today and watched me contend with the *Thugs*."

"An Englishman?"

"I thought it would interest you."

"You mean you suspect that this man may be connected with the death of Umrao's benefactress in Lucknow?"

"Then she has told you?" Sergeant Abdul said to Henry.

Henry nodded. "But I don't see why that death should be connected with what has happened in England?"

"There is obviously a connection," Sergeant Abdul replied. "We were all present when the *Thugs* challenged me and that same man tried to follow me back here to learn where we are hiding. It took all my knowledge of London's back streets to lose him before returning. That is why I am late."

"Do you think that this man is Akhtar Devi's killer, Uncle?" Umrao asked.

"You have not been listening, Umrao. It is possible. Beyond that, I don't know. It is of the last importance that I get this inscription translated. So that we can anticipate the Thugs rather than find their victims after they have done their dreadful work. This scrap may tell us what lies at the heart of these deaths. If we knew that, we might anticipate them and perhaps apprehend them. Fortunately, in the course of an eventful day, I have thought of one other person who may help us. You know him, Umrao. Colonel Hasan Ali Meer."

Umrao made a face. "A wicked man, I think. With perverse appetites."

"Yet, he is qualified to help us. I know that he did a lot of work with Major General Sleeman in helping to trace the connections of the *Thuggee* families. For that, he must have known Ramasee."

"Is he truly a colonel, sir? I did not think any Indian had attained so high a rank," Henry said.

"He styles himself so. He is vain of any English

honours he can attribute to himself. He likes to pass as an Englishman."

"A completely false man," Umrao put in with a shudder of distaste.

"Yes," agreed Sergeant Abdul. "But useful. In addition to his knowledge of Ramasee, he is now putting his interest in *nawabi* culture to good use here in London. He has brought a handful of Lucknow dancers and singers to England and engages them to perform in front of wealthy patrons."

"Rather, say his interest is in the girls, not their dancing," Umrao said.

Henry took her hand and said, "And what is wrong with that? I am interested in a certain *nawabi* dancing girl." He smiled at her.

"No. This man is a half-cast who had an evil name even among the lowest of the low. He would hire *takaiyas* in Lucknow and even beggars off the street and pay for the right to abuse and hurt them. He enjoyed giving pain. I don't believe he cared anything for dance or music or poetry. The thought of him disgusts me."

"Well, we shall have to deal with him," the Sergeant said. "I am quite certain he knows Ramasee."

"And why should he help us if what Umrao says is true?" Henry asked. "And do we dare trust him with the knowledge that may be contained in the inscription?"

"I would have preferred it if Sleeman's heir had known Ramasee, but now we shall have to. I also believe that the *Thuggee* would not leave a simple message even in their own tongue. It will probably be only part of the puzzle whose pieces we shall have to assemble. The Colonel will help us for one reason: money. Umrao, for performances by someone of your gifts he could get large sums from his clientele. You would be a voice from another age for these old *Lahknavis*, voice and *mudra* that would set their memories and dreams spinning once again and carry them back to the gay, extravagant nights in the Qaiser Bagh, times that are gone forever. He may even be able to lead you to the one you seek. Who knows what dark corners of Lucknow this man crawled through before coming here? Once I thought of him, it actually occurred to me that he would be a good place for you to start your search, regardless of the *Thuggee*."

Umrao gave a little shiver of distaste. "It is like befriending a python."

"Wait," Henry said. "Is there any danger to Umrao from this man if she sings and dances for his clients? If there is even the slightest jeopardy, I shall not allow it. I shall go right now and turn myself into the police."

"But I would go to meet him anyway, Henry," Umrao said, touching him gently on the shoulder "if he could lead me to my mother's killer. I would do it even though the thought of him makes my flesh creep."

"If Lucknow courtesans are the great singers and dancers, will this old man's clients expect more than singing and dancing from Umrao?" Henry asked.

"I can make it plain that she offers only her art and not herself," Sergeant Abdul replied.

A long silence ensued while all three thought of the dark necessity that they were facing. Finally, Abdul looked at Henry closely.

"Stand up, Henry," he said.

"What is it, Sergeant?" Henry said, rising. Have you thought of something?"

The little Sergeant walked all around the tall Englishman and scrutinized him from head to foot.

"Would he do for a Sikh, Umrao, with a little stain on his face?"

"My attendant," Umrao said clapping her hands together. "He could carry my boxes and guard me. No one would even notice him. Do you think you can do it, Uncle?"

"It is Henry who would have to do it. Could you be a silent native servant, Henry—at all times— no matter what you see, no matter what is said?"

"If it enables me to watch over Umrao, I could walk through fire."

"It is also an excellent way to hide you from the English police," Sergeant Abdul said. "As a Sikh, you will be invisible to Englishmen. My only concern is that you will not be able to bear the indignities you will meet with as an Indian."

"I find it hard to think it will be bad as all that," Henry said. "But no matter what, if silence allows me to watch over Umrao, I shall play my part."

Umrao turned and put her arms around Henry's neck and hugged him quickly.

"It is decided, then," the Sergeant said. "We will transform Henry into a Sikh and I shall introduce you both to Colonel Hasan Ali Meer."

The staining mixture was made by Sergeant Abdul out of various ingredients he got from Covent Garden. He cooked the mess over a bunsen burner which he had brought from his home. The result of his labours was a sticky, odd-smelling brown liquid which Umrao painted all over Henry's body. When she was done and sponged off the excess, she looked at Henry and said,

"You make a beautiful Indian man, Henry. Hmmm." And she kissed him on the neck. "I have to make sure it doesn't come off," she said, looking at him slyly. "How quickly does your beard grow?"

"Must I grow a beard?"

"Sikh's have beards. You must have one. Your own will be much more convincing than a false one. We are fortunate your hair is so dark and glossy," she said running her fingers through his hair.

"I don't know, I.."

"I have his clothes," Sergeant Abdul called from the other side of the door.

Umrao opened the door and received an old brown suit made of a very crude cloth, something like fustian.

Once Henry donned the clothes, which fitted him quite well, Umrao picked up something from among the fabrics heaped on her blanket.

"This is the crowning touch, to make a pun," she said smiling, and she put a weather stained turban on his head. "That is absolutely correct," she said surveying him carefully. "With a black beard, no one will know you are not a Sikh, as long as you don't talk." She opened the door and called to Sergeant Abdul.

"Come and see our Sikh, Uncle."

"Very good," the little man said as he looked Henry over and made him turn around. "This is the last item in his costume." And he threw a pair of worn Indian sandals onto the floor.

"Do I have to wear those?" Henry asked.

"It completes the picture, Henry," Sergeant Abdul said. "No one would believe an Englishman would wear such things in London. When your beard is grown, the disguise will be complete. But you must not..."

"I know, I must not speak," Henry said. "Umrao has already told me."

Without replying, Sergeant Abdul suddenly grabbed one of Henry's heavy boots and threw it at his bare foot.

"Oh, bloody..."

"You have just given yourself away, Henry," Sergeant Abdul said. "A grunt of pain is permissible, speech, even exclamations, are dangerous."

"I understand."

"We are going to teach you a few words of Urdu, so Umrao can give you commands in front of other people. If anyone else speaks to you, you are not to react at all. This will be understood as an aspect of your complete devotion to her. You don't even hear anyone else."

So, for a week and a half, Henry found himself learning to recognize strange words when Umrao spoke them. Rather try to teach him more, Sergeant Abdul told him to stand straight and still whenever he and Umrao were not alone.

"You will be like a soldier on guard, watching any action that could affect Umrao. You must project that this is your only interest in life."

"But it is," Henry said. "I should ask nothing better than to watch over her forever, sir. Perhaps this is not the time to say it sir, but I should like to marry Umrao."

"Oh, sweet, Henry," Umrao said. "It is not time for that."

"Yes it is. I want your Uncle to know that I consider myself engaged to you unless you send me away."

"Very well, Henry," the Sergeant said. "I understand your feelings for Umrao. Even though I am not her guardian in the usual sense, your declaration has been heard and acknowledged—without a reply, as yet."

"Without a reply," Henry agreed. "I shall wait until, until,—until the Ganges freezes."

Umrao came over to him and kissed him on the cheek. "Dear Henry, that is a vow worthy of your patient tenderness." And she put her arms around him.

Finally, the conspirators were ready to see the Colonel of evil repute. It was a warm sultry night when they set for the lair of this strange ally. Sergeant Abdul had a four wheeler waiting for them outside and he had apparently instructed the driver. They set off the moment Henry pulled the door closed after tucking Umrao's *sarangi* next to him. Acting as her porter was part of his duties as a fanatical Sikh guard.

"We certainly aren't passing through any of London's fine quarters to reach this knavish Indian," Henry thought, as the cab crossed Borough Street and turned into Long Lane and then dashed toward the river. Next, they skirted the rail yards below London Bridge and finally drew up in a very disreputable looking street which ran among other equally dirty and miserable thoroughfares off Noows Fields.

As he opened the door, Henry was glad he had insisted on carrying his ironwood stick. If he was supposed to be Umrao's guard what would be a more natural primitive weapon than a stick?

Rain had begun pelting down sometime during their journey and Henry made a tent out of his jacket to keep the rain off Umrao as Sergeant Abdul pulled the bell wire in front of a door whose paint was cracked and peeling. It seemed a dismal place to Henry and he thought suddenly of how his mother must have felt when she was shown into the house where she had her *rendez-vous* in Lucknow.

The door swung open and a well-dressed *khit-mutghar*, bowed low before Umrao, who had assumed a haughty, worldly air which Henry didn't like, even though he knew she was acting a part.

"You are expected, Begum Umrao."

With an arrogant toss of her head, Umrao threw

off the plain old cloak she had worn and her jewel bedecked jacket and pajaymas were revealed. If ever she had look like one of the supernatural maidens of the Ginn who danced through the pages of the *Arabian Nights*, it was then. Henry was staggered anew by the barbarous beauty of the role she had adopted, a beauty which now had an edge of cruelty brought out by the haughty set of her features.

"I do have much to learn about my beloved," Henry thought as he stooped to pick up Umrao's cloak and then followed the *khitmutghar* as he led them down the hall.

They were escorted into a large chamber furnished with certain items which reminded Henry of his mother's description of the apartment where she met her lover. There was a very thick expensive carpet on the floor that deadened all sound and over it was laid the tiger and antelope skins. The ceiling and walls were draped with rich, heavy fabric and the shape of the building or any windows were lost in the folds of rich fabric. Five soft lights were lit in each corner and in the center of the room. Under the central lamp sat a huge engraved *hukkah*.

A cadaverous man with an eye patch, wearing an Indian embroidered silk shirt sat puffing on the *hukkah*, sending gusts of fragrant smoke into the room. His skin and hair looked bleached into an unhealthy pallor, which made it difficult to determine his race. He rose with surprising ease when he saw Umrao.

Henry noted that behind the Colonel, against the far side of the room stood two bearded Indians, each wearing sabres.

"Begum," the Colonel said, bowing. "Let me offer you some pan," he said in Urdu.

"I prefer my own handiwork, Colonel," Umrao

replied in the same language, as she settled easily onto one of the cushions thrown on the floor around the *hukkah*. She was being deliberately insulting.

With a courtly nod to her, the man offered her a lacquered wooden box.

Henry could not see what was in the box, but Umrao seemed to take several things from it, combine them and then put something in her mouth.

The Colonel sat down again and sat close to Umrao. He took her hand in his and Henry had difficulty restraining himself.

"You are even more beautiful than I was led to expect. When I last saw you, Umrao, you were merely a pretty child who sat on my knee. But now," the Colonel said. "If the stars came down from heaven to be your jewels, you could not be more lovely. If your art is equal to your appearance..."

"If my art is equal to my appearance," Umrao said interrupting the man with a purr in her voice, "we will both make a lot of money," as she finished, she threw off his hand from her own. "For, money is all I want from you, old serpent. You tried to pull me onto your knee when I was a child, but Akhtar Devi upbraided you for trying to fondle a little girl."

Henry could follow nothing of what was being said in Urdu and when Umrao detached herself from the Colonel so abruptly, he was ready to act. He looked over at Sergeant Abdul, who shook his head negatively, in an almost imperceptible gesture.

"Very well, then," the old man said in a haughty way, his vanity pricked. "Let me hear you perform. What? You play as well as sing? That by itself is a singular accomplishment."

"I'll not disappoint your wise old ears," Umrao said pouring some balm on the wound she had just inflicted.

The music, though not entirely unfamiliar to Henry had none of the effect on him that it had on the Colonel, who sat as though he had suddenly been turned to stone the moment Umrao began to sing and play. As the older man sat listening, obviously spellbound, Henry was astonished to see tears start to roll down his leathery cheeks.

When the music ceased, the Colonel touched his forehead to the floor in front of Umrao's feet.

"I am abashed," the Colonel said when he sat up. "One of the *houris* of paradise entertains me in my house. I mistook her at first for a woman. Not even in Wajid Ali Shah's gardens in the Qaiserbagh was there a voice and such playing as this," he said to Sergeant Abdul. "Tell me, goddess," he said turning back to Umrao, "do you dance as well?"

"I am a better dancer than I am a musician, old serpent. But I do not want to make your heart stop today, so I shall not dance."

"Who trained you, goddess? You are obviously the queen of all Lucknow courtesans but I hear the sweetness of Benares in your music as well. Akhtar Devi had none in her house who could teach such as you."

"I should prefer you talk to my Uncle about fees."

Abdul thought for a moment that his niece might be over doing her contempt for the old man, but he also knew she was trained for just this sort of drama. This lack of respect was part of her artful *nakhra*, too.

Henry had no idea what was being said, but even he could read the contemptuous expression on Umrao's face. He hoped this face was a completely false one for he could feel an edge of bitterness in her expression. There was so much he didn't know, he realized as he watched her. Seeing her in her brightly coloured embroidered clothes, smoking a *hukkah*, her painted face a beautiful mask of cool, distant irony, he thought of what she had told him about romantic love: that its essence was mystery. Would he ever know her and see all there was to see? He doubted it. She shone like the gemstones sewn to her costume, throwing off a different pattern of light each time she moved. Who was she, really, he wondered? He watched her, fascinated, as she and Abdul spoke to the old man. He, too, felt that she exerted some mesmeric power over him, not through the music but through her person. Then she laughed and the silvery sound broke the spell. Apparently the negotiations were over. Sergeant Abdul and Umrao got to their feet. He saw the old man smoking, his heavy-lidded eyes watching Umrao intently, even greedily, as Henry wrapped her old cloak over her shoulders, covering the beautiful costume. Then, he picked up the *sarangi* and wrapped it, too, as Umrao had shown him.

Once they were in the cab and rolling away, Henry could no longer contain himself.

"Well, is he going to translate the inscription for us?"

"Yes, but first he wants Umrao to give three concerts. He will take his fee out of the proceeds." "So we will know nothing of the *Thuggee's* plans for some time," Henry said.

Abdul shrugged. "This is how it has been written for us. We must be patient. But I still believe there is more to be learned from your mother's diary. I urge you not to put it aside."

"I don't see how there can be any connection," Henry said. "But I will certainly continue reading. I would in any case. I must say, I didn't like the way that old man kept looking at Umrao."

Umrao put her head on his chest. "You have nothing to fear from him, dear Henry. A great French writer once said about such a man, 'He pretends to be a past which hopes to be a future but will never be a present.' And he is only part of my past because he used to come to make love to my benefactress, Akhtar Devi, when they were both young. She got great sums of money from him. He only became perverse when he got older. He will do nothing more than flatter me and pretend to be my lover to flatter his own vanity. He is nothing, Henry. A toothless old serpent."

"I still do not like the way he acts with you," Henry said in a surly voice.

Chapter 12
The Journal of Jane Booth

Fourth Reading

Entry date: November 12, 1856

"The bath I soaked in had a refreshing, healing aroma and I felt a pleasant languor spread through me which helped comb out my tangled thoughts and feelings. My mind became empty and the only feeling that stayed with me was that somehow I was safe and would be cared for. As I drew comfort from this feeling I also marveled that, under the circumstances, I should be convinced of its truth. If there were even the slightest whisper of my transgression against the laws of God and Man, I had no doubt that my husband and everyone I knew in India and at home would cast me off, and for all I knew, the Deity himself had cast me off. Yet, I felt peaceful, wrapped in the mist of the fragrant, warm water. I think I may have slept for a few moments, for when I opened my eyes again I saw a beautiful embroidered robe hanging on the back of the door. I thought of the woman who waited for me in the next room, rose from the water, dried myself and put on the robe.

When I opened the door, the woman sat as I had last seen her, seeming not to have moved even in the slightest degree.

"You feel better now, don't you Mrs. Booth?" she said. Her voice was low and soft in a way I found soothing. Her little attendant was so still, she might have been a statue. I could not but admire the child's very long black hair and beautiful dark eyes.

"Yes, I do, thank you. It is so odd, being here, it feels so, so safe."

The woman smiled. "This house is a refuge for women."

"A refuge? I thought it was a, a, brothel."

"Yes. But it is a refuge, too. Sit down. I will tell you. Would you like some coffee or tea?"

I shook my head negatively, sat down and waited for her to speak.

"You see, child, the women who come here are often in circumstances like yours."

"Like mine? Whatever do you mean?"

"They have husbands or families who abuse them. I have seen your bruises while you were asleep."

I felt myself blushing very deeply. My face grew hot.

"Do not feel ashamed. It is the men who cause this damage who should be ashamed."

"I thought most women in places like this were sold into them like slaves," I said.

She laughed and the sound of it surprised me, a round, full belly laugh that was infectiously carefree. It made me smile, in spite of myself.

"This is not so. Most women come to me or houses like this because men have used them cruelly.

They come here to hide, to rest. Some stay. Others do not. You have the same choice, now."

"You mean I could stay here?"

"Yes."

"But I would have to, to, be..."

"One of us. Yes."

I was silent. I felt very drawn to the older woman. And the house felt very peaceful. But the thought of what I would have to do was too repulsive to me. I couldn't possibly bring my little boy here. The thought that she was asking me to become a prostitute was disgusting. If the suggestion had come from anyone else or under different circumstances, I would have been mortally offended.

"I appreciate your kindness," I said, "but I couldn't possibly. I..."

"Think," her voice cut through my own thoughts and feelings. "Here you would give yourself to men and keep a large portion of your own money. We have sisters who help us put our wealth into businesses with good returns. With a husband, you will never have anything that is yours. He will own you and all you possess. Which is more free?"

"I simply couldn't...," I started to say.

"You already have a lover in addition to your husband. Keep him, if you like, though I advise against it. With your appearance, you could choose your own clients very selectively. If you were younger, I would train you. But I think the Englishmen of Lucknow would all want you. So the fact that you could not entertain except with your body would not be a great shortcoming."

"I do play the piano rather well—when I am in practice," my pride could not help saying.

"A valuable accomplishment for an English

clientele. You would never have to fear any of these men. No one will ever harm you here. You will be protected. Are the blows of your husband and the false position he provides really better than that?"

"I couldn't possibly become a prostitute. If you had not already been so kind, I should be incensed by your suggestions. My religion, everything forbids it."

She shrugged. "You will think of it. Though, there are many who do very hard labour rather than come here, that is true. I just thought that since you already had a lover..."

"No. Thank you. I know you are trying to be kind in your own way. But for a well brought up English-woman it is a disgusting alternative and out of the ques-tion. I can't improve one crime by committing a greater one."

"Very well, then. Many Moslem ladies feel the same. Are you ready to go home? I can have a *palanquin* downstairs in minutes."

"But I have to get dressed in my own clothes and put on my *burqa* so no one will see me on the street."

"Very well, child," the woman came over and kissed me on the cheek. "You shall always be welcome here as a visitor or as a resident."

I said nothing and simply waited for her and the little girl to leave.

Midnight

I am lying in my bed at home listening to Broderick snore on the sofa in the sitting room. If he should wake and come to me, I don't know what I shall do. After the beautiful, loving touches of my friend, I am not sure I could tolerate Broderick's hurtful hands on me. I brought a knife from the kitchen up to my bed. It is one

Sita uses for cutting up meat. It is very sharp.

　　As I lie here, sleepless, writing, I cannot help but think of the woman who spoke to me at the brothel. Her proposal was, of course, disgusting, but, much of what she said was true. With a husband, even back in England, I never should be free. As long as Broderick stays away from me, I may be able to maintain my position here. But now my situation seems much more tenuous than before. I am a married woman. I have a native lover and I have been offered work in a brothel. But those are only the outer facts. The way I feel is also something real. My friend makes me feel so very beautiful and respected. It is those good feelings that makes me feel less tolerant of Broderick. I know that I am in sin by taking a lover, but it cannot be wrong to want more than the empty, fearful life I have been living with Broderick. George Sand had many lovers, but she has made her own life with her writing. That is what I must do. I must become someone in my own right. I must stay home tomorrow no matter what and start my article on Lucknow. I pray that I shall have the talent to become the mistress of my own fate. Otherwise, what is left to me? I must act.

　　It will be easier while Henry is younger and I am still attractive. If I were to lose my looks now, as so many women do in this climate, no one would be interested in me or in helping me. Then, I should be truly lost. If I were an author, however, it wouldn't matter nearly as much.

November 13, 1856—Dawn

I see the light of a new day breaking. I can see the ruddy colour it lends to the Gomti, but I can find no such light in my own life. I know what I must do, but can I do it?

There is nothing else but to try. Consequently, I cut some pens, for I do not like a metal nib, and begin.

11:00—morning

Most people will be having *tiffin* served soon, but I have no fear that Broderick will come home to eat as he used to do. I have been writing for hours and hours and con-stantly consulting my friend's sheet of facts about Luc-know. I believe I've made more than a good start. I must sleep now so I can read it over with a clear mind later in the day. It is too unutterably hot even to move at this hour. I am too exhausted even to call Sita and have the boy work the *punkah*.

4:00 —afternoon

I have written to my friend and told him that I am working on my article and will not meet him today. If he is really the friend he claims to be, he will not be put out by my desire to write today. He will realize that my determination to make my own way is genuine. I know he is staying in Lucknow so we can meet more easily, but surely he will spare me this single day. He must.

6:30 pm—evening

He has written back and tells me he is called back to Bithur and we shall not be able to meet until next week. He wishes me inspiration for my article and reiterates his willingness to help me! How glad I feel that I am not mistaken in his goodness. In a few hours, I shall com-plete my first draft and then begin to re-write. It must be well-polished before I submit it to my friend. I am sure he has high standards. I want him to be proud to submit my work to his famous journalist friend.

7:30 —evening

I hear Broderick in the house, but I shall stay in my room and continue working through dinner. I feel exhilarated by the act of writing. I have not seen my little boy once today, but I know he is in good hands.

9:00—evening

Broderick's tread was heavy and angry, but he is gone out now, and I believe I can finish tonight. I am working furiously. Discarded paper and broken pens litter my room. I am still in my dressing gown. I feel a kind of exultation I have never known before. It gives me a palpable feeling of strength. I have no sense of fatigue, though I have worked harder and longer than at any previous time in my life. It now seems slightly less surprising to me that George Sand is able to write so many books.

Midnight

I have finished! At least, I believe I have. I suppose I shall not really know until it is read by some perfectly neutral person. Unfortunately, I don't dare show it to any of the ladies I know.

11:00—Late morning

I have slept late but I still wake with a feverish desire to have someone read my work and to hear their opinion. My friend will be back in Lucknow in another day so it hardly seems worthwhile to send my writing to him in Bithur. I can do nothing today. I feel so impatient. I long for my life to change. I hope what I have done is good enough to make a start. It is so hard to have so much depend on this one effort, but I can't imagine living here with Broderick for much longer.

3:00—Late afternoon

Even the heat of the day cannot quell my restiveness. I feel like a caged beast, myself. This evening, Henry and I will sit outside and he can tell me all about what he has been doing while I have been working. I even return to my pianoforte whose pitch has suffered horribly in this climate. Anything, to make the long hours of the searing afternoon pass. Thank heavens my friend will be back tomorrow and will read my work and give me his judgment. I don't think I could bear a longer postponement of a verdict.

Dec 22, 1856

As I woke this morning my one thought was of seeing my friend today. I just pray that Broderick's stalking around the house yesterday was not the beginning of a new way of arranging his day.

6:00—evening

Broderick has not come back for dinner. I am free. I am certain the *palanquin* will arrive soon.

Midnight

What a wonderful evening I have had! My dear, dear friend greeted me so warmly. Even the native footmen that are employed at the house seemed friendly and pleasant to me, in spite of their huge, curling mustachios and fierce, dark faces.

The *rendez-vous* with my friend was in the same room where we met last time. My friend again showed his consideration by not trying to possess me before reading my work.

He ordered coffee for each of us and we sat and read together for some time while I leaned on his shoulder. He made many thoughtful comments and, though I was disappointed that he recommended so many changes, I appreciated the thoroughness of his reading and could not disagree with the points he made. He must be fully satisfied if he is to present it to his friend with conviction.

After we had finished with the article, I lay down on the cushions next to him. I felt my own appetite for him had increased since the last time we had been together. I was puzzled at first by what he did. He made me sit on my heels and bend forward.

He removed my under things without disrobing me fully. Then there was a pause and I looked back to see what he was doing. I watched while unfastened his flies. I have never watched Broderick do that. We both kept most of our clothes on. There was something very naughty about it and it gave our play additional piquancy and stimulated me even more. Perhaps I felt less guilt. Perhaps it was our having already been together before. We even took a short nap while remaining joined. Waking that way was particularly delicious. Everything he does with me, he does with patience. Everything Broderick does with everyone, he does impatiently.

Later on, I was very surprised when my friend brought up Henry. He asked me when I was planning to send him home, meaning, of course, England. I said I didn't know and he said, he felt it should be soon.

"Why?" I asked.

"He is getting of an age when he should start to benefit from English schooling. Also, political events here are, I believe, approaching a crisis. Were he our son, I would insist on sending him soon."

I meditate on these words even now. I know my friend is very knowledgeable about politics and his thoughts trouble me. There have been rumors about the natives of Oudh losing patience with our rule. Perhaps Henry would be better off leaving soon. Broderick would probably applaud the idea. Especially, since my cousin in London has such excellent connections. Henry would certainly get a better start in life there. Though my family complained of supporting me, my cousin and her husband, who is a Dean, will take Henry as a Christian duty, I am certain. Now that I have the affection of my friend, it is easier to contemplate losing Henry. And though it is very hard to think of giving up my only child, I know it is inevitable if I want the best for Henry. Perhaps I shall speak to Broderick about the matter.

As I left the room where I met my friend, wearing the *burqa* and stepping into the hall, I glimpsed an Englishman walking ahead of me. It was only just a glimpse and the halls are so shadowy, I would not know him again, but it gave me a strange feeling to think that so many come to this place to satisfy their carnal appetites. But I do feel that, with my friend, there is something more. It is not for our physical experiences I come here, not simply for that. It is the feelings which underlie these experiences, feelings which I know women are not supposed to acknowledge openly. Yet, I know that other women come here.

Akhtar Devi has told me that other women who are outwardly respectable pay her well for the privacy and protection of her walls. Our own feelings are not permitted us! Is this really what God wants for women? There seem to be so many barriers for us. I wonder if I shall ever be free?

December 23, 1856

Broderick is, thank heavens, working today. It is of the last importance to him not to lose his position as a civilian member of the company. It is rare for men to have the chance to go from the army to the civilian service without having to go to a frontier outpost, and Broderick appreciates that. His knowledge of Oudh both linguistically and geographically makes him unique here. His outstanding army record and my family's connections made it possible for him to change to the civilian service, but few men have that opportunity, and if Broderick gets behind on his work, he could be replaced with one of the bright young men coming out from Haileybury. I never had to suffer the stigma of being an army wife when I was in Calcutta. If Broderick were to fall from his position, that is what I would become. We might even have to leave the Residency. Due to my family connection and due to the fact that Broderick was a *bona fide* hero, we knew only ladies and gentlemen in Calcutta. Of course, I never would have deigned to be the wife of an ordinary soldier. Life would be insupportable here as an army wife. Those poor women! I saw one wandering about the bazar the other night, as I left in my friend's *palanquin*. She was drinking with natives and smoking *bhang*. What she will be in a few years, heaven only knows.

At least, the Englishwoman in the Residency are ladies. We have been fortunate, Broderick and I, and I know Broderick will exert himself to keep up our position. Just when he seems about to lurch over the edge of social propriety, he is able to take himself in hand and regain his balance. Thank heavens he is not such a drunkard as to lose his grip on what we have. I do not want to stay with him or stay in this Residency but I do not want to slip lower, either.

If he does come home after a short day at his office, I shall speak with him about Henry's return to England.

December 25, 1856

Christmas, a very strange day. Henry, Broderick and I may not even see each other today, let alone sit down to a dinner together. Henry doesn't mind. I made certain that he got some very nice gifts and he will be playing with them and his *ayah*.

Broderick has disappeared somewhere, supposedly to his office, though I am certain there are celebrations at the Residency. So, I went to see my friend again today. As I passed through the house to go to our room where I meet my friend, something rather unpleasant happened.

I saw Akhtar Devi, the older courtesan, whom I like so much, with a man. I could see from their behaviour that he was a client. The thought of that dignified lady going with the ugly half cast was terrible to me. His skin was lighter than most natives but looked almost blanched and his hair had unnatural streaks of white in it. He wore an eye patch and was extremely thin, yet he could not have been much over thirty. He might even have been diseased. I found it very disturbing that such a fine woman could give herself to such a creature for money, in spite of what she told me about freedom and marriage.

Once I entered our room, I put it out of my mind, for I was pleased that my friend had read and accepted the latest draft of my article about Lucknow. He was very complimentary. He particularly praised my descriptions of people, mentioning specifically the degraded army wife I had seen and included in the article, along with suggestions I had made for helping such women. In talking with my friend about this woman, I said something about Akhtar Devi and the ugly man with whom I had seen her. He told me that the man was well-known in Lucknow. He is a kind of *impresario* for the native dancing girls. He is apparently very wealthy. He has an evil name, my friend said, for abusing women. Though, my friend felt certain that the man would not dare mistreat the madame of the house. He would never leave the house alive after such a transgression, and Akhtar Devi would certainly take enormous sums from the man before she was finished with him.

Then my friend warned me, "It is better never to repeat to anyone anything you see here. This is a house of secrets. You do not know whose life could be affected by making even apparently innocent incidents known."

I thought of our own situation and promised him and myself that I would never divulge anything I saw there. Already, I had come to prize the absolute secrecy of my meetings with my friend. Even the nondescript *palanquins* that took me to the house were owned by Akhtar Devi. The bearers who carried me were under her control, as well. All was managed with such skill that even among the ladies of the Residency, the sharpest tongued gossips in Lucknow, there was not a whisper of my secret crimes. All that was ever talked of was Broderick's ill-treatment of me. His visits to the woman I had seen him with were known and remarked upon by the ladies, but probably ignored by the men. The Resident would say nothing. He is a practical man and as long as Broderick keeps his behaviour within limits, the Resident will keep him on. Broderick's languages and army reputation are useful to the Resident."

Chapter 13
Out of the Kotha

Immediately after reading the foregoing, Henry got up walked to Umrao's door and knocked. The sonorous notes of the *sarangi* stopped and the door opened.

"Umrao, was your benefactress named Akhtar Devi?" he asked.

"Yes. How did you know?"

"My mother knew her. In fact, it was in Akhtar Devi's, ah, house that she used to meet a certain man with whom she carried on shamelessly. Though, when I read about her life with my father, it is hard to blame her, especially knowing how it all ended for her."

"Then your mother was a British *khangi*. I know they existed in those days and probably still do."

"What is that term? What does it mean?"

"They were respectable women who paid the *chaudharayan*, a woman like Akhtar Devi, for the use of a well-protected room in the *kotha*."

"Were you often with Akhtar Devi?" Henry asked.

"Oh, yes. She would not let any of the nawabs sponsor me. I did not attend the *Parikhana* like many other talented girls who caught the *nawabs'* eyes."

"Why would she not let you be sponsored or go to this place?"

"Sponsorship would have given a *nawab* exclusive right to me. I would have become his in all ways. Akhtar Devi did not want to share my company with a *nawab*. She was too fond of me. *The Parikhana* was the school that was created by Wajid Ali Shah. Girls who went there would, of course, be at the ruler's beck and call. She trained me herself in song and dance and literature. Only on the *sarangi* and languages did I have separate teachers. She loved me very much, and kept me by her whenever possible."

"Then, I think you may have met my mother, Umrao, when you were still a child. Here, I shall read it to you," and Henry read out loud the passage that described Akhtar Devi and her little attendant on Jane Booth's first visit to the *kotha*.

"Yes, yes," Umrao cried excitedly. "I remember her. A sad beautiful lady with pale hair. So different from any of us. She was tall, taller than Akhtar Devi who was herself, tall. But what I remember most about her was her sadness. I saw her in the *kotha* many times. She used to meet a tall, slender Moslem man who wore western clothes. I remember him because he once gave me a gold coin and said I was a rare flower even in the garden of Akhtar Devi's *kotha*."

"How strange it all is," Henry said ruefully. "To think of you meeting her, then coming here and our meeting." He was silent for a moment and then burst out, "But wait—then—it is Akhtar Devi who was murdered. It is her killer you seek here in London."

"Yes, my more than mother" the girl said, suddenly looking very small and delicate to Henry.

"I am sorry, Umrao to call up these shadows from the past that make you sad, but Sergeant Abdul told me to look for clues in my mother's diary. I think I must trace all this history."

"Yes, I understand. It is only that I loved her much," and as she spoke tears began to run down her cheeks.

Henry put his arms around her. "My poor darling," he said. "We both have lost our mothers."

Umrao nestled against him for a few minutes and then looked up. "I shall be all right, now. If there is anything else..."

"No. I understand," Henry said. "I shall keep it to myself."

"No. I want to know. It may lead me to her killer."

"Well you already know she used to see the Colonel and as far as I can see, he should be high on the list of possible killers."

"Yes. I shall watch him carefully to see if he might betray himself to me."

"But, dearest, you must be very careful not to provoke him. Everything I read of him in the past makes me uneasy about him."

"If he is the one I seek, he will not escape me."

"But you must realize that he may be a very dangerous man."

"But I, too," she said with emphasis, "am a very dangerous woman," and suddenly, seemingly out of thin air, she conjured a wicked looking curved knife.

"This is how my mother's killer will die," she said, her face transformed into a savage mask. The blade disappeared a moment later and she looked once again like herself. Then, she shifted the *sarangi* and bow to her other hand and closed the door. Her fierceness on this one subject and the weapon she carried shocked Henry. It once again reminded him how different Umrao was from any woman he had ever known. She had the heat of the subcontinent in her veins and it could be roused in hate or love.

Left to himself, Henry continued to mull over what he had read. He would certainly be sure to discuss it with Abdul. Umrao was so set on dispatching her mother's killer that he did not trust her judgment. He wanted to hear what Abdul would say about the possibility of the Colonel being a danger to her. The diminutive sergeant usually looked in at least once a day, though it was difficult to anticipate him because his schedule of calls was so varied.

The ways in which past and present had converged led Henry to think once more of Mary and the Suttons. How were they faring in the terrible crisis that had struck them down? Losing Charles would be trying beyond measure for Mary and Amelia. He must find some way to see and talk to them. He couldn't bear the idea that they would think him callous toward them. Perhaps his disguise would make it possible for him to approach the house and talk with Mary or even Smythe-White. In spite of his feelings for Umrao, the Suttons were his family. He must find a way to see them. He would discuss the idea with Abdul.

Umrao practiced all afternoon and time hung heavy on Henry's hands. He felt that for the time being he had absorbed all he could of his mother's diary. It still pained him to read of her immoral behaviour, in spite of the justifications for it. If he condoned her adultery, where did it end? It would seem to be the end of religion as he had known it. It was difficult enough to realize that Umrao had been trained as a prostitute and that he had relations with her that should only take place between husband and wife. He had broken his word to Mary, but it would have been much worse if they had been married. For, if one began to accept the breaking of divine law, what was left? Yet, his heart ached for his mother's loneliness and sorrow. Her unhappiness magnified the suffering of her horrible death. How strange that he should learn all these intimate details years later, and find Umrao as a result of receiving his mother's journal. Where would this strange road take him? How could he stop Umrao from killing the Colonel, if he was, indeed, the murderer of Akhtar Devi? And how could he prove his own innocence to the authorities? So much rested on learning the intentions of the *Thuggee*. Would they commit more killings? Could they be caught? The grotesque cult of death sounded like an utterly fantastic invention, yet Sergeant Abdul assured him there were many, many files filled with facts regarding the *Thugs* at India House, files which the Sergeant had helped Major General Sleeman compile. The possible outcome of all these threads that were now woven through his life occupied his thoughts for hours.

Finally, as the sun was sinking into a fiery looking canal, Sergeant Abdul appeared. The powerful cry of the *sarangi* still emanated from Umrao's room.

In spite of the fact that the Sergeant looked tired, Henry couldn't hold his tongue.

"Sergeant, I learned today that my mother met Umrao and Akhtar Devi many years ago. Umrao was just a child at the time, but she remembered the incident clearly. That is all I have been able to learn today. But I have spent all afternoon thinking about our difficulties. I have come to the conclusion that I must see my family and find out how they are. Do you think my disguise would allow me to get past whatever police might be watching the house?"

The sergeant said nothing for a few minutes. He put down his bag and sat down heavily on the wooden crate. Then he looked up at Henry.

"You have a much better chance in light such as this, young sir. If you go late at night, you might run the risk of being arrested as a prowler in a respectable neighbourhood—a chance made more likely with your dark skin."

"Then what do you advise, sergeant. I must see them and find out how they are."

Sergeant Abdul stood up and began to pace. "I understand your need, young sir, but you must be careful for Umrao's sake. Your lives are connected now. She needs you as well."

"I know Sergeant. I have been feeling all afternoon how divided I am between my two families, Umrao and the Suttons, between past and present. But I cannot desert those who have raised me. "
Sergeant Abdul looked thoughtful.

"Perhaps, we could make ourselves look like porters by carrying an empty box between us. That would be a fitting reason for two dark-skinned faces to appear in a fine neighbourhood. If we are pursued, we could drop it and run. What do you say?"

"I had no intention of involving you with my risk, sir," Henry answered.

"We are each dependent on the other, now, young sir. Umrao, of course, will stay here."

"Of course," Henry agreed. "I should be pleased to have you with me if you think it best."

"I do think so, Henry. I am too tired to go now. But at around this time tomorrow, we should set out."

"I had another thought, as well, sir," Henry said. "I thought I might give the inscription to Smythe-White and see if he could translate it for us. That way we might remove the need for the Colonel."

"But of course you realize that Umrao will pursue a connection with the Colonel in any case, until she is satisfied that he is not her mother's killer. He already knows about the inscription and I am not happy to tell someone else of it. The fewer who know we have it, the better. We are still in the dark but the *Thugs* know the exact meaning and value of it. So we are blind and they are sighted."

"Very well. It's just that I don't like what I heard and read about the Colonel. I am much more inclined to trust someone from my own family."

"I understand. But Umrao now knows that the Colonel is here in London. She will not rest until she is satisfied he is innocent of her mother's blood. You cannot turn her aside, Henry."

"I realize that. I just wish she was not so violent in her desire to exact her own vengeance."

"She is from a different world than are you, Henry. She has not known the chill breezes of this island long enough to cool her blood."

"Yes. I know."

"If there is nothing else, then, I shall go until tomorrow."

"Good evening, Sergeant. Be careful."

"Good night, young sir."

Shadows began to fill the corners of the room as Henry sat at the window and looked out at the opaque, turbid water. As the sun sank lower, extinguishing itself in the canal, melancholy overtook him. Gradually, the water became darker and finally as black as ink. The *sarangi* was quiet, but Umrao did not come out of her room. Henry thought about his possible meeting with Mary the following day and his unease made it impossible for him to knock on Umrao's door. He would have liked to shelter himself in her arms, but it seemed somehow unfair to both Umrao and Mary. So he sat for hours looking out at the river and listened to the sound of water lapping against the quays, the small waves catching faint slivers of light from the distant lamps of carriages which occasionally broke the otherwise complete darkness of the moonless night. He thought of the strange dream he had on the first night they had slept above the opium den. Part of that dream had already come about: Umrao did now fill his life as her cloak had filled the horizon in the dream. Was there some way in which his mother would return from the grave? Or had the image of her resurrection from the well at Cawnpore simply referred to the revelation of herself through the diary itself? She had come back to him through her written words, and he knew her now much more completely than he had at any time during his life. The vague, bittersweet memories he'd carried with him since childhood were slowly starting to merge with the woman who spoke to him about herself in the pages of the diary. In that sense, the dream had already been fulfilled. As he lay down on the several thicknesses of blanket folded on the floor, Henry's sense of his mother's presence was very strong. He fell asleep expecting to dream of her.

The next morning, Henry woke without the anticipated dream. He heard rain rattling against the metal roof of their chambers and saw Umrao kneeling next to him. She kissed him very tenderly on the lips the moment his eyes opened but said nothing. Then she rose and went back to her room. Moments later, the cry of the *sarangi* wound through the rhythm of the drumming rain. At moments it seemed as if the *rag* she was playing was actually conjuring the rain, so perfectly were the *tal* of the beating rain and the *sarangi* intertwined.

The day continued rainy, gray and unutterably slow for Henry. His nerves were strung tight in expectation of seeing Mary that evening. Umrao seemed aware of his mood and its connection with his former love. She played for hours and left him to himself. He could do nothing but count the minutes and hours until Sergeant Abdul came for their expedition. Finally, as dusk approached, he heard the door scrape over the bowed wooden planks of the floor.

"Good evening, young sir."

"Good evening, Sergeant Abdul."

"You are ready? I have a growler below. We will take it to the vicinity and walk to your family's house." Henry paused for a moment on the threshold of the apartment and looked back at Umrao's room. As much as he wanted to take leave of her, he could not on his way to see Mary. Then, he followed Sergeant Abdul down the old stairs.

They rode in silence, each man apparently lost in thought. Henry was entirely taken up with his reunion with Mary. What would he say to her? Should he tell her about Umrao immediately? What was the fair, the kind thing to do? As he had done all day, he played out various scenes of their meeting in his mind, but none seemed to satisfy him. Then, he heard Sergeant Abdul thump on the ceiling to signal the driver to stop.

"Come, Henry. Help me with this box. Remember, it is our disguise."

Henry realized he had forgotten the ruse they had discussed the night before.

"We are going to walk from here in the rain?" he asked.

"What about my skin colour?"

"Don't worry. It will not wash off and your whiskers are your own."

So they both got out of the cab in the pelting rain some blocks from the Sutton residence.

"Now, remember to walk as though the box is heavy," Sergeant Abdul exhorted.

"Right."

As they walked, trying to sag under the "weight" of the chest, Henry spoke.

"Do you think I can just ring the bell?"

"No. We do not know who is in the house. There may be policemen inside."

"Then what do you suggest?"

"You know the house, well. Perhaps we could look in some of the windows where people are likely to be. Where do you think a policeman would be stationed?"

"In the front hall, I suppose. I have no idea what has transpired in the house since Charles was murdered."

"Is there some way, then, you can see into the hall without being seen?"

"We could get behind the shrubs and walk between them and the house," Henry answered. "I just hope no one sees us. It would certainly look suspicious."

"I doubt very much that anyone would be looking out on such a night, or that they could see us from a brightly lit room. I shouldn't worry."

Henry nodded his agreement.

"Is this not the house?" Abdul asked, putting down his end of the box.

"Yes. But let's leave the box near the path so that it looks like it may belong to the house. Certain carters sometimes do that, even though they are only supposed to leave goods at the kitchen entrance. Let's approach the gardener's path from here," and Henry led the way behind the shrubbery to a narrow gravel path which the gardener used to tend the plants on the side closest the house.

"Most of the curtains are drawn," Abdul commented softly.

"Yes. But there is one round window near the door which I think I am tall enough to see into, and it has no curtain."

It was fortunate that the shrubs were almost continuous on the front of the house and hid them well from the eyes of neighbours. Two men peering into windows would eventually be noticed by someone, even on a dark, dirty night. They made their way silently along the house, walking nearly half its width until an oval window glowed with interior light. Henry got up on his toes.

Things looked much as normal. Gibbons was asleep in his chair before the entry fireplace. Fortunately, Archibald was not with him, or he might well have barked. Henry turned to Sergeant Abdul.

"Things look quiet inside. Sometimes we leave the curtains and window open in the back sitting room. It is badly ventilated and becomes very stuffy, otherwise. I should like to see if we can look in there before attempting the bell."

The Sergeant nodded and followed Henry back the way they had come. They then skirted the end of the semi-detached house and saw that the windows were dark, but when they turned the corner of the building, voices from within could be plainly heard.

Henry drew closer to the window and looked inside. He could hear the voices of Smythe-White and Mary. The pair, for so they seemed, were holding hands and sitting on the sofa across from the window. The scene made Henry wince, for a moment. Then he thought of his passionate nights with Umrao.

"Perhaps it is better, thus," he said inwardly. "She will feel my desertion less if she has Wilfred to stand in. And what can I tell her to relieve her mind about Charles? Smythe-White was with me. He knows I could not have possibly done any harm to her father."

But Henry had to admit to himself that standing outside with the cold rain dripping down his back,

looking into what had once been his home and seeing Mary and Smythe-White together made him very
sad. He turned away from the window and gestured to
Sergeant Abdul to go. The return trip to Swandam Lane
was as silent as the trip to the Suttons. The Sergeant
asked nothing. Henry got out of the cab without saying
a word. He was wet, cold and heartsore.

"What a fool I am," Henry said to himself, as he
paused in the driving rain while the cab pulled away.
"I have been completely disloyal to Mary, yet when I
see her finding harmless solace with another man, I am
pained by it. And all the words I was going to say, die
before they pass my lips."

But no matter how he exhorted himself as he
climbed the old steps, he felt sad.

He opened the door and saw Umrao, who had
obviously been waiting for him. She rose and came to
him.

"My poor, wet, Henry. You'll catch your death of
cold from the icy English rain. You must get out of those
things right away." And she began tugging at his wet
clothes.

In a few moments, he was naked before her. She
took him in her arms and he found himself crying as
Umrao kissed him. She guided him into her room and
they lay down on her blanket. She covered him to make
him warm, then removed her clothes and crawled next
to him. There were still tears on his face.

"I don't know why I am so sad," he said. "It is so
stupid. I want no one but you."

"I know why, sweet Henry."

"No. Really," he said pulling away from her to
look in her face. "It is not Mary..."

"No, I know it is not." Umrao said, interrupting
him. "It is losing the past. We mourn for it even when

235

our memories are of something that never existed. I expected you to come back to me feeling this way. Now, no more thoughts. Only love," and she drew him to her again.

Umrao's patron

Chapter 14
Umrao's Concert and what befell

In spite of Umrao's tenderness, Henry woke with a feeling of loss and regret which he knew he must keep to himself. Umrao would need to spend the day preparing for the concert before the Colonel's patron that night. Having played the organ in the Church of St. Michael's at Christ Church, Henry knew what a strain a public performance could be. But Umrao was smiling and happy when he came out of the room where they had slept. The *sarangi* rested near her and she was eating some eel soup which she had apparently gone out and purchased for their breakfast. She was carefully picking out the the pieces of eel.

"Good morning, sweet Henry," she called to him. "How is my darling today?" she asked as she put down her bowl and kissed him.

"Much better, dear girl," Henry answered somewhat lumpishly. "Tonight is the concert. Do you feel up to it?"

Umrao wrinkled her nose at him. "The old serpent and his pet worm will get what they have paid for. I have no fear of not pleasing such as them. How I should like to go for a walk today among some trees and flowers," she said.

Henry sat down and looked around the room.

"I know what you mean. This place does not exactly improve upon close acquaintance."

Umrao laughed and threw herself into Henry's lap. She seemed as playful as a kitten.

"You are in a jolly mood this morning," he said.

"Yes, for today is a real beginning for us."

"You mean the concert?"

"Yes," she answered curling up almost into a ball as she leaned against him.

This easy physical intimacy was something he enjoyed with her very much. When they were alone, she would lean on him, sit on him or take his hand with no constraint whatever. It was light-hearted, almost childlike. It was hard to imagine an English woman ever being so relaxed. He thought for a moment of Smythe-White and Mary sitting stiffly on the sofa holding hands. They had not looked comfortable together. It was not a generous thought and he dismissed it. Wasn't Mary entitled to her own kind of happiness?

"You look so serious, Henry."

"I imagine we have different ways of seeing this concert tonight. I am concerned about your safety and what these men may expect of you."

"Ha," she cried. "These are men who live in the past. They want to recapture their former glories. That is what they want from me. To remind them of the past. Their desire is to be reminded of a time they barely re-member. Those are the feelings they want me to touch."

"How do you know?"

"I know because I grew up in Akhtar Devi's *kotha* and I have often seen men of all ages in pursuit of pleasure. Now, will you trust me that there is nothing to worry about—except your own temper—you will be silent and trust me—and not be a stupid man who tries to catch the sunshine in a net? You must promise, or we might lose all. And remember that my Uncle will also be present."

"Yes. I promise. I shall be a silent Sikh. Believe me, I understand what is at stake."

"Good. Now, I would like to go to one of your famous parks."

"But..."

"You are disguised. We shall just be a pair of blacks. No one will pay the least attention to us."

Henry thought for a moment. "It is true that if the *Thuggee* knew where we were living, we should have been molested before this. So we shall not be followed from here. They would have no way of picking up our trail...very well."

"Please, let us go out my dearest," Umrao pleaded like a child. "We shall picnic on the lawns at the Regents Park, and you will buy me that cold delicious food, ice cream, yes?"

"Oh, all right, I suppose it's safe enough."

"Look, dearest Henry, at how the sun shines for us."

So for the first time, Henry found himself among English crowds disguised as an Asian. Both he and Umrao were literally invisible to the white faces everywhere. People pushed them aside on the pavement and made rude remarks about "the stupid wogs, the damn niggers," and so on. Henry listened in amazement to the abuse.

He said nothing in reply, for he knew that to reply would be to break his incognito, but he nearly struck a man when he overheard him and his friend who were walking behind himself and Umrao.

"I say," one of them remarked, "that little nigger girl's got a saucy bottom. I wonder what she'd charge to take both of us on."

"Go and ask her," his friend said, chuckling.

Henry wheeled around and glowered at the men,

each of whom were a head shorter than he was. They immediately crossed to the other side of the street.

"Disgusting louts," he remarked watching their retreat.

"Henry, you must not be so easily provoked. Not when you are a Sikh."

"I apologize for my countrymen, Umrao. I did not know what people of colour had to put up with in this country. I thought it was only in India. I am shocked and disgusted by my own people."

"What does it matter if we have a nice day?" she answered.

"Yes, my dear. You are right. Let's enjoy the promenade. We could go to the zoological gardens as well. They have quite a few Indian animals there. Have you ever been?"

"No. I would like very much to see the animals of my country once again. I am homesick, Henry. It is so different here than at home."

But after a tour of the snake house, and the lions and tigers of the cat house, Umrao was too dispirited to continue.

"All these poor creatures look so miserable in their cages. It makes me sad to see them trapped here in the midst of all this noise and strange smells. Bengal tigers are particularly solitary, I can only just imagine their misery among these crowds and strange smells."

"You talk as if they were pets," Henry replied.

"No. Though, there are Rajahs who keep tigers and leopards as pets. But they are noble creatures and I am certain they feel demeaned in these cages, surrounded by this foreign evil-smelling city."

"Perhaps it is you who feels this way," Henry remarked.

"I do, but I am certain the animals feel it as

well. The English try to put so many things in cages, themselves, most of all."

"You mean their feelings."

"Yes. Even between children and parents I see little joy and affection."

Henry turned and looked around at the crowd which streamed past them. After some moments he said, "It is a very different way of life. Much less elemental."

"I do not know that word."

"There is less of the natural world here. Man has touched the environment and life much more heavily here than in India."

"Yes. That is certainly true. Let us go out onto the green and away from these poor beasts."

"Very well," Henry replied. He could always count on Umrao for an utterly different way of seeing the world.

In the course of the afternoon, Henry found he had to answer myriad questions about people in the park. She thought perambulators a particularly strange invention.

"How can a baby who does not feel the warmth of his mother's body have warmth in her own?" she asked and, "Why do English women squash their breasts and stomachs with whalebone? I could never wear such things."

"They do it to have a silhouette like yours," Henry said, smiling.

"But when the gentlemen take the ladies' clothes off, they will be disappointed."

Two middle-aged ladies who were walking by heard Umrao's comment.

"They're just like animals," one remarked to the other, and the pair turned away in a huff.

"What is the use of pretending these things

do not happen in life?" Umrao said in response to the women, but they were already out of earshot. "I don't understand this pretense," she said to Henry. "When we use pretense in the *kotha*, there is a purpose, usually to get more money. But here, it has no reason. And the English Christians are always telling us we must never lie."

In a way, Henry thought, she is right. Yet, if we did not have these pretences what would life be like in a city where millions were jostling each other's elbows day and night?

Umrao's comments exposed the falseness of British prudery but they also made him wonder if a life in England with her was possible. She was like one of the great cats in the zoological gardens, at once more full of life's elemental powers than those around her, yet a prisoner of British habits and expectations as long as she remained in their society. Could he live among the musicians, dancers and courtesans of Lucknow's *chowk*? It was a strange thought. There seemed to be almost a kind of fatality in the idea, returning to live in the place of his mother's disgrace. As he mulled it over, he became outwardly more quiet than usual.

Finally, Umrao asked: "Have I said something to offend you, Henry? I am not always sure of your ways, though I have tried to learn most of them."

"I would not want you to learn all of them, Umrao. Then you would lose something essential to yourself. I could not love you more for being more English." But, he thought, it might be easier for us to find a society in which we could live. For he was not at all certain he wanted to spend his life as a bawdy house musician in India.

But as far as his relationship with Umrao, the die was cast. They belonged to each other forever. They must marry and he must turn her away from her plan to kill her mother's murderer. He knew that it would not be easy. The shadows lengthened and the air grew cooler. It was soon time for Umrao to return to their rooms and dress for the concert.

<hr/>

When they got back, Umrao opened a large tin box she had brought from Sergeant Abdul's.

"I have not opened this since I left India," she said.

"I wondered about that box," Henry remarked.

"It is made of tin to keep the white ants from eating my clothes. They will devour anything but they like cloth best. And my costume is very costly."

She showed him a magnificent semi-transparent jacket and pajamas embroidered with something that glittered like diamonds or rhinestones. When she put it on, and did a pirouette, she was literally dazzling, indeed a vision out of the *Arabian Nights*. Her beauty made Henry proud to be her lover. He felt desire stir within himself and put his hands on Umrao's shoulders.

"No, no," she said. "Not now," she said smiling. "I have not time."

"But," Henry began.

"No. I do not want us to be making love when my Uncle returns. We should be dressed and ready."

"I am dressed and ready," he said.

"But I shall not be if I let you stay with me," she said as she pushed him toward the door.

Left alone in the outer room, Henry sat at the window. Visions of a naked Umrao kept flitting through his thoughts.

"When the beast in us is roused, there is little else," he said out loud. He had never had feelings like these with Mary. It would have been unthinkable and,

243

the fact of that inner prohibition he had felt with Mary now seemed very strange to him. He thought of his mother. Was there some peculiarly animal attraction between light and dark races, he wondered? He could not recall that his mother had expressed any such feeling. Finally, Umrao emerged and rescued him from his ponderings. The paint she wore was almost like a mask, intended to be seen from some distance. Henry was surprised to find that the heavy paint made her even more beautiful, unearthly and remote. Her eyebrows were darkened and her high, broad cheekbones were emphasized with very evident rouge. Her jacket and pajamas were not simply diaphanous white fabric but sparkled with the hundreds of little gems sewn to it. At moments she seemed almost naked but when he tried to really look at her, the illusion disappeared in a shower of scintillating lights that seemed to wrap her in a shower of stars. She whirled around the room like a galaxy that threatened to set the earth on fire. The only response Henry could think of was to applaud as Umrao pirouetted across the room. When she came to a stop, she was holding her *sarangi* in her arms.

"Bravo," Henry cried. "You are the most beautiful creature I have ever beheld."

Umrao smiled. "That is my art. To be admired by men."

"No, by one man. Me," he said huskily as he griped her upper arms.

"No, for you I am really myself only," and she took a piece of cloth from her sleeve and wiped her face blurring her elaborate paint.

"What? You spoiled it. Why did you do that?"

"To show you that for you I am only myself. Whatever other men might see tonight. I want you to see me." And she suddenly fell at his feet and put her cheek against his feet and then kissed his instep and looked up at him.

"I love you, Henry, with the love that only comes once to anyone. No matter how I may seem tonight remember that only you have been my lover, and only you shall be. I am a singer and a dancer but no longer a courtesan."

Her sudden change of mood was very strange to Henry, though he was enough in love with her to be glad of her pledge and to lift her to her feet. Then he kissed her smeared face. She was so passionate, he thought, sometimes like a character from the age of Greek tragedies when people killed and died in wild, extravagant ways for love. What nineteenth century English woman would ever offer such incendiary passion? Certainly not Mary, nor any other he had ever met. He thought fleetingly of an account he'd read of one of the last acts of *suttee*, the self-immolation of a widow on her husband's burning funeral pyre. The love of such a woman was not a tame, quiet gift but a blazing sun that could scorch the wings of angels. For the first time, he felt profoundly responsible for Umrao, for her happiness and well-being. He had never before felt this kind of burden. It made him want to weep and be joyful at the same time.

"You are extraordinary," he whispered, holding her close.

She pulled away to look at him and he saw that tears were streaming down her cheeks.

"Don't ever stop caring for me, Henry. I could not bear another loss so grievous. I must repair my face paint now," and she darted into her room.

A few minutes later, Henry heard Sergeant Abdul's knock on the door. He stepped into the room carrying a very large bag, which obviously contained an enormous musical instrument. When Henry stared at it he said, "It is called a *tamboura*. Umrao will use it when she sings tonight."

"Umrao is almost ready," Henry said as he greeted the Sergeant.

"And are you ready? To play the dumb guard tonight. You must see all and say nothing."

"Yes, I know, Sergeant. I frankly hope this man is not the killer of Umrao's mother. Somehow I must turn her aside from her desire for revenge. It can only end in disaster for all of us."

"I think there are many things in play in all this, Henry. And the likelihood is that if Umrao continues to sing and play among the Indians and Anglo-Indians in London, she will encounter her mother's killer. How events from the past will play out in the present is beyond guessing at. All we can do is wait. Be watchful tonight."

Just as the Sergeant finished his exhortation, Umrao came out of her room. She had wrapped her gorgeous costume in a plain, gray cloak. The paint on her face was hidden as much as possible by a hood on her cloak, which covered her head. She handed her *sarangi* to Henry.

"I am ready," she announced.

Henry was surprised to find that the cab took them west rather than east. As they rode through the Regents Park he said to Abdul, "This must be a wealthy Indian indeed if he lives north of the Park at this end of the city."

"He is an Anglo-Indian, what they call here a Nabob, which, ironically, is a corruption of *nawab*.

"I remember people in the Residency talking of the *nawabs*, mostly with contempt," Henry said.

"Orginally, *nawab* meant "governor" when the S'hite court of Oudh was supposed to be ruling in the name of the Mogul king in Delhi. They soon broke away from the Moguls only to end with a much harsher master in the British. Theirs is a sad history. And they were gay, happy rulers, too."

"I think anyone who saw Lucknow before the Mutiny, feels some nostalgia for those days, at least for the loss of some of the beautiful buildings," Henry said. "But isn't it surprising that an Anglo-Indian is a connoisseur of *Hindustani* music?"

"The colonel tells me that our patron is tonight is what was politely called in English society in India, a *Eurasian*, a person of mixed racial parentage, like the colonel, himself. Some became very rich and came to England to live as Englishmen. But, they are as rejected here as they are in India. What do you think about wearing a dark skin?"

"I must confess," Henry replied, "I am deeply disappointed in most of my countrymen. I had no idea of the universal disregard that dark-skinned people suffer here. I thought it was strictly confined to India."

"Well, young sir, you may make other sad discoveries about such things before we are done untieing the knot of the past and present."

"It is very possible," Henry agreed.

Then, the two men lapsed into silence and watched the handsome houses they passed along the western edge of the park. Finally, after what seemed a very long ride, the cab stopped in front of one of the extremely elegant villas on Park Road on the north western edge of the Park, just behind St. Dunstans. These large, elegant homes faced a row of well-kept trees which lined the other side of the wide avenue. Only the very wealthiest people in London could enjoy such a bucolic view from their windows.

Henry and Abdul both admired the building and environs, but Umrao seemed unimpressed and even disinterested. They were taken through a lofty entrance hall where Umrao left her cloak. Directly off this hall was the sanctuary of the *nabob*, the *Jahlsagar* or music room, where the old man held court in one of the most beautiful chambers Henry had ever seen. A roof of glass covered one end of a large court which seemed half room and half garden. The floors were paved with beautifully painted oriental tiles. Rich fabric cascaded in folds across the windows. Plants grown to the height of Sergeant Abdul were placed around the area in large white tubs. A pool containing multi-coloured fish, probably baby pike, was the centre around which the room was arranged. At one end was a dais covered with an extraordinarily thick Chinese carpet. Around the dais were large glass tanks which held flickering oil lamps. The shimmering effect made it seem the light was coming from the water, since the glass that actually held the oil was virtually invisible. A beautiful carved wooden chair, inlaid with brass and ivory stood at the front edge of the dais. This, presumably, was where the *nabob* would sit during the concert. However, like the Colonel, he rose from a large pile of cushions thrown on to another beautiful area rug, woven in the Persian style of Isfahan. The entire room was suffused with the odours of flowers and aromatic shrubs. Henry thought the man might have been any *Eurasian* from an Indian regiment. He was light haired, dark skinned, wore a huge turban and looked about the same age as Henry. He was shocked since he had expected another old man who was stuck in the past.

The *nabob* had been smoking a beautiful silver *hukkah*, which stood in front of his cushion. His teeth were red from using betel leaves. As Umrao approached, he bowed low.

"Good evening, Begum," the man said in Urdu. "You are more beautiful than a starry sky. Will you sing some *ghazals* of your own composition?"

Umrao bowed and said, "Some which I have written just for you, honoured gentleman. For I have been told you are a great connoisseur."

"You bring me joy, Begum. If your voice is half as beautiful as your eyes and figure, I shall have a rare treat tonight. May I lead you to your place of honour?" And he took Umrao's hand and led her up to the cushions on the dais.

Henry followed close on her heels and as he stepped on the stage, the patron turned on him angrily,

"Who is this oaf who steps on the place prepared for the loveliest star in the heaven?"

Henry had no idea what had been said. Only that it expressed anger which was directed at him.

"Pay no attention," my lord," Umrao said to the man. "He is my porter and is deaf and dumb. He is nothing but a slave and brings my *tamboura* to my place."

"Very well. But he is certainly a tall oaf."

"A lackey with a strong back and an obedient heart, my lord," Umrao answered. She took the *tamboura* from Henry and sat in the nest of satin and velvet cushions that had been provided for her. Then, she waved her hand at Henry in a gesture of dismissal. He stepped off the dais and stood against the wall which backed the platform. He did his best to be truly oriental in his immobility.

Once Umrao was seated another Indian came out from behind a curtain, carrying some small drums, which Henry knew were *tablas*. Another man followed carrying a long necked instrument with a bulbous shape at one end. This was the *sitar*. These two with her own instrument would be Umrao's accompaniment.

Henry had gathered a tiny smattering of knowledge about the complex music of which Umrao was such a master. He would try to follow transitions between the different *rags* and *tal*, the different scales and rhythms that would be used during the performance.

Because the music was often in musical intervals smaller than the half or whole tone of western music, he found it very difficult to grasp its subtleties most of the time. But he had set himself the task of learning, for his own improvement and to be able to share Umrao's art with her.

Umrao removed the *tamboura* from its sack and laid it across her knees. The notes it produced when she lightly touched the strings was a drone, some of the most individual sounds Henry had ever heard. As Umrao touch the strings in a preliminary way, Indian servants in richly brocaded coats and pajamas snuffed all the lights except for those floating in the tanks on either side of the stage. In her glittering coat, which increased the number of sparkling highlights thrown on the walls and ceiling, Umrao looked like the goddess of an oriental myth. She closed her eyes for a moment, opened them and began. She stroked the strings and against the droning strings her own voice began to quaver in an intricate series of sounds. Then, the *tablas* began and finallly, the *sitar* was added.

Their host soon closed his eyes, but he was smiling a very tender smile as he listened to Umrao sing. He remained motionless for what seemed a very very long time to Henry.

Umrao's shimmering costume sent sparks around the room with each movement. Henry felt the hypnotic power of the music, but it made him sleepy as though he were being mesmerized. It was difficult to remain standing and keep his eyes open. He, Umrao, the *nabob*, Sergeant Abdul and one servant in a black brocade jacket were the only people in the room, so there was little for Henry to observe. He could not exchange glances with Umrao for he stood behind her and off to one side, and she was raised up on the dias. Eventually, for Henry, the evening became nothing more than a struggle to remain awake.

Every so often, Umrao stopped to twist one of the pegs that lined one side of the *tamboura's* neck. Henry had learned by now that singing and playing the *sarangi* was a virtuoso feat that often surprised connoiseurs of Hindustani music. The *tamboura* was a more common instrument of self-accompaniement.

These breaks helped interrupt the trance in-duced by the music. Henry felt his sleepiness disloyal to Umrao, but he could not help it. By the end of the concert, which seemed to last for hours and hours, his desire to sleep had become a torture.

When Umrao suddenly stood up, stepped off the dias and handed the *tamboura* over to him, he was so numb, he nearly dropped it.

The *nabob* got up and approached Umrao, who was walking toward him. He took one of her hands in his and muttered something in Urdu. The two talked for a while in low voices and finally, Henry saw the man shrug. Abdul stood up and Henry took this as his signal to leave his post and follow the sergeant as Umrao led the way out of the splendid room. Henry felt only gratitude as they entered the cooler air of the hall. His expectations of an eventful or dangerous evening had evaporated in the numbing monotony of his role. He must learn more about Umrao's music.

Outside, on the front steps, the fresh air finally woke Henry, and not a moment too soon. As the party started to descend the steps to the coach and four which had been offered to them by the *nabob*, four men rushed around the door of the coach. They were all carrying long white scarfs in their hands.

"*Thugs*," Abdul cried as he whirled around with his cane and struck the closest of the men across the head. The man staggered back and fell as the others closed on Henry, Abdul and Umrao. Henry spun around and felled another one of the villains and looked over his shoulder just in time to see that one of the *Thugs* had Umrao by the wrist and was dragging her away from himself and the sergeant. In two leaps Henry was on the would-be abductor, seized him by the throat, lifted him and threw him into the street. When the man got out of the gutter, he ran. The fourth man had already departed.

"Well," Henry said watching the men run into the trees, "that puts the colonel squarely in the dock."

"What do you mean, Henry?" Umrao asked.

"Well, who else knew we would be coming here? The *Thugs* don't know where we have been staying, otherwise we would have been molested before."

"Yes," Abdul responded. "They knew we would be here. But don't forget the nature of *Thuggee*. They may even have accomplices in that house, unbeknownst to the *nabob*."

"The *nabob*'s house?" Henry asked.

"It is not impossible. When you are dealing with *Thuggee*, no villainy is out of the question."

"Well, it seems simpler to me to just assume it is the Colonel and stay away from him."

"No, Henry," Umrao said. "I will not do that. I must know about Akhtar Devi. I must know if he is the man. I will give concerts with him until I know. And then..." She let her voice trail off.

By the time Henry and Umrao returned to their rooms, they were both exhausted.

Umrao looked drawn and gray, as if she had spent some essence of herself during the concert.

"You must go to bed right away, Umrao," Henry said. "You look utterly done up."

"I am. But you must come with me. I need my brave knight next to me while I fall asleep."

"That is a pleasure and hardly a duty, my love," Henry said. "Let us go, then."

The exhausted woman was asleep in just moments after Henry kissed her cheek.

Then, he got up and found his mother's diary. Tired as he was, the attack made him want to press on with getting more answers from the past. He must, before some thing fatal happened in the present.

Chapter 15
The Journal of Jane Booth
Fifth Reading

December 27, 1856—evening

Everything has been decided for me. Our lives are being turned topsy turvy and perhaps it will be for the best. I certainly look forward to almost any change. Broderick has been reposted to Cawnpore and I shall lose my little boy before we settle in our new quarters. Henry is to go home to live in London.

It really does seem like the workings of Providence that so many things just fell into place. A clergyman here just happened to write to Charles Sutton about the rumors of native unrest here in Oudh. In the same letter he also wrote about several people who were sending their children home. In his next letter, without being asked, Charles Sutton offered to take Henry into his elegant home near London University. It is a marvelous chance for the little man. Charles is very well-to-do and has very high connections in the Church. It could be the making of our son. But how I shall miss him! If it were not for my friend, and the fact that only ten miles lie between Cawnpore and where my friend lives, I think my heart would break.

Little Henry will take the long sea voyage around the Horn as I did. Why papa thought a six-month sea voyage was better for me than the overland route, I shall never know, though I must admit, the P&O steam vessels had not been running as long, then, and I had my pianoforte with me. Henry will also go the long way. I have chosen that route for him because there will be no danger of him being lost at any of the transfer points. He will board in Calcutta and arrive in London. I know it is dreadfully long. But even so, I believe he will be safer. Broderick likes the idea because the long journey is cheaper.

Of course, I shall bring Henry to Calcutta, which means I am to have several months of holiday while Broderick stays here and arranges the logistics of our move to Cawnpore. I must meet my friend once more before we go. I will be away from him for over two months!

December 28, 1856—evening

Henry and I shall go by an army ship down river from Cawnpore to Calcutta, which will take about three weeks in each direction. I'm told the trip can be quite pretty at this time of year. There will be pelicans and other water birds on the river as there were when I went to Cawnpore on my last visit. And, I may have several weeks in Calcutta before the ship sails. But for all I know, these few weeks might be the last time I shall see my child. So many people die unexpectedly out here, and even East Indiamen have been known to sink. But I must be brave and not make Henry afraid. At least, whatever happens to me, I shall know that Henry has a good start in life with the Suttons. They can do much

more for him than Broderick or I could, and Charles
is really a good and generous Christian. My cousin did
very well when she married him.

I give Broderick credit for his willingness to let
his son go. He knows the Suttons can give our son a
good life and he does not want to stand in Henry's light.
I have just written to my friend to tell him of the changes in my life.

January 3, 1856—evening

My friend has written back promptly to say that he can
meet me next week at Akhtar Devi's *kotha*. He will
write when he reaches Lucknow. He says that he knows
it may be difficult to get away, but he must see me once
more before I go. I do believe he really loves me.

January 10, 1856—afternoon

I am trying to spend more time with my precious little
boy, and to my surprise, so is Broderick, but Henry is
like a quick young bird who must be watched all the
time or he will dart away in an instant. Usually the *ayah*
watches over him, but Broderick took him on a business call to the Qaiser Bagh, where the *Nawab's* home
is located. In just moments, Broderick told me, Henry
disappeared. Broderick was frantic, not knowing what
the *Nawab's* retainers would do to a white child found
in the *Nawab's* compound. The grounds of the Qaiser
Bagh are enormous with a multitude of ornate courtyards and buildings. Broderick looked and looked. After
an hour of anxious searching, he finally found Henry
standing in front of an absurd two-story pigeon house
that one of the *Nawabs* built for his birds. Broderick said

Henry was mesmerized by the birds entering and leaving their elaborate dwelling. And of all things, the *Nawab* himself was watching Henry watch his prize birds.

The *Nawab* and Henry were each throwing handfuls of grain down on the ground for the birds. The *Nawab* was laughing each time Henry tried to grab one of the birds who came for the grain. Broderick was astonished. The *Nawab* caught sight of Broderick and picked Henry up and handed him to his father.

"Who was the greater child of the two, I should like to know?" Broderick said when he told me about the incident. "It is no wonder that this country is in such a state of chaos when its king can find nothing better to do than play with pets and children."

But I thought it was very kind of the *Nawab* to play with Henry and let him watch the birds.

January 13, 1856—morning

The letter from my friend arrived today, naming the hour for our *rendez-vous*. As usual, he will send the *palanquin* in the late afternoon. I only hope that Broderick does not alter his habits to be home with me and Henry. Will he give up his pleasure so readily? He may, since I am going to be away for a long time. He will have a great deal of time to have whatever native woman he wants. I have even seen him cast an enquiring eye at little Sita.

No. All is well. Broderick sent a note to say he would be away. It seems our imminent parting as a family has at least made him more considerate.

January 15, 1856—late evening

A very horrible visit to the *kotha*. I scarcely dare to write
of it. All was well with my friend and I. We took as
much pleasure in each other, as usual. He was very kind
and attentive. I believe he will miss me frightfully and
that he is very glad that we shall be so much nearer each
other when I return. The horror came afterwards:

As I prepared to leave, I did not put on my *burqa*
immediately, so safe had I come to feel in the hall near
our room. As I stepped outside...I saw...it was ghastly...
the hallway was quite dark, as usual, but the door to
the room across the hall was open about six inches and
inside the room was well lit. I could see Akhtar Devi,
quite clearly, her head hanging backwards off the foot
of the bed, her long dark hair streaming onto the floor.
It was not at all a normal posture and I knew it immediately. But the most horrible thing of all was that her
eyes were wide open and staring at nothing. They were
utterly devoid of life, and from what I could see, she
was naked. I could scarcely believe what my eyes were
seeing so I took a step toward the open door to look
more closely. When I saw that she really did look dead,
I wanted to run back into our room, but horror had
rooted me to the spot. Before I could move, a man came
out of the room, he was putting a white scarf into his
pocket. We looked directly at each other. We stood only
a few feet apart and with the light from the room falling
into the hall, he could not mistake me anymore than I
could him. He was an Englishman but even worse, we
were known to each other! We could see each other
clearly!

My heavens, what a moment that was. His look
held me for a moment. Then he glanced toward the
room I had been using, following the sounds my friend

was making while getting dressed. The Englishman must have realized that someone was close at hand or I believe he would have slipped the white scarf around my neck, too.

He looked back at me and I almost felt I could hear him say in my mind, "Neither of us is supposed to be here, so we had better forget we ever saw each other." I was as astonished to see him as he was to see me. But there was real menace in his look. He was some...no..I will put no name down after what my friend has told me about keeping the secrets of the house. I turned away suddenly and reentered our room.

My eyes must have been wide and staring; perhaps I was breathing hard. My friend asked me what had frightened me. I told him. I told him everything, even the name of the man.

"Never, never, say a word of this anywhere on this side of the grave," he said when I had done. He told me what the white scarf meant, but he said he was astonished that the weapon of a *Thug* had been used by an Englishman, but then he smiled, somewhat ironically and said, "But perhaps in these times it is not so strange."

He told me to re-bolt the door, get undressed quickly and lie down with him. I did not understand but I did as he said. A short time later there was a scuffling in the hall and then a heavy fist fell on our door, and a voice cried something I could not understand. My friend sprang out of bed.

"Keep the covers pulled up to your eyes," he snapped at me. I did as he told me and he opened the door completely naked. The two fierce, black mustachioed men from the front door barked at my friend in their strange tongue. He said something back and closed the door.

"Now, hurry," he said to me. "Get dressed quickly and put your *burqa* on."

It was evident that he expected more callers and was trying to get me clear of the place before anyone saw me. I had time only to peck him on the cheek and run down to the place where the *palanquin* usually was. As I got into it, I just prayed that Broderick was not yet home. The disorder of my clothes and hair would certainly give me away.

Fortunately, the bungalow was dark when I got home and I slipped into my room before anyone saw me.

Several hours later

I have now been home for some hours and have been asleep. I woke dreaming that there was something around my neck. At first, I thought I was awake and that the bed clothes were wrapped around my throat. But the pressure on my throat became greater and greater and was finally unbearable. There was a man standing over me. I could not breathe. I tried to cry out but could not. Suddenly I truly woke, gasping for breath.

I lay awake in the still night and fought back my feeling of panic. What if the man I had seen at the *kotha* decided that he could not count on my silence? If he were a *Thug*, would he not be able to have me murdered and buried before anyone knew of it? I had heard terrible stories of how these killers had haunted India even in the recent past. Many people, even English people, believed they had supernatural powers. And what could it mean that this *Thug* had been an Englishman? The idea was too horrifying to contemplate. It seemed almost as if my dream and waking life had somehow been mixed together.

When I next see my friend, I must ask him about

all this. All I can do for now is to stay in my bed with the lamp burning and try to quiet myself by writing. The persistent terror of the dream refuses to leave me. If I did not feel it was against his interest, I would go to Henry's room and wake him up to keep me company. My future now seems very tenuous to me and I really wonder if I shall ever see Henry again once I put him on the ship.

Perhaps all this is a presentiment of the end. At moments I wonder if I shall live long enough to take Henry to Calcutta. Even my friend seemed frightened when I told him about the white scarf.

Shah Nujuf, Lucknow

Chapter 16
The shadows of the past deepen

"Heaven protect us!" Henry exclaimed. "What kind of fatality pursues us over so many years and at such a distance? What do these fiends want? And who is this Englishman who is worse than all the dark-skinned *Thugs* of centuries past?" He sat quietly for a moment and then muttered,

"Could all that has happened be because my mother saw this man commit a dreadful crime? Is that why they are pursuing the journal? Perhaps, if my mother and this man knew one another, this English *Thug* might be afraid she could have named him in these pages. Perhaps that is why he wants the journal."

He would have liked to wake Umrao and tell her about Akhtar Devi, but the poor girl was thoroughly exhausted. She must get her rest, especially if she was determined to perform again and place herself at risk. Perhaps they should try to capture one of these *Thugs*. According to Sergeant Abdul, the *Thugs* that Sleeman caught were readily turned to approvers and gave information on their fellow cult members most willingly.

But this Englishman, who was he? What white man would ally himself with such a terrible gang of killers? It was difficult to imagine who he could be. If his mother's diary had not been so patently real and true, he would doubt that such a man could exist. But if she hadn't lied about other things which put her own character in a bad light, why would she lie about this?

Sergeant Abdul said that the reason Major General Sleeman was able to defeat the *Thugs* was because the English were better organized and more methodical, where the *Thugs* simply continued practices that were centuries old and easily anticipated. But if an Englishman were working with them, what then? What if English method and strategy were combined with the ferocity and blood-thirstiness of the *Thugs*? What a formidable and terrible combination. Most important of all, why was he and his mother's diary being pursued by these fiends? Did this white man fear exposure? The diary had been dropped on the lawn outside of Charles' window, but probably accidentally. The *Thug* might have been frantically looking for something specific in the book, such as the passage Henry had just read. Then, when he was unexpectedly pursued, he dropped it.

Until Henry could answer these questions, he and everyone who associated with him was in danger. This last thought made him start to pace up and down the room. Perhaps he should leave Umrao in the Sergeant's care. His own presence might endanger her. The protection he was trying to provide for her could be far outweighed by the danger that seemed to stalk him.

Sergeant Abdul had the presence of mind to change from the *Nabob's* carriage to a cab and to change cabs three times before actually coming back to Swandam Lane from the concert. But if these killers should ever find him, Umrao would be at risk, too. He would wait for Abdul that night and then discuss what to do next, though, he believed it would be best to separate himself from Umrao.

He was so lost in his speculations that he did not even hear Umrao come out of her room, wrapped in a blanket.

"Henry, is something wrong?"

"Gracious, you startled me," he said. "I have made astonishing discoveries in my mother's diary, Umrao. I have learned that she knew the identity of your mother's killer. He was not only an Englishman, he was also a *Thug*."

"What? An Englishman who was a *Thug* killed Akhtar Devi? And your mother knew him?"

"Yes."

"Do you think that is why the *Thugs* are after you?"

"It could well be. Perhaps they think that I now have the same knowledge my mother did, now that I have the diary. Don't forget that all this started when I received it. There was no sign of any trouble before that."

"Yes. But I thought the *Thugs* left the diary on the grass when they killed your stepfather. Would they not have kept it?"

"I think it was dropped by accident. I think the man wanted to look into it immediately. But when he heard me open the window in hot pursuit, the killer's first thought would have been to get away after murdering Charles. In any case, dear girl, with all these dark dangers hovering around me I must leave you with the good Sergeant. He will look after you and will not draw any danger to you."

"No," Umrao cried. "If you leave me, you won't come back. I feel it. I fear it. You must stay with me."

Henry put his arms around her. "Well, in any case, we must take counsel with Sergeant Abdul and see what he says. I think he will be very interested in what I have learned. If only we had the inscription from the painting translated. It might give us the key to understanding the actions of the *Thugs*."

"I want you to stay with me, Henry. I will be more frightened for you if you are alone. You must stay in your disguise and you, I and Sergeant Abdul must continue to help one another."

That evening when Sergeant Abdul finished his rounds, Henry put the case before him as it now stood. The Sergeant, too, was very struck by the fact of an Englishman actually working with the stranglers.

"I know that there were many highly placed and wealthy Indians who assisted them in various ways. Certain *Maharajahs* protected them in their territories. There were some very rich Indian bankers whose affiliations with the *Thugs* we uncovered. But an Englishman, never. I am bowled over. I wonder who he is? We must find out. His presence makes our enemies that much more threatening. That man knows his own country and will certainly be able to give the *Thugs* valuable help here, if he is not their actual leader."

"Their leader!" Henry and Umrao exclaimed.

"It is hard to imagine an Englishman following an Indian Thug, is it not?" Sergeant Abdul replied.

"Well, I, for one," Henry began, "think that the attack last night puts the Colonel in the dock. He is perfect for this role. We know my mother knew him by sight. And we know he visited Akhtar Devi."

"I am not convinced that your mother would have described the Colonel as an Englishman, Sergeant Abdul said. "How does she describe him when she first saw him with Akhtar Devi? Let us consult the diary."

Henry picked up the book and rapidly thumbed through the pages to find the incident to which the Sergeant adverted.

"Here," Henry said. "She calls him both an 'Englishman' and a 'half-caste,' so she might have been referring to the Colonel."

"Then we must admit the possibility that he is our man," Sergeant Abdul said.

"I am convinced of it," Henry said. "His bad character would certainly fit with the sort of man we are seeking, or who is seeking me and the diary. It all fits together. Have you shown him the inscription from the painting?"

"Not yet. I only told him I had an old paper from Major General Sleeman that was written in Ramasee that I wanted him to translate."

"That was thoughtful, Uncle," Umrao said.

"Whenever one deals with Ramasee or anything touching on the *Thugs*, one must always be thoughtful. Umrao," he said in a changed tone, "what happened in the *kotha* after Akhtar Devi died? I mean, what happened to the house, to you, your training. What events transpired? Anything you can remember may be of importance."

"Well, I told you when I came to England last year, Uncle that in some ways very little changed outwardly. For a long time, my heart was sore and I thought little about anything. The house was left to me in Akhtar Devi's will and Bismullah was left in charge until I was of age. Bismullah is a good woman, but she has not the style or polish of Akhtar Devi. Fortunately, I was able to continue my musical studies with an old *sarangi* player, a man, who, it was said, had worked in Lahore in the *Shai Mohalla*, as an accompanist to courtesans and as a pimp. He was ancient, but what a voice he could pull out of his old, battered instrument. He knew all the styles, those from Delhi, Benares as well as Lucknow, and that is very rare. Usually a musician only has one *Ustad*, one master, and learns only one style of playing. This was the one good thing that Akhtar Devi's death brought me. I loved the *sarangi* but because *sarangi* players were often pimps in places outside of Lucknow, Akhtar Devi would not have one in her *kotha*. She hated pimps who made profit from women. She had relied on other players for accompaniment. But once Akhtar Devi was gone, the old man, whom everyone simply called Babaji, which means, revered father, because of his vast musical knowledge, was allowed to teach me. Bismullah had to hire a *Maulavi* to continue my studies of literature. I already knew English well, but my Persian was limited and still is. Outwardly, my life changed little, except that I was alone a great deal more and I harboured a deep hatred for the man who killed my mother. Every day in my prayers, I swore to avenge her. I still do.

Bismullah kept me apart from the clients of the *kotha* because she knew that had been Akhtar Devi's wish. My greatest happiness was singing and playing the *sarangi* and taking instruction from Babaji." She paused and then said, "This does not seem very helpful."

"No," Sergeant Abdul said. "I know most of the rest, in any case. You applied to come to me as a reputed blood relation on your father's side. Bismullah runs the *kotha*, still. No. There is not much to find in the rest of your tale, Umrao."

"I still think the Colonel is a thorough black-guard," Henry said.

"He may be," Sergeant Abdul said. "But we cannot force him to translate for us. He could easily deceive us and we would have shown him what we have."

"But sooner or later, that is exactly the situation we shall be in," Henry said, "unless we can find someone else to read this text from the painting."

"What do we gain by waiting?"

"I do not know," Abdul said. "But I would like you to finish the diary before we do anything. It has already given us facts of importance. I would like to be in full possession of the past before we try to march blindly into the future."

"Very well, I shall finish it tonight. I'm fairly sure I can do that."

"I shall tell the Colonel we need more time after this attack. I will not mention *Thuggee*."

"And Henry shall not go away from me?" Umrao asked.

"Where would he go?" Abdul asked.

"I felt that perhaps I should leave her since it is myself and the diary that the *Thugs* seem to be most interested in."

"But we can all see that both of you are connected, in the past as well as the present," Sergeant Abudul replied. "There is a strong karmic bond between you. The future we don't know, yet. But, you cannot mend a carpet by cutting the warp thread. If the *Thugs* knew you were here, you would both be in danger. The absence of one will not protect the other. That is why, whenever I come to you from my patients I take a very circuitous route. Finish reading the diary, Henry. Our way may then be clear to us."

Chapter 17
The Journal of Jane Booth
Sixth Reading

March 1, 1857

A very busy, even feverish, time has passed. I have been packing things for Henry which he might need on his journey. He has been such a little man about it all. He caught me sniffing back some tears while I filled his chest with some of his favourite things. He came over to me, put his arms around my waist and said, "Don't worry, Mother, I shall be all right."

He has such a good heart. And I believe in the Sutton's house that his goodness shall be encouraged by theirs. It should really be my family that take Henry in, but, of course, they plead poverty. Broderick has no family, and therefore, no resources in England to offer his son. In the end, I believe that Henry will be much better off with the Suttons. They are such devout Christians, without being at all severe, and they have a little girl close to Henry's age.

Cawnpore March 3, 1857

We are on our way and already in Cawnpore where I make this entry.

We have the same room at the Residency that I had when I was last here. It makes me think of my friend, and what I thought of him when I was last here. I could never have imagined where things with him would lead me.

No, wait. That's not really true. If I am scrupulously honest, I must admit that if I hadn't been so shocked at my own feelings, I should have known then how things would be with us.

Henry enjoys the water birds so much. I suppose all children love animals. Every afternoon, he feeds the pelicans which land on the terrace where I danced on my last visit. He is excited about his journey and is looking forward to it. Our parting, perhaps forever, has not really entered his thoughts. He talks of what WE shall do on the ship; how WE shall cross the desert up to Suez and so on. I suppose it will not seem real to him until we say goodbye in Calcutta. It breaks my heart when I think of his sorrow, then. How alone he will be!

March 10, 1857

A group of officers shall be leaving here sometime in the next week and we shall be on one of the flats which their steam vessel will tow down the Ganges. I suppose we shall have accommodations to ourselves.

I don't imagine we would be expected to share such

close quarters with soldiers, even officers. At this time of year, in the cold weather, such a trip is supposed to be quite a pleasant excursion. Henry can't wait to be out on the river. He sees nothing but an adventure in all of this. And I must help him sustain his high spirits as long as possible.

How different everything seems since I first went up-country with Broderick, though it is hard to say where the greatest difference lies. Is it in the outward events or myself?

We came up by *palanquin* then, and the weather was hot. There were swarms of blister flies. It was quite miserable. We had to travel at night to avoid the heat. I shall never forget watching the torches of the bearers as they made their way through the jungle. Every so often we had to stop because one of them thought he saw a snake. Broderick had to get out of the *palanquin* and give them a dressing down to get them to go on.

     Now, I have lived in this land of natives, snakes and wild animals for nearly ten years. I gave birth here. I thanked God for the English doctor at Lucknow, when I had Henry. Now there is also a little brown skinned surgeon who looks after the poorest natives and low ranking army men. I have heard he is very good. The new Resident, the famous Major General Sleeman, even consults him, I am told.

Good or ill, the years have gone by in a kind of trance, it could all be a dream during one blindingly hot after-noon— or a lifetime. The proof that it is a lifetime, my lifetime, is that I am seeing my own son off for home. If it were not for my friend telling me constantly that I am beautiful, I should feel like an old woman.

Women do get old rapidly in this climate and people die very easily, a little scratch, a snake, cholera, damp air with the ague in it, any one of a thousand things can carry one off. I remember when I first arrived in Calcutta, I was shocked at how many people were talking about acquaintances who had died recently and suddenly. I wonder if I shall see Henry grown up?

If it were not for my friend, I would feel that all my happiness and good years were already ended.

There is more and more talk about the possibility of some trouble with the natives in Oudh. That is why we are moving to Cawnpore. Broderick is doing something secret there with the army. Whatever the reason, I look forward to living in a more civilized cantonment.

March 12, 1856

It soothes me to write. The river is quite placid. The jungle grows right down to the water and from under the roots of the mango trees. I see crocodiles slithering back and forth to sandbars further out in the water.

What a profusion of vegetation lies all around us! At night, I hear all manner of jungle birds, their strange voices crying out at us from behind the curtain of the heavy, tropical darkness. I don't like to write at night since with the lantern on I can see that the netting of our tent is alive with insects who want to get at us.

Henry begins to be bored with the journey. He is even growing used to the crocodiles; seeing one no longer excites him. I have to stop him from running across the flat a hundred times a day. As pretty and comfortable as the journey is, for India, Henry and I are both resorting to the books we brought for ourselves.

March 13, 1857

There is something about being on a vessel surrounded
by placid water that creates an illusion of timelessness. I
think it must be the closest experience of Eternity that
we get in this life.

No matter where I look or what I think about, it brings
me back to my imminent separation from Henry. It is
really a kind of death. Most parents here must face this,
or see their children seriously disadvantaged by growing
up in India, if they do not get ill and die.

My friend has said that we English have created a very
strange fate for ourselves by trying to rule a country
which is so foreign to us. He said that even when we
take more of India away from its people, we lose more of
ourselves.

When I think about this in in the light of my own present situation, I must agree with him. We shall never
conquer this country. We can only be strangers in a
strange land. My son and I shall pay the price for that,
soon.

We are all exiles from our home and from this land,
even though we dwell here. I wonder how the Queen
thinks of Her subjects here, or if she thinks of us at all,
or merely counts the revenues from Her eastern colony.

Later the same day

Henry is resting. Each day is like the last. We float

through the days and nights. My little son whom I have just been holding close to me is the only fixed point in the compass, and soon he will be gone.

Will he remember me when he is grown and living among the green hills and meadows of home? Perhaps it would be better if he did not remember anything of India at all.

March 15, 1857

The days are too featureless to write about. I can't wait to see Calcutta again, even if it is the place where I must say goodbye to Henry. We shall see his namesake, too, my brother, the only member of my family with whom I feel any sympathetic connection. He has done well out here. Well, it is a man's world, though I know poor Akhtar Devi would not have agreed with me.

March 31, 1857

We arrive tomorrow. What a strange mixture of emotions I feel: relief from boredom, sadness at soon losing my son, happiness that he shall have a better start in life than either of his parents, happiness that he shall be away from Broderick's uncertain temper, away from the dangers, the heat, the dust, the smell and the narrowness of Anglo India.

Those last words certainly belie the "interesting" article I wrote about the *chowk* in Lucknow. If I had had the remotest idea of what India was really like, I probably would have been ready to work as a governess at home rather than come out here. Now, however, the only people with whom I could share experiences are

Anglo-Indians. That is only one of the reasons I send my son away, now, before he gets India in his blood and becomes a life-long exile.

April 1, 1857

—We arrive in Calcutta. I had heard that a new branch of the Calcutta police had been formed to keep corpses out of the water near the harbour. I must say, I am not impressed with their efforts. The bloated corpses are not a pretty sight for a little boy to look upon.

As usual, there was a forest of masts on the river. There were well-trimmed American ships with ice in their holds, merchant ships flying the flags of many countries, and Chinese junks with an eye painted on either side, so that the ship could "see" where it was going.

Green goose-shaped budgerows used by Europeans for river travel were in abundance. I called Henry's attention to these things and tried to make him forget the half-decayed forms floating in the river, however, the stench made it difficult.

Early evening of our arrival

Our rooms at Spences Hotel are quite satisfactory. After being up country for so long, I might even say luxurious. Henry rushes from one thing to another, uncertain which new thing fascinates him more. His excitement makes me glad, for it shows me the happiness he will get from having new experiences and friends—even if I am not with him.

If it were not for the man my brother is sending to

England, I should really be in fear for Henry on the journey. I don't know the man, but my brother says he is reliable and has made the trip often. I know he won't give Henry any comfort, but at least, he will make certain that he does not fall overboard .

April 2, 1857

We have been to my brother's factory. He looks prosperous, much as a successful merchant at home would look. He still has a good figure and people commented on our resemblance. He is tall, fair and does not show his age.

His house is handsomely decorated and has very large airy rooms with mahogany furniture, all elegantly upholstered in red damask. He has a multitude of servants who wait upon him.

Today, I met the man who is to accompany Henry on the voyage. His name is Joshua Tree. He is quite young and won't mind having a childish companion, I think. He is nice looking in a slightly rotund sort of way. He even threw Henry's ball a few times in the commodious courtyard that surrounds my brother's house. Since my brother is Mr. Tree's employer and the man's prospects with him are good, I believe he will take good care of Henry, until the Suttons meet them in England. He seems like a responsible young man.

April 3, 1857

It seems we shall only have five days here. My brother's cargo is packed and Mr. Tree is anxious to leave and return with a young woman who will be his bride.

My brother has proposed that Henry and I stay in his house until we leave. He has always been a very kind, gentlemanly man and I am quite overwhelmed with the attention he shows me and little Henry. Given his manly appearance, manners and good prospects, I am sure he will be married before he is forty. He will be well established by then and will be able to have his choice of any of the women coming out.

I believe Henry is beginning to realize that we shall soon be parted. He keeps speaking of the things I must do to be safe and well. He tells me I must watch out for snakes. He is so good-hearted. All his concern is for me. When I see him being such a brave little man, I feel my eyes fill with tears, which I do not want him to see.

My kind brother senses our impending sorrow and seeks to distract us by offering a tour of the city and some money to buy things in the shops. We begin our round of amusements tomorrow morning with the horse races in front of Fort William.

My brother actually owns two of the Arabs that are racing. He is wealthier than I thought, if he can bring horses from the Persian Gulf and partake in the sport of kings. Henry is delirious with excitement. I daresay he'll not sleep much tonight.

April 6, 1857

My dear brother is going to great lengths for us, and tries to make certain there shall be no dull or introspective moments before Henry leaves with Mr. Tree. Today, he proposes to take us to the *Sans Souci*, a playhouse where they are putting on "The Rivals." It is a chestnut to be sure, but it has been so long since I have been to the theatre, I am as excited as Henry at the prospect.

April 7, 1857

For our next outing, my brother says we must see the improvements made at the Eden Gardens. There is now a bandstand, tall palms and red poinsettias. There is a fine, winding artificial lake with a beautiful arched bridge. In the centre of the Gardens is a replica of a Burmese pagoda, made of white chunam. The pagoda runs up into a spire upon which one night, the local wags have it, a British tar put a soda water bottle, which nobody has ever taken down. My brother says we must time our visit so that we meet the promenade at the end of the day. Then, we shall hear the band play *God save the Queen* in the twilight.

Night

A wonderful day! God bless my dear brother. Whatever happens, Henry and I shall always have this day to cherish.

April 8, 1857

I shall not go to the ship with Henry. I do not think I could do it without showing some signs of my distress. No doubt, I am weaker than many other women who have to let their children go. I am fortunate to have my brother to help me in my weakness. He does not judge me for it at all, as I know Broderick would.

April 9, 1857

We rose early this morning. It is the day of Henry's sailing. I hugged him to me upstairs. I did not feel I could say goodbye in front of the household. I told Henry I would watch his carriage from my window. I thanked Mr. Tree again and then left them and ran upstairs to my bedroom window. My brother's well-varnished carriage glinted in the sunlight and was quite visible for some time. Now, I can write only, he is gone! My little son is gone! My eyes grow blind with tears. I do not think that taking leave of my own life could be more difficult.

Night

How I long for my friend in the still watches of this sad, sullen night, knowing my child is being borne away from me, perhaps forever.

No matter what happens, I shall never see him again as a child, as my little boy. If we meet again, he will be a stranger. We would be strangers to each other. That is our lot.

My heart craves my friend's gentle, intimate touch. I loathe the thought of returning to Broderick. Along with greater proximity to my friend, there will be many more eyes to watch me at Cawnpore.

April 28. 1857

For the last three weeks, I have watched the thick green jungle, bejeweled with brilliantly coloured birds, and the sluggish brown river flow around me like one watching an unpleasant dream, from which one cannot wake. The muddy, turbid water, the moist air and even the beautiful early morning mists, all seem unreal and menacing. A dozen times a day, I take out the remarkable photograph my talented brother made of Henry. I hide it from myself again, but a short time later I take it once more from my luggage and stare at it. Everything in my life seems like the picture, intangible yet absolutely clear. My image was also taken for Henry to carry home with him so he will not forget me. The picture of him was supposed to remind me what my son looks like, but no matter how clear the image, all I can see is a little boy in a dark suit against a light background.

Henry is a stranger to me in the stillness of the picture, the glass an impenetrable barrier between us. Across the bottom, my brother has signed Henry's name and the date. His inscription makes me think of an inscription on a tomb. Again, I tell myself I shall not look at it.

I wonder how I shall feel when I get to Cawnpore tomorrow? Shall I wake, or go on living like a sleepwalker? The hot season is approaching and I have heard that Cawnpore is known for its dust storms in the hot weather. They say that great clouds of brown dust blast through the town at the temperature of a furnace. I don't think even these shall bring me back to life. The only thing that might wake me is the touch of my friend. We shall see.

May 1, 1857

Broderick has done me the courtesy of not meeting me at the pier. But he did send our servants to help with my things. How different everything looked, knowing that it is to be our home.

May 3, 1857

I am settled in our new bungalow and I must say it is
an improvement over the one in Lucknow. Our compound is larger and we are within sight of the river.
The rooms are similar. Sita has moved with us, and I
am very glad to have a loyal servant who knows the
secret of my friend. Meeting in Cawnpore will be more
difficult because there are more Europeans and they are
more spread through the city. My friend will be aware
of all this and will find a way for us to meet. He becomes more and more important to me the longer I am
here. I seem to have wakened from my stuporous state
to think only of him. Otherwise I am alone most of the
time in a darkened room with no one to talk to except
Sita.

People here are worried about the native troops turning on us. My friend has also warned me of this many
times. "The English pretend to be a friend," he says.
"But keep stealing from us."

From what I have seen at Lucknow and the way we
have treated the former King of Oudh, I must agree
with him. Broderick says that Lord Dalhousie would
ride rough-shod over every native in India if it would
put an extra hundred pounds in the Company coffers.
That doesn't seem to bother Broderick. But it does
bother me and I don't see how it can go on. I am so
glad Henry is gone. If he were here now, with the disquiet that is spreading across the cantonment, I should
be very worried for him. Many of the mothers here are
worried for their children. On the other hand, perhaps

my disquiet is simply my own loneliness. I don't know. I still am hoping to make a writer of myself and become independent, and to develop a stronger sense of the purpose God has for me.

May 5, 1857

I have seen my friend! With Sita's help and the intense heat of the mid day, he slipped into our bungalow without being seen by anyone. It was so good to be with him again, and meeting in my own house made what we are doing seem less guilty and wrong. I know that in the eyes of the Church, that is not so. But the Church seems so often to support the wrongs we commit against the Indians. It makes me ask myself if the Church's view of right and wrong is always the most true.

Without telling me anything definite, my friend says that there will be a great change in India very soon. He tells me that I need not worry because when the time comes, he and I shall be together and safe.

May 6, 1857

I have no idea what Broderick is doing, but he is closeted with General Wheeler for hours at a time. I have it in mind that Broderick is some sort of link between the civilian and the military branches of the Company in Oudh.

May 15, 1857

It has happened. The thing everyone has dreaded has happened. Broderick told me that General Wheeler has received word by telegraph that troops at Meerut have mutinied and have gone to take back Delhi. When Broderick came home for a very short nap in the horrible mid-day heat, he made the comment that at least the mutineers had turned away from us, not toward us.

Certainly, it will be terrible if there is war, but when I think of the injustices we have committed and the calm certainty of my friend, I begin to think it would be as well to get the war over with. We must lose, I think. My friend says so, and I believe in him more than all the generals of the East India Company. We have stolen such a vast amount from this country. We should have gone home long ago.

Thank God, Henry is in England, or soon will be. It seems less likely than ever that I shall ever see him again, but at least I can think of him being safe, well and happy. The Suttons will give him a better home than Broderick and I ever could have done."

By the time he reached this point in his Mother's text, Henry's eyes were filled with tears. He felt he had only come to know his mother through the pages of her journal. Now, he knew, her death was not far off. He wiped the moisture from his face and pressed on to the terrible, inevitable end.

May 16, 1857

"Broderick says there are rebel fires burning around the perimeter of the entrenchment that General Wheeler has set up around the barracks. He says that it will only be a few days before I shall have to leave our house and come to the comparative safety of the entrenchment.

May 21, 1857

Broderick and I had a terrible row when he came home and tried to force me to move into the entrenchment. He says that everyone is coming in, "who has any sense."

But I refused to leave our bungalow. Once I am in the entrenchment, I would be cut off from my friend. Whatever is coming, I prefer to meet it with him at my side. Broderick left in a fury, calling me filthy names as he went out the door.

My friend must fetch me soon if we are to stand together in the rising tide of war. If he doesn't, someone with more authority than Broderick will certainly force me into the entrenchment. It is only because I am so new here and know so few people that I have not had more pressure on me to join the others. Then, too, our bungalow is somewhat isolated. I hope these things will make it easier for me to leave Cawnpore with my friend, though where we shall go, I have no idea.

I can feel the tension in the air outside the bungalow. Like the horrible blasts of brown dust and heat that sweep over Cawnpore, the fear and the presence of danger is palpable outside. I cannot believe my friend has abandoned me. If he does not come soon, someone shall take me away, my own people or the mutineers. If that happens, I should never discover the special purpose George Sand says that every life has. This would be my greatest regret: that I had lived without knowing to what end, other than to give birth to my son.

Every day that passes makes it more difficult to justify

my presence here rather than in the entrenchment.

June 3, 1857

A neighbour who was gathering things from her house told me that many English corpses have been seen floating down the Ganges.

Later in the day, Broderick tried to drag me out of the house. He has no compunction about laying hands on me, but I struck him with heavy metal tray and he left, cursing me and calling me a fool.

Midnight June 3, 1857

I write in breathless haste. My friend is coming for me! He bids me be ready.

Thank God, we shall fly together. I have no idea what sort of life we shall have, but at least I shall be with a man who has real regard for me. If we are to die together, I am reconciled to it, knowing that my son is safe. If my friend had not warned me, I don't know if I should have let Henry go when the opportunity arose. I might have tried to keep him for another year or two. Another reason why I shall always be grateful to my friend. I

The text now continued in a different hand, which Henry recognized as his Uncle's.

April 1874

Dear Henry,
the above is the last entry your mother wrote. This diary was found in the *bibighar* after the slaughter, and sent

to me in Calcutta. I have tried to clean it up. It was badly stained when I received it. While the last entry seems to point to her not having been in the *bibighar* on July 15, 1857 when the massacre took place, a number of people saw her taken along with other women who were known to have died there. Given the condition of the diary and the undeniable fact that is was found in the *bibighar*, I am sorry to conclude that she was almost certainly present during the atrocities and was one of the victims.

I have not read the text of your mother's journal. After glancing at the first few entries, I felt it too private a thing, but nor would I take the decision to destroy it. These are your decisions. I felt it better to leave these ambiguities alone while you were growing up. For, even if your mother were not present in the *bibighar* it is hardly possible that she survived the Mutiny. We certainly should have heard from her.

I hope you will not hold it against me that I have reserved all this until now. Your recent letter made me feel that this was the time to send this. Believe me, I am faithfully your friend and uncle,

Henry Franklin

Chapter 18
The search for Jane Booth and where it led

"Great heaven, she is alive. She must be." Henry cried as he snapped the diary closed. The photograph of Harry Clayton's mother seemed to float before his eyes, as tangible as if it were printed on the blank wall of the room where his eyes rested.

"His mother and mine are one and the same, Harry Clayton must be my half brother. There is no other explanation. Umrao," he called. He threw open the door to the other room.

Dawn was just adding a ruddy tinge to the gray shadows. Umrao did not stir at his approach. He sat down next to her and gently shook her. She rolled over and continued sleeping heavily.

"Perhaps I should just go," Henry said to himself. But, no, he must leave a message for Sergeant Abdul in case he had not returned from Oxford by evening. He shook Umrao harder.

"Uhh," she said without opening her eyes.

"Umrao," he said shaking her again. Without opening her eyes, she reached up for him and put her arms around his neck.

"If you are going to wake me, you must kiss me, Henry. It is the only thing that will make waking possible."

He kissed her quickly, the first perfunctory kiss in their short history.

"Umrao, my mother is alive. I am certain of it."

"What?" she said sharply as she sat up. The sheet fell from her perfectly shaped breasts and then the long coil of her blue-black hair slipped across her and covered them once again.

"My mother is alive, Umrao. She did not die in the *bibighar*. I feel sure."

"Why? How can you know?"

Quickly, he told her of his first meeting with Harry Clayton and then the way the diary ended and his Uncle's note.

"So you see," he ended. "I must be on the first train to Oxford this morning. I must see Clayton and confirm my guess. Then, I'll find out exactly where she is right now. Explain all this to Sergeant Abdul when he comes later. He can make some excuse for your performance tonight, I am sure. I simply must do this without any delay."

"But you shall come back tonight?" she asked somewhat anxiously.

"Probably, but, Umrao, dear girl, surely you realize what this means to me? I must follow the trail until she is found."

"But what of our plans?"

"Let us discuss it when I return. Let me see if this bears on our plans at all."

"Well, certainly it will have some effect," Umrao said.

"If, as is unlikely, I cannot come back myself, I shall send a wire. I promise you shall hear from me, Umrao. Now, I must make myself ready to leave," and he rose, went into the other room and began to change his clothes. A moment later Umrao came through the door. She was completely naked and she came and put her arms around Henry's neck. Her skin was warm from the bedclothes and her scent stirred him.

"What if she does not like me?" she murmured.

"How could she not like you? I'm sorry dear

Umrao, there is no time for this, now. Do not worry. We shall be together, I promise."

"But already she separates us," Umrao said somewhat petulantly. "You are going to leave without giving me a true kiss," and she pulled herself against him and kissed him deeply. She felt him melt in her arms and start to kiss her back, then she pushed him away.

"There," she said, "you can think of me all the way to Oxford. I wonder how she will like your black skin and beard?"

"Oh, my goodness. I forgot about the dye."

"It will not wash off," Umrao said.

"Then I shall go this way."

"Just remember how you look. Though, I daresay, your countrymen will remind you."

He finished dressing and at the threshold, he turned to look at the naked woman who watched him,

"I shall be back by tonight," he said. "And if for any reason I am not, I shall wire. I promise," and he ran down the stairs.

Henry trembled with impatience as the train lumbered out of Paddington and progressed from gray city to the green hills. As the country passed his window, it was not the green hills of southern England he saw, but the dusty plains of Bengal.

Images of Lucknow overlapped his final days in Calcutta with his mother. Her lovely face lay superimposed on all the scenes in his mind. He thought, too, of Clayton, how they had met and become friends so quickly. His own brother! And he now had a step-father, as well, that shadowy figure in his mother's diary whom she had not even named. Were they still together, he wondered? They must be. The man must be Clayton's father. And no matter what had happened in the past, he and Umrao still had the British *Thug* and his band of killers to deal with—not to mention the police. Could his mother identify the killer she had seen, the British *Thug*?

Was there even a connection between the British *Thug* and the inscription that Sergeant Abdul was trying to translate? Would it explain anything? Where was she, now? When would she next be in England? His mind was in a feverish whirl by the time he arrived in Oxford.

If necessary, Henry thought, I shall go to Anatolia to see her.

The short ride from the station to Clayton's rooms seemed to take an eternity. He ran past the lodge before anyone could stop him and burst into the building where Clayton was resident. He charged up the stairs and hammered on his friend's door.

"Who the devil is it at this hour?" Clayton called.

"It's Booth. I must talk to you."

"Very well. Just a minute."

Clayton was still wrestling on his dressing gown, but as soon as the door swung open Henry burst out with no preamble, "Clayton I have made the most astonishing discovery. It closely concerns both of us."

He walked straight past Clayton into his chambers, went to the table and picked up the photograph of his mother and said, "This is my mother, Clayton, as well as yours."

"What? Are you mad?"

"No. I have finally finished reading her diary, written at the time of the Mutiny and before. Prior to meeting your father, she had another life with my father. He was a brute who treated her badly, an army man. That is why she let us think she was dead."

"How can you possibly be certain..." Clayton

said.

"I have read the whole story of her meeting and love affair with your father. I know where they met, how they met, everything."

Clayton was quiet for a moment. "Then, then, are you saying that we are brothers?" he finally said.

"Exactly," Henry answered, clapping his friend on the back. "Amazing isn't it."

Clayton fell down into his own chair. "I'm staggered," he finally answered. "I hardly know what to say. Are you quite sure?"

"Absolutely positive," Henry answered. "There is no other explanation that fits the facts I have come across. They admit of no other interpretation."

"I am dumbfounded," Clayton said.

"I can imagine," Henry said. "You are feeling as I did when I first saw her picture on your table."

"Something very like, I suppose," Clayton replied. He shook his head. "I can't understand why she never told me that I have a brother."

"I believe I understand," Henry said pulling up another chair. " She was a married English woman who ran off with a native practically on eve of the Mutiny. You know what a narrow society one finds at an Indian station. A short time later, my father, a British officer, was killed in one of the bloodiest battles of the war. Her actions might have been open to the worst possible construction, disloyalty that was morally if not legally, desertion. Given the mood that prevailed throughout the empire after Cawnpore, criminal charges might have been laid. People were mad with the desire for revenge. It was not something she wanted to talk about. And as far as you were concerned: why throw you off balance by divulging all this? She probably wanted to spare you any embarrassment. It was simpler and kinder to say nothing."

"I hardly know what to say," Clayton replied slowly. "Do you think she behaved dishonorably? I can hardly think that of her."

Henry shook his head decidedly. "When I remember how badly my father treated her and think of how lonely and miserable she must have been, I can forgive her anything. My father was a brute, I tell you. He hit her and called her names."

"How disgusting," Clayton said.

"It was disgusting," Henry agreed. "That's the only reason I can forgive her for letting me think she was dead all these years. She knew I was being taken care of, living with one of the best families in England. I know it was the hardest thing in the world for her to send me away from her. I know because I have read her pain written in her own words. And your father had a hand in that. He sensed what was brewing among the *sepoys* and warned her to send me away. His concern for her and her child was genuine and disinterested. I am glad if she has found happiness with your father."

"My mind is spinning, I am truly agog." Clayton said. "But if she were married to your father, how could she have been legally married to mine?"

"As far as I know, my father did die at Cawnpore. So say the army records. So she would have been free afterwards. But our mother left with your father just before the entrenchment was sealed off by General Wheeler. So when they were first together, their liaison would have been illegal and immoral, another reason she would not have talked about it. But, your father probably saved our mother's life."

"Incredible," Clayton said, " yet, perfectly plausible."

"It's more than plausible. It's fact. I have read

everything about it in her own words. I shall give you the diary so that you can read for yourself. I didn't bring it this morning. I've developed the habit of thinking of the diary as a dangerous thing to carry around."

"After what happened here," Clayton said, "I can understand why."

The slender dark skinned man stood up suddenly. "After what you have disclosed," Clayton said, "There is something you will be interested to know."

"Yes?" Henry said.

"Our mother is arriving in Oxford tonight."

"What?" Henry exclaimed springing to his feet as though galvanized.

"Yes. My father has some business interests in China which he is anxious to develop. They have talked for some time about settling there for an indefinite time. Apparently, they have decided that the time is now. They have come to say goodbye to me and—perhaps—our mother wanted to see you before she went so far from Europe."

"That's very kind of you, old man," Henry said. "But I don't' think our mother ever had any intention of seeing me again. I can understand it in a way, but it does hurt me, I confess. I suppose she thought it was better that she remain in the honoured grave of the Memorial Well where I thought she had been resting all these years."

"She is such a warmly emotional person," Clayton said. "I find it hard to imagine that she would abandon her son and leave me in ignorance of my brother."

"Well, I suppose now we can ask her," Henry said.

"What a surprise for her," Clayton replied. "Perhaps we should see her separately at first. So that she doesn't feel overwhelmed."

"I think that's an excellent idea," Henry said. "I am concerned about meeting her at all right now."

"Why? What do you mean?"

"Clayton, I have not given you my full confidence before now because it seemed unnecessary to discuss family matters with a school friend, but now I must tell you everything. Do sit down again."

"Is this going to be another shocking revelation?"

"I'm afraid so," Henry answered. "It will take some time to tell you."

So, beginning with his being sent down from Oxford, Henry explained his involvements in two murders, and his meeting with Abdul and Umrao. He also provided a few more details he had learned from the diary.

"The *Thuggee?*" Clayton exclaimed when Henry told him of Abdul's ideas about the murders. "A British Thug? I've never heard of such a thing."

"Yet it is revealed in our mother's diary. You can ask her about it, Clayton."

"Oh, I believe you. But it is extraordinary. Like everyone else, I assumed that Major General Sleeman had wiped them out."

"I'm afraid not."

"And you are afraid that there might be further danger from them?"

Henry nodded grimly.

"We must tell our mother and my father at the first opportunity," Clayton said.

"Do you think so?" Henry asked. "I do not know what our mother is really like now, nor do I know your father."

"Oh, he is equal to anything," Clayton said. "Our mother will be all right as well, I believe. From what I have observed, she is not a fearful woman."

"From her diary, I think you are right. But I don't really know her. It's very odd, all this. I used to think of her with the memories of a child. Then I got to know her in the pages of her diary. Meeting the living woman will be strange. Does she still look like this photograph?"

"The last time I saw her. The photograph is only a year old."

"Really?"

Clayton nodded affirmatively. "A present for my last birthday. Don't worry, old man," Clayton said watching Henry look at the photograph with a mingled expression of fear and excitement. "It will be all right. Remember, If there is trouble ahead, we'll meet it together. I have spent enough time in the jungle that I have come to regard danger as the savoury seasoning of life." Clayton held out his hand.

"Thank you, Clayton. You are a stout fellow. Though, I don't like to draw others into my trouble." Henry answered shaking hands heartily with his newly found brother.

"I think you can hardly own it all as yours, alone, old man," Clayton replied.

"Perhaps, not," Henry said. "When is her train due?"

"Six-ten."

"And they're probably not even finished serving breakfast in the dining room yet," Henry said. "It's going to be a long day."

"I have a lecture I must attend," Clayton said. "I'm sorry, but it's quite important."

"I understand. I show up here, first thing in the morning and disrupt your entire life. Of course, you must carry on with whatever you need to do. I shall look after myself. I'll go out so you can get dressed without my being in your way. Probably better for the scout not to see me, in any case."

They shook hands at the door once again and Clayton managed to find an extra key for Henry.

"Thanks awfully," Henry said. "I'll see you later."

"Do be careful, Booth—ah, Henry. If those *Thugs* are still around..."

"Quite. I shall be watchful and I do have my stick with me," and he turned and started down the stairs.

The rest of the day had, for Henry, a strange, dream-like quality, though he did not forget to send the promised wire to Umrao from the station. He sent it care of the owner of the opium den so it would be delivered there. The two *lascars* were rough characters but had given no cause for anxiety.

"Great good fortune," he wrote. "Mother due in Oxford this evening. Must be here to greet her. I adore you. Wire after we meet. Be careful. Henry."

After that, as he wandered around the city, he could hardly think of anything but his coming interview with his Mother.

Memories of Lucknow once more took possession of him as he sat on benches along the Isis or next to the public walks. There were moments when he could swear to faint scents of jasmine in the air. But mostly, he thought of her, burying his face in her beautiful golden hair, feeling her strong, finely made hand in his and the confidence it had given him as a child.

He also felt again something long forgotten: the pain of their parting in Calcutta, and his agony when news of the *bibighar* massacre reached England. These dark storms of childhood passed over him swiftly now like the shadows of fast-moving clouds, leaving him unscathed, exciting nothing more than the anticipation of seeing her again. It was strange to feel excitement rather than any of the old pain these memories had evoked in years past. One part of him wondered how his adult self would see her, another felt such joy that it was difficult to sit still at times; yet another felt utter disbelief that he was actually going to be with her in a matter of hours. Not once in all those hours did it seriously occur to him that he might be wrong about the true identity of "Mrs. Clayton." He especially wanted to tell her about Umrao. He hoped that she would see his choice as the strongest possible approval of her own marriage to an Asian. He hoped it would demonstrate that he felt no blame or bitterness about her choice of Clayton's father, a native. He would not have to tell her about the complication of his former betrothal to Mary, since she knew nothing of it.

"After all, " Henry thought, "Mary chose someone else when trouble came to me. Perhaps Mary and Smythe-White would go to India and be missionaries, as Mary had wanted to be.

He and Umrao would go to Calcutta, work with his Uncle Henry and make money for their future together. His Uncle was a pleasant, good natured man, whom Henry knew from many letters and the contact in childhood. He had never married in spite of the good position he had attained and Henry now wondered if he had a liason with a native girl. He could picture his uncle quite clearly, thanks to a photograph that was only five years old. But when he tried to retrieve a semblance of Calcutta from his memory he could only draw from the few days he'd spent there with his mother before he left. He had a dim recollection of the walled villas and the grandeur of the Governor General's Palace, but his clearest memory was of the horse races in front of Fort William, when his uncle had picked him up and put him on an elegant dappled Arabian which he owned and which had won the day's races. The narrow face and arching neck of the noble creature was clearer to him than anything else in the city of palaces.

In one corner of his mind, Henry knew that he was dreaming of a future that would never come to pass if he did not clear himself and Umrao from the dangers that hovered around them. But the sun was warm, the air fresh and in his mind, he leapt over the dangers facing him as easily as a new Oxford man discounted the dangers of drifting through the term in a punt.

"Besides," he told himself, "has not my mother returned from the grave? If that miracle can occur, why not others? She has seen this English *Thug* face to face, perhaps she can tell us something about him that will enable the authorities to catch him. Once he was in custody, would not the other *Thugs* admit their part in the crimes he had been blamed for? They had certainly given evidence against one another when Major General Sleeman caught the leaders back in the forties."

In the light of his coming reunion, it seemed not too far-fetched a hope. Who could tell what would come out of this meeting? Perhaps, like Alexander cutting the Gordion Knot, Jane Booth's knowledge of the past would slice through his present perplexities in a single stroke. But then a truly dreadful thought fell on Henry like a blow: Would not his mother's knowledge make it very dangerous for her to be in England? If the *Thugs* became aware of her presence, they would certainly try to kill her. She might be the only witness to a murder committed by the English *Thug*. She knew what he looked like. In a court of law, her testimony would put the man's head in a halter! Surely, the English *Thug* would spare no trouble to eliminate her, even if their meeting was many years ago. That must be the motive for the death of the college president and Charles Sutton. Anyone who read Jane Booth's revelations would be pursued and killed. Did she have any inkling that the man was in England? Probably not. He and Clayton and Clayton's father would have to be her protectors and shield her from these murderous devils. What a terrible cloud for her to be under! And just at the time when mother and son were to be reunited. The thought catapulted him into action and he began to jog back to Clayton's rooms.

"If I had been less excited about seeing her, I should have realized the danger for her right away," he thought as he ran. "Perhaps Clayton can wire her and tell her not to come. She can't possibly know that there are *Thugs* here, killers who know about and are interested in her diary—in what she saw all those years ago."

Henry slipped into the New Building and leapt up the stairs two at a time. If he were seen on college grounds, the authorities might be called, but no one accosted him. He knocked and then let himself in with the key Clayton had given him. The rooms were empty. Henry closed the door quickly and bolted it. The *Thugs* had been here before, seeking the diary. They knew of the place, so he and Clayton would have to be extremely careful. There was no way their mother could come to these rooms, even if they hid her from the scouts.

Now, there was nothing to do but wait in the hot, south-facing rooms just beneath the leads.

He paced, he read, he looked at his mother's photograph to his heart's content and finally there was the rattle of a key in the door.

"Clayton?" Henry called. "Wait. It's bolted. Clayton? Is it you?"

There was no answer. The silence was deep and sinister. With each passing moment it became more sinister. Who but the *Thugs* would have tried the door? There was nothing cheerful or pleasant about the afternoon sun, now. Henry's heart hammered against his ribs.

"If Clayton comes now," he thought, "they may take him completely off his guard and break his neck. I must go out and take my chances. I have better odds with my single-stick than Clayton will, in any case. I hope that my call frightened them off."

He picked up the ironwood shaft and snapped the bolt back. He put the stick through the doorway first, bracing himself for the tug of a noose, but none came. Slowly he looked out onto the landing. It was empty.

"We must make certain we are not followed from this place," Henry muttered.

He leaned over the railing and listened in the stairwell. All was quiet. He went back inside, bolted the door and passed the afternoon pacing like a caged animal, wondering why, in heaven's name, he had not asked Clayton what time his lecture was over?

The rooms were at their hottest, the day verging on the beginning of evening when the bells of Magdelan Tower tolled five o'clock. Henry heard steps on the stairs and a moment later a key in the lock.

"Clayton?"

Henry heard the door tried as someone pushed against the bolt after turning the key.

"What the deuce" he heard Clayton say in the hall.

"Just a minute, Clayton," Henry called and stepped forward to pull back the bolt.

"What in the world is going on?"

"I just had another brush with the *Thugs*."

"They came here, again?"

"I'm afraid so, Clayton. I've put you in danger."

"Well, if it has to do with our mother, it is part of both our histories."

"Where are we going to meet her?" Henry asked.

"I am to wait here until she sends for me. She was emphatic about not coming to the rail station."

"Perhaps she, too, is alarmed about something," Henry said, " But I don't know how she could know that the *Thugs* are here."

"You are getting quite wrought up, old man, do try to relax. She was only thinking of me standing around at the station, I'm sure."

"I know. You're quite right. But it's devilishly difficult to feel easy under the circumstance."

"I can barely imagine what you are feeling. If I hadn't seen her for thirteen years and thought her dead...Yes, it must be very hard. It's been three years since the last time I saw her in Calcutta, and that seems long ago."

"So all of you must be great travellers," Henry said. "It sounds as if you are continually coming and going from different continents, not just different countries."

"I suppose it is a bit of an unusual way to live. But I wouldn't want to leave India, except to come here, of course. Their lives are centered around Istanbul, though my father is often in Calcutta. It is the nature of his business, I suppose, that makes him so peripatetic. At any time he might hear of a remarkable antiquity that he can get his hands on—and off he must go."

"It must be rather exciting. Rather like a perpetual treasure hunt."

"I wouldn't like it," Clayton said. "I like to immerse myself in something, not dart about as my father has to do."

"I suppose it is entirely a matter of temperament," Henry said. "Oh, heavens," he said pulling out his watch. "Another three quarters of an hour before her train gets in."

"And that means it could be another hour or two before I hear from her," Clayton said.

"I shall be mad by then," Henry said rubbing the back of his neck. "You mustn't..."

A soft knock on the door interrupted him. The two men looked at each other.

"It doesn't sound like the scout's knock," Harry said in a whisper.

"We'll, we've got to look. It could be anyone. A messenger even, telling you where to meet our mother," Henry replied as he picked up his stick and stood to one side of the door.

"You open it," he whispered. "If it's a foe he will soon regret his trespass."

But as the door swung open Harry Clayton cried out excitedly, "Narinder!" and threw himself into the arms of a slender, elderly yellow-skinned man with a short white beard.

Henry watched as the two greeted each other with a great show of affection. The old man wore a sort of robe that left one shoulder exposed. His face was very seamed from the elements and his movements were absolutely noiseless. But the most arresting thing about the old man were his eyes which were literally glowing with love as he looked at Harry. Henry felt the man's gentle magnetism, as well.

"Narinderji, this, this is my brother, Henry Booth. Henry, this is my teacher and friend, he is a renunciate of the lineage of the great Ramakrishna. He returned with my father from one of his journeys. I did not know he would come to England. What a wonderful surprise."

The slender, elderly man made a graceful slight bow to Henry with his hands pressed together in front of him. Henry tried to respond in kind.

"How do you do?" he said. Henry observed that the old man showed no surprise at the word "brother."

"Your mother is waiting," the old man said. "And there are men outside watching this place with evil intentions in their thoughts."

"How do you know?" Henry asked.

"I saw them. Even in their western clothes, they cannot hide the fact that they are *Thugs*. I remember when the devotees of *Bhowanee* haunted the lonely roads and jungle paths all the way up to the high passes of Sikkim and Bhutan. As soon as I saw the two men waiting below, I knew they carried the *rumal*."

Something in the man's voice made the *Thuggee* seem more present and threatening than ever. Henry felt a shudder of fear pass through him.

"What shall we do?" Henry asked. "We mustn't endanger our mother."

"How can he be so sure?" Henry wondered silently.

"Both men are very stupid," the old man said as if in answer to Henry's thoughts. "It is not difficult to cloud the vision of such dull minds. Shall we go?"

Henry's heart leapt at the thought of seeing his mother so soon. But, in fact, it was not as soon as he anticipated. The three walked out of Oxford on the Banbury Road and soon left the city behind. The old man led them toward the village of Woodstock, past the gates of Blenheim Palace and strode into the fading light ahead as if he had lived in Oxfordshire for years.

Henry thought of what the old man had said about the lonely roads of India and the *Thuggee*, but they went on without incident. They walked through several villages, passed between ancient hedgerows and still they went on. It became pitch dark all around them. It wasn't long before Henry was lost among the twisting country lanes that the old man followed so confidently. Finally, they turned into a very narrow lane that was little more than a path and abruptly they were facing the yellow windows of a low, brightly lit, thatched cottage.

Henry's heart began beating like a steam hammer. When he spoke, there was a tremor in his voice:

"Ah, Harry, don't you think I should wait out here while you go in and speak to Mother. Tell her that I have come with you."

"It is not necessary," the old man said.

"Still," Henry answered, "I should feel better." Harry clapped him on the shoulder.

"I'll tell her, Henry."

"Thank you," he answered as the two men opened the door and Harry stepped inside, leaving Henry by himself. There was a dull click as the old door shut on Henry and he found himself alone in the soft air of the early autumn night. It had been raining lightly while they walked and the air was now very fresh, redolent with the smells of earth and fallen leaves. A large, yellow moon had risen. Henry could see the ivy growing up the side of the building in front of him, the edges of the leaves traced by the moon. He began to imagine the scene inside, his mother reacting to Harry's revelation of his presence.

Suddenly, he felt a horrible pain in his throat as life was tugged out of his body. He got his hands inside the noose but it tightened inexorably. Life began to slip away from him and everything dissolved into darkness.

At first, it seemed that everything had been extinguished by oblivion, but then she emerged from the utter darkness. First, he saw her golden hair, catching points of light in the way that it always had. Then, he saw the light in her eyes, a light of tenderness that went straight to his heart, and for a moment he was once again walking with her through the groves and meadows of his infancy. The smell of jasmine seemed to pervade the moment. An intensely bright Asian moon illuminated her face. A moment later it was a kerosene lantern that was being held near him.

"Mother?" he said, hoarsely. "Is it really you? Or am I dead?"

He felt himself clasped to her warm bosom and heard her say, "No, my sweetheart. You are not dead. I am with you." And he felt a light kiss on his forehead.

As his eyes came into focus he could see that she was kneeling beside a chaise on which he was lying. His collar had been loosened. The slightest movement of his head sent a stab of pain through his neck.

"Oh," he cried. "Mother?" he said, hoarsely. "I can hardly believe you are here with me."

"I am here, my dear," he heard her say.

"But they know where we are, where you are." Henry said, sitting up in spite of the pain.

"He did know," Narinder said. "But he no longer remembers anything. He is having a pleasant walk in the country. That is all he will remember when he returns to his friends."

"Are you certain?" Henry asked looking up at the elderly Hindu. "In spite of what you said earlier, he followed us."

"I don't think so, Mr. Booth. I believe he was

already waiting here."

"Then my mother is not safe at all. We must move her."

"Thank you, dear Henry. But you know nothing about my errand here, what I must do."

"No. I do not. But you must not be put at risk, especially if I am the one who has brought the danger to you."

"But you aren't, Henry. These *Thugs* have been following us for years."

"What?"

"Yes. My husband has something they want. It makes the *Thugs* follow us but afraid to kill us before they know where it can be found."

"Mother!" Henry exclaimed."How can you speak so casually about being killed when I have just found you again?"

"Ignoring the truth of our situation will not im-prove it," she said. "I know what these men want and I have come to England to get it for my husband."

"Can't we contact the police?" Henry asked. "I can't, but..."

"No," she said sharply. "I can have nothing to do with the British authorities. It is British greed that has put us all in the situation where we find ourselves."

"I don't understand," Henry said.

"Henry, there is a great deal you don't know about me," his mother said.

"I read your diary," he said, studying her face for the first time. Her cheeks were thinner, and there was sadness in her eyes. It was as if the youthful woman of his childhood had been refined by privation.

"Mother, there is so much for us to say."

"Perhaps, Henry. But we cannot change the past and that diary was written a long time ago and contains only a small part of the truth," she answered. Then, very abruptly, she asked, "Where is the journal now?"

Henry could not mistake the eagerness in her voice.

"How did it come to be found in the *bibighar*?" he asked.

"This is not the time or place for those questions," she answered in a tone he had never before heard. There was no tenderness in it. It was a rebuke from one adult to another and it shocked him inexpressibly, though he knew she was right in her assessment of their situation.

"We should leave this place, now," Narinder put in. "We don't know how many *Thugs* there are. One or two would not attack us, but in this lonely spot, at night. It is their chosen venue for murder."

"I shall be safe until they get what they want from me," Jane said, "But the rest of you are at risk. They may use the threat of your deaths to learn what they want to know from me."

Jane Booth bit her lips with vexation. For a moment, she looked to her son like an old woman, older than she was. He suddenly glimpsed her troubled life during the many years that had passed. The brash, unhappy young woman who had "thrown the book into the fire" had been scorched by the flames. She had evaded the terrible death in the *bibighar*, but there was some sense in which Jane Booth had died. There was a curious foreign quality about her now, he realized.

She wore an Indian shawl over her shoulders in the style of native women and her head was covered with a scarf, like a Moslem. His vision of her shining hair must have been seen only in his own mind. He felt a sudden gulf between them, almost as deep as the terrible well in Cawnpore and for an instant he felt a wave of sadness sweep over him. He didn't know what to do to cross all the lost years, so instead, he concentrated on the present.

"Mother," Henry said, "Would it not be wise to leave England immediately, at least for now? Don't you agree, Harry?"

"There is something I must do first," she answered. "And I shall not have another opportunity. My husband and I are going to China, Henry. You and I were fortunate to become acquainted with each other, now. For I am quite certain we shall not meet again. Once I leave England this time, I shall never come here again. I would never have come now if it were not to help my husband rid us of the *Thugs*."

There was a bitter tone in her words.

"Not even to see me, again?" he asked.

She reached out and touched his face, tenderly.

"You were once my greatest, my only, treasure, Henry. I know that is what you remember and perhaps long for even now. But I tore myself away from you and sent you to this cruel island to become an Englishman, a species I no longer like or respect. The relationship you crave is just a child's dream. You can no longer be my whole world or I yours. The shadows of an empire separate us now. "

"No they don't, Mother! Please don't speak so. I have not yet even told you about the woman I am going to marry. She is Indian."

"Indian? You are going to marry a native?"

"Yes. She is an extraordinary woman, a musician and dancer. You met her when she was a child at the house of Akhtar Devi."

Suddenly all the colour drained out of his mothers's face. "You will marry a Lucknow courtesan?" she said.

"Yes. I know all about it..."

"You know nothing," Jane's voice cracked like the blow of a whip. "Such a choice will bring you many of the same difficulties I have suffered. What happened to Charles Sutton's little girl?"

"Mary prefers another man."

"So you will leap into the bed of a courtesan and bring a lifetime of trouble on yourself. You grieve me, Henry."

"I thought you would realize that I am not an English bigot and be glad."

"I am glad you are not a bigot, Henry. But there is so much that you don't yet know."

"Then tell me. So I can know you and feel closer to you."

"We must leave for London, now" she said, suddenly turning away. "Narinder's hypnosis won't last forever and the man may find his way back here. But I am afraid to take the train I'm sure they will be watching at the station."

Henry suddenly looked away. Some new thought had just entered his mind.

"Clayton, can you handle a scull?" He asked.

"I've done a little training. I'm sure I am not in your league."

"That doesn't matter. Mother, you'll leave Oxford by water. I know where we can find good boats and oars. Can you swim, Mother?"

"A little."

"Narinder?"

"I grew up on the lakes of Kashmir."

"Then, that is how we shall go."

"All the way to London?" Jane Booth asked.

"They would never expect it," Henry said. "The

river is little used for speedy travel since the railways were built. And we will stress urgency in the message we will send to the *Thuggee*."

"Message?" Harry broke in.

"Narinder will go to the train station and buy tickets. He will ask how long the trip is and when he hears it is short, he will be relieved and say, 'Thank heavens, my mistress must get to London as quickly as possible.' The *Thugs* will overhear this. There are many inns along the water. Traveling by water also prevents anyone finding us at the railway station in London. Paddington is where I was first attacked by the *Thugs*. Where is it you have to go in London, Mother? And why would the *Thugs* attack you now, when you say you have been safe from them for years?"

"We draw near to what they seek. I think your idea of traveling by water is a good one but how do we do it?"

"You must tell me your destination, first. Then I can tell you how we shall get there."

" I must go to "Glyn, Mills, Currie & Co, in Lombard Street," she answered.

"My father's London bankers," Harry said.

"Yes, Harry." Jane answered. "I must retrieve something there and take it away with me. An old trunk containing a valuable antiquity, The Glass Tiger of Lucknow."

"I've never heard of it," Henry said.

"Few have. It was a gift to Asfad ad Dauli from the Chinese Emperor and was stolen by the British from the Bara Imambara in Lucknow when the British sacked the city after the siege of Lucknow was finally lifted."

"This is what the *Thugs* want?"

She nodded. "Their lust for it has kept me and

my husband alive. As long as the *Thuggee* believed we might lead them to it, they postponed our murder. But, enough ancient history. Where are the boats? And how do we get to them?"

"So that is why they have not killed you even though you saw the face of their leader in Ahktar Devi's house?" Henry asked.

She looked away from her son's searching gaze and nodded."Where must we go to board the boats?" she asked again.

"Folly's Bridge," Henry answered. "We have to go back to Oxford."

"Then I shall pack and we shall leave."

"It would be better to go at first light," Henry said.

"Very well. Then I will go to bed. Narinder will take care of you both."

Henry was tempted to solicit a further interview with his mother but he could see how fatigued she was. There would be time on the river. He could ask her all the questions he desired.

"Clayton, I think we should take turns watching tonight," Henry said after their mother left the room.

"I agree. Narinder will take a watch, too."

"Then, I guess we can go to bed. I will take the first watch," Henry said.

"Are you sure? You were pretty shaken up before."

"Really, I couldn't sleep, just now. Leave me to watch," Henry said. Leave me to myself and my own thoughts, be a good chap."

"Call me in three hours, then."

Chapter 19
The River

The night passed uneventfully. Naridinder was the only one awake at six, the hour when they had agreed to leave. Both the young men overslept. Narinder woke everyone. All of Mrs. Clayton's things were packed and efficiently piled near the front door, waiting to be loaded into the carriage, which Narinder, seemingly omnipresent and omniscient when it came to practical details, was about to do while the others ate the breakfast of porridge, toast and tea which he had waiting for them. Henry looked appraisingly at his mother's things and pronounced,

"We're going to need something rather more than a scull for all this and ourselves."

"A punt?" Harry suggested.

"No. This will be a long trip and we should have a proper boat. I'm pretty certain there will be one we can rent near the Bridge. Salter's may have something. There may be someone about the boathouse whom I can rouse. They know me well."

"How shall we keep the *Thugs* from following us onto the river?" Harry asked.

"I'm afraid we shall have to rely on the ever-resourceful Narinder for that. Remember the message we will send them? I'm certain the *Thugs* will be watching there. Narinder will speak his part. He will be told that it is sixty-three miles. He will breathe a great sigh of relief and say he is glad it is so close, that it is of the last importance for his mistress to reach London as soon as possible. Mother will stay here while you and I, Harry, shall go to Folly Bridge and find a suitable boat. Then we shall push off as if we were going on an excursion on the river and meet Mother's carriage, driven hell for leather by Narinder to a spot just past Iffley lock. By the time we meet you, Mother, we shall be too far from the bridge for the *Thugs* to get another boat and catch us up. First, they will be busy watching Harry and I and the train station. They can't have brought an army down here. They only have so many men to watch us."

"It worries me to put you boys in danger," Jane said.

"But clearly, we are all in danger as long as you and the *Thugs* are in England," Henry said. "The best thing is to finish your errand as swiftly as possible while we try to think of some way to get the authorities to listen to us."

Mrs. Clayton looked very ill at ease as she toyed with a buttered scone. "I haven't had one of these in an age and now my stomach is in such knots, I can't eat."

"Don't worry, Mother," Henry said, taking her hand. "We shall be all right, shan't we, Harry."

"I've no doubt that in broad daylight we would best these blackguards," Harry said.

"I hope you are right," Mrs. Clayton said. "I hope there are not more than a couple of *Thugs*."

"Even if they had ten men on the river," Henry said, " with a short head start we are sure to leave them far behind. The subcontinent isn't known for racing oarsmen, is it?"

"Not really. The crocodiles, the current and the sandbars tend to mitigate against it on the larger rivers like the Ganges."

"There you are, then. Once we put a couple of locks between us, we have more than a fighting chance.

It will be impossible to catch us."

"On the other hand," Harry said, "if they do get on to us at any point we should be easy prey in any one of the thirty-odd locks between Oxford and London. I have a horror of sitting immobile in the lock as the water rises or falls and these villains close around us."

"True, but they would have to find us alone, which isn't likely on the river at this time of year. And their particular method of dispatching—killing—isn't really well suited to boats, except perhaps at night."

"What shall we do at night?" Harry pressed. "We can't have Mother sleeping in a hedgerow."

"I have slept rough many times," Mrs. Clayton put in. "I am not a porcelain doll."

"There is a multitude of decent inns all along the river between Oxford and London, Mother," Henry said. "We shall have our choice of ambience and cuisine. None of us shall sleep rough."

"You make it sound like an excursion," Mrs. Clayton said.

"I'd like it to be for your sake, Mother," Henry replied.

"The only thing that bothers me about your plan is that it relies entirely on stealth," Harry said as he was about to take a bite out of his third kipper. "If they see us once, the hue and cry shall be raised and we could be a long way from our destination."

"But we can always get a train," Henry countered. "There are many stations where we could leave the river and send the boat back to Salter's on the train."

His salient objections voiced, Harry fell silent.

"Well?" Henry pressed.

"Yes, well, I suppose you have won the debate. It is just the thought of sitting in a lock waiting for the water to rise or fall while these devils creep around the lock and ambush us."

"If we take a train we would be even easier to get at, and we know they will be looking for us on the train."

"Very well, then let's go to Salter's and get our boat."

"What do you say, Mother?" Henry asked, "river or rail?"

"I think what you've said is sound, Henry. It has been so long since I was here, everything seems very strange."

"Of course it does. Harry remarks on it often, don't you?"

"Well, the green and the wet is rather a change from the baked plains around Calcutta. The only green one sees there is where it has been planted and irrigated. And in really hot weather every leaf turns to leather, thirsty for the monsoon."

"I should like to see Calcutta again, the Chowringchee and palace," Mrs. Clayton said wistfully. "It has been many years and—I suppose one always longs for the place where one was young and carefree."

There was an awkward silence for a few moments and then Henry rose.

"Excuse me, but I think we should get under way. I shall just go to the kitchen and have a word with Narimder."

As the two young men left the house in another quarter hour Henry said, "I hope that hypnosis of Narinder's doesn't fail. What if those blackguards come back here while we are gone?"

"I don't think you need to worry," Harry replied. "I have seen surgery performed on men Narinder has hypnotized."

"One never sees that in England anymore," Henry said. "Chloroform is so much easier."

"But when one doesn't have chloroform, hypnosis is preferable to pain. Narinder is a good hypnotist. I give you my word. The man will not remember where he went on his walk last night."

"Mother's life will depend on it."

"Yes, I realize. I still say, trust to Narinder."

The two young men met on the front walk. The morning was scrubbed fresh from the rain the night before, a crisp, but not uncomfortable wind was blowing as they set off to walk back into town. They walked in silence for some time. Until Harry said, "It is lovely, here."

"Oxford is putting you under its spell," Henry said smiling. "Really, most of the Thames valley is picturesque."

As if to support Henry's assertion, when they left Salter's boat house with a sturdy broad beamed boat, the sun broke through the clouds and lit the water behind them with a beautiful glow. Under Henry's expert strokes, the boat glided quickly forward and Folly Bridge slipped away, it's heavy, bulky form soon fading into shadows. Along one side of the water some of the white painted college barges were moored, looking like gilded cakes in the reflected sun. The trees still retained some of their leaves, half green, half gold, an interesting lace trimming the horizon.

"This is beautiful," Harry said appreciatively. "I don't believe I have ever been here before. Not at this hour in any case."

"Well," Henry replied, "I believe you shall see many such sights on our journey, though I confess, this stretch is exceptionally pretty. I will feel much better when we meet Mother and Narinder."

"Really, old man," Harry said, "Don't worry about her so much. She is a very resourceful woman. I have seen her in tight places."

"Really? Like what? I am quite jealous that you know so much more about her than I."

"Well, I remember one evening we were returing from the bazar in Istanbul. I was about seven. A man started to follow us and some of the lanes we had to travel down were quite empty. But Mother was quite unflappable. She didn't lose her head for a moment. In fact, she actually let the man draw closer to us. When he got right behind us, I was expecting anything. I felt quite frightened. Anything can happen in those dark, narrow streets—but Mother suddenly let go my hand, wheeled around and threw the cayenne pepper she had just bought into the man's face. We left him there, staggering around the lane, quite blinded. And she did it in cold blood, didn't hesitate or become afraid for a moment that I could see."

There was a long pause in their conversation as Henry pulled even harder on the oars. Finally he said, "How fortunate you are Harry to have had her with you all these years."

"Of course, I never thought about it. But I can certainly see it from your point of view. Oh, look, there's the carriage with Narinder in the box."

"Then it looks like all is well."

"We've still got a hundred and twelve miles to go before I will think we are all in the clear," Harry said. "And Henry, I will try to give you some time for *tête à têtes* with Mother. Keep out of your way—that sort of thing. So you can get to know her better."

Henry smiled at his half brother's earnest face.

"You are a good chap, Harry," Henry said as he

applied himself to finding a good place to land and load the boat.

Moments later, Narinder and Mrs. Clayton stepped out from behind a tree, appearing as if by magic. The old man expertly helped Henry moor the boat. Mrs. Clayton carried luggage closer while the two men prepared the boat.

"There were two *Thugs* at the train station," Narinder told Henry.

"You're sure?"

"There are not that many Indians in Oxford. And these two looked like bad men. I made sure they heard me say we would leave on the six oh five tonight to Paddington."

"And no one followed you here?" Harry asked.

"No sir. I am certain. No one. Now, you want me to drive back to the house and act as if we are going to leave tonight. I shall pile portmanteaux and chests on the carriage and drive to the station, load the baggage and get on the train. Where shall I meet you in London?"

"Do you know London, Narinder?" Henry asked.

"From many years ago when I was a student."

"Then go to the India Office in Whitehall and find a friend of mine. His name is George. He wears skirts, kilts, like a Scotsman. I shall make sure he knows where we are."

"Good," Narinder said.

"You've quite a talent for this sort of thing, don't you, Henry?" Harry said.

"Practice makes perfect, Harry. I am almost getting used to being pursued."

"Yes, I suppose so. Mother, mind the mud. I couldn't find a dryer place."

"It is a river bank, Henry," Mrs. Clayton replied.

"I shan't melt." And she gathered her skirts around her and took a long stride into the boat from the muddy bank. Henry watched and found her very graceful in the awkward place.

The boxes soon followed and Narinder drove rapidly away, realizing the carriage would attract attention of anyone nearby. A few moments later they were gliding over the bright water which mirrored the sky.

"Don't let Henry do all the rowing, Harry," his mother said.

Harry chuckled.

"He could row to London and back without getting tired, Mother. I would be exhausted in a couple of miles. He is a leading member of the Magdelan rowing team."

"You are an athlete, like your father, Henry."

"I suppose I am."

"He was a famous heavy game shot when I first came out and could stay on horseback all day without tiring. At least, he could when I met him."

It was the first reference to the past that Henry had heard her make. There was so much he wanted to know about that time yet, he felt diffident about asking questions of the handsome stranger who sat opposite him in the boat. Henry thought Mrs. Clayton still far more than merely pretty. She must have been a great beauty when she was young, he thought.

"Henry," Mrs. Clayton said, "what are you thinking of? If you were not my own son, I should say you were ogling me."

Henry felt his face turn beet red. "I was, Mother, I mean, I was just thinking how beautiful you still are."

She laughed and it was a sound he remembered. The last time he heard it, they had been playing on the Residency Hill in Lucknow. The clear, bright tone of her laughter also made him think of Umrao's voice, which was huskier and darker but just as ringing and clear. They had been reunited less than twenty-four hours! With every pull on the oars, Henry could feel the soreness in his neck loosening where the *Thug* had throttled him.

"It is a very long time since a handsome young man has rowed me in a boat and paid me compliments," Mrs. Clayton said. " I very much like that it is you, my own son. And that you are— as you are. I had always hoped you would be when you were little—and not like your father."

"And what about Harry's father?" Henry asked. "How do you get on together?"

Mrs. Clayton's face became still and cold, a mask to hide feelings.

"What an idiot I am," Henry thought to himself. "Utterly lacking in tact."

She said nothing but dipped her hand in the water as the boat glided along the river. Henry thought each moment that she would speak, but she did not. She seemed literally lost in her own reflections, peering into the water. Henry thought the pensive mood suited her and made her seem even more beautiful. He wondered what she was feeling. Was she disappointed with her life? What had happened in the *bibighar*? Had she been present when the *untouchable* Hindus hacked the other women and children to pieces—and if so, how had she escaped? Like the water flowing by, his thoughts slipped through his mind without offering any point of purchase, any place to grab hold and turn the endless flow into words that he could say to her. He felt a great deal, but didn't know what it was. And he could not bring himself to say a word about his perplexity to Mrs. Clayton. He felt shy with her, and he found that strange.

"Umrao could explain what I am feeling," he thought. "I wish she were here. I hope she is safe and well."

That night they stopped at the little town of Abingdon, some seven and a half miles from Oxford. In his own mind, Henry favoured it because the town lay at the Thames' intersection with the River Ock. He could not help but think about routes of escape if they should find themselves pursued.

The Crown and Thistle was a pleasant house which, like the town, had no special characteristic other than cleanliness and comfort. They ended the day dining in Mrs. Clayton's room on some fresh caught barbel, local ale and some locally grown marrows. They were all hungry from being out on the water all day.

"Mother, you should wear a hat with a broad brim to keep the sun from your face," Henry said.

"It is of no consequence, Henry. Don't you see how brown I am? Harry and I are used to a much hotter sun than an English one. Aren't we, Harry?"

Henry watched his brother's dark eyes soften with affection as their mother addressed him.

"It is much hotter and brighter in India and even in Istanbul," he replied.

"But you are not brown, Mother. Is she Henry?"

"He's right Mother, you are still a peaches and cream complexioned Englishwoman."

She reached out across the table and took each man's hand and pressed them affectionately.

"I have such gallant sons," she said smiling.

"Truthful sons, Mother," Harry said.

"Well said, Harry," Henry replied as he smothered a yawn "But I must row tomorrow and need my sleep."

"Then, away with you, both," Mrs. Clayton said.

To Henry, she sounded almost lighthearted. He gave thanks that night for a pleasant and uneventful beginning to their journey. Their rooms were on the second floor and he had made his mother bolt her door while he and Harry stood outside to hear the metal click and know she was secure, even though she insisted she was safe until the *Thugs* got what they wanted.

Henry and Harry had a room on either side of hers. As Henry turned toward his own door Harry spoke to him:

"A good start, old man. If we go on as we have started, we shall have a pleasant excursion."

"I want at least to double our distance tomorrow," Henry answered. "But we don't seem to have any *Thugs* around us. That makes it a very good start. Narinder is certainly a brick. He carried off his part today, superbly."

"He always does," Harry said.

"Well, good night, Harry."

"Good night, old man."

As Henry lay in bed listening to the mice in the thatch of the old building, he found it hard to believe that he had spent the day in his mother's company. He had so often thought of such a day, believing it could never be, that it now seemed curiously unreal. It was difficult to make a composite of her from the diary, his own childhood memories and the beautiful, silent woman who looked into the river as if reading a secret text in the ripples his oars made in the water. He was glad that the bond between Harry and Mrs. Clayton was strong. Whatever her relationship with her second husband, she had an affectionate son by her side. It also relieved Henry to think that if anything happened to him, Mrs. Clayton would still have Harry.

As they pushed off the following morning, Henry said, "Harry, remind me if you see me wool-gathering. When we get about a mile and a half from here, near the Cullam Lock, I must keep the boat to the towing path side. The cut leading to Cullam Lock tends sharply to the left."

"What is our next port of call today, captain?" Mrs. Clayton asked gaily as Henry handed her into the boat. She was wearing a pretty print dress and, in spite of her words the previous evening, carried what must have once been a very elegant parasol but which now looked rather worn. The parasol was somehow familiar to Henry. He wanted to ask Mrs. Clayton about it but did not want to see the gaiety dashed from her face as it had been yesterday by an impolitic question. In the sunlight and in her happy mood she looked remarkably young, almost as if all their years of separation had never occurred and all the shadows she alluded to were dispelled.

"If we had the time," Henry said, "I should like to stop at Day's Lock and wander into Dorchester," he said. "The town was a roman station of some importance. Sinodun Hill commands extensive views and the abbey church is remarkable for its architectural qualties. More important, after a day of rowing, is that the White Hart is famous for its ale. But I think we had best try to get to Wallingford. That place also has things to recommend it. Saxons, Romans, Britons and Danes have all left their marks there. It was a borough in the time of the Confessor."

"I believe he knows every cow pasture and mud hut along the Thames," Harry said, grinning.

"I have rowed it many times," Henry answered, coolly superior to the barb.

"You are very much the man of action, Henry.

As your father was. Don't ever become a fixture in a dusty office. That sort of life destroyed your father."

Once more Henry felt an urge to ask her about the past: had she seen his father fall at Cawnpore? Did she know, absolutely, that he was dead? But the smile on his mother's lips sealed his own. There would be time later for painful questions. She looked so young and happy in the sunshine, almost exactly as he remembered her.

Not a shadow of any kind touched them during their days on the river. They had certainly lost the *Thugs*. Henry congratulated himself on his strategy.

On the fourth day out from Oxford as Mrs. Clayton dozed in the back of the boat, Harry said, "You are a good general, Henry. Your scheme has worked marvelously. Not a *Thug* in sight and I have not seen Mother look so young and gay in years. It is an excursion, and it is doing her good. She admires your prowess tremendously."

Feeling somewhat embarrassed Henry answered, "And she has told me while you were sleeping, that she thinks you one of the most intelligent men she has ever known. She is exceedingly proud of you as well, old man."

"Well, we don't have to compete for our mother's affection," Harry said. "There is enough for both. She has a true, womanly heart."

"Yes," Henry said slowly, "yet, at moments, I feel—I am not even sure what it is. Perhaps it is only my own desire to cross question her about the past and the feeling that she doesn't want to have it raked up. Have you ever asked her about her life when she first left India, just after the Mutiny?"

"No. I really had nothing to ask," Harry said.

"Probably a mare's nest," Henry said. "I just remember—something—something about her is different, though obviously it would have to be after all this time and all that has happened. I don't know."

"Of course," Harry said. "But I already know you well enough to know that when you get something under your saddle, you won't leave it until you can draw it out. Give her some time and talk to her openly."

"Yes, Harry, you're right. Give it some time and then talk to her about the past. Say, who's the elder brother here? You giving me advice?"

"It's good advice."

"I know it is. And I will take it. Thank you, Harry. You have had so many more years with her than I. I feel you know her a great deal better."

"Oh," Mrs. Clayton said, sounding startled as she woke in the back of the boat. "Something nipped me."

"Did you let your hand slip into the water?" Henry asked.

"Yes, I must have."

"Just a fish. No crocodiles in England. Though pike can bite."

One day glided lazily into the next as days on the water can do, and the reunited family had a wonderful time. Henry showed them every point of interest on or near the river all the way into London. Each inn on this busy section of the river was well-appointed to receive guests. Most of the river traffic was made up of pleasure craft. The 'excursion' was an unqualified success. Even as they rowed through the oily dark water of the London harbour, dodging steam launches and large ships, the excitement of arrival made up for the end of their idyll.

Chapter 20
Harry is lost in the City

After having grown accustomed to the clear air and sunshine of the beautiful country along the river between Oxford and the suburbs of London, Lombard Street, where Mrs. Clayton's bank was located, in the centre of the City, looked particularly gray and dismal. Henry hoped that the boat he had left in charge of the proprietor at the rental dock near the Old Swan Pier would be safe. He and Harry both commented on the soot and cinders of the commercial centre of Great Britain. Mrs. Clayton said nothing about the metropolis, though she looked carefully at the streets and the men and women. Henry felt she was particularly observant of the women's costumes and comparing them to her own. Her expression was melancholy as they took a four-wheeler deeper and deeper into the City. She looked at London with disquiet and unease.

The Glyn, Mills & Co bank was a flat-faced, architecturally uninteresting building of five storeys, typical of the London in late Victorian times. Since both Clayton and Henry regarded the errand at the bank as their mother's very personal business they waited outside for her and watched well-dressed City men measure the pavement with brisk, purposeful steps.

"By the by," Henry said to his brother , "How do you feel after all that rowing? Are you sore or stiff?"

"I must confess to feeling both. Ordinary movements are somewhat painful. I need a Turkish bath."

"I can only imagine...here, what's all this?" Henry was commenting on the fact that three different carriages had suddenly come into Lombard street not far from where their cab was stopped. The drivers were all Indian and were talking excitedly to each other.

"That lot is certainly animated," Henry commented. "Do you know what they are saying?"

"Sorry, it sounds a little like Persian, but there are over one-hundred languages spoken on the sub-continent. I can only speak English, Urdu, Hindi and Turkish. The first three are the most useful languages in India, I should say. The lingo of those chaps is entirely beyond my ken. They do sound excited, though."
"They do indeed."

At this point in the conversation, Henry saw his mother emerge from the bank followed by two porters who were carrying a small steamer trunk for her. It had obviously just been retrieved from some little-used vault in the bank. The black leather and brass which bound it bore streaks of dust from a hasty cleaning. From the way the porters handled the trunk it looked heavy.

"I say, those porters don't look any too strong," Henry remarked. "I think I'll give a hand. I'll take one end and you take the other, Harry."

"Right," the other man said as they got out of the carriage and approached the porters. Both of the young men had forgotten the arguing Indian jarveys. They didn't realize that as they approached the trunk, three of the Indians were walking right behind them, following on their heels.

"Mother," Henry called out, "We'll take it from here. Just put it down," he said to the porters.

As the trunk touched the ground, the three Indian drivers sprang forward. Henry seized one end of the trunk and Harry the other.

"What the devil?" Henry exclaimed as the three men tried to seize the trunk from them. "They're *Thugs*," Henry called out.

One of the Indians drew a wicked looking curved knife. Keeping the trunk between him and the man with a knife, Henry swung the heavy trunk with Harry and managed to slam it into their assailant. Just as he went down, Henry felt someone leap on his back. In order to throw him, Henry had to put down his end of the trunk.

"Harry," he called, "whatever happens don't let go your end." Then, he attended to the business of throwing the man on his back to the ground. As the man began to be dislodged, he tried to slip a white scarf around Henry's neck, and failed. Henry threw him hard and when the man tried to get up from the street, Henry finished him with a neat right cross. He then looked around just in time to see two other men dragging Harry and the chest toward one of their waiting carriages.

"Hold on, Harry. I'm coming," and he sprinted across the few yards between himself and the men.

Unfortunately, Harry was losing the tug of war for the chest. His two opponents were dragging him in-exorably toward one of the carriages. As they drew close to it, another Indian ran from the other side, got behind Harry and pinned his arms from behind. Harry's end of the chest fell to the ground and Harry was bundled roughly into the carriage by two men. The remaining men were carrying the chest to the boot when Henry caught them up and got one of the trunk's handles in his grasp. With a huge effort, Henry tore the trunk away from the jarveys. Harry, however, had been dragged into a different carriage and was out of sight. Henry had hold of the trunk when one of the drivers sprang to the box of the carriage Harry was in and lashed the horses. In moments, the coach careened around a corner with Harry in it and three Indians clinging to the boot and the sides. The other two carriages were left standing in the middle of the street.

"I shall be right back, Mother. Watch the trunk until I can get the bank porters out here," he said as he raced into the bank. In seconds he managed to raise the alarm in the bank and reappeared with two flustered porters at his heels.

"Just keep watch on it until I return."

"We could take it back inside, sir..."

"Yes, fine. Mother," he called as he raced toward their cab and jumped onto the box next to the driver, "I must try to overtake them."

Henry was fortunate that the man driving his cab was a seasoned London cab driver who raced through the traffic with the utter disregard for life and limb which is peculiar to his tribe. Henry tried to stand to see farther ahead, but the pace was too furious and he was forced to sit or be thrown when they turned the next corner. In spite of their breakneck speed, it soon became clear that the other carriage was completely out of sight, lost in the great cross roads at Cornhill in front of the Bank of England, one of the most crowded inter-sections in London.

When Henry saw the milling crowd ahead of them he told the driver, "Go back. Return to Lombard Street."

After the wild, bone -jarring ride, it seemed as if the cab crawled back to the bank.

He found his mother standing on the pavement in front of the bank. She was white-faced and looked ill.

"Mother, let me take you somewhere we can get a restorative for you," Henry said as soon as he saw her.

She shook her head.

"Let us just get away somewhere safe with the accursed trunk," she said. "If you'll go to the porters and direct them. I should be glad to get into the carriage."

"Of course, Mother," Henry said, taking her hand and placing it in his arm as he led her to the four-wheeler. He handed her into the carriage and he saw that she sat away from the window. He was afraid she was going to cry.

"Mother," he began as he approached the window. "Perhaps..."

"Just get the trunk and let us leave, Henry."

"Very well," and he withdrew from the window and turned to the bank entrance. Inside, he gave instructions to the porters, as a senior clerk rushed up to him, and said, "We are very sorry, sir, for the outrage. I can send a boy to the police station if you would like."

"No. We just want to get our valuables away."

"Again sir, on behalf of the Glyn, Mills bank, please accept my apologies. I shall see you out, sir."

"No, no," Henry answered. "The porters have things in hand. Good day."

"Good day, sir," the unctuous clerk said, finally letting Henry go.

Henry emerged from the bank in time to watch the porters secure the trunk in the boot with straps. Then, he gave them each a few pence and got into the carriage.

He found his mother dry-eyed but looking strained and overcome.

"Mother, where would you like to go now? To a good hotel?"

"Henry, do you not realize that your brother is now in the hands of the *Thuggee?*"

"It would seem to be the logical explanation for that hugger mugger. But how can you be so certain? Shall we go to the police? I cannot go, but you could."

She laughed a very brittle, bitter laugh. "I cannot go to them, either, Henry."

"Why ever not, Mother?"

"Oh, there is so much you do not know, Henry."

"I am all attention, Mother."

"Let us find someplace safe. Where I can speak freely and long."

"An hotel?"

"Henry, those *Thugs* could be anywhere. There could be others. We must hide, Henry, away from even the most respectable eyes."

"Very well. Then I shall take you where I have been staying. It is rough and coarse, Mother..."

"I don't care, Henry, as long as we are safe there. I must be safe before I can think clearly about this disaster." Henry called out the address on Upper Swandam Lane to the driver and the cab began to move.

As soon as she felt the motion of the carriage, Jane Booth let her eyes close. A few moments later her head rolled to one side. Henry looked at her blanched, exhausted face and thought, "Poor Mother, she looks thoroughly done up. What a way to return home. But at least, we are together. She is alive. And we shall have a chance to know to one another. But what are we going to do about poor Harry? Would the blackguards kill him? No. That is too dreadful to contemplate."

Then, he thought of the fact that he would soon see Umrao again. He had hoped for better circumstances for the introduction of his mother and the woman he loved, especially after the things Jane Booth had said on the river about marrying a *tuwaif*, a Lucknow courtesan. In her Anglo-Indian mind, apparently, nothing could have been worse, in spite of her own choice. He could see it would not matter that Umrao was an artist. It wouldn't matter that she had not yet been introduced to her first client, or that the first man she had ever known was Henry. In fact, when Henry had mentioned dancing, his mother had cried out, 'A *nautch* girl'. Henry, don't you know that those dances are used to arouse men in the bordellos so they are more easily gulled?'

He knew it was not going to be an easy meeting, no matter what happened. His mother was absolutely against him marrying a native woman no matter who she was, but the fact that Umrao was a *tuwaif* made the dreadful prospect even worse.

"She must feel some bitterness about her own marriage to hold such attitudes," he thought as the carriage rolled through the east end. He looked over at her exhausted face and thought, "She seemed ready to weep when she heard about the events her diary had set in motion. And he had not even told her about Charles' death. Now all of this. And why, did she say, 'accursed trunk' a short time ago? Why would a priceless relic belonging to her husband be cursed? Or did she mean because of Harry?" He looked over at her once more. "Perhaps it just meant that she was exhausted."

He tried to push all speculation out of his mind and concentrate on Umrao. Of course, in the small confines above the opium den, he would not be able to make love to Umrao with his mother present. That would be difficult, too. He had been longing for her for some days. It would be hard to be with her and not touch her.

His mother woke.

"Oh, my heavens it was not a dream. The *Thugs* have Harry," she said.

Trying to soothe her Henry said, "You can't be

certain they were *Thugs*, Mother.

"Yes, I can," she said, dabbing her eyes and making a great effort not to cry. "I recognized one of them from Ahktar Devi's kotha. He was a doorman there."

"Are you really sure?"

She nodded wordlessly.

"We'll get him back, Mother."

"You don't know them. They are brutes."

"How do you know?"

"I know them."

"Mother, how can you know a cult of killers? What do you mean? I think you are overwrought."

"No. They helped my husband and I escape from India after the mutiny."

"Escape? Who were you escaping from? I thought your husband rescued you from the mutineers."

"We were escaping from the British. They were after me. I was suspected of assisting the mutineers during the siege at Cawnpore."

"What? How could they think such a thing?" Henry asked, sitting up abruptly and grabbing the strap on the side of the carriage. "What are you saying, Mother?"

"Your father was so angry at me for leaving him for a native, he told some of the officers at the entrenchment that I and my present husband had given information to the mutineers, that we were traitors. This story was repeated after the siege and we were pursued all over the country and up into the mountains, even through the dead land of the Terai plateau."

"Oh, my heavens," Henry exclaimed. "What a blackguard. And they believed him?"

"Yes. You forget, your father was an army hero and according to the gossip his remarks started, I was an unfaithful wife who had run off with a native. He did

333

not have to make any formal charges when the siege was broken. He was dead by then anyway, hit by a ball during the fighting. The gossip he had retailed in the mess was enough. At that time, Henry, anyone with a dark skin could be hung on any excuse. My husband was lucky to get the help of the *Thuggee*. Without them we would not have gotten out of India."

"So there is a connection. How horrible to be indebted to those grisly killers."

"The British, too, were dreadful killers. I have never seen such mindless slaughter as during and after the mutiny. I hope you never live to see a man blown to pieces from the front of a cannon. Terrible wrongs were committed by both sides, but at bottom, Henry, make no mistake, it was British greed that made the situation incendiary. And now, God help us all, all of Europe is about to do something equally horrible—and all for money and power."

"But what about the *Thugs*, Mother?"

"Yes, the *Thugs*. They got us passage on a ship and we agreed to pay them a large sum, a very large sum. When I heard the figure mentioned, I thought to myself, "My husband must be much wealthier than I thought." She paused.

"And was he?" Henry asked. "Could he not afford to pay them?"

"Their payment is in the chest we just took from the bank. You will see."

"But you said it was a stolen art treasure—a glass tiger."

"That is just a code for what is really in the chest."

"What is in it?"

"A king's ransom in precious stones."

"So that is what they were after today. And

that's why the Indians attacked us."

"Yes. My husband also suffered from what seems to me to be the besetting male sin: greed, the desire to own and control anything one can."

"So now you are indebted to the *Thuggee* and now that we have the treasure, we shall be stalked." She nodded. "I believe that some servant in our house in Istanbul was in their pay and told them of our plans to go to China. My husband sent me here so we could take our wealth with us."

"Why didn't he come himself? It seems a mean thing to send you into such danger."

"He will never set foot in England, again. That is all I can say about his judgment."

There was a long pause while Henry digested what she had said. Finally he spoke, "Mother, you recognized the man you saw kill Aktar Devi, the Englishman. Who was he?" Henry asked.

She looked up at him, her eyes wide and startled, her face drained of any colour. Even her lips were pale.

"That is a secret I have kept so long and which is so dangerous that I cannot give it up to you, now. There is no reason for you to know. It will do you no good and would place you in even greater danger. Can you understand? Can you understand that I am a mother and feel a mother's responsibility toward you and Harry. I must do any small thing I can to protect you both."

Henry nodded. "I understand. But then, tell me were we not in any danger as we went down the river?"

"We were certainly in danger. Look at what just happened to Harry. *Thugs* have always been ready to ransom a really wealthy victim. They would have kidnapped either myself or Harry and used that to pressure my husband to bring them the treasure. The only reason they did not is that they had no idea where, in this foreign land, the treasure was. And what is worse, we did not give them the payment we said we would. How they knew exactly when and where I would come, I can't imagine. It all took place so long ago but now, the horrors of the Mutiny suddenly seem much more in the present. All these years we've been living in the shadows under a false name have fallen away."

"Your husband's name is not Clayton?"

"No. We both changed our name before we left India."

"So it is a complete pseudonym?"

She again nodded without speaking.

"So in a sense, the *Thugs* are trying to collect a debt?"

"Yes, I'm afraid so."

"They certainly seem like the wrong people to cheat. I can't imagine what possessed your husband."

"And me, Henry. I am also to blame. So you see," she said breaking down and sobbing, "I have destroyed both my sons. You, by abandoning you and instilling a foolish longing for India and Harry by coming here. Oh, God, what am I to do. I am the most miserable woman in the world."

"There, there, Mother," Henry said putting his arm around her shoulders. "Where there's life there's hope. We'll win through. I feel certain."

"Oh, Henry you are sweet but you understand so little about the world's injustice and cruelty. How can we possibly find Harry and get him back?"

"That seems fairly straightforward. They want money. We've got it. We'll give it to them. We'll ransom Harry."

"But we don't even know where they've taken him."

"I admit that there are difficulties," Henry said.

They were both quiet for some time. Then, as the metal wheel rims of the carriage clattered northward toward the opium den he began to think once more of Umrao. For the first time he felt a stab of apprehension about her. Was she still safe in the hideaway Abdul had found for them? Danger seemed to press in on them from every side. It was now more important than ever that they not be found.

When the carriage finally stopped in front of the seedy building on Upper Swandam Lane, Henry turned to his mother.

"You wait here," he said. "I want to make certain all is well before you enter. If I am not out in ten minutes..."

"I shall not go quietly away. I have lost one son today. Do you think I would tamely lose another?"

"Mother..."

"You cannot control me, Henry. Your Father tried and failed. I shall act as I think best."

"Very well." He got out, took her hand and kissed it. "I love you, Mother."

"I know, Henry. I hope that is always so. God bless and keep you."

Then, he turned away from the carriage and started down the worn wooden staircase which sagged at every step. He prayed that all would be as he had left it. In the dim well of the staircase, he could see the red flame of the oil lamp. This, at least, seemed a good omen. The lamp was undisturbed, and in a moment, tendrils of the heavy brown opium smoke seized him by the throat. The disreputable entrance was reassuring: all appeared unchanged. He walked through the tartarian cellar with winking orange points in the darkness. No one stopped him. He could not even see that he was watched. He saw the same slack features and twisted limbs he'd seen when he first passed through the den. Surely someone was on watch, but Henry did not see the watcher. He approached the stairs at the back of the Tartarian gloom. He heard no music or singing from the second floor apartment, no sign that anyone was there. He pushed open the old door and heard the familiar scrape across the threshold. He stepped inside. The apartment seemed deserted. Umrao's door was closed. Was she here? Had she been taken, too? he wondered, his heart skipping a beat as he approached the door. He looked in.

Umrao was fast asleep, curled into a ball, an ivory kitten among the dark, tattered blankets. He sat down next to her and was unable to resist touching the beautiful curve of her naked back.

"Ummm," she said, her eyes still closed. Then, suddenly realizing his presence, her eyes popped open and she leapt to her feet, throwing both arms around him.

"Henry, Henry, where have you been? I have been so worried. Are you all right? Are you safe?" She punctuated each question with another hug and a kiss on his face or neck. "It is so good to feel you next to me."

"Umrao," Henry said disentangling himself from her embrace, "my mother is waiting outside in a carriage. We have had rather a nasty shock. The *Thugs* have just kidnapped my brother and my mother is very distraught. I made her wait outside to make certain everything was safe here. I should go out and bring her in."

"She is coming here, to this dismal place? But I have nothing to serve her. I have no way to entertain her. I must dress." And she jumped to her feet.

"How could you do this to me? I did not know she was coming with you."

"Nor did I. There was simply no alternative."

"How could she possibly like me when she sees me this way."

"What do you mean?"

"I mean I can show her no honour or hospitality. She will think I have no manners at all. She will think I have been badly brought up. I, who have been trained in all the protocols of the *Nawab's* court. It is terrible to meet her like this. In my country, a husband's mother is a queen."

"Don't fret, so, Umrao. Just dress. She is a little concerned about your profession. So, please, don't be too demonstrative. Remember, she has lived as an Anglo-Indian for years."

"Now, is it you who thinks I am ill-mannered? I would never touch you in front of her, not in any way. You offend me, Henry. I was trained to understand every nuance of social behaviour."

"I'm sorry Umrao. But can we just let it go for now. It has been a very difficult afternoon. I, I guess I'm not always sure what to expect from you."

"Don't concern yourself, Mr. Booth.," she said frostily as she began to unceremoniously pull on her clothes.

"I'll just go out and get her, then," Henry said. " Don't be angry with me, please."

"Kiss me then. No. Really kiss me. Mmmm, that's better. Now you can go, but stay outside with her for a quarter hour," and she abruptly pushed him away.

After their long separation, Henry was as charmed with her as ever, but how would she seem to his mother, he wondered? He took the key to the second door from the nail on the wall. He was glad his mother would not have to pass through the opium den. In a few moments he was at the carriage door.

"Everything is well, Mother," he said as he handed her out, and with the driver's help pulled the trunk out of the boot. Heavy as the chest was, Henry felt he could carry it up the stairs unassisted so he paid the driver, and heaved the trunk onto his shoulder and walked into the alley where the second door was to be found.

"This way, Mother. I'm sorry for the roughness of the place . But I believe we are safe here."

"I have been in many rougher places than this, Henry. One doesn't survive a war without getting one's shoes muddy."

Henry heaved the chest onto his shoulder and trudged up the rough stairs. With each step, he was afraid the old wood might give way under the combined weight of the chest and himself, but they reached the top without misadventure. He prayed that Umrao was in readiness and pushed open the door for his Mother. He was very surprised by what he saw. Umrao was wearing western clothes, a very simple skirt and bodice cut from dull coloured cashmere. It was the same costume she had worn when he first met her. She looked as demure as a school marm. Her hair was piled on her head and except for her dark skin, she might have been English. By anyone's standards, he thought her very handsome.

"Mother," Henry began, "this is Umrao, my fiance. Umrao, this is my Mother, Mrs. Clayton."

Umrao made a very pretty curtsey. "How do you do?" she asked.

"Very well, thank you. And yourself?"

"I am well, madame. Thank you. Allow me to apologize for not being able to offer you refreshment."

"Please don't trouble yourself. I should just like to sit down."

"All we have to sit on is that old crate, Mother," Henry said.

"Thank you, Henry," she said, "I believe I would rather stand."

Then for a moment, they all stared at one another. Henry felt a strange creeping sensation at the back of his neck when he thought of all the time he had spent in this room thinking of his dead mother. Now she was here, like a materialization of the past, a living presence out the pages of her own diary. It was a waking version of his dream of the first night. There was something uncanny about it.

"Henry, I am sorry to be abrupt," Mrs. Clayton said, forcefully, " but we must do something about Harry. Immediately."

"I have been thinking about that, Mother. I think we can advertise to the *Thugs* in the agony column of four or five different papers."

" How would you do it?"

"Give me a few moments to compose something and I shall read it to you."

Henry walked to the window, took out his pocketbook, put it on the sill and began writing.

Mrs. Clayton and Umrao said nothing to one another as Henry wrote. They each stood very still and silent. The tiny Umrao was head and shoulders shorter than the statuesque figure of Mrs. Clayton. The tall blonde Englishwoman and the tiny black haired girl could not have been more dissimilar. Each reinforced the most salient characteristics of the other. The only sound in the room was the scratching of Henry's pen as the two women eyed one another, each making a searching feminine assessment of her opponent.

"Here," Henry said. "I think this will do it: "Reward to five Indian jarveys, who on Monday last were seeking re-payment of a long-standing debt in Lombard street in front of Glyn, Mills Bank. You shall be paid when our relation comes home. Contact HB through this newspaper."

"But there is nothing in what you have written to tell them what their reward shall be," Umrao said. "Would it not be more enticing if you mentioned a price?"

"Mother?" Henry asked his Mother. "What do you think?"

"Anything you think may help. Tell them an even division will be made, say, ' as promised long ago.' "Those were your original terms with the *Thuggee*?" he asked. Mrs. Clayton nodded. "My husband never should have tried to cheat them."

"Well, that is over and done," Henry said. "But offering them the original terms might get a quick response. Let me add to what I have written," and he once more took out his pocketbook and leaned on the window sill and quickly scribbled a line.

"Here is how it now reads, he said: 'Reward to five Indian jarveys who on Monday last were seeking re-payment of a long-standing debt in Lombard street in front of Glyn, Mills Bank. You shall be paid when our relative comes home, unharmed. You will be paid according to the same terms agreed upon long ago. Contact HB through this newspaper."

"That was well-thought of, Umrao," Mrs. Clayton said.

"Thank you," Umrao returned.

"All that remains now is to insert it into the papers," Henry said, "which I shall do right away. I don't like to leave you both but...Oh, Umrao, where is

Sergeant Abdul? Have you seen him since I've been gone?"

"No. Henry. I have been very worried about him. I feel if he had been able, he would have come many times to see me. If you hadn't left me money, I should have starved."

"Worse, and worse," Henry said when he heard this black news. "I hope he has not been taken."
"Is this Abdul also someone from the past?" Mrs. Clayton asked.

"Yes," Henry replied. "A surgeon from Lucknow."

"Ah, yes. I remember him, well. How curious that he is here, too."

"Only he is not here now," Henry said. "That is the material point. I don't think he would have gone missing of his own accord."

"Pardon me, Henry. I want to understand your use of the newspaper, better. The publishers will provide a post box where you can be contacted?" Umrao asked.

"Oh, yes," Henry answered. "These columns are used for this type of message, frequently. All that remains now is to place it in the papers. I think I'll use *The Telegraph, The Chronicle, The Express and The Evening Standard. The Times* would not be read by these people."

"Whatever you think best, Henry."

"Mother, in all probability they will actually be watching these columns, hoping that we might communicate. That's what they will do if they are not fools. And I believe the man in charge of these *Thugs* is not a fool. Is he, Mother?"

"I think not," Mrs. Clayton answered looking chagrined.

Suddenly, Umrao leapt across the room to stand

in front of the other woman.

"You, you know my mother's killer!" she said in a voice that was almost a growl. "I had forgotten. You know the British leader of the *Thuggee*. Tell me who he is."

"Who is your mother?" Mrs. Clayton asked. "Many years ago I met a British man who carried a *rumal* as a weapon. That is true but..."

"Who is he?" Umrao replied in a trembling voice. "Tell me at once. My Mother was Akthar Devi. I have come to this cold island to find her killer. What is his name?"

"You were the child I met at the *kotha* so long ago. I see. How extraordinary we should meet again like this."

"I was. And Akthar Devi was murdered by an Englishman, as you know. Tell me who he is."

"I am sorry, I do not know his name. I know only his face," Mrs. Clayton answered.

Henry said nothing, allowing the lie to pass without comment. He thought Umrao too hot-blooded to be trusted with the identity of the Thug leader. If his mother thought it too dangerous for Henry, telling Umrao would be like giving black powder to a child. In any case, he knew he would not be able to change his mother's mind.

"I am sorry for your loss. Akthar Devi was a good woman. She was very kind to me— at a time when I badly needed kindness."

"Then you will tell me his name."

"Henry, what can I say to her? She seems unable to grasp what I am saying."

"She has searched for this man a long time, Mother. I believe she is simply overwrought. Umrao, my mother could identify the man's face. But she was never given his name. She only knows him on sight. I am sorry."

"Then, how am I to find him on this dirty crowded island?" she asked in a tone of mixed pain and anger.

"He shall be found, Umrao. I promise you," Henry said.

"You give your word?"

"I give you my word," Henry answered. "But right now we must try to get Harry back and negotiate with these blackguards. Their leader is the man you seek, Umrao. I feel sure of it."

"Then find them," she said.

"That is what I am going to do, with the help of the press."

"Henry, please put the notices out for Harry right away," Mrs. Clayton said. "I am sick with worry."

" I shall be back as soon as I can," he answered and kissed each woman on the cheek. Suddenly, he stopped moving toward the door. "I think we should know exactly what is in this trunk before we offer payment to the Thugs. If we are going to treat with them, I want to be sure we can meet any commitments I make. Mother, do they think that this is an art object that needs to be sold, the glass tiger?"

"I no longer feel sure of what they might know. My husband might have told them things that I don't know. He was in England in 1855 and fearing a war, he left this trunk here for safe keeping. He asked me to retrieve it."

"If the Thugs know that, they know it can't be something stolen by the British during the sack of Lucknow in 1857," Henry said.

"Yes, it must be so."

"I should feel better if we opened the chest and

took an inventory of what is actually here," Henry said.

"Then open it," Mrs. Clayton said. "But I have no key."

"Then I shall break the lock," Henry said. "I only hope my knife is strong enough."

"Use mine," Umrao said tugging at her bodice and finally drawing a knife from a flap of fabric. "It is very strong."

"What a wicked looking thing," Mrs. Clayton commented as it was passed to Henry. The thick curving blade, sharp point and glittering edge did give the knife a bad character. It was obviously made to be an instrument of death.

Henry fumbled at the lock and then said, "I got the edge jammed into the hasp. The knife looks thick enough, but I might break it."

"It is all right, Henry," Umrao said. "Do what must be done."

"Very well. Here goes," and he threw his full strength against the blade, half expecting it to snap at any second. Instead, the hasp sprang open. Henry straightened up.

"Mother, this is your property, do you want me to lift the lid?"

"It doesn't matter, Henry. All that matters is getting Harry back, and time is of the essence."

"Very well." And he lifted the lid. Everyone gasped. The iron bound trunk had been reinforced with metal sides and was filled to the top with the most fabulous gems they had ever seen.

"My heavens, Mother, where did all this come from? Is your husband fabulously wealthy?"

"Not on this order," she said. "All I know about this trunk is that I was first told it was supposed to contain a work of art stolen from the Imambara at Lucknow by the British when they sacked the city, a near life-size glass tiger. My husband told me he would sell it for a great deal of money. Half of the proceeds were to be given to the *Thuggee* for getting us out of the country after the war. My husband brought this chest here in 1855 when he visited England on business."

"But if he brought it here in 1855, how could it have been stolen by the British during the sack of Lucknow in 1858?" Henry asked.

"Wait," Umrao burst out suddenly. "This is the treasure that has already crossed the sea."

"What are you talking about Umrao?" Henry asked.

"I succeeded where you and Abdul failed, Henry. I got Hasan Ali Meer to translate the Ramasee phrase from the back of the painting."

"Hasan Ali Meer? When have you seen him?" Henry asked.

"He has come here twice to try to hire me," Umrao explained.

"How did he find us? And does this mean the Thugs know where we are?"Henry asked.

"I, I believe one of Ali Meer's men followed us here, but I do not think Ali Meer is interested in the treasure or knows any *Thugs*. He is interested in me. He wanted me to give what he called an intimate and private performance for him."

Henry's face took on a dusky colour and when he spoke his voice sounded choked with suppressed anger.

"How many times has he been here?" he said grabbing Umrao's arm.

"Henry!" his mother exclaimed. "Unhand that woman immediately. You, of all people, should know that violence against a woman is something resorted to only by the most vile men."

"You are right, Mother," Henry said. "Forgive me, Umrao."

"Your jealousy makes you stupid, Henry, and less of a man than you are," Umrao replied. "I've told you that before. I shall take your apology this time. But do not behave this way again."

"I am glad you have spirit, Umrao," Mrs. Clayton put in, walking over to the smaller woman and putting her arm around the younger woman's shoulder...and a healthy amount of self-respect."

"Thank you, Mrs. Clayton."

It was the first time Henry had seen the two women united in any way. For the first time, he could imagine that they might become friends.

"I beg the pardon of you both," he said, and then added, "I can certainly see why the *Thugs* would kill for this wealth—which means that somehow they knew what was in the trunk. But I suppose Hasan Ali Meer is cleared of involvement by the fact that he translated the inscription—if his translation was a true one. It could just as easily be a blind to win you over, Umrao. And his interest in you could also give him an excuse for coming here to find out when and if the treasure has arrived."

"I never thought of that," Umrao said. "I dislike him so much that I was largely thinking about warding him off in a personal way. No, Henry, he did not try to touch me. He would not do that unless a price was agreed upon."

"I could believe that a *Thug* would use such a ruse. He may still be the man who has Harry and who killed your mother, Umrao. He may have been waiting to see if the treasure came here. Now that it has, we cannot let him in again. If he is the one, once he saw the treasure, there would be nothing to keep his blood-thirsty minions from us. You must not let him in if he comes while I am not here. You must promise me."

"Yes, I understand your reasons, though I think some of it is also jealousy."

"But you agree there may be a very good reason not to open the door to him?"

"I shall tell him I am sick. I got what I wanted from him anyway: the translation of the inscription. If he is the one I seek, he will die. But I must be sure."

"We can't allow him to be near the treasure."

"I agree," Umrao said.

"Well, these gems certainly make things easier in one respect," Henry said as he looked at the enormous pile of carbuncles, diamonds, pearls, emeralds and other precious stones. "We do not have to sell an *objet d'art* to turn it into money to make it divisible. We can simply give the Thugs half of what is here. But it is possible that since you and your husband broke trust with them, they may want more than half."

"I don't care," Mrs. Clayton said. "All that matters now is getting Harry back."

"I quite agree, Mother. But let's not offer more than necessary to begin with. You may need money. I'll leave my advertisement as it is. If they want more, I'm sure they will tell us."

"You don't think they would just hurt Harry?"

"Why should they? " Henry said. "If they harmed him they would have nothing to trade with. They want the gems. And we'll make certain Harry is all right before we let them have the gems. I'll ask that he write a comment, in his own hand, on that day's Times editorial page. But there is another concern, an even greater one. You can identify their leader, Mother. That means that as long as you are within their grasp, you will not be safe. He will not let you live if you can put his head in a halter."

"He must die," Umrao said coldly. That is the correct solution."

"No, Umrao. That is not the correct solution. We must keep Mother hidden and get her out of England before the *Thugs* can locate her. They will probably try to arrange the ransom so they can seize her."

"My life is not important," Mrs. Clayton said.

"Mother! Don't say that," Henry cried. "It is important to me. All those years, I thought you were gone...I never want to feel that again. And I am certain that Harry would be profoudly affected as well."

"I only meant that Harry's safety comes first," she replied.

"I feel sure, if we are careful, we can free Harry without exposing you to danger."

"I shall have to wire my husband and tell him what has happened. I must tell him that his gems will have to be used for ransom. Incidentally, Henry, do you have the diary my brother sent you? Is it here?"

Henry felt he divined an odd tone in her voice.

"I hope you will not ask me to part with it," he said. "It is sacred to me. It is how I came to know who you really are."

"Is it here or not?" she asked in a flat, cold peremptory tone.

"The diary, again," Henry thought. "I shall not surrender it even to my mother until I know its true importance."

"No. It is not here."

"Then where?"

"At the Suttons."

"Can you get it, soon?"

"No. The police are watching the house. Or, they were."

For a few moments, the vexation written on her face was plain to see.

Henry added: "Until I can prove that the *Thugs* were responsible for the killings and not me, I cannot go there. One type of noose is as effective as another."

She ignored his remark and said, "It is time you went to place the advertisements, Henry. And I should like you to send this wire to Mr. Clayton in Paris at the same time." She handed him a piece of paper which had three words on it: Gems are gone. Henry looked at the paper and said, "But, Mother..."

"It doesn't matter. I shall do whatever is necessary to save Harry. I just feel that I owe it to him to tell him, first. If they want them all, I shall give them and he will already know the worst. If not..."

"Yes, I see," Henry said. "Then, I think we are ready."

A few moments later when he took the folded paper from his mother and opened the door, Umrao stepped outside with him.

"Mrs. Clayton, excuse me for a moment," she said looking back over her shoulder. "I shall return, momentarily. Bolt the door after me. I shall knock and call to you."

"What is it, Umrao?" Henry asked after the door was closed.. "Why are you coming out?"

"Shh. Let us go down to the bottom of the stairs. I don't want to be overheard."

They walked down the short wooden flight of exterior stairs which led into the alley.

"Henry," Umrao said, "There is some great burden on your mother's heart. I do not know what it is, but I feel she is very sad."

"She is worried about Harry."

"No. There is something else consuming her.

Something she has lived with a long time. Almost like an illness, not of the body but of the mind.. It is very deep, and eating away at her. I don't know what the cause is. If I can find out, perhaps we can help her. I shall try to find out while you are gone."

Henry took her hand and looked deeply into her dark eyes.

"You are a remarkable and curious woman, Umrao. How are you able to see so far and understand so much and at the same time be talking about committing murder yourself? I can't grasp it."

She gave him a light kiss on the cheek.

"Sorrow. Sorrow, is what makes us wise," she answered as she turned to go back inside.

"Is that another *ghazal?*" he asked.

"No. But it would make a good subject for one."

Chapter 21
The Final Parting

B y the time he returned to Upper Swandam Lane, Henry had placed six advertisements in papers that included one or two east end papers as well as those that had the widest circulation in the City and west end. He could only hope that Harry's captors would be watching the agony columns for a response. The fact that their leader was reputed to be British gave him hope. The man would know that this was the only way they could communicate. If the British Thug was aiming at a ransom, Henry felt the man would be watching the agony columns. He could only hope that it was so. Hasan Ali Meer was another conundrum. If Mrs. Clayton saw and identified him, they would know if he was the man who committed the murder in the *kotha*. But, to allow him to enter the apartment when the jewels were there could ruin their negotiations—if he was the "British" leader of the Thugs. Henry felt it best to keep away from the man until negotiations through the newspapers had taken place. If Hasan Ali Meer was not a *Thug*, he was simply irrelevant. But if he were...

The next three days were very difficult for the inmates of the small apartment above the opium den. Out of respect for his mother, Henry slept in the outer room by himself and Umrao slept in the bedroom with Mrs. Clayton. In spite of her unconventional past, the older woman was still an Anglo-Indian of a generation who strongly disapproved of any kind of sexual misconduct, at least publicly. In spite of Henry's strong desire for Umrao, the thought of any physical contact with her in such close quarters with his own mother was abhorrent to him. He felt at times that his mother was even abashed by her own past, by her readiness to leave her first husband, in spite of his abuses. For her part, Umrao felt it would be extremely ill-mannered to flaunt behaviour that would be offensive to Mrs. Clayton, especially with the strain they were all under.

As they waited for word from Harry's captors, Mrs. Clayton was very agitated at times, wringing her hands and even shedding quiet tears. She blamed herself for what had happened to Harry.

Henry wanted to ask her many questions about the past: what had happened in the infamous *bibighar* where so many British women and children died? Had she been there and escaped? If so, how? Each time he had been about to ask, something had prevented him from pressing her for what was bound to be a difficult and painful narrative. Since Harry had been taken and Mrs. Clayton's every nerve was strained beyond endurance, it was now unthinkable to ask her about terrible events of the past when the present was so painful. At times Henry wondered if his mother were berating herself for her decision to leave her first husband, but this question, too, went unasked.

The only good in the situation was that the two women, living at such close quarters, had developed some tolerance and respect for each other. Henry felt that his mother must now see that Umrao was not a woman of loose morals, even though she had been raised in the *kotha* of a Lucknow courtesan.

When Umrao rehearsed her singing and dancing, Mrs. Clayton had even shown interest and appreciation. She told the younger woman, "When I lived in Oudh, I knew nothing of *hindustani* music and dance but my husband is something of a connoisseur and has taught me enough to distinguish what is good and what is not. You, I think, he would judge very fine, a true artist."

Umrao glowed with pleasure. "I am very glad to have your good opinion, Mrs. Clayton. Thank you."

A few exchanges like this gave Henry hope for the future of a relationship between the two women. In general, however, each day that passed increased the tension, putting all of them more on edge.

At times Henry wondered if the *Thugs* had already murdered Harry. Such a loss might be doubly tragic, for Henry was afraid for his mother's health and sanity if anything happened to Harry. Each morning, when Henry went out to check the post office, Mrs. Clayton would see him to the door with two bright spots of hectic, feverish colour in her cheeks. When Henry returned empty-handed she was crest fallen and usually shed a few tears.

"Poor fellow," she would murmur a few times.

Then she would sit in silence for the rest of the day unless she was spoken to. Each day that passed seemed to weaken her, and Henry felt that her sorrow was breaking down her health.

On the third morning of the advertisements, Mrs. Clayton asked, "How many days shall we run the notices, Henry?"

"Why, we'll run them until we get an answer. I feel sure that we shall, Mother."

But his heart was in his boots when he spoke

these brave words. Finally, on the fifth morning, Henry returned at a gallop. The door burst open.

"We've had a reply," he announced breathlessly.

"I ran all the way back from the post office. But I took a very circuitous route to prevent anyone following me—in case someone was watching the post office."

Both women looked at him, expectantly. Mrs. Clayton's face was the colour of chalk. Her eyes were dull and frightened.

"What does it say?" she asked.

"They agree to give proofs of Harry's safety..."

"Oh, thank the Lord," Mrs. Clayton burst out and began to cry violently, releasing the strain of the last five days. Umrao put her arms around the older woman.

Henry said, "There, you see, Mother. I told you it would all come right. We'll get Harry back. But the knaves do want all the treasure and say so at the outset."

"I don't care," Mrs. Clayton said, recovering herself, somewhat.

"Well, it is very bad of them, I think, and..." Henry said.

Both women watched him expectantly.

"Yes," Mrs. Clayton said, "what is it?"

"They make a condition that we will not—cannot—entertain."

"What?"

"They want you to bring the ransom yourself—alone. And before you say anything, Mother," Henry said holding up his hand, "You must realize that their only purpose is to remove you as a threat to their leader."

"I don't care, Henry," his mother said. "I would

trade my life for his."

"Mother, surely you realize that they would only kill you and then kill Harry. You would do him no good."

The young people could see all the spirit dashed from Mrs. Clayton's face in an instant.

"Yes, of course you are right....but if there is even the slightest chance...Then we must go to the police," she said.

"I cannot," Henry said. "I am wanted by them. I have been blamed for two murders committed by the *Thugs*."

"Two?" Mrs. Clayton exclaimed.

"Yes, Mother. I did not want to tell you but Charles Sutton was murdered in his own study."

"Oh, heaven help us. How many crimes will spring from my original one?" Mrs. Clayton asked and then burst into loud wracking sobs.

Her few words spoke volumes about how she regarded the end of her first marriage.

"Do try to quiet yourself, Mother," Henry said. "This is not your fault, and I could not possibly allow you to put yourself in the power of the *Thugs*. I know that they would kill you the moment they had the gems in their hands. It is not to be thought of."

"Henry, you must tell me where they are," Mrs. Clayton said with a wild look in her eyes I must go there. I must, I tell you I must. Nothing must happen to Harry. I cannot abandon another child. Oh, please, please tell me and..." she began weeping and clawing the air. Then, suddenly, she fell down in a dead faint.

Henry lifted her in his arms while Umrao opened the bedroom door. He gently placed her on the blankets where she had been sleeping. She was as pale as a corpse. Even her lips were nearly white. He would

have been glad to see the bright, feverish spots of colour on her cheeks. Henry touched her forehead. It was
burning hot.

"Good heavens, feel her, Umrao. She has a fever. The shock of all this has been too much. She may
have brain fever. Oh, I wish Abdul was here."

"I very much fear we shall not see him again,"
Umrao said sadly as she crouched over the unconscious
woman. "You are now the only one I have left to depend on and help me," she said.

"Dear girl. You know I shall do whatever I can
to help you. But first we have to finish our present business. I'm afraid you may be right about Abdul. These
Thugs are fiends," he said. Murder is nothing to them.
"I could not possibly let my Mother go to them."

"Of course not," Umrao agreed. She placed
her hand on his arm as they both stood over the sick
woman. "Henry, you have acted for the best in all
things. Do not blame yourself for any of this." She put
her arms around him.

"Thank God, I still have you, Umrao," he murmured. I don't know how long I shall have Mother.
But I must think, carefully, about what to do next."

"It is not so difficult," Umrao said, looking up at
him. "The ransom must be paid. Your mother cannot
do it, so you must do it. What else can we do? Did they
send an address?"

"No. They instruct me to put my answer in the
agony column again."

"Then, do it."

"Yes, you're right. There is nothing else to do if
we are to save Harry."

"The dangerous time will be after they name a
meeting place. There is no point in going by yourself,
Henry. They could just take you and have the gems as

well."

"I would not be so easy to take."

"Sometimes I really do forget that you have all the prejudices and foolishness of your sex. Henry, they are many. You are one. You must be sly."

"How?"

"Take me with you. But not in a way that they will know that we are together. Just as we did before," she added quickly cutting short his objection. " I shall dress myself as a schoolgirl, a mere child, and follow you at a distance. When you go to meet them, I shall watch. If they try to betray you, I shall go for the police."

"Your bravery is extraordinary, Umrao. But before we only thought that we might be watched. This time I would be taking you directly into the clutches of these fiends. Even if you brought the police, they probably wouldn't believe anything I said."

"If the police took the *Thugs* along with you and you told your story, who would they believe, the natives or an Englishman?"

"But what about their white leader," Henry muttered, thinking out loud.

"Do you think he would chance putting himself into the hands of the police? Do you think him that brave? I do not. He kills by stealth only."

Henry was quiet for some time. "I agree. Perhaps your plan could just give us the glimmer of a chance." he said finally.

"Any chance is better than no chance at all," Umrao said.

"Yes, but it puts you in danger."

"Not if I look like a child and keep my distance until the alarm is raised."

"Mmmm. Perhaps."

"What else can we do if we are to save your

brother? It is better than walking into a tiger's den by yourself."

"I must think some more."

"Henry, no matter what, you will have to act—and soon."

"If I can't think of a better way, I shall adopt your plan."

"We should go back and see how your mother is," Umrao said, having gained her point.

"You're right," he said, and turned away and walked to the bedroom door. Mrs. Clayton was still unconscious, but her colour was better and her breathing regular.

"Rest is probably the best thing for her," Henry said.

"Yes, I don't know that a doctor could prescribe anything better," Umrao said. "Now, you should answer the *Thugs*, Henry...before..."

"Yes, all right. You are right. Here." He squatted down took out his pocket book and wrote a few words: "Terms agreed to. Name a location. Reply by letter to General Delivery, Lombard Street. HB."

"You are not going to tell them your mother is not coming?"

"Why tell them? It could do nothing but anger them and perhaps make them not want to meet me."

"That's true," Umrao said.

"All right," Henry said getting to his feet. "I'm going to put this in the papers for tomorrow. I'll be back soon with some food, too."

"No pork, no eel" Umrao said.

"No pork. No eel. Some fruit and cheese?"

Henry paused at the door of the bedroom and looked back at his mother. Umrao squatted next to her.

"Don't worry," Umrao said looking up. "I shall

watch over her. If she wakes and needs anything I'll get it for her." He nodded and left.

This time, the *Thuggee* answered the following day: "Mrs. Clayton will come to Hubbard's Wharf below Broad Street, Limehouse at 8:pm, tomorrow night with our goods."

"Do you know where that is, Henry?" Umrao asked.

"Not precisely. I believe it is in an area of small commercial wharfs, which will probably be deserted at night."

"Your description sounds dreadful."

"And perfectly in keeping with the blackguards we are dealing with."

"I'll put some soot on my face and remove my shoes. I'll look like a ragged street child. In a place like that no one will look at me twice."

"What about your hair?"

"I'll plait it in a single, long braid and hide it under a disreputable bonnet."

"I shall be so frightened for you, Umrao."

"And I should be frightened if I were not there," she said, kissing his cheek.

"I am going to try to get to know the area better by looking at an old map. It may be of the last importance to know the ground well."

"What are you whispering about?" Mrs. Clayton's voice called from the other room. She had wakened that morning feeling much better. When Henry went out for the paper, she had been taking a nap.

"Nothing, Mother," Henry said as he looked into her room. "We didn't want to wake you, that is all. You look much better."

"Oh, yes. I feel a great deal better."

Henry thought, "In a way it is too bad she is not more enervated so that she would sleep when we go out tomorrow night."

"Tell me what you were talking about."

"Nothing important, Mother."

"But you sounded like conspirators to me. What were you talking about?" Mrs. Clayton persisted from the other room.

"What to get you for a nice dinner, that's all. I want to celebrate your recovery." Henry answered as he walked to her open door.

"You spoil me, Henry."

"Yes, just look at this magnificent palace I have put at your disposal," he answered smiling. He wondered how they would keep her in the apartment when they left for their sinister meeting with the *Thugs*.

"No word from the kidnappers?" she asked, anxiously.

"Not yet," Henry lied.

"You will tell me?"

"Of course, Mother. Now try to rest."

On the day the ransom was to be paid, Henry was on edge all day. He kept peering at an ancient copy of *Greenwood's Map of London*, though he was well aware that it was nearly sixty years old and probably very out of date. They had found it in a cupboard of the crumbling apartment. Still, it had all the major roads in the area, and he really had nothing else he could consult. He did not want to leave the two women to go and buy a newer map.

The day seemed to crawl by. Umrao dressed Mrs. Clayton's hair and talked to her in soothing tones, a breath of domestic normalcy in the midst of their nightmare. By late afternoon, Henry felt worn out with tension. Umrao had fallen asleep with Mrs. Clayton in the other room. Henry felt his own eyes grow heavy as he continued to pore over the map and the *Thugs'* instructions. His head drooped and he fell asleep with the letter and book next to him.

He woke with a start. It was dusk. There was enough light to consult his watch without a candle or lamp. He thought he had heard something. He sat up and walked barefoot to the door of the bedroom and looked inside. Umrao was fast asleep, but his mother was gone!

"Dear God, Umrao, where is she? What happened?"

As always, Umrao woke slowly, in spite of the alarm she could hear in her lover's voice.

"What is wrong, Henry? Oh, Mrs. Clayton. Where is she?" Sitting up quickly.

"That's just what I was asking you," he said.

"She must have wakened. Perhaps she went to the water closet."

"I hope you are right," Henry said. "Will you go down and see?"

"Yes, of course," Umrao said as she got up, yawned and stretched. Together, she and Henry walked into the main room.

"Oh, my heavens," Henry said. "She didn't go to the water closet. She went to meet the *Thugs*. Look, my letter from them was right next to me when I fell asleep. Now it is gone."

"Oh, Henry. What can we do?"

"Follow her as quickly as possible to Hubbard's Wharf, Limehouse, and hope we get there ahead of her.

Hurry. We'll have to walk to Mile End Road before we can get a cab. It will take too long to walk from here.

"Aren't you going to take the treasure? I see your mother left it."

"It was too heavy for her in all likelihood. But I shall leave it here, too. I fear that this will certainly be the moment of truth for us all. For my mother, for Harry and for you. You may see your mother's killer face to face."

In grim silence, they trudged to Mile End Road and waited until they saw a cab amidst the snarl of wagons, horses and foot traffic that choked the thoroughfare.

Henry thought of the wicked looking knife he had seen Umrao wield.

"Umrao, do you have your knife?"

"No, it is back in our rooms."

"Good."

They rode in silence for some minutes then Umrao asked, "Henry why are you scowling so?"

"We must get there ahead of my mother. If we do not, I am afraid of what might happen."

He reached up and struck the roof of the hansom with his singlestick.

"Hurry, driver. A pound for your best speed."

They clattered toward the water on Burdett Road at break-neck speed, barely dodging other conveyances and pedestrians. Henry held Umrao close to him and hung onto the strap for dear life. As the cab careened through the streets, Henry looked out and tried to remember each turn of their route. From Burdett Road they shot into Commercial Road East where they had to dodge really heavy traffic until they swung into the much more narrow White Horse Street and Butcher Row. These streets led them south to Broad Street which ran along the very edge of the wharfs. They raced past the repair wharf, Ratcliffe Dock, the Marine Brewery and lurched to a halt at Hubbard's Wharf, a narrow slit of water that lay between high, tarred wooden walls. Half a dozen lighters and a handful of rowboats were moored in this narrow ill-favoured waterway. The hulls of the small boats caught the flotsam and scum that eddied in from the harbour and trapped it between them. Alongside this sour smelling inlet was a narrow street. Looking out on the tiny thoroughfare were rows of brick warehouses which were so gnarled and twisted they seemed to be leaning over the street trying to catch a glimpse of the water, though to what end no one could tell. There were no gates to prevent access to the boats, but Henry surmised that there must be hidden guards somewhere close by. His mother was nowhere in sight.

"This is a dreadful place for your mother to come alone, Henry," Umrao said when he finished paying the driver and the cab drew off.

"Well, let us hope she has not yet come here, so we shall meet her."

"Look," Umrao said. "All of the buildings are shut up tight but one."

Henry looked along the row of Hubbard's warehouses and saw that she was right. All were shut up for the night, all but one whose gaping double opening gave forth a weak reddish light. The narrow lane where the warehouses stood seemed to trap and hold the bad air of the metropolis, making the darkness seem even darker. The red glow of the single oil lamp seemed to struggle to leave the open building, falling into the street exhausted and nearly spent. With each minute the lane grew darker, the dirty brick buildings less distinct as the fog rolled in from the water.

Without thinking, both the watchers faced

away from Broad Street and toward the faint light of the warehouse. Broad Street was deserted. Suddenly a woman's cry broke from the gloom in front of them and without exchanging a word, they both ran into the narrow lane toward the noise. As they ran, several more sounds followed in quick succession: a crash as of something falling and then several loud thumps. Each one issued from the open warehouse.

Henry raced up the lane and then, as he reached the warehouse door he seemed turned to stone. The horror of what he saw numbed his mind and body for moments that seemed an eternity.

The reddish light within fell on a man who had a white scarf in his hands, which was tightly wrapped around Mrs. Clayton's throat. Her eyes bulged and her face was darkened.

Henry thought, "She is already limp." And then he suddenly jumped toward the man who looked up when he heard Henry.

Another shock jolted Henry, but this time he did not stop. The man holding his limp mother's neck in a white scarf was Smythe-White!

"You!" Henry hissed as he jumped toward the man. But the momentary pause had done its damage, and Smythe-White, knowing his ground and each and every obstacle in the warehouse sprang into the darkness away from the lamp. In an instant, he had vanished.

Henry swung around and saw his mother lying on the dirty floor of the warehouse, the white scarf still wrapped around her neck. Her eyes were open and glassy, reflecting the lamp. It recalled her own description of Akhtar Devi's eyes when she was murdered by the unnamed white man in the *kotha*. As he knelt beside her, Henry already knew that she was dead. He felt her wrist but there was no pulse in it.

"No, no. Please. Mother..." And he threw himself down beside her and sobbed.

Then he quickly sat up and raged, "Those fiends, those foul fiends. I always knew Smythe-White was not what he pretended. I shall get him. I shall. I swear it, Mother."

He felt Umrao's arm slip around him and she drew him to her tenderly, opening a new torrent of grief.

Finally he said, "How dreadful. How perfectly dreadful."

"Then, let us leave this place," Umrao said.

"No. We've got to look for Harry. He may be here somewhere. I have to search this warehouse."

"We have to be careful in this place," Umrao said. "We don't know if the *Thugs* are about or not."

"Their leader is gone. Why would they stay here at the scene of a murder where they could be caught? No. They are gone. I have to look for Harry. My mother died trying to save him."

And once more, his voice broke as he moved toward the lantern that hung from a long square nail, driven into one of the building's wooden uprights.

The ancient warehouse which looked small from the street seemed very large indeed as Umrao and Henry moved through the shadows cast by their lantern. The ceilings were high, so that all above them was shrouded in darkness. Crates and heavy canvas lay all around them. Henry insisted on looking into or under anything where a living or a dead body could have been placed.

The sputtering light of the old lantern made their work very slow, illuminating only a circle of about six feet around them; beyond that circle all was gloom and menace. For, in spite of what Henry had said to Umrao, it was difficult not to be apprehensive among the shadow shapes and creaking floors and scuttle of rats in the dark building. The heavy smell of creosote was everywhere, used as a maritime preservative on the wooden crates and cases all round them. The broken knots in the old boards caught at their feet and once or twice even Umrao cried out at getting a splinter in her tough feet, which were callused from years of dancing. It wasn't until the black interior of the building began to turn to gray that they realized they had searched all night. Outside, carters could be heard.

"Henry," Umrao said, "We must leave. Someone may come here soon."

"Yes, you're right. I don't want to be blamed for yet another *Thug* murder."

They climbed down through two floors of the old building on rickety wooden ladders and once again found themselves at the scene of the monstrous deed. Mrs. Clayton's eyes were no longer staring, since Henry had closed them before he went upstairs. He knelt down beside her as Umrao looked on.

"Mother," he said, "I hate to leave you in this horrid place, but I can't take you with us. I don't want to be taken by police before I have found Smythe-White. I, I really don't know what to do. This is not the way I wanted us to say, farewell."

"Henry," Umrao said, "in India people know that death is merely another door through which we must all pass. *Hindus* believe those doors are countless and result in many lifetimes. Moslems, like your Christians, believe in a just reward for the dead. But they all agree that the body is not the soul and is of no great value once the soul has left it. Is that not so? Please, come away, now. Come. That is no longer your mother."

She accompanied her imperative with an attempt to lift him to his feet. Reluctantly, he stood, never taking his eyes from the dead face which a short time ago had been so full of life. He held the lantern over her and took one last look.

In death, all the signs of trouble and age had gone from her and she once again looked like the mother of his childhood. It made the parting doubly difficult.

"Look," he said, "Do you see how peaceful she looks, now?"

"Yes, Henry. I see. She looks happier than at any time I have seen her. When I first saw her in the *kotha*, she looked troubled. When she came to us in London, she also looked troubled. Now, she is truly at rest, and we must leave her so. Come." And she tugged at his arm and drew him away toward the door.

Once out of the dark building, Henry's spirits seemed to lift. He had a settled purpose which hardened in him. He would catch Smythe-White and break him. He would see him punished for the deaths of those he had personally murdered, and for those killings done at his command.

He turned to look at Umrao.

"You don't seem that upset that Smythe-White got away. Isn't this the man you have sworn to kill?" he asked suddenly as they walked in the emerging day along Broad Street, next to the water.

She smiled, a supremely confident smile. In the golden light of reflected sunrise she looked an ageless golden idol. In spite of her tiny size, her concentrated expression of confidence made her seem capable beyond the limits of human endeavour. Her patience and determination were somehow one with the timelessness of India itself. But such qualities hardly engendered a feeling of intimacy. It made him think of a force of nature or even, *Kali*, the Hindu goddess worshiped by the *Thuggee*. At the same time, he was proud of Umrao's strength and knew that somehow before the end, she would help him achieve his purpose.

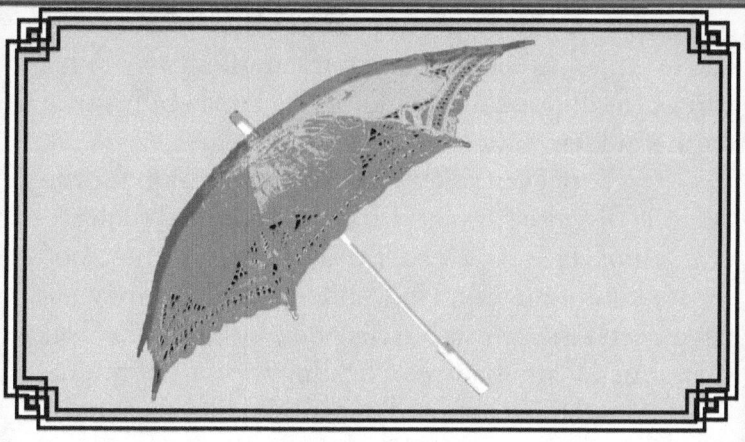

Chapter 22
Mary

In the days following the terrible events in the warehouse, Henry spent every waking minute thinking about Smythe-White and how to avenge his mother's death. It hurt him deeply that he could not stay with her and see that she had a Christian burial, but he did agree with the things Umrao had said about the primacy of spirit. He had felt, even as he looked at his mother lying on the floor of the warehouse, that death had already erased all that made her who she was. Her real self lived in his heart and with God. There would be no "miraculous return" for her this time.

Perhaps this final farewell was a little easier because he had said goodbye to her twice before, in Calcutta as a child of seven and again when he arrived in London and learned of the massacre at the *bibighar*.

The sorrow he felt drove him back again and again to the one subject that offered him some scope of action: the capture of Smythe-White. The man had been living a public life, raising funds and fooling someone as wise and intelligent as Henry's stepfather. He had even helped countless Asian families in Britain as part of his disguise and so doing, he had kept his true nature hidden.

Henry even felt a grudging admiration for the diabolic disguise Smythe-white had adopted to mask his evil genius. He was a leader truly worthy of the blood-thirsty cult of murder. He wondered if Sleeman would have been so successful in his prosecution of the *Thugs* if Smythe-White had been leading the cult of murder in those days. He seemed to have all the bloodlust of his native brothers, but he also had a keen mind, an excellent education and an exact understanding of British society and its forms of organization. With the notable exceptions of the atrocious Nana Sahib and Azimullah Khan, Smythe-White deserved to go down in history as the worst monster ever born within the precincts of Great Britain or her dominions.

After considering for several days how best to catch him, Henry could only think of one person who might know enough about Smythe-White's habits and haunts to help track him down: Mary Sutton. He hated to approach her on such an errand but, catching Smythe-White was of the last importance, for his own future and for Umrao, and to protect others from the murderous gang. So Henry resolved to take his mother's diary with his own notes to Mary. She could then decide for herself about helping him catch this fiend in human form. The fact that he had hidden his horrific crimes behind the shield of the Church's sanctity would, Henry believed, more than anything else, turn Mary against him. He had no direct evidence of Smythe-White's involvement in her own father's murder, but he had seen him kill Mrs. Clayton with his own eyes and would swear to it. His mother's diary gave Smythe-White a clear motive for killing her and showed that he had killed more than once. If Mary wished it, Henry would would swear any oath she chose.

After he had arrived at his plan to go to Mary, he discussed it with Umrao, who, to his surprise became petulant and irritable.

"What help can that pale child offer?" she asked derisively. "I cannot believe she will help you. I don't like you to go there. Our enemies could be watching that house. Perhaps the little Christian girl has been twisted into their evil purposes."

"I don't think so, Umrao. Mary is very devout and she was off balance, confused and she thought Smythe-White was a genuinely good man."

"And you think she would not follow this good man into the Christian Hell? You are foolish, Henry Booth. You trust women too much."

"Umrao," he said, taking her hands in his. "You have no reason to be jealous of her or think that I could ever prefer her to you."

"How do I know that?" she asked.

"Umrao, surely you can see my plan is the best opportunity we have. If you can think of a better, tell it to me."

"You are too soft-hearted with women. I am afraid she might bend you like wax in her fingers."

"Don't worry. There is nothing to fear from Mary."

But one real danger did exist in going to Mary's house: the police. Henry had told his mother that the house might be watched by the authorities. Part of his reason for saying that was because he had not wanted to return the diary. But he did believe the house could still be watched. Yet, he felt he had to risk it. He had to see Mary and talk to her. She was really the only person who could help him gain an advantage over Smythe-White by telling him more about the imposter's haunts and habits.

"What do you hope for from this child-woman?" Umrao said. "How can she help, and if you are taken how shall I save you?"

"You are my concern if I am taken," he answered.

"No. You have nothing to fear for me. No one wants to hurt a poor dancing girl. If you are taken, I shall get the man who killed our mothers. You may depend on it."

"No. You must promise to return to Lucknow. You must not pursue this man on your own."

"Shall I agree and tell you what you want to hear, or shall I tell you the truth?" she said. He did not answer but kissed her on the forehead and left.

Henry had conflicting feelings as he set out for the Sutton's house and left the vile alley where he and Umrao hid, like vermin in a hole. Perhaps Umrao was right. Perhaps he was a little afraid of feeling more for Mary than he should. He thought again of the long ago day of his arrival in London when Mary had taken his hand for the first time. The day he went to seek her help was the same sort of chilly, windy weather as the spring day they had first met on the pier as children. That past could never be altogether erased for Henry. At the same time, Umrao was already a part of him in ways that he felt could only result from physical intimacy. If he closed his eyes, he could smell her scent and feel her hair between his fingers. Tiny details of her facial expression, vocal tone and the stance of her athletic body now seemed as much a part of him as the gardens of Lucknow. Her music was audible whenever he wanted to hear it, and the rhythms of her dancing

feet beat in his very pulse. If he felt divided between the
two women it was a division of his English and Indian
aspects, a reflection of the same ambivalence he had
always felt about India and England. It seemed he could
not escape from a love of the heat, colour and danger
of India nor an appreciation for the cool precision of
English science and industry. He now understood why
Anglo-Indian parents tried to send their children home
before their seventh birthday. It was more than just
concern about falling behind in education, it was fear
of their children being permanently ensorceled by the
beauty of the subcontinent as he had been.

Henry had not been in the west end since the
day that he and Abdul had masqueraded as Indian
porters and he had overheard Smythe-White and Mary
talking together, as the rain dripped from the eaves and
trickled in a chill stream down his back. Had he
known then what he now knew as he approached the
familiar house, he should have leapt on the villain and
throttled him. Those moments came back to him and as
he lifted the knocker. He wondered how she would
react to his revelations about Smythe-White. He also
wondered if he would be seen and seized by the police
when he entered or left the house. There was no help
for it, if it should it happen.

In a few moments more, he confronted the
startled look on Gibbon's face.

"Mister Henry," he cried with genuine pleasure,
as he opened the door wider to admit him.

"Hello, Gibbons. It is very good to see you."

"And you, sir. Is, is the trouble over?" he asked
in a lower tone.

"No Gibbons, in some ways I fear the trouble may be worse. Is Mary at home?"

"Let me go and see, sir. Won't you wait in the parlour, sir?"

"Thank you, Gibbons," and he showed Henry in to the same room where he had sat with Mary when he was first sent down from Oxford and all their trials began. It was odd to look around at the familiar objects and furnishings and find them utterly changed. All his homely associations with the place were gone, replaced by his desire to find the man who had murdered his mother and Charles, and by the nagging anxiety that at any moment the police might rush into the room and take him.

Looking across the back of the house, Henry could see the curtains covering the window he had leapt through after Charles' murder were the same. The wall there probably still bore the small, dark mark where his foot had hit as he catapaulted onto the lawn. How would he feel when Mary came if these little things could affect him? She gave him a half hour to consider all these questions.

Perhaps, Henry speculated, the interview was as trying for her as for him.

He sat on the same couch where he and Mary had sat when they were last together. He nervously rolled and unrolled the pages he had brought for her to read. Apart from his emotions about the past, there was the very tangible fact that if Mary refused to help him, he and Umrao were at a dead end. They might then have to sneak out of the country and return to the subcontinent as if they were criminals. The mere possibility of such an outcome made him angry and determined to bend Mary to his will. He had no idea how things stood between Mary and the monster who had murdered his mother in cold blood. Were the two lovers now? Would she not have been subject to new influences since the last time they met?

After what seemed a very long interval of speculation, he finally heard a faint rustling in the hallway and the door opened.

Mary's small, fine-featured face wore a deadly pallor and he suddenly remembered how white she always became when any strong emotion gripped her. After becoming accustomed to Umrao's bold features and colouring, Mary looked doubly pale and refined. He thought of his recent adventures and reflected that the mere strain of them might have killed someone like Mary. He felt the same desire to protect her that he had always felt while they were growing up. It didn't matter if he was rescuing her from a harmless garden snake or keeping her dry in the rain, she always elicted from him a tender regard which Umrao had commented on when they first went to the opium den. He felt Mary's need for him and it drew him. Umrao would always be, in some corner of her soul, self-sufficient.

All of these thoughts passed through his mind in less time than it took Mary to walk from the door to where he sat.

"Hello, Henry. How are you?" she asked as he stood to greet her.

"At least, still alive," he said awkwardly. "But how are you?"

She gave him one of her quiet, gentle smiles and said, "Well, we have had rather a bad time since Papa died. Mama doesn't come downstairs anymore. Not even for dinner. She keeps to her room now and reads the Bible. She is unable to comprehend how such a man as my father could meet such an end. We have seen no one since the funeral."

"No one?" he asked.

"Oh, one or two of the more intrepid Church dignataries have paid very formal calls after services on Sunday. But that is all. I have not gone farther than the garden in all the months since you've been gone."

"And Smythe-White, you've not seen him, either?"

She sat down and became even more pale. She looked so delicate that her face seemed almost transparent, lit from within. He had to admit that he found her very handsome.

"Would you play for me?" she asked, suddenly.

"The pianoforte?" he asked.

"Yes, there is some Chopin on the stand I have been struggling with. There is something wrong with my tempo. You must know how much I admire your musical talent. You play so much better than I."

"*The Preludes*," he remarked when he saw what was on the stand. "Musically, these are very difficult. I did not know your taste ran to his more obscure works."

"In these last months I find I am very drawn to their austere melancholy."

Though he chafed under the constraint of the conversation, he felt it was of the last importance not to press her too hard. He had to approach his subject gently.

He played badly, woodenly. He was out of practice and his heart was not in the music. He apologized as he rose.

"Thank you," Mary said. "I believe I see what I have been doing wrong. There must be a strong enough pulse in the music to carry through the long pauses. I must count unceasingly in those places. I could see that you kept the pulse effortlessly. What are those papers you carried to the pianoforte—and that volume?"

"They are for you to read. But I must take them away with me. So I would like to you read them now—all of them?"

"Did you write them?" she asked.

"Some. The bound volume is my mother's diary."

"The start of our troubles," she said.

"So, it seemed that way to you?"

"How could it not? I shall read it. I should like to know what sort of fatality has been pursuing our family."

As Henry handed her the bundle, he said as calmly as he could manage, "You will find out some things about Smythe-White that you won't like."

"He told me about the money he stole from the congregation at Lucknow. I know the worst. And I think it is very ungentlemanly of you to berate him after all we have been through."

"Very well," he said, coldly. "Please remember that I did caution you. There are shocking things in those documents."

"Shall I get us some tea and sandwiches before I begin? This looks like some hours of reading. I know you like cook's cucumber sandwiches."

"Yes, thank you," he answered, feeling that she would read in a more receptive state of mind if he responded to her hospitality. As she rang for the parlour maid, Henry went back to the pianoforte to relieve the strain he was feeling. He took some different music out of the piano bench and thundered his way into Chopin's *Revolutionary Étude* and several other *bravura* pieces before Gibbons wheeled in the tea cart. Mary, too polite to read while he played sat passively until they began to eat. Then, she began turning pages. She soon had a remark to make.

"I never believed you were guilty of murder, Henry. And I didn't try you in the 'court of public opinion.' But Mr. Smythe-White did tell me how you took to your heels when there was mention made of the police. He told you to stay, but you ran away down the lane like a criminal. I know the police think you guilty, but I did not. I know you would never do violence to father."

"That is not what happened, Mary. Please read on and learn the truth.

He could feel himself growing hot as he thought about the villain she was defending, but he knew that if he wanted to achieve his end, he would have to remain calm. Mary had always said he was too choleric and he did not want her prejudice against his character to affect her openness to the facts.

After about half an hour of reading, He saw her face flush red and she said to him, "I never knew you had so much lust in you, Henry. I really find your antics with this harem girl disgusting." She frowned and looked genuinely pained. "I don't know why you gave me this to read. It hurts me to think of you so."

Once more, he reined in his thoughts and feelings and said nothing. He was only grateful they had not married. He now had the experience to imagine how cold their conjugal relations would have been.

Sometime later she asked, "What is this mark here?" She pointed to the manuscript.

"That means you must turn to the diary," he replied and handed her the small volume.

"What an unhappy woman," she remarked after some time. And a little later, "I should like to read the novels of George Sand, though she is not popular anymore. Mr. Zola's realism has carried all before it in the matter of French novels."

Later, she put down the diary for a moment and said: "It is shocking, Henry. One clearly sees how a good woman can be drawn into sin, all the while feeling perfectly justified by her own discomfort."

He bit his lips and made no comment. He thought of his poor, harried mother lying on the floor of the rundown warehouse, but poured cold water on the hot rage that was rising in him. He was waiting for Mary to read about the murder of Ahktar Devi and of his own mother, her cousin. That's when he believed she would begin to understand what kind of demon had been masquerading in the trappings of sanctity.

After what seemed a long, weary time he finally heard her say in an incredulous voice, "This can't be true. She must have been mistaken. She even says the halls were very dim."

"I'm afraid it is true, Mary. And there is worse to come."

"But he couldn't have fornicated with that native woman, and, and killed her for pleasure."

Henry could no longer contain himself and jumped to his feet.

"He not only did what is written there. Only two days ago, I saw him with my own eyes brutally murder my mother because she had witnessed this murder."

"That is impossible," she retorted, herself, flushing with anger. "Henry, you are mad. You frighten me. Your mother died at Cawnpore years ago."

Without thinking, he grabbed her by the wrist and put his face close to hers.

"I tell you, I saw it. I can take you there. To the very spot where my poor mother breathed her last."

"Henry, you're hurting me," she cried.

Without intending to, he had squeezed her arm harder and harder as he spoke.

"And," she continued when he released her, " I am truly afraid of you now. I fear for your reason. We all know your mother died at Cawnpore. Your attack on me makes me wonder what you are capable of. Please go."

"My mother..." he began.

"Please go, Henry. I can't bear to see you like this. It pains me deeply to fear you."

There was no choice, he realized. He picked up his papers and started toward the door. On the threshold he turned, "Mary, I tell you, he is a killer. He will brush you aside like a fly when he no longer needs you."

"You are mad, Henry. I have heard him speak often from the pulpit. He has a great heart and has a true love of Christ."

"He will use you to gain his ends and then discard you. I really fear he may hurt you, Mary..."

"You are the one who has attacked and hurt me. Please leave or I shall have to call for help. You put me in fear of my life."

"Do you truly know me so little after all these years?" he shouted as he left the room.

Once outside, Henry walked through the daylight like one blind. He was stunned by Mary's complete rejection of everything he had written and said. After all their years under the same roof. She was entirely in the power of that dangerous villain and there was nothing he could do about it. To make matters worse, he would get no help from her to trace Smythe-White's present whereabouts. He and Umrao were once more thrown back entirely on their own resources. The thought made him glance around the street in front of the Suttons. It was of the last importance that he not be followed, now.

The only card he and Umrao had to play was the treasure, which the *Thugs* wanted. If Harry were still alive, it was desperately important that the *Thugs* not find the treasure before it could be used as a ransom. Consequently, Henry spent hours finding his way back to Umrao, winding through every deserted square and lane between the west and east end. By the time he arrived in Upper Swandam Lane he had passed through many open places where concealment would have been impossible. He felt certain he had not been followed.

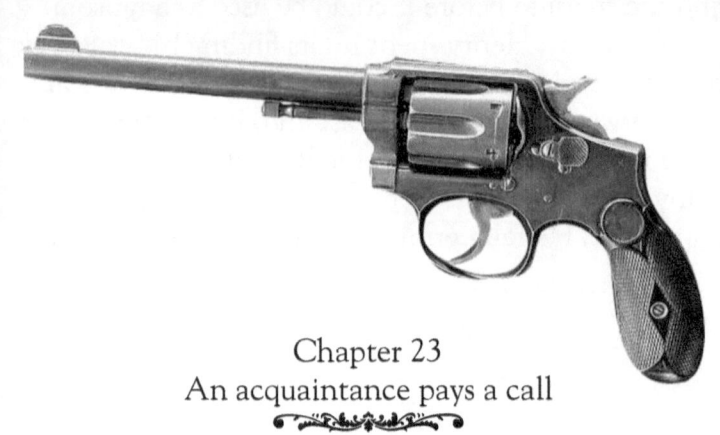

Chapter 23
An acquaintance pays a call

B y the time Umrao saw Henry, his spirits were quite depressed and he was feeling sorry for him-self and worried about Mary and Umrao. After one glance at him Umrao said, "She will not help."

"No. And even worse, she regards herself as engaged to that hound."

"Does that make you jealous?"

"No. Merely sad—and fearful for Mary's sake."

"What will you do?"

"Perhaps we should just go back to India. I'm sure my Uncle would be glad to see us— both of us. He would be happy to give me a good post. It is where I would have gone eventually, anyway."

"And you would leave this white *Thug* unpun-ished?"

"He has bested us at each turn. It now seems like a checkmate. And—I don't want anything to happen to you."

"*Bapre Bap*! You disappoint me, Henry. Where is my English knight?"

"Only in your imagination, I fear."

"You also forget that I have sworn to avenge my more than mother, Akhtar Devi."

"You won't leave England, then, to return to Lucknow?"

"No," she said folding her arms across her chest and staring up at him defiantly.

In her colourful waistcot and payjamas, her out-thrust chin made her look like an angry child at bed-time.

"Well," he answered, I had to try."

She slapped him lightly on the shoulder. "You were trying to see if I would bend."

"Yes. He was very dangerous before. Now, he will be on his guard. He shall try to kill us the moment he feels sure of the gems.

"Do you want to leave then, and let your moth-er's killer go free?" she asked.

He sat down heavily on their crate.

"I have mixed emotions about it," he said. " I want you to be safe, but I want to see Smythe-White in a halter. He is the murderer of my Mother. Providence preserved her from the horrible massacre of women and children by the arch fiends of the Mutiny. Why should he be allowed to take her life without retribution? Natu-rally, I should like him to pay the ultimate penalty."

"Then, he shall. We shall make him pay it."

"There is no 'we' involved in this, Umrao. I shall do it, alone."

"Henry, now you are being a stupid man again. Instead, be a general. You have a very small army, but I am here to serve you. Permit me to do so. You have no other allies and I am as able to kill a *Thug* as you are—perhaps more so. I am not unfamiliar with danger. And—if you do not permit me, I shall do it anyway.

There is nothing you can do to stop me."

He knew she was right, and knew how determined she was. He could not exclude her from the danger. He put his arms around her.

"My dear brave girl," he said.

"How will you start to pursue him?" she asked, pulling away from Henry's embrace.

"We cannot pursue him and we have only one thing that can bring him to us," he said. "The treasure. That's what this is all about. Perhaps he regards it as 'his' for having helped my mother and her lover get out of India. In any case, that is what Smythe-White and his minions are after. We must offer it to them once more."

"How?"

"In the same way we did last time. They did respond to our notice in the papers. I shall place another advertisement in the agony columns of the same newspapers. It will be an exact copy of the first ad I placed. That way, there will be no mistake about who has placed it. Then, we shall have to wait. I am not even certain that they will respond again, though I think they will. The death of my mother cost them nothing. In fact, it eliminated someone who could have been a danger to Smythe-White. They probably believe they have nothing to fear from us and—they may be right."

"No, no, we shall get them in the end. It is written. You will see."

"Then I shall go and place the notices."

"And I shall come with you."

"No. There is no reason..."

She put her finger across his lips. "You are a general, yes? I will dress as a child and watch to see if you are being followed when you go out. The *Thugs*, might they not watch the newspaper offices? No one will take any notice of me. Wait here."

In minutes she returned. She had perfected her original costume: now she truly looked like a dark-skinned school child. Her breasts had disappeared, her hair was twisted into a bun so tight that it fit under a school cap. She wore a faded school jumper and broken brogues. From her appearance, anyone would have judged her age to be twelve at most.

"Where did you get those clothes?" he asked.

"I bought them from an elderly man I saw on the street. He was passing with a cart of old clothes and it occurred to me that such a costume might be useful."

"It is a complete transformation," he said.

"Thank you, my general," she said giving him a quick kiss. "Now, let us start the campaign."

The newspaper offices where they needed to go were all at the western edge of the City so it took them some time to walk there. Umrao did a wonderful portrayal of a child playing with a ball as she drifted after him on the pavement. Her capacity for dissimulation was astonishing and they had agreed that as long as they were out of the house they would pretend not to know one another, so they did not speak at all. Henry was so worried about being traced back to the treasure, no precaution seemed too great. Without the treasure, their hand would be empty and he had no doubt that the *Thugs* and Smythe-White would simply fade away after murdering Harry.

They made their rounds uneventfully until, as Henry left the last newspaper office and returned to where Umrao was "playing" on the pavement, she suddenly ran up to him, seized his hand and began to run with the air of an excited child. They had agreed that this is what she would do if she saw someone watching them. In spite of his athletic training, Henry had to work hard to keep up with Umrao's short legs. She ran like the wind itself and he was determined that nothing should separate them.

In spite of their gallop she managed to say, "A big man with yellow hair in a brown coat was waiting outside the last office."

"I didn't see him," Henry acknowleded. He turned his head as they continued running. "I don't see him now."

Henry thought how strange they must look: a dark skinned man who no longer looked quite like a black, since the dye had faded somewhat, with unkempt hair and beard, and a shabby black schoolchild, holding his hand, who ran much faster than any child ever could.

In any event, no one stopped or molested them, though many turned to stare after them until they got into the quieter and shabbier streets of the far east end.

When they got near to Upper Swandam Lane, Umrao said, "I shall go on ahead and make certain no one is watching our refuge." She slowed, took out her ball and appeared to wander off with the aimlessness of a child. Once again, her portrayal was perfect.

Henry was ill at ease as soon as she was out of sight and could not help but hurry his steps to bring her into view once more. It was not many minutes before he saw her playing in front of the alley entrance to their refuge, a dark slit between the two buildings which Henry now regarded as a perfect place for a *Thug* to throw a noose around their necks. He did not really believe that they could have traced them. Yet, he was relieved when they once again stood in the ugly rooms and he saw the treasure chest standing undisturbed in one corner. They had no choice but to leave the door unlocked when they went out. There was no way to secure it from outside. He did not know that the ugly reputation of the lascars who oversaw the opium den for Smith offered them considerable protection from local thieves.

"Your portrayal of a child was remarkable, Umrao."

She looked pleased by his comment and replied, "Yes, I am an artist."

"So modest, too," he said grinning.

She shrugged. "What is the use of false modesty? It is just a lie."

Henry could not argue with her.

Once the notice was placed in the papers, there was nothing to do but wait. Both of them found the enforced idleness very difficult. They were both sick of being shut in their rooms, the broken walls with the lathe showing through the plaster and the damp of the canal rotting the floor.

Henry chafed under his eagerness to clear his name and bring Smythe-White to justice. Umrao gave no sign of the restlessness Henry was sure she felt. She was capable of a truly oriental impenetrability. She played the *sarangi*, danced and sang and began giving Henry some of the finer points of Hindustani music and dance. She tried to explain the meaning of the stylized gestures of *Kathak* dance and the moods and meaning of different *rags* and *tals*, but he could not concentrate and her commentary seemed to slip away from him. Like much of Umrao's thinking, the laws that governed this complex and ancient music seemed peculiarly fluid, even metaphysical.

She told him, "The British approach life with the idea that things are either this or that, true or un-true, yes or no, but for deep knowledge of any subject one must be able to understand that even things which appear dissimilar may also be alike. Instead of this or that, we should think of this and that."

He knew what she meant by her comment yet, her mode of thinking would often frustrate his logically structured, western mind, and when they spoke about abstract things, he often felt he was groping in a dark room. But Umrao was a very patient teacher, and after several weeks passed, Henry began to 'feel' things with more of his senses, instead of struggling to comprehend everything with his mind. She encouraged him to believe that he was becoming more sensitive, and certainly their intimate life grew even richer than he could ever have believed possible.

At times, Henry thought of Mary's white face and realized how little warmth she had and was shocked that he had ever wanted to wed her, though he still quailed when he thought of her with the villain they were stalking. If Umrao and he were successful, Smythe-White would come to a terrible end. If not, there was a good chance that the fiend would prevail and kill Henry. How would Mary feel about that? Either way it seemed a dreadful future for her. Would the day come when she would see Smythe-White for what he was? Painful as it was certain to be, Henry knew that the sooner she comprehended Smythe-White's true character, the better.

Henry had placed the notice to run until he canceled it, but after two weeks went by, he began to think Smythe-White would elude them. Then, one afternoon, there was a soft knock on their door. Even Umrao looked startled by the unaccustomed sound. Henry's first thought was that they had been discovered by the Thugs. He jumped to his feet and grabbed his singlestick, determined to defend himself and Umrao to the last. He signaled to Umrao to get behind him.

In another moment heavy blows fell on the door. "Police. Open up."

Henry's heart sank. He felt no compunction about breaking the skull of a *Thug* but, hitting a policeman would only make their situation worse. And who was to say it was not the *Thugs* trying to take them off their guard? They had come up through the establishment below, though Henry was certain that whoever it was had covered the other door as well. He and Umrao looked at each other for some long moments before

Henry finally called out, "If you are police, identify yourself."

"Inspector Lane, Mr. Booth. It is in your best interests to open at once." He could never have imagined he could be glad to hear the name of the bored, tired police inspector who had come to the Suttons in the middle of the night, yet he was glad, very glad. He knew Umrao, at least, would have nothing to fear from him. He drew the heavy iron bolts at the top and bottom of about.

Lane looked as bored and rumpled as ever, but Henry had seen his keen brain in action and knew that his appearance was a pose.

"Come in Inspector. I'm glad to see you."

"Considering who you're playing...oh, I didn't see you, miss," he said tipping his hat to Umrao. "You stay in the hall, Mulligan," he said to his thin, nervous sergeant. Then he stepped inside and closed the door.

"You're a hard man to find, Mr. Booth."

"I wanted to be, Inspector Lane."

"He nodded. "The last time we met you were not exactly in good odour with the law, so if I say I would like to make an accomodation with you, will you understand me?"

"I'm afraid not, Inspector."

"I will not arrest you— if you cooperate with me and play a part I want you to play."

"I don't understand, Inspector," Henry said again, feeling quite amazed by the policeman's proposal.

"I am not actually working as a policeman any more. I have been seconded to the Home Office and I should like your help— in the interests of the Queen and Her realm. Will you help?"

"The Home Office wants my help?" Henry asked feeling incredulous.

"Yes, sir. It's these *Thugs*..."

"Then you do know about them?" Henry exclaimed gripping the other man's forearm. " So you must know that I did not commit those murders."

"We've always known that, sir."

"You've always known it?" Henry cried. "Yet, you nearly dogged me to death."

"There were and are larger interests than yours involved in all this, sir."

"Yes," he replied. "That is true. The *Thugs* must be stopped. If they should ever prosper here as they once did in India, London would be as dangerous as the forests of Bengal...Their present leader is an Englishman, you know."

"We know who he is, sir. But we have nothing on him. The Church is all for him and without something very sound, we don't dare bring him in. He's a canny lad is Mr. Smythe-White."

"That he is. But I saw him commit murder with my own eyes."

"Who, sir? Whom did he kill?" The detective asked, suddenly waking out his apparent torpor.

"My own mother. He murdered her at Hubbard's Warehouse less than a fornight ago. She had seen him commit a murder years ago in India. And, the crime had taken place in an Indian bordello. Something he would not want his highly placed friends in the Church to know. You can use my testimony to try him on. Not about the past obviously, but for my mother's death. I am ready to go before a magistrate to swear out a warrant, immediately."

The big man shook his head slowly. His face was creased into a frown. "I'm afraid it won't do, sir."

"What do you mean? Why ever not?" Henry asked indignantly.

"Isn't he now engaged to the same young lady you were once engaged to, sir?"

"Yes, poor Mary."

"Poor indeed if that devil gets his way with her."

"But I don't see..." Henry started to say.

"Well, you have what a barrister could make out as a very good reason for trying to put his head in a halter. Besides, where's the body? And, there are things you don't know about your mother."

Henry started. "The body?"

"Yes sir, we followed you both to Hubbard's Warehouse and after you and he and the young lady left, we went inside. There was no body. We never saw your mother, living or dead."

"What!"

"Nothing there, sir. We searched every inch of that building."

"It is the art of the *Thuggee*," Umrao suddenly said. "In India they were known for making their victims utterly disappear. There were never any bodies. Therefore, there were never any crimes. Ignorant people believed they fed their dead victims to *Kali*. Actually, there are special *Thugs*, *lughaees*, whose special art is making bodies disappear. The *lughaees* do nothing but locate hiding places for graves and dig them in a way that no signs of the digging can be seen. "

"How do you know so much about *Thuggee*? Lane asked quietly. Did you have relatives who were *Thugs*? "

"No. When I was little, Ahktar Devi had a client who was very rich, an Indian banker who was head of a family of *zamindars*. He was one of the great Hindu land owners of Oudh. He was one of the bankers the *Thugs* used. He told Ahktar Devi some of their secrets. He was very powerful and helped my mother make money. He wanted to sponsor me at the *Parikhana*, the *Nawab*'s school. But Ahktar Devi would not allow it. She was one of the few people in the kingdom of Oudh who could say, 'No,' to *zamindars* who did business with the *Thugs*."

"Still," Lane put in, "very dangerous. Especially if the *Thugs* thought she had been told more than she really had...and if it can still have a bearing on Mr. Smythe-White, and if it bears on him...."

"If it bears on him— what?" Henry asked impatiently.

"I'm afraid I'm not at liberty to say. It does not concern you directly and I have already told you more than I should."

"Then what part are we to play?"

"Proceed with the plans you have already made, and if they lead us to Mr. Smythe-White, you will have done your country a great service. If we are successful, we shall see what we can do for you—to right any wrongs that might have been done. For now, we must stay very much in the background, but you will be under our surveillance."

"You will protect us?"

"Not exactly, sir. You see, we are playing a double game. One, you can see. One you cannot. We want to apprehend Mr. Smythe-White and his minions, but the

the game we really want to win has results that can affect interests that are on a national, even an international scale... " He let the sentence hang in the air and then said, suddenly "Incidentally, what ever happened to that diary of your mother's? Do you still have it?"

"No. I'm afraid it was lost in the waters of the Thames somewhere between Tadpole Bridge and Rushy Lock when we rowed down from Oxford." Henry was not entirely sure why he lied. But he feared that Lane would try to take the diary from him.

"From the beginning of this whole business, " Henry thought, "someone had been trying to get hold of my mother's diary, and I still do not know why."

"A pity after all the trouble it has caused you, sir, Lane said," seeming curiously ill at ease.

"So," Henry said, "are we never to know what this is all about??"

"I am sorry, sir. I have already told you more than I should."

"Then what part are we to play?"

"Take this," and so saying he reached out his huge hand and dropped something very cold and heavy in Henry's hand, a well-oiled service revolver. "This is the only protection I can give you, Mr. Booth."

He slipped through the door and left Umrao and Henry gaping at the massive revolver. Their difficulties had just taken on a graver and even more desperate tone. Henry didn't know what to think, but Umrao did.

"He is using us," Umrao said, her dark eyes blazing. "He is using us the same way a *shikari* uses a tethered goat to draw out a tiger. If the goat is eaten it doesn't matter as long as the *shikari* gets the tiger."

Henry thought about her succinct analysis and

said, "It could be. I am sorry to draw you into so much danger."

"It is my danger, too," she said sharply. " Ahktar Devi has not yet been avenged. That is what brought me to England, to the danger—and to you. It is my fate and I would not have it any other way."

At least we know we are not altogether alone," I said.

"Small comfort to the goat knowing the tiger will be shot after it is already in the tiger's belly," Umrao said.

"We must not be eaten," Henry said.

"And how are we to avoid that if the tiger springs?"

"By finding out what this other, this secret game is that Lane alluded to. The more we know about what is going on, the better our chance to survive."

"Now you do speak like a general," she said. "We must out-fox the British fox— the police— and we must kill the lurking tiger as well. "

Henry could see there was a fierce gleam in her eyes, a kind of savage pleasure which he had glimpsed before. It's ferocity repelled him, but also made him glad to have her as an ally. In the contest that was about to be joined, she might well be a better player than an Englishman with an Oxford degree. He knew she would not shrink from any eventuality. But how, he wondered, could they see where the tiger was lurking— before he sprang?

While Umrao retreated into her music by picking up the *sarangi*, Henry tried to see into the problem more deeply. He reviewed everything that Lane had told them. Lane said that he revealed more than he should have. Did that imply that there was a hint he had dropped that could help them? Henry considered that idea as he recollected the conversation. Suddenly, one of Lane's comments came back to him with a peculiarly poignant sharpness: "There are things you do not know about your mother," he had said. It was poignant because, in the last months he had just begun to feel that he did know something of his mother's true character and former life—after many years of feeling permanently separated from her. Prior to reading her diary and meeting her again, she had been a golden dream, a child's faery queen. He had spent most of his life longing for her and feeling that he would never know her—until very recently. Now, he had been told there was something terribly important and deadly about her past that he still did not know. So far, all of his adventures had sprung from her past. Was it not also reasonable to assume that her past was where the greatest danger had its genesis—rising from the shadows and secrets of the *kotha*, but able to overtake them in the present? What could it be? What dreadful secret would bring the Home Office into all this? Something of national, even international importance, Lane had said. And the policeman had asked for the journal, too. Henry was baffled.

The Journal again, why, he wondered? If his other assumptions were correct, should there not be some clue in the Journal? The Claytons left India under a cloud and their escape had been aided by the *Thuggee*. Is this what Lane was referring to? His mother had been very vague about the reasons why the British had been pursuing her when she left India. Henry never did learn how she had escaped from the *bibighar* if, in fact, she had been there at all. He now reproached himself with his own delicacy in not pressing her about what had happened in the grisly house of the *bibis*. Surely, there was no doubt that the deliberate slaughter, the dismemberment of British women and children by the minions of the mutineers was the most horrific crime ever perpetrated. But how could it matter so much fifteen years later?

He went over to a certain floorboard near the trunk of gems, lifted it and reached into the darkness underneath where the gas pipes were joined. The loose board was a pipe fitters' access but quite invisible to anyone who didn't know it was there. Umrao had discovered the hidden place while she was dancing and stumbled on the loose board. He pulled his mother's diary from the hollow. Lane had shown no interest in seeing the gems, but he had asked directly about the Journal. He knew of the gems and was satisfied that they would draw out his quarry. That was his only interest in the treasure. But he'd been genuinely curious about the diary, and had been deeply disappointed when Henry had told him it that he did not have it.

There must be some clue or code in the journal that he had missed before. Henry picked it up and sat down near the window where he had first encoutered the written record of his mother's innermost thoughts. Then, her words had been precious personal revelations to him. Now, he skimmed the entries quickly, no longer interested in his mother's states of mind but only in some factual detail that could connect past to present.

But no matter how he pored over it all, he could find nothing that might explain Lane's visit and his revelation about the interest of the Government itself. He felt it was of the last importance to untangle this knot of the past and present. In some ways, it felt like a task he had been essaying all his life. Now, however, it could be death to him and Umrao if he failed to comb out the secrets of their tangled histories. He even had the fleeting thought that Umrao might know something about the past that she had kept from him. She had been present in the *kotha* when his mother had come there. She was probably close by when Akthar Devi's murder took place. Perhaps she had seen something or knew something whose value she didn't realize. He quickly pushed his suspicious thoughts away and dismissed them as the result of looking for danger and shadows in every direction. But as he put down the diary and looked at the enormous revolver at his feet in the gathering gloom of the afternoon, he resolved to ask Umrao to search her memory. He would not accuse her of any deliberate act of omission. And logically, that seemed unlikely. What possible motive could she have for hiding something from him, something which might help them flush out the "lurking tiger?" He picked up the diary again to chase away his thoughts about Umrao and just happened to come upon the seduction of his mother. He thought of Mary's comment about "black lovers" and wondered, "Were we, my mother and I involved in some kind of repetitive and dangerous attraction to natives?" That was an undeniable connection between past and present, her Indian lover and his. Both of them had been, literally, seduced by Indian natives. His mother had at least had the excuse of her situation with his father. What had his excuse been for betraying Mary?

He threw the diary down in disgust. He was a rider lashing an exhausted horse.

His thoughts about Umrao were nonsense. He rose and went over to where she sat and kissed her cheek.

"Are you going to play all afternoon?" he asked.

"Oh, you are done thinking by yourself? Are you ready for me then, *sahib*, sir?" and she put her hands together and bowed from her seated position.

"Have you thought of anything new?"

"No."

"Then give me a kiss in earnest. Do not dare to be tepid with a *deredar tuwaif*."

Chapter 24
The trail runs hot for a while

The evening of Lane's visit, Henry's love-making with Umrao was very passionate and in the calm after the storm it was not difficult to advert to her early life in the *kotha*.

"I was thinking, my love," he began, "about Ahktar Devi and the powerful people she knew. I wondered if there was anything about any of them that might be connected with the policeman's visit. Can you think of anything? Any person or event that you might have overlooked as a child? Because it seems to me that like the *Thugs*, the hidden danger that threatens us must come out of the past, the early history of Akhtar Devi or that of my own mother. I have gone over what I know of my mother's life but I thought perhaps that living in the *kotha* as a child and petted favourite, you might have seen something, heard something, perhaps seemingly unimportant, that could lead us to the dangerous secret that Lane would not tell us, and which has now involved the British government."

"I have been wondering the same thing," she said sleepily. "Something has pulled at my memory ever since the policeman was here, but I can think of nothing, now, except what a wonderful man you are. Let us sleep," she muttered as she curled into a ball and pressed her back against him.

Henry knew that Umrao loved her sleep and that he would get far more help from her in the morning, so he lay awake and looked at the ceiling and wondered how they would defeat the hidden forces ranged against them. Abdul, unfortunately, seemed to be gone for good. Another crime to put to the discredit of Smythe-White. He would have been the counselor Henry would have sought if it had been possible. He had been a part of his parents' past and a good friend in the present. With his desire to finish the work of his friend, Major General Sleeman, Henry could easily imagine the little man facing Smythe-White and his *Thugs* in a premature and dangerous confrontation. That he had not survived the encounter seemed only too clear. For a moment, Henry was tempted to get up and pore over the diary again but the comfort and warmth of Umrao's back kept him from moving. He had been over the diary with great care and still found nothing. But there had to be some critical clue hidden, somewhere. He feared that not seeing it would be their downfall but, no matter how minutely he had examined the past, he could see nothing. He finally drifted off to sleep but slept badly, experiencing many fragmentary dreams.

When he woke, it was light outside and the bed was empty. He rose to find Umrao and talk to her. As soon as he entered the other room she came to him and said, "I have remembered something. Something about the great British Government, itself."

"Tell me then, what did you recall?"

"It is actually about Abdul. Did you know that he used to come to the *kotha* to treat the women when they were sick?"

"No. I didn't know."

"Most of the time it was just some stomach powder or salve for rashes. But I remember once, I must have been very small, before I met your mother, another English lady came to our house. She wore heavy gloves and was dressed in a burnoose that covered her from head to toe—except unlike a Moslem woman, her face was partly exposed. I glimpsed it only briefly. But there were odd patches of thick white skin. It was leprosy, I am sure. You know how common that disease is in India. She also had a strange smell. She was taken off to a separate room which the *kotha* kept for the sick. Ahktar Devi sometimes even took in one of the poor from the street and let them die in this room. There was something about this woman that caused a stir in the *kotha*. She was not merely another *khangi*. No. She came to us for treatment and I found out later that she had come all the way from Delhi. More than once while she was with us, I heard Abdul's voice in the hallway in the middle of the night. The whole mood surrounding this woman was strange and secretive. Even Ahktar Devi seemed flustered by her presence, and that was very unusual. In fact, I don't think I ever saw her react so strongly to anyone. When I asked her about the lady she said she belonged to Geegee. That was even stranger, for Geegee was an old monkey that Bismullah kept. In my childish mind I decided that the stranger must be somehow related to *Hanuman*, the monkey god who is so important throughout India. I was awed by this as a child, and thought our visitor was of supernatural origin. Everyone treated her like a supernatural being and within two weeks she left and I thought no more about it. In my adult life, the odd visitor has been merely a memory of distant childhood. But now I think I know who she really was. She was the wife of the GG, the Governor General of India. They used an abbreviation so I would not understand what was said. And she had come to seek help from Abdul because he was known to treat native illnesses that no English doctor could. I feel certain now that the wife of the Governor General of India came secretly to our house and that she had leprosy."

Henry listened almost breathlessly to her narra-tive. It did seem the kind of thing he had been seeking. Only, he could not see the incident's connection with the diary or the *Thugs*. But there was no question that he must follow it up and resolved that day to go to the India Office to see what he could learn about the former Governor General's wife.

On his own, he probably would not have had much luck. After all, he was making inquiries of a personal nature about the family of a once-important servant of the Crown. But Charles Sutton had a friend in the India Office on whom Henry had called before. He and Henry both wore the same school tie (or would have worn it if Henry had not been sent down) and Henry felt sure he would help. Living the life he did, this man probably knew nothing of Henry's troubles. He was a librarian by training and had become the unofficial keeper of the massive records of the English East India Company. He lived more in the past of John Company's India than any man living. His name was Plimpsol, George Plimpsol, named out of his parent's sympathy for the third monarch of that name, George III. This monarch was not really mad, insisted Plimpsol. Merely misunderstood. Setting aside this one freak of character, George Plimpsol was a first rate scholar and librarian. If anyone could help Henry uncover obscure facts about officials of India's past, it would be George.

It was a fairly long walk to Whitehall where the India Office was located. Umrao stayed at home, guarding the treasure and Jane Booth's diary with the service revolver while Henry slunk through the streets, constantly glancing back to see if anyone was following him. Without the diary and the gems, they had nothing. He was hoping to see a plain clothes police agent close at hand. Or, at least, not to see any *Thugs*. He took a very circuitous route which wound through many quiet streets and squares, but saw no one.

He arrived in Whitehall at around noon and so of course the street was clogged with civil servants, politicians and other officials walking out for luncheon. He had asked Umrao to cut his hair and he had tried to make himself look less shabby, but as he pushed along through the crowded pavement of well-groomed men, he felt an outcast.

Finally, he stopped and fixed his eye on another looter of the subcontinent who stood guard outside the building which was his destination. Clive was immortalized in bronze and stood directly outside the India Office building. Henry approached, pulled the bell and opened the door. The other minor odditities about Plimpsol were that he favoured kilts and, unlike the archtypical librarian he was a strapping athlete, a first-class oarsman and long-distance runner. Athletics was the other bond Henry shared with him. But outside of this interest, it was unlikely that George ever gave a thought to anything that had happened in the last few decades.

"Mr. Booth," he boomed at Henry," when he looked up from the old manuscript he was perusing. His great voice had never learned to whisper, but there was no one to hush him. This was his kingdom: shelf after shelf of the records of The English East India Company, originally chartered by good Queen Bess.

Henry was generally used to being the tallest man in most gatherings but George was a good four inches taller. George's huge hand enfolded Henry's and he shook the smaller man's whole frame vigourously.

"It's good to see you, George. I see you have been on the river already." The giant was already as brown as a berry and it was early in the season.

"Of course, of course. What little problem have you brought me this time?" he asked. "You never come without setting me some pretty little tidbit to search out."

"First, let me ask you about a friend of mine, an Indian chap, Narinder, by name. Has he come here at all, looking for me?"

"No."

Henry thought of the stalwart service the dignified Hindu had given them and his heart sank. Would his be another murder that could be credited to the *Thugs*? He hoped not. But now he had to press on with his other business.

"Well, there is something I need to know," Henry said. "Though, I don't think even you will be able to dig out what I am looking for. I want to know about the medical condition of the wife of the Govenor General in 1856."

"Clemency Canning," George said immediately.

"The very one," Henry said. "Do you know anything about his wife?"

"Died in Calcutta, November 1861. She's buried in Barrackpore. She was born in France, you know."

"No, I didn't. Do you know what she died of?"

"I believe the entries I've read say only 'fever.' God knows there are enough varieties of it over there."

"I need to know exactly what she died of. Can you help, do you think?"

"Egad, that is a thorny one. I mean, there may not be anyone who actually knows. The old boy himself survived her for only a year, though he made it back here to die."

"So what would you suggest? I must learn as much as I can. I am trying to trace a woman who was treated in Lucknow, and may have had leprosy."

"Leprosy? That would have been ghastly. Why do you need to know this?"

"It is a very long story, George. Suffice it to say that I have an eye-witness who has described the appearance of an English woman in '56 in a way which seems consistent with leprosy. My witness says she was rumoured to be the wife of the Governor General. Families are often very ashamed of anyone who contracts this illness. If they ever wanted to return to England, that person would certainly be kept strictly isolated. I thought perhaps Canning may have tried to hide it from the world. During his last years in India, I imagine it would have been fairly easy. No one expected a woman to expose herself to the risk of God knows what at the hands of the Mutineers. I doubt that she would have had to make many public appearances."

George was quiet for a few moments. He frowned and pulled at his lip. Finally he said, "I don't think you'll ever know. If the family were trying to hide the condition, it would be extremely unlikely to be mentioned in personal letters or other family papers."

"So you think it's hopeless?"

"Well, if you would settle for probabilities rather than historical certainties, there is some place you could go."

"Yes, I'll settle for anything, George. I'm sorry I can't tell you why this is so urgent."

"Then, you don't want an archivist. You want a medical man, a specialist in tropical diseases. Someone like that might be willing to give an opinion on what Charlotte Elizabeth Stuart would have been most likely to die of in Calcutta in 1861. Mind you, even then it will be purely speculative on his part."

"Give me a name, an address," Henry said.

"Just a minute, I'll look it up." He went out of

the room and returned a few moments later with a piece of paper in his hand. He handed it to Henry.

"Sir Morton Oakdale," he read out loud, "Eighty-six Harley Street."

"Apparently, he is the top man when it comes to tropical diseases of the skin."

"Can I give him a reference so I can get in to see him?"

"Oh, very well. Give him my name. We are both members of the Conservancy."

"The...?"

"The Conservators of the Thames to you, sir. With the amount of time you spend on the river I am surprised you are not a member. You should be. However, the doctor is a member and so am I, so you can use my name."

"God bless you, George. I shall try to come back and tell you why I need this."

Henry snatched the slip of paper and rushed headlong out of the building and back onto the crowded street where he dashed at the first hansom he saw. During a short time which seemed an eternity, he was riding down Harley Street on the southern edge of Regents Park where all the most successful medical men had their consulting rooms.

As the cab clipped along, he tried to think about what he what reason he could give for his enquiries. Unfortunately, he battened on to just about the first thing that came into his mind: Trying to authenticate a bequest of an estranged family member who had died in Calcutta. Since the whole inquiry at this point was entirely theoretical, nothing mattered except the age, general health and disease to which my "aunt" might have been exposed in Calcutta and which might have carried her off. In other words, was it even plausible that Canning's wife could have died of leprosy?

The house was, of course, elegant. The servant could have put a bishop out of countenance let alone a shabby young fellow like Henry. But George's name got him into the physician's study where he found the doctor writing at a grandly imposing desk made of carved teak. It was obviously of Indian manufacture. The man to whom Henry had to prevaricate was not the easiest inter-locutor he might have had. The doctor was over six feet in height, slender, weathered and looked hard as flint.

"Do you wish to speak to me on a Conservancy matter? I have not seen you at any of the meetings"

"No sir, my errand is rather an odd one," he said. With that preamble, he launched into his story about an Aunt who had died in '61 in Calcutta and who had left an obscure will. We, the family, were trying to make some kind of educated guess at her mental condition when it was written and in order to do that, we had to have some idea what had precipitated her end."

As Henry told his impromptu story, the doctor's long face grew even longer. Henry could see that he was not doing well with him. However, the doctor did not cut him off but waited until he had finished.

"Let me see if I understand you," he said in a sour tone. "You want me to make a diagnosis at a distance of ten-thousand miles, a decade after the patient has al-ready died."

"I know it sounds rather absurd, sir, but..."

"It doesn't sound absurd, young man. It is absurd."

"I suppose it is," he said.

"Then what is the real reason for your call?"

Without allowing himself to be completely swept aside by the doctor's penetration, Henry answered, "You see our aunt was described to us as suffering from lep-rosy."

"Ah ha," the doctor cried triumphantly. "You would be surprised how often I am called in to make this terrifying diagnosis for people returned from our eastern possessions."

" She was described to me by an eye-witness. If I repeat that description..."

"It will still not be a diagnosis, young man, but let me hear your 'description' and perhaps we shall make a start toward arriving at the truth." And as he said the word 'truth' he fixed Henry with a very deliberate look.

"She looked blanched, sir, with great patches of thickened white skin on her face."

"The person you describe may be suffering from leprosy."

He spoke in the present tense and had apparently decided that Henry's "aunt" was alive, now.

"Please do not think for an instant I believed your absurd story. However, what you describe may also be a case of *ichthyosis* or pseudo leprosy. Which of these two could only be determined by a first-hand examination. You must know the outcome of leprosy. *Ichthyosis* is more benign and may even be cured altogether. Now, I must insist that you bring this person to my consulting rooms. Even the remote possibility of leprosy is not to be trifled with. Good day to you, sir, until you bring the patient with you."

"Good day, sir," Henry managed with his last shreds of dignity.

"So what have I learned," Henry asked himself as he walked back through the pleasant streets near the park. He had not been up this way since visiting the zoological gardens on the other side of the park with Umrao. What a carefree innocent time that seemed, now. He felt a sudden stab of anxiety for Umrao, for he believed that it was just a matter of time before the

Thugs found them, especially if he went out to buy food and go on errands. They had many eyes watching for a sign of the treasure, he was certain. But how could they force the hand of the *Thugs*? And where was the "lurking tiger" of Umrao's metaphor? It seemed that his trip to Harley Street had not fulfilled the promise of Umrao's recollection. They were back to the Journal and the agony columns.

With that thought, he turned into Lombard Street where the main post office was and where he had taken a post box. A few minutes later, it was with trembling hands that he drew out a greasy looking envelope from the box. There was a dirty thumb print on it and the handwriting looked sloppy and illiterate as it had on the first reply. He did not read it but put it into his pocket book and hurried home, as quickly as caution would allow.

He pushed open the door to their threadbare lodgings which, in spite of their lowliness, had served them well and allowed them to remain hidden from their enemies. Umrao hurried to greet him.

"What did your friend say?" she asked.

"It might or might not have been leprosy. But I have been thinking: suppose it was leprosy, then what? Suppose the Governor General's wife did have this horrible disease, what does it have to do with us, my mother's diary and the government's interest in us? It is not enough that Mrs. Canning was married to a high member of government, we must see what the connection is and that has eluded us. It has eluded me all day. Without that connection, assuming there is one, of course, we still cannot 'see the tiger,' to use your phrase. But we have heard from him, at last," he finished dramatically, drawing out the envelope with a flourish.

"What do they say?"

"I have not read it yet. I thought I should read it with you." He turned it over in his hands and noticed for the first time that the flap had been lifted and re-gummed. "Someone has read this before we have," he said. "It can only be Lane and his people from the Home Office. No one else would dare to tamper with the Royal Mail for a letter."

"How do you know?"

"Only Lane could gain access to the Royal Mail, open something, read it and replace it. It is his way of keeping us under his watch without arousing the suspicions of Smythe-White."

"What does it say?"

The note was terse and surprising. "Be at the top of Glastonbury Tor on the night after you receive this. Bring what we want and you may be spared."

"Glastonbury? Why? And not even a trace of pretence about turning Harry loose," Henry growled. "Oh, Lord. They must have already killed him. Poor, poor fellow."

"I am so sorry, Henry," Umrao said drawing close to him. "What shall we do?"

"I must keep the appointment. Lane knows about it and would want us to draw out Smythe-White for him. I must play the goat to Lane's *shikari*—and hope he is a good shot. There is simply no other choice. You shall stay here."

"No, I shall not," she said in a voice of granite. "I shall watch your back, as the English say. That policeman may do nothing to help us. He said so, himself."

"But I begin to feel that he may be our only hope of getting to the bottom of all this. If I cooperate with him, he may help us. He said that, too."

"So now you've decided to trust the *shikari* who

is tying you up before the tiger? He may help us but he may also behave like most of the English officials I have known: extend the hand of friendship while holding a weapon in the other hand."

"Then what do you think we should do?"

"Take a look at your watch."

For a moment, he could not understand her. He thought she had taken leave of her senses. Then her meaning became clear, "The moon, you want to know how much moon there will be tomorrow." He pulled out his watch, a farewell present on going up to Oxford. He had shown it to Umrao and she had thought it remarkable. It showed the time, date and the phases of the moon. The face of the moon had been beautifully worked into the face of the watch.

"A very new moon," he said looking at the dial. "There will be hardly any light at all. What there is will rise late and set early."

"Good. Now what is this place mentioned in the letter?"

"It is out in the country in Somerset on the edge of a little town of about three thousand souls. The grand Abbey next to the town was sacked centuries ago and is now nothing but ruins, though many Christians believe it is a sacred place, even the burial place of England's most famous king, Arthur. The Tor is reputed to be a centre of spiritual power."

"But have you been there? What is it like, will we be inside or outside, trees or no?"

"Oh, it is mostly open ground at the bottom of the Tor. But the Tor itself is a strange mound, rising above the flat plain all around. It is bare of trees but covered with grass. It will be quite a climb with that iron bound box on my shoulder," he added. "I wish I had some way to communicate with Lane, even though I

413

know he is aware of our meeting."

Umrao pulled a sour face. "Dismiss him from your mind, I tell you. But I am glad it is a sacred place," she added. "Greater help may come from that quarter."

"You constantly amaze me, Umrao. Here, I thought you were laying out some bold plan."

"I told you it is written that we would prevail over our enemies. It is even more likely in a sacred place."

Chapter 25
The Isle of Glass and the Vale of Tears

What odd, perverse twist put Smythe-White in mind of the Glastonbury Tor as a venue for the confrontation, Henry could not guess. But, when he thought about it, he had to admit there were good practical reasons for the choice. It was safer for Smythe-White to meet in the Somerset countryside than in London, especially if he sensed that Inspector Lane was watching him. It probably would be safer for him to depart the country with the gems from some port other than London, perhaps Bristol. On the Tor, under the pale light of a new moon it also might be easier to convince Henry that one of his own men was actually his half-brother—before they attempted Henry's life.

Of course Henry hoped against hope that Inspector Lane was wrong and that Harry would be present. This consummate villain had also timed the delivery of the meeting time and place with nice judgment: Henry had received it on the day before the meeting, giving him little time to make plans of his own. Finally, there was the fact that a lookout on the Tor could see for miles in every direction across the mostly open ground of the Salisbury Plain. Whatever the practical reason, he believed Smythe-White's choice of the Tor also revealed something of the man: in spite of the foul beliefs of the *Thuggee* whose ghastly rites he observed, Smythe-White had for many years previous to reorganizing the *Thugs* been a good cleric from all he could gather. So whatever else may be said of him, he was a believer in unseen powers: the best and the worst, and like the man, the place he had chosen for a venue had always been marked with a curious mixture of the Christian and pagan, a place hedged round with legends of Celtic Britain, while being venerated by Christians as the site of one of the oldest churches in the world.

The Tor, a terraced elevation reaching nearly five hundred feet above the level, grassy Salisbury plain which stretched for many miles all around was, according to Celtic legend, supposed to be the home of the Lord of the Underworld. Two thousand years ago, the sea washed right to the foot of the Tor, nearly encircling it. Over the centuries the ocean was succeeded by a vast lake. An ancient name for the Tor is *Ynys-witrin*, the Isle of Glass; "isle" because, after the ocean waters receded, from most angles of approach, the lake and island would have looked like an island of glass set in the level plain. The Tor, or the isle that stood in the vast vanished lake was also known as Avalon, a name derived from the demi-god Avalloc or Avallach, who ruled the land of the dead. In Celtic lore, Avalon was an isle of enchantment, a place where the separation between realms of living and dead was permeable. On Avalon, legend said, the living and dead could meet and converse.

Henry wondered if the choice of venue had a symbolic significance, the knowledge of which might offer some strategic advantage. Surely, Smythe-White knew the legends of the place better than he. The Sutton family had Celtic blood, but Smythe-White's gift for languages had allowed him to master Welsh and Old Irish, the language of the first mention of King Arthur in the seventh century tale, *Chulwich and Olwen*. Smythe-White had even used 'Ynys-witrin' in his note. It was a signal that he was done hiding the fact that he was the prime mover of the events in which they were participating. Henry felt it was also a signal that he was planning to leave England. Obviously, no Indian *Thug* would have known of 'Ynys-witrin'. Smythe-White was ready to cast his false Christian skin. The note was in his own handwriting even though the address on the envelope was not.

When he was younger, Henry himself had been drawn to the Tor by the romance of the place. He had last visited it just before going up to Oxford in his first year. He had galloped across the countryside on his own horse just so he could climb the Tor at sunset because, supposedly, one could still see the lake and Island as it had once existed in this world and still existed in the Celtic Otherworld. Because of these deeply personal associations with the place, Smythe-White's choice of the Tor as the place for their final encounter had chilling overtones. It is universally known that Avalon was where Arthur's fatally wounded body had been taken after his last battle.

"Perhaps," Henry thought, "it was also chosen to unnerve me."

There was something uncanny about the place and when Henry had looked out from the Tor on that sunset visit, he did feel that he was looking out over a vast lake. The evening mist had a bluish cast and gave the impression of very transparent water lying above the fields far below. The evening he visited the Tor as a lower classman, he was young and had been highly susceptible to its enchantment. That the Tor should be chosen by Smythe-White as a meeting place was strange indeed.

Henry told Umrao about King Arthur and the Celtic legends associated with Glastonbury as they rode out from Paddington to Castle Cary, the closest station to their destination. There they would have to hire a dogcart. She listened to him wide-eyed. He had never seen her so entranced as by these ancient legends. He omitted the part about the Tor being a meeting place for the living and dead because he realized that she was profoundly superstitious and took such things very seriously. When he told her how Joseph of Arimethea's staff had taken root in Wearyall Hill, close to the Tor, her dark eyes became as big as saucers. She looked like a child listening to hearth side tales. She combined a wonderful innocence with a surprising toughness of mind. He was glad she was absorbed in what he was saying. He could not entirely shut out his awareness of the revolver's weight in his pocket. He feared for them both and wondered how he could get Umrao to stay behind while he went up the Tor. This night was to be the crisis in their adventures, he felt certain; it would almost certainly be a deadly one.

Finally she said very seriously, shivering slightly. "Those are all excellent omens for us."

"How do you know that?" he asked. "Smythe-White is the one who chose the meeting place. Why would they not be good omens for him? You told me that *Thuggee* are great believers in omens." He spoke in a light teasing way. But Umrao was in deadly earnest. He noticed that she shivered again.

"Are you ill, Umrao? I saw you shiver."

She ignored his question and said, "The omens are good for us because the place is good and so are we. The others are the evil ones." She delivered her line of thought as if Henry was missing the most transparent thing in the world.

They were alone in the compartment so he slipped his arm around her neck and kissed her. She nestled against him like a kitten. After a long time listening to the wheels of the carriage clicking over the rails she sat up, looked at him and said, "Don't worry Henry, you shall triumph. It is written." And she shivered again.

"I saw you shiver twice. Are you ill?"

"No," she replied. " It is just that talk of spiritual things moves me deeply, that is why I shivered. I wish I could help you more tonight."

"The thing that would help me most is to be certain you are safe." he said. And feeling that no better time was likely to present itself, he went on,"Would you consent to stay down at the bottom of the Tor?"

"If it helps you," she said off-handedly. "I needen't have put my pajamas on under my skirt."

"Oh, Umrao, you relieve me inexpressibly. Thank you."

"You care so much for me?"

"You know I do."

"And you are not just being a knight of the round table, a knight who will go back to the English girl to rescue her—afterward?"

He hugged her to him and said, "Never my dear, sweet child. You are the companion of my heart—forever."

She looked very pleased with the answer and once again settled into the crook of his arm.

They said little else during the rest of the trip,

but basked in the warmth of their closeness. On the seat directly across from them was Mrs. Booth's trunk filled with a vast fortune in gems.

At Castle Cary they got off the train and Henry got the chest onto a dogcart. He still had a dreadful picture in his mind's eye of his mother's bloated face as Smythe-White finished strangling her and dropped her to the floor of the warehouse. He would have to govern himself carefully when he saw the killer and false friend. He knew his immediate impulse would be to fall on him and beat him within an inch of his life—which would do nothing to save Harry. So he turned his thoughts to the practical question of getting the chest up the steep, uneven sides of the Tor. A barrow or cart would only make the job harder. He could see nothing for it but putting the chest on his shoulder and struggling up the steep side of the grass that covered Tor. He felt quite equal to the task, but it would make it harder to be vigilant on the way up and began to wish they had come earlier. Smythe-White and his men would have a good prospect of his climb while he would be preoccupied with the trunk and unable to see them on the heights. He wondered if that could be part of his reason for bringing him here.

Henry left Umrao sitting on a stone near the bottom of the Tor in a small declivity. A heavy fog was now moving across the plain toward the Tor. He watched it for a few moments. It was moving quickly and would probably engulf the Tor around the time he gained the top. On the plain, all would be obscured by fog. At the top of the Tor, it probably would be clear. From where he stood, the layer of fog didn't look that deep, but it would certainly hide Umrao. In the dark, it would be impossible for the *Thugs* to find her.

He climbed about fifty yards, put down the trunk

to rearrange it on his shoulders and turned to look at Umrao, already considerably below him.

In the final glance before he started upward again, he thought her more mysterious than ever: child, woman, sibyl, lover, a wood nymph in a demure English costume of brown alpaca with a single long braid, sitting among tall grass as naturally as if it were the carpet of her own drawing room. He never loved her so much as in that moment when he glimpsed her in the gathering darkness. All traces of light were fading rapidly and her dark dress was beginning to melt into the space around her. He thought fleetingly of what she had said about the importance of mystery between men and women. He felt a pang of fear at leaving her alone but he muttered to himself, "It is written," under his breath and lifted the trunk onto his shoulders.

Strong emotion, darkness and uneven ground made it difficult to judge the length of his climb. The fog seemed to climb with him, however, and soon all would be cloaked in obscurity, perhaps even the crest. His hope was that he would be the first one up the Tor. It was a good hour before the time Smythe-White had named. It would have been pitch dark if he had fulfilled his instructions to the letter. Still, he feared an attack of some kind as he climbed, though he knew that because of the chest resting on his shoulders, they could not throw a noose around his neck. He had to pay close attention to the uneven sloping ground, and was continually trying to look downward as he balanced the chest. It seemed to him that he was crawling up the Tor, some kind of odd insect creeping through the grass.

The physical struggle to bear the weight of the treasure and not to fall was more than matched in intensity by the emotional struggle that buffeted him like a ship at sea. He wanted to kill Smythe-White himself,

yet knew he must be diplomatic. Henry was furious at
the false friend who had insinuated himself into his
family. He had never liked him, always disbelieving his
elaborate piety and the obvious ways he had ingrati-
ated himself with Charles Sutton. But having seen him
kill his mother and being forced to treat with him for
Harry's life enraged him. For years, Smythe-White had
hidden behind the church, using its respectability to
mask his horrific crimes. And while Henry had never
been pious, Smythe-White's villainy and sacrilege
moved him to fury which would have been great even if
he had not seen the white *Thug* with his hands around
his mother's throat.

Now, he told himself, must come the reckoning.
Now the monster must be made to pay. First, though,
he thought, trying to regain control of himself, he must
find out if Harry is alive or dead. He did not want to
do anything that would reduce the likelihood of his
half-brother's survival. If Harry was not present, Henry
would assume that anything Smythe-White said about
him would be a lie. That the scoundrel would be plausible he had no doubt.

It then occurred to him that if not for Smythe-
White and his *Thugs*, he would not have met Abdul
or Umrao and his whole life would now be different.
He wondered, how much of the old *Thuggee* network
of families and money was still in existence in India.
Did Smythe-White control any part of the vast *Thuggee*
kingdom that had been at least partially disbanded bySl-
eeman? How large was it now? Or were Smyth-White's
men only the handful he had seen here in England?
Questions, perhaps, for the future. First, he told himself,
he must hope that Harry is among the living. Second,
he must get him away from the *Thugs* unharmed. Then
and only then could he consider the luxury of revenge,

perhaps through the agency of Inspector Lane.

The weight of the revolver was, he felt certain, stretching and ruining his jacket. As he had this banal thought which would have made Amelia Sutton proud of him, he gained the top of the Tor. A moment later a sharp voice cracked the darkness, a voice he recognized and which made him hot and cold all over.

"Put down the chest," Smythe-White ordered in a tone Henry had never heard from him before.

"So your villains can throw a noose around my neck?" he asked with more bravado in his voice than he felt. "Where is Harry." He thought briefly of using the gun that tugged at his pocket but realized that it would be a sure way of killing Harry.

"Oh, we have Harry, Henry. You may rely on it."

" I rely on nothing you say, you fraud. You are a liar and a cowardly murderer."

"Umm," Smythe-White murmured. "But you didn't come here just to insult me, did you? The treasure is really in the chest?" And for a moment Henry heard the uncertainty in his voice. He wanted to be sure the ransom was here. He felt rather than heard other men slipping through the darkness and fog, surrounding him.

"Put down the chest, Henry. It is all over. You will soon join your friends."

"And Mary, shall you kill her as well?"

"No. I am leaving England tonight. Mary was merely surety in case the treasure slipped through my hands. She will marry with a considerable settlement. I have had access to all of Charles' papers."

"You are a foul degraded creature," Henry said, spitting the words from between my teeth.

"Perhaps. But if you don't put down the chest, your death will be slower and more painful than need be. Do put it down like a good chap. I shall dedicate your death to *Bhowanee*. She will be glad to receive you."

At the mention of *Kali*'s cult name, Henry heard mumurs of assent coming out of the darkness. There were at least ten *Thugs* with Smythe-White. Occasionally, he could glimpse their forms moving like shadows against the whiteness of the rapidly thickening fog that was rising all round.

Henry bent down to unburden himself, intending to throw himself on Smythe-White a split second later but, as he straightened up something very soft dropped around his neck. Before he could spring on his enemy. The *rumal* tightened around his throat inexorably. His assailant stood behind him and Smythe-White was within a few feet of him, smiling, obviously enjoying his struggle to breath. Henry's position had not allowed the *Thug* to break his neck. A noose would have broken his neck, instantly, but the *rumal* would slowly choke the life from him.

Then, as he fought for breath and felt himself sink under Smythe-White's smirking gaze, out of the darkness he heard a blood-curdling scream and saw a tiny figure rush out of the fog. A moment later, the grip around his neck lessened slightly. Smythe-White scowled and leapt toward him. At first, he could not imagine what had happened, for in her fury, Umrao's voice was unrecognizable. He heard spitting, unintelligible curses and then the grip was broken enough for him to spin around and confront the man. Henry and his assailant were so close, he could see his glassy eyes already aware of his own death as Umrao, mounted on his back thrust her knife into him repeatedly, hissing like a cat. It was too dark to see her weapon, but Henry assumed it was the wicked, curved knife he had seen her wield. She had lied about having it with her.

In just moments the *Thug's* light coloured suit showed large, ink-like marks . However, the *Thug* was not alone and split seconds later, Umrao was dragged off of him into the darkness. Then there was commotion on all sides of Henry as he lost consciousness. He awoke with his head propped up by someone's knee.

"Umrao?" he asked.

"I'm afraid not, son," Inspector Lane said as he poured brandy between Henry's lips.

"You, here? So you were following."

"Just a few moments too late. The fog was not something we had reckoned with, you see."

He could tell that the big policeman was trying to soothe him and he sat bolt upright.

"Where is Umrao? She was here a few moments ago. She saved my life. Where is she? Umrao!" He called as he staggered to his feet."

"She's dead, son. The devils broke her neck. It was quick, at least."

"Oh, no. Oh my God. No," he heard his own voice as if from a great distance.

The thick fog blanketed everything and seemed to make any sound more distant.

"I'll kill him. Where is that monster! I'll kill him," and he lunged blindly into the darkness.

"I am ashamed to say that he slipped past my men," he heard Lane say in a flat tone. "But we'll get him. That little oriental girl died to save your life, sir. If it were not for the fog she should not have died."

"Umrao!" he screamed and fainted. But as he fell to the ground, for an instant he saw an ephemeral likeness printed on the thick fog. It was Umrao, smiling at him as he lost consciousness.

"It was written," he heard her say, and then knew no more.

When Henry next became aware of himself, he was shocked to find himself in his old room at the Suttons' home in London. The gas was turned down low and it was night. Mary was dozing in a chair not five feet away from him. She looked like a fragile porcelain doll in her repose.

How, had he gotten here? The inspector's men must have rounded up the other *Thugs* and carried him to the train. He could only remember odd fancies about making love to Umrao. They had been back in their broken old rooms on the canal. They talked about many things that he couldn't quite remember. The more awake he felt, the farther away she seemed, which made him want to sleep the same eternal repose where she lay. The more he woke, the more pain he felt. His sorrow for Umrao was like a fist in his chest, stopping his breath and heart. He thought he would surely stop breathing at any moment. Instead, he started to weep, softly at first, then in great wracking sobs that woke Mary. She came to him but he pushed her away.

"I am so sorry, Henry. For everything," she said as she sat down next to him on the bed. She tried to put her arms around him as one would to comfort a child but he roughly pushed her away, almost striking her with clenched fists.

"You don't know," he howled. "That cursed monster. Your friend," his voice rising in volume. "A fiend in human form," he screamed at her. "And he got away. Did they catch him, yet?" he yelled and tried to jump out of bed. But he was feeble and slipped backward, pinned by the bedclothes upon which Mary was sitting.

Mary's composure broke and she said. "I'm so sorry, Henry. I didn't know what he was. I still can't believe it. I am so sorry," she sobbed. "Inspector Lane, told me, you see, when he brought you home. Forgive me."

"Sorry?" he yelled. "You're sorry? Umrao is dead. At the hands of your fiancé. And I saw him strangle my mother with his own hands. He smiled at me while one of his *Thugs* was squeezing the life from me. If not for Umrao, I should be dead, too. I wish I were so that Umrao and I would be together," and then, he burst out crying.

By this time, Mary, too, was sobbing loudly. Both of them wept uncontrollably for what seemed to an endless length of time. Henry fell asleep and woke to see Mary's sleeping face on the pillow next to him. But he would not soften. He refused to acknowledge any of her sorrow. What was her loss compared to his? She had been saved from a dangerous villain, He had lost the dearest, wisest heart that ever beat!

Mary also had the misfortune to have a complexion which was not improved by tears. She had red blotches on her sleeping face. He got out of bed and found himself surprisingly unsteady on his feet. In fact, he lost his balance and fell against the bed.

Mary woke and looked at him, "Henry, what are you doing? You shouldn't be out of bed. Gibbons can bring you the chamber pot." She rose and helped him back into bed.

"No. I don't need that. But, I am so weak. Why am I so weak?"

"You have been in the grip of a delirious brain fever for more than three weeks. You must get your strength back. That's why Inspector Lane brought you here. So you could convalesce."

"I don't want to get better. I wish he had let me die on the Tor with Umrao."

Mary took his hand as she had when he was a

very little, lost boy and new to England.

"Tell me about her, Henry. Could you do that, do you think? Should you like to?"

"I don't want to cause you any pain," he said. Then, recalling the circumstances on the Tor he said, "I must telegraph to Lane at once to find out what has been accomplished while I have been lying here. Surely after three weeks they have caught the villain. I hope they hang him soon. Do you know anything?" He snarled at the girl who was weeping softly next to him.

"No. Inspector Lane has not been here since the night he brought you. Please, don't be angry with me, Henry. I am also your sister, you know. Please be kinder to me. Can't I comfort you in any way? Won't you take my hand again and let me be your gentle sister? Tell me about her, Umrao," the name sounding awkward on her lips.

"I don't know," he said sulkily. "I don't think you could bear it."

Mary's head drooped but she slipped her hands over the covers, captured his hand and held it tightly in both of hers.

"Now I shall feel braver no matter what you say, Henry. Remember when we were little and I had to do something hard I always asked you to hold my hand?"

He said nothing. His heart was frozen and hard. Her appeal to the past touched him not at all.

After a long period of silence she said, "I know I have made many mistakes. But shall you not be at least my friend if not my brother any longer? Do tell me about her."

She sensed immediately that her request was the first thing that had reached him.

He began thinking about Umrao and their time together. He realized he did want to make her more present by talking about her. It didn't matter who Mary was. He would have talked to the dog, just so he could speak about times that would not come again. The temptation to recall Umrao from the vagueness of death was too great to be gainsaid. By the time he'd had enough, the sun was filtering into the room. Mary reached over and turned the lamp out well before he was done. He omitted nothing. He even told Mary about his intimate moments with his *deredwar tuwaif*. He talked about *rags* and *tals*, about the tone of the *sarangi*, about Umrao's voice and her grace when she danced, her hands fluttering like two quick birds, while her silvery ankle bells beat out the rhythms of the *Kathak* dances. He wanted Mary to know how irreplaceable Umrao was, and he wanted to show her that no one else could ever again make him happy. Above all, he wanted her to know that she could never possibly stand in Umrao's place.

He was unkind, angry at everything: at Lane for not moving more quickly through the fog, at Mary for ever having anything to do with Smythe-White, at the monster's wiliness that let him slip away from Lane and his men, even at God for allowing Umrao to die. He felt angry and bitter toward anything that pretended to peace, happiness—anything good. How could anything in this world ever be good when his dear woman-child was gone from it?

He poured out all his love, bitterness, rage and disappointment.

Once he fell silent, Mary blushed more deeply than he had ever seen her do and said, "If we had been married before—before all of it—I would have been happy with a tenth part of the love you have felt for her. I should have thought myself a very fortunate wife, indeed."

Unfortunately, he still had some bile in him and he wanted to hurt Mary for showing her affection toward him. Those were his excuses for what he said next:

"A tenth part is all you would have gotten. Umrao was a poet, a sibyl and wise about love and life in ways you will never comprehend. What she taught me I could never have had with you."

When he looked back on this conversation at a later time, he wondered if Mary deliberately offered herself as a victim of his rage and hurt. At any rate, he knew he had behaved abominably.

She finally could not tolerate any more, burst into tears and ran from the room. Almost immediately, he became aware of his exhaustion and was soon fast asleep.

Chapter 26
The astonishing secret of Jane Booth's Journal

Mary came no more to the sick room, but Amelia took up the task of providing whatever little nursing Henry still required. She must have known about his bitter words to her daughter, yet she offered him none in return. When Henry begged her to send a wire to Inspector Lane, she did it immediately, taking the message to the office herself, rather than entrusting it to one of the servants.

His message to Lane ran: "Have you caught that evil man, yet? If not, why not? Is there anything I can do to bring about his demise?"

It was sent, but no reply came, not for some time. Henry never could have guessed the form it would take.

Amelia was as kind to him as the day he met her on the East India Dock. She sat with him for hours, patiently working away at some embroidery she had on a frame.

She was thinner and paler than before. After all, she had lost a husband whom she revered and had doubtless heard about the death of her cousin at Smythe-White's hands. That must have been a terrible shock. She had even suffered through the rancor that came between Henry and Charles at the last. To say that she bore it all gracefully is an understatement. Of course, she now dressed in black all the time and even though she was still attractive, Henry was certain she would never remarry.

Henry rapidly grew stronger, tried to gain control over his thoughts of Umrao so that they affected him a little less like a knife thrust. Within two weeks of his first long conversation with Mary, he was up and about and taking meals downstairs. Archibald fawned on him and Gibbons welcomed him home by giving him the wine list. There were moments when everything felt as it had been, though he and Mary made certain they were never alone. He knew he had to leave as soon as arrangements could be made. But his first order of business was to visit Inspector Lane and berate him for not writing. He had to know what steps were being taken to bring down Smythe-White. Now that he had some strength back, he could not rest. One evening, the evening he had vowed to go to Scotland Yard the next day, Gibbons came to him in the drawing room where he was reading the *Times*.

"Sir, are you at home?"

"To whom, Gibbons?"

"An Inspector Lane. He has been here twice before, I believe."

Henry stood up at once and led the way to the hall where he found the Inspector.

He, too, looked more worn. Henry could see at a glance that their adventure had not left the policeman unscathed. They greeted each other like friends.

"You are looking very well, Booth. I have been waiting for your health to improve before I gave you a report." He held out his hand which Henry took without hesitation.

"That is why I haven't heard from you?"

"Mrs. Sutton strictly forbade me, sir. She is not a woman whom one disobeys."

"Come this way, Inspector," Henry said leading him into the drawing room. To his surprise, he found Mary sitting, waiting for them. It was the first time he had seen her since the stormy interview weeks earlier.

"I should like to hear what Inspector Lane has to say, if you have no objection, Henry?"

"Of course, Mary," he said in the gentlest possible way. Even at a few days remove, he deeply regretted his words to her.

"Perhaps afterwards you would stay to have a word with me?"

"Of course.

"Do sit down, Inspector. What can you tell us about Mr. Smythe-White?"

The big man looked pained. "I am ashamed to say, sir, very little."

"You mean he has gotten clean away?"

He nodded. "I believe we have the rest of the villains. Of course I recognize that they are nothing to you, sir, but I am glad to have such practiced killers behind bars."

"What is your opinion then, Inspector about *Thuggee*? That is, do you still think that Sleeman eliminated them?"

"I should say, no, sir. He certainly wiped out a vast number of them but, it was naive to think that a long-standing association based in many cases on family ties of many generations could be destroyed in a few years. How much Mr. Smythe-White has done to restore them, I couldn't say, though his accomplishments in that line seem prodigious."

"Then are you of the opinion which I hold, that Smythe-White has probably decamped to the subcontinent?"

"Henry," Mary said, "You never told me that was

what you thought."

"I wanted to speak to the Inspector, first, Mary."

"I see."

"Mr. Smythe-White is a very clever villain," the Inspector continued. "He had his escape very well planned. I have been able to trace him as far as Suez, but there his tracks disappear into the wastes of the Sahara. He is as bold as he is resourceful and will probably cross the wastes and take a boat from another African port."

"I am certain," Henry said, "he will return to India. All of his lieutenants and resources are there. He can dispose of the gems to the friends he doubtlessly has among our enemies, the Russians."

"You think like a policeman, Mr. Booth."

"I've had time to do little else but think, recently. I want to see that man fitted up for a halter."

He saw Mary turn very pale.

"I am sorry, Mary," he said as he went to stand next to her seat. "But the villain must pay for his crimes. Not the least of which may be his revival of the most terrible organization of murderers the world has ever seen."

Mary took the hand he had placed on her shoulder and held it.

"I know, Henry. His crimes are horrible."

"Well," Lane said, "my opinion is that he is a long way from being taken."

"No," Henry said. "He is not. I am going after him. I had a strong presentiment of what your report would be and have thought of little else, lately."

Mary again turned pale and said, "You said nothing about leaving, Henry."

"I'm sorry, Mary. I had wanted to tell you in a different way, only the opportunity didn't present itself."

He could see that she was mastering some very strong emotion, though precisely what it was he didn't know.

"That is a bold resolve, sir," Lane said.

"Not really. There is no other purpose in this world that can have a prior claim over this one."

"I understand, sir. But I have some other things to impart to you. I think it might be as well to do it in private." He glanced at Mary, who got up to leave.

"Please sit down, Mary," Henry said. "Anything Inspector Lane needs to tell me, he can also tell you. You are, after all, my sister. You have suffered the loss of your father in all of this."

A faint smile managed show itself on her face.

"Thank you, Henry."

"Miss," Inspector Lane broke in,"without disrespect, there are things it would be better if you did not know. Terrible things that are quite shocking."

"If Henry permits me, I shall stay," she said stubbornly.

"As you will, Miss," he said.

Lane was quiet for a moment and then said, "I am sure, sir, that an intelligent man like yourself will realize that there are several pieces more to the puzzle of recent events. Is that not so?"

"Yes."

"Then I assume that you would like to have possession of those pieces."

"Yes."

"Then allow me to preface what I am about to tell you—and your sister— is not for anyone else's ears. As I told you, sir, there are state secrets among the disclosures I am about to make. You both will be very shocked."

After this dramatic introduction Inspector Lane paused and studied their faces. Then he went on, apparently satisfied with their solemnity.

"My disclosures have to do with your mother, sir."

Henry quickly sat down next to Mary who automatically took one of his hands in one of hers.

"Do you know anything of the circumstances of your mother's departure from India after the Mutiny?"

"Very little. I restrained myself from questioning her when I had the chance—something I now sorely regret."

"Well, I shall begin by saying that she left under a very dark cloud indeed."

Henry felt all the blood in his body rush downwards into his boots. His mouth was suddenly dry.

"Yes?" he said in voice like the squeak of a mouse. Then he managed to clear his throat and say, "Was she really at the dreadful *bibighar* in Cawnpore? And if so, how did she escape?"

"That is an excellent starting point for what I have to say, Mr. Booth. Yes and no."

"I should have known I would get no plain answer to this mystery," Henry said to himself.

"It isn't plain because what happened was most extraordinary and we know only part of it. Do you know, sir, whom we believe was directly responsible for the slaughter of women and children that terrible day?"

"I know it was reported that the rebel general Tatya Tope gave the order? Didn't he give the order?"

"Yes, he did. But I mean the man who plotted and planned and cajoled Nana Sahib into taking arms against us, the man who wanted to make Nana Sahib our irreconcilable enemy."

"Azimullah Khan?" Henry said.

436

"Yes, sir. That one. Even though it was Tatya Tope who gave the orders for the murders of the women and children, Khan was the evil genius behind that foul undertaking."

"What about him, then?" The hair on the back of Henry's neck was standing up, as if his body already knew the incredible truth.

"Your mother was brought to the *bibighar* by him, personally," Lane said.

"You have proof of this?" I asked.

"We have a letter which I am not permitted to show you. Suffice it to say that it is from your mother written to Azimullah Khan. It proves that he brought her to the *bibighar* and shortly afterward"—his face took on an extremely pained expression— "he became her lover."

Henry knew of course, from reading the dates in his mother's diary that Lane was wrong but, in that moment, something else gripped him. All mention in his mother's diary of "my friend" suddenly fell into place. The nameless Indian man she had met in the *chowk* in Lucknow, the man who had taken her to the *kotha* and there seduced her was none other than a man who bore one of the most reviled names in all of British history: Azimullah Khan, lieutenant to Nana Sahib and co-conspirator—and some said originator—of the Indian Mutiny! This was the man his mother had loved. This was his half-brother's father—one of the worst traitors in the kingdom's long history!

He felt something next to him on the love seat and looked over to see Mary in a dead faint, her head had fallen back and her eyes were rolled up in their sockets. He grabbed the bell-pull and immediately rang for assistance. Gibbons came a moment later.

"Smelling salts, Gibbons, in Mary's room."

"Right away, sir" and before the door was closed we heard feet running upstairs.

"Hurry, Faith," Gibbons called after the young girl he had sent on the errand.

Henry gingerly patted Mary's hand until Gibbons appeared with the smelling salts.

"Allow me, sir. After forty years of overseeing a house full of servants I know something about the use of smelling salts."

"By all means, Gibbons."

Mary came around immediately, which made Henry think that no serious damage had been done. After Gibbons left he turned to Mary and said, "Are you all right?"

"Yes—but—how horrible, Henry."

"I do apologize, Miss Sutton," Lane said. "But I did tell you it would be shocking. And I am afraid, Mr. Booth, there is more."

"It must be an anticlimax after what you have already stated," Henry remarked.

"I suppose that depends on your point of view," Lane said, grimly. "Perhaps less sensational. But only just."

"But wait," Henry said, "do you know if my mother was actually in the *bibighar* at the time of the slaughter?"

Lane shook his head in the negative. "She told us that she wasn't."

"She told you? When? What have you to do with her?"

"That is getting a little ahead of my story," he said.

"But clearly, Khan got her out of the country?"

"I should say it was the other way round, Mr. Booth. Your mother and the fact that she was English got *him* out of the country. They went by the name of Clayton."

"Thank God Harry is no longer alive," Henry said. "I take it that is a fair assumption," he added looking at Lane.

"I believe he is gone, sir, though we've found no body."

"The Lord works in mysterious ways," Mary said.

"He does indeed, Miss," Inspector Lane said.

They were all quiet for a moment.

Then Henry looked up at Lane and said, "So Harry had no idea about this?"

"We don't think he did," Inspector Lane replied.

"Thank God he never knew," Henry said. "He just thought his father was a dealer in gems and antiquities."

"Well, he was, in a way," Lane said.

"What do you mean?" I asked.

"Those gems in the trunk which Smythe-White and at least two of his men got away with were from Nana Sahib's house in Bithur."

Henry smacked his thigh with the flat of his hand. "Of course, Bithur. When I read my mother's diary something about that name struck me but I couldn't place it. Nana Sahib's home. What did he call it?"

"Saturday House."

"Yes, that's it."

There was another long silence and then Henry said, "I must ask you something else about Nana Sahib. Did he have strong ties to *Thuggee*?"

"We don't believe so, sir, but the thought is intriguing. What makes you ask?"

"My mother told me that she and her 'husband' owed these gems to the *Thuggee*, who had helped them leave the country. Of course, that was long before

Smythe-White was ever connected with the cult."

"Then that is one small missing piece of this story that we had wondered about: how Mr. and Mrs. Clayton had slipped out of the country, probably landing in Russia, before settling in Turkey. How that villain made friends with those enemy nations—I can't guess. It was enough for him that they were our enemies."

"Yes, I imagine if they had the aid of the *Thuggee* getting passage on a boat bound for Russia would have been a great deal easier. Money, papers, everything they needed could have been supplied to them."

There was again a long pause as we all digested the revelations, then Lane spoke, "Sir, you once told me that you had lost your mother's diary, somewhere between Rushy Lock and Hampton, I believe."

"Yes," Henry said.

"That wasn't really true, was it, sir?"

"No."

"May I see the diary, Mr. Booth."

"I am afraid, Inspector, cordial as you have been I still do not want to surrender the diary to anyone. I can't see how it could be of any use to anyone now. After all she is dead."

"But do you have it in your possession?"

"I can lay my hands on it." Henry said in a truculent tone.

" I don't want to read it, Mr. Booth. But I want to show you something about the diary itself which will surprise you. It is quite important, sir. I shall only take it from you for a couple of minutes and I shall not remove it from this room. Would you bring it here, sir. It is a matter of some moment for the War Office."

"The War Office?" Henry cried. He and Mary looked at each other, utter astonishment plainly written on both their faces.

"Yes, sir. Will you do it?"

"If for no other reason than my curiosity is piqued beyond all measure."

"Could you bring it here tomorrow by about five o'clock?" the policeman asked.

"I couldn't resist your mystification in any case, Inspector Lane. And your promise that you'll not take it from me. I'll do it."

"Thank you, Mr. Booth. I shall see you tomorrow at five."

When Henry promised to bring the diary to Inspector Lane he had not thought about the fact that in order to get it he would have to return to his old rooms overlooking the canal. Of course, their things might have been removed by Smith or by thieves, but he doubted that anyone would tear of up the floor boards. Yet, he knew he would not look on the rooms he shared with Umrao without strong emotion overtaking him.

After Lane left, Henry and Mary had a brief conversation. She was anxious to discuss how all of this would affect her mother, who had already had such great losses. Dared they tell her that her estranged cousin had been the lover of—not just a native—but of the arch fiend of the Mutiny, Azimullah Khan? It only took Mary and Henry moments to agree that the answer to the question was a decided 'no.'

"It is not just that it is shocking in itself," Mary elaborated, "Mother was actually great friends with the Lady Lucy Duff Gordon."

Henry looked at her blankly.

"Lady Gordon was a very unconventional, well-connected lady, whom papa used to call ' a cigar-smoking radical'. Against all likelihood, she and mama were great friends, sharing a strong interest in literature. But the end of their friendship came when Lady Gordon sponsored Azimullah Khan when he came to London in the early fifties. The odd pair were so inseparable that many people believed they were having an affair. Mama thought so. Lady Gordon introduced him to the best society of the metropolis and mama broke with her over it. Mama told Lady Gordon that her behaviour was improper. So you see, if her own cousin..."

"Oh, yes," Henry said. "That would be bitter, indeed."

"Yes, very bitter" Mary added.

"My poor mother," Henry suddenly said. "She seems to have been in a trap from the beginning of her life in India. A short time of happiness with my father and then all went sour. How sad. She wanted so much to rise above the foolish prejudices of society. Her intentions were noble, even high-minded. She wanted to be something more than women are allowed to be—except..."

"Except?" Mary said with a question in her tone.

"Except in the *kotha*, among the society of courtesans, a society of outcasts who achieved a kind of equality with men."

"But surely you can't..." Mary began, then, remembering his relationship with Umrao, she coloured and was silent. Then she added "The judgements of society can be very harsh and exacting," Mary replied. "And Cousin Jane certainly set Anglo-Indian society at defiance by her impulsive actions."

There was no way Henry could explain to Mary what he had learned from his mother and Umrao. Both women would have given anything to live according to their own beliefs rather than assigned roles. Umrao stepped out of even the unconventional role of a courtesan when she vowed to avenge her mother's death. He could not help but think of the lines from George Sand that his mother had taken as her catechism: "We cannot tear out a single page of our life, but we can throw the whole book in the fire."

He thought, no one had told her or Umrao about the risks attendant upon throwing the whole book in the fire. At least, he thought, she had aimed at something higher than the narrow world in which she had found herself, even if her efforts were doomed. Mary's sanctimonious tone annoyed him. Jane Booth had risked all and lost all— but not through her own wickedness. Azimullah Khan had used her discontent and her love for him to make her his tool, a tool for taking him to a safe haven after tearing the subcontinent asunder. It was he, not she who was to blame for what had happened—and for the end at Hubbard's Warehouse, even though the hand that struck her down was Smythe-White's. Khan had sent her into the danger.

Henry suddenly realized then that when he returned to India, he would be hunting two quarries. He stood up suddenly, surprised by a thought that struck him. Mary sat silently, watching him closely.

"That trip must be when Khan met Lady Gordon and must be when he brought the gems to England. He probably told Nana Sahib he would use them for bribes, though it seems likely that Nana supplied him with a great deal of cash, too. I remember hearing from Sir Joshua that Khan had come to England to argue Nana's right to inherit a Company stipend from his predecessor. Sir Joshua said he spread a great deal of money around the City during his stay."

Henry was quiet for a moment and then added, "I wonder how much of this Mother knew? I can understand why she ran off with this fellow. Everyone who ever met him thought him charming, especially women. My father was a brutal beast. But I can't believe that she would help him steal, even from Nana Sahib."

"I am sure Cousin Jane would never do anything like that," Mary said soothingly. "And, if, if Khan was having an affair with Lady Gordon and Cousin Jane knew it she would surely have broken with him, Mary said."

"She did not have many options open to her. I'm not certain what she would have done if she thought her lover was unfaithful."

"Oh, but really," Mary said. "This is dreadful, speculating on the degree of Cousin Jane's culpability, when she was so recently taken from us in such a horrible way."

"Yes, Mary. You are right. Let us not walk on mother's grave, wherever it may lie. I have to fulfill my promise to Inspector Lane and there is no time like the present for doing a difficult task. I must go and fetch the diary."

She must have read some kind of pain in his face for she reached out and touched him on the arm and said, "Do you want me to come, Henry?"

"No, dear sister. I must gather Umrao's things, if they are still there. I'm certain strong emotions shall overtake me and I do not want to inflict them on you."

"I understand," she said. "But if it would help you, I should come anyway."

"No, thank you, Mary," and he bent to kiss her on the cheek before leaving the room.

Henry took the Sutton's carriage to Swandam Lane and was not surprised that as the ugly narrow streets came into view the pain of his loss overcame him afresh. The alley was unchanged. He could believe that not one mote of dust had been shifted or changed in the malodorous approach to their rooms. The steps creaked in exactly the same places and the door stuck in the usual way. Everything was the same except—except—that Umrao was dead and buried in a handsome plot which Lane, under authority from the Home Office, had arranged for her in a country churchyard not far from Glastonbury. There she would rest for all eternity in the cold island that she disliked so much.

The rooms were also unchanged. The dust was a little thicker but nothing had been stirred at all. The sight of Umrao's colorful robes which she had pinned to the walls overwhelmed him and he fell onto their old pile or rags and pressed them to his face as he wept for a long time. The jasmine based scent that Umrao had worn clung faintly to the tattered bedclothes. He clutched them against his body, mingling his tears with his memories of Umrao and the hours they had passed in the dingy little room.

Finally, he was able to rise and began to gather her scanty possessions. Most of what was in the rooms was hers. Last but not least, he went to the loose board, pulled it up and reached down into the dark hole. The Journal was gone! he was literally staggered and fell against the wall with the shock. He did not know the full purport of his loss but he did know that people had been trying to take the diary from him since the beginning of his adventures. There was only one man to whom he could attribute this theft. He had gotten away with the gems, Jane Booth's Journal and Umrao's life. In that moment in those dusty rooms, overpowered with rage, he swore that Smythe-White would return everything— everything that could be returned—and pay for that which couldn't, with his own life.

In the grip of these overwhelming emotions, he returned to the Sutton home.

"Where is mother?" he asked.

"She is out overseeing one of father's favourite charities. She is mending clothes for poor Indian children in the east end."

"Really?" he asked unable to hide the surprise he felt.

"I know. But you know what father believed and now that he is gone, every one of his undertakings has become sacred to her. She supports all his interests that she is capable of supporting."

"My having the carriage must have inconvenienced her. I am sorry."

"It didn't matter. She had a ride with another lady. She will be back for dinner. It would be nice if you dressed for the meal. Mother would appreciate it."

"Of course, Mary. It has been sometime since I had my own clothes."

"Yes, I realize that. But Mother has always taken such pride in your appearance. I do, too."

"Really? I never knew that."

"Now you do. Don't let it make you vain," and she smiled.

So in a short time, Mary and Henry were more reconciled than they could have hoped after Henry's harsh words.

They dined together as a family and both women withdrew to their rooms early, while Henry spent half the night pacing up and down speculating about what Lane would say when he heard of the theft of the diary. While he paced Archibald watched him with close attention, his long ears spread out over the carpet, no doubt speculating, in the way of canines, about Henry's agitation.

Henry could not stop wondering what he would learn on the morrow. Everything had turned on his mother's Journal. It's delivery started their troubles with the *Thugs* and it seemed to haunt them still. Why? He could not begin to come up with a credible reason. He certainly hoped that Lane would tell them tomorrow. in spite of the fact Henry no longer had it. It was past three before he could fall asleep on the love seat.

"I yielded to an overpowering instinct of outcry and rebellion which God had implanted in me, God who makes nothing that is not of some use, even the most insignificant creatures, and who interposes in the most trivial as well as in great causes."

—George Sand

Chapter 27

The following morning, Henry and Mary had a few words in the drawing room after breakfast. They agreed that neither of them would tell Amelia about what they had learned from Inspector Lane. Neither of them wanted to keep her in the dark but, the truth would have been hurtful to her, indeed: to realize that her own cousin had been lover to the arch fiend of the Mutiny. Amelia had suffered enough. She knew nothing of Umrao's true history, only that she and her Uncle had helped Henry through a bad time.

After their talk, Mary and Henry spent the rest of the day waiting, waiting in the drawing room, waiting in the yard, waiting in their own rooms, but always waiting for Inspector Lane. At a quarter to five, as they waited in the front hall with the footman, the two agreed that it had been the longest day of their lives.

At five exactly by the hall clock the bell rang and though they had been waiting all day, Mary and Henry both started at the sound. Then Henry lunged at the door and opened it.

Before Lane had even crossed the threshold,

Henry blurted out, "Inspector, the Journal has been stolen."

Henry had expected some strong reaction but the usually placid detective was literally staggered, as Henry had been when he made the discovery.

"Blast him, the clever fiend," the Inspector said a moment later, his light complexioned face turning bright red.

"Smythe-White?" Mary asked.

He nodded, "Who else? Though how he learned about it I can't imagine.

Unless..."

"I don't understand Inspector."

"Let's speak somewhere more private," he said.

I opened the door to the drawing room and Mary led us inside. As soon as the door closed behind us, Lane said, "This is an unmitigated disaster, Booth."

"I knew you would feel that way, Inspector. But I don't really know why. I don't know why everyone has been trying to steal this Journal from the day it arrived in England."

The big man was so absorbed by the loss of the diary that he fell into a chair while Mary was still standing.

"No, no," he said absently. Of course you do not know why everyone tried to steal it. But I see now that we are dealing with two of the wiliest criminals to ever do business in our island.

"I had the same thought myself, sir, this afternoon," Henry said. "That there were two rather than one."

"They certainly fooled me," he said.

"Inspector Lane, if you could just tell us why you wanted to see the Journal—and why everyone has been trying to steal it, we would feel greatly enlightened,"

Henry said a little more sharply than necessary.

"It's a bitter dose to lose the Journal," Lane said shaking his head. "But yes, of course I'll tell you. "

"We are all attention, sir," Mary said, sitting on the edge of her chair.

"None of this must ever leave this room," Lane said in his most official voice.

"We understand," Henry acknowledged.

"Do you realize that Europe is increasingly an armed camp? The world's five great empires, us, the Turks, the Russians, the Italians and the Germans are carving up the rest of the world. It is a race to see who will come out with the greatest prizes. Right now, we are in the lead. Our potential enemies of greatest importance are the Turks and the Russians. The Russians, we believe pose an even greater threat than the Turks. Both are well- positioned to interfere with our routes to the subcontinent. To a handful of far-sighted men in the Home Office, it is a question of when and where the war will start, not if. It could be five years, ten years, even more, but eventually these great powers will be at war. And that diary contained secrets of incalculable value to Great Britain, secrets which could save tens of thousands of lives and hundreds of thousands of British pounds—in the event of a European war. German improvements in naval technology, in weaponry, sizes of deployed troops, all this and more."

"Is that what this has been all about?" Henry cried. "You are all mistaken, sir, I have read the diary from cover to cover. There are no such state secrets in it."

"But you never read what was in the covers," he said.

"What do you mean?" Henry asked.

"Hidden within the covers was a wealth of

written information on the true state of the Russian and Turkish fighting forces."

"But that's impossible," Henry said.

"No Henry, you see, for some years, your mother has been our secret weapon in maintaining the British advantage in the European balance of power."

Lane saw that Henry was agog and too stunned to speak so he went on: "Ever since Azimullah Khan went to the Crimea in the fifties, we knew he had made alliances with the Russians and the Turks. How he was able to serve both of those masters, we do not know. But he and your mother traveled widely in Russia and Turkey, ostensibly for his work as a dealer in gems and antiquities, but actually as an espionage agent, a secret agent—plotting, as he always has, to bring about the ruin of Great Britain."

"You astonish me Lane," Henry said.

"Then let me astonish you even more, Mr. Booth. What Khan didn't know was that your mother approached us through our people in Istanbul after hearing certain conversations with members of the Russian government and offered her services to us. Not for pay, mind you. I was not ever privileged to meet your mother, Mr. Booth, but it is in her dossier that her reason for helping us was that she felt such profound revulsion for the atrocities committed at the *bibighar*. She did witness some the horrors...

"But I thought she hadn't been present, she said..."

"It is a government policy not to release *any* information regarding the atrocities committed in the *bibighar*. It is too inflammatory. In the eastern empire, people died just for making assertions about what had happened, Your mother was simply doing what we asked when she said she had been absent. You see, Khan was late getting her out of the *bibighar*. On the day of the massacre, Khan had to put her in with the other English women to satisfy his own fanatics. They had to believe that she was going to die with the others. So she glimpsed the beginning of the slaughter. Then, Khan managed to get her out, himself. But she had no idea that her lover was the man responsible for what she saw. She only learned about his role after they had left India.

After she knew what Khan had done, she could hardly stand to be in the same house with him. But she only learned the full extent of Khan's part in the *bibighar* butchery some years after the fact. It was through a letter from one of the leading mutineers, that she learned that Khan had given direct orders to Tope that the women and children were to be destroyed without mercy. She was almost killed herself because Khan was late taking her away. She did witness the beginning of the horrors as she was leaving. What she saw, we believe, was why she was willing to do almost anything to undermine Khan once she knew the truth. Once that ghastly deed was done, Khan knew there could be no turning back for Nana. When your mother saw the letter that outlined the chain of command, she came to our people in Istanbul to get papers to leave Turkey and Khan forever, but when she arrived, we told her how she could help us and she agreed to think about it. Shortly afterwards, during a conversation with some Russians, she overhead things which she knew would be of use to us. She came to us with the information and agreed to work with us. She said she was doing it for the little ones she saw die. Needless to say it was with the utmost difficulty that she returned to Khan's house and played at being his wife. I can't imagine how she must have felt. She must have been an incredibly strong woman. Heroic is the only word that seems appropriate. I would imagine that seeing what she had seen would have given her a nearly superhuman determination to be avenged for being involved in the slaughter and for being lied to by her lover. It is probably what enabled her not to see you, Mr. Booth, until the pressure of circumstances forced her to. She kept her life separate from yours rather than endanger you in any way."

"What you tell me is the most astounding thing I have ever heard," Henry said after a long interval of silence. "My poor mother. No, wait, actually," he said suddenly. "It was what she had wanted. I remember what she wrote in her diary several times. It was a quote from George Sand, the French author. I believe it went like this:"

"I yielded to an overpowering instinct of outcry and rebellion which God had implanted in me, God who makes nothing that is not of some use, even the most insignificant creatures, and who interposes in the most trivial as well as in great causes. She wanted above all else to find that great purpose."

"I believe she certainly found it, Mr. Booth," Lane said.

"Yes," Henry said. Her strength of character overawes me, though I had glimpsed hints of it in her diary. I tell you, Lane I disagree with much that Britain has done in India, using the people and the subcontinent so we could enjoy our tremendous wealth at home, but against the other European powers I back our people completely. I feel a thrill of pride to know that my mother was such an extraordinary woman."

"Now you see," Lane went on after a long pause, "why it was of the last importance that nothing should happen to reveal your mother's true work."

"Yes, but the *Thugs*..." Henry began.

"Were a ghastly interference and a complete surprise to us. In some ways I think that Smythe-White is one of the most brilliant criminals I have ever encountered. He ranks way above Khan as an intellect. From the beginning, he has been two steps ahead of us. And now, this final *coup de maitre*, stealing the diary to auction it to the highest bidder, which will probably be us, will make him even richer. When he sells Nana's gems he will have tremendous power. Imagine his wealth in the service of his criminal contacts and knowledge of the subcontinent." Lane shook his head. "I have much to answer for."

They were all quiet for some time, numb with shock. Then Lane said, "Did you have any idea that the *Thugs* had found your hiding place, Mr. Booth?"

"No. Every indication was that we were safe."

"Did you go out at all, close to the time that you got a reply from Smythe-White?"

"Yes, yes I did. I was following up something which I thought might lead me to answering the riddle you had set me when you mentioned the Home Office. I went to the India Office."

"That," Lane said emphatically, "is when they saw you and found your hiding place."

"Wait," Henry said. "Why was this information hidden by my mother in the covers of the diary in the first place? And why was it sent to me?"

"Sending the information she had for us in the diary through your Uncle in India was a touch of genius," Lane said. "The information was so valuable to us that she dared not take any chance of it not reaching us. If she brought it herself, she could have been followed and exposed. She was aware of both the *Thugs* and her own husband's confreres from Turkey and Russia. Getting that information to us was a perilous difficulty for her. So she hit on this plan."

"You mean she sent this information to me without telling me? After not seeing me all these years? That seems very odd."

"She tried to tell you, Mr. Booth. If you recall, you actually got two packages from India."

"Yes. I'd almost forgotten. The empty package of pasteboard was the first one I received. I couldn't imagine why my Uncle had sent it."

"It was supposed to have contained a letter to you, Booth, from your mother, explaining what she wanted you to do. The first package must have been intercepted by Smythe-White. He opened it and removed the letter. Knowledge about the diary was the card he waited to play until the very end of his little charade."

"How could he have intercepted it?"

"Not in the mail, so I would guess that one of your college scouts is much richer now than he used to be."

Henry smacked his knee, "That blackguard, Bannister."

"Of course, the scout knew nothing of the whole plot. He must have been terrified when the college president was killed. By then he was involved and would have done anything to avoid being connected with the murder."

"But what about Azimullah Khan?" Mary asked. "Will he and Smythe-White divide the money? Are they united?"

"United only by their willingness and desire to enrich themselves by theft. Otherwise, I would guess them to have very different motives. Khan wants to destroy us. He has never gotten over waiting on British officers when he was a servant after graduating from a British charity school. Smythe-White is a different sort. He is a career criminal and loves wealth for the sake of power. That's how I read him. They will start down the same road but I doubt they will remain together, two such villains."

"But how would they have known that I would be at the India Office?" Henry asked.

"That I can't begin to guess," Lane said. "But think of the many possible connections between the archives of the Company and the people with whom we have been concerned. Perhaps one of them saw you there quite by chance."

"If I'd only realized how damaging my search for information would be."

"You did a good job of keeping our followers off of you, Booth. You can pride yourself on that."

"I was followed?"

"From the day we finally located your hiding place, which was the day I came to you there."

"Tell me," Henry said, "was Abdul working with you?"

"No, but we knew about him, of course. He had been Sleeman's *aide de camp* in his last years in India. He knew more about *Thugs* than any man alive, so we watched him closely. He knew he was being watched, however, and never led us to your retreat. Now, you can also understand, sir, why you had to remain a felon until the business was concluded."

"No, perhaps I am dense but that escapes me."

"All right," Lane said. "We weren't entirely sure about three things. First, the location of the diary. It never occurred to me that you would keep it in those unguarded rooms—not after the events in Oxford. I was certain it was in a bank vault somewhere in the City. The second thing we didn't know was the exact relationship between Smythe-White and Khan. We still don't know that. We could do nothing that might let Mr. Khan know how to lay his hands on the diary. If he knew of its existence, he could have sold it back to the Turks or the Russians, and your mother would have been sacrificed. Khan would have done away with her if he had any hint that she was working against him with us, the British. I assume that only Smythe-White was involved in stealing it. Khan has kept well out of Britain and probably knows nothing of the diary's recent history. All of that was Mr. Smythe-White's work."

"Why would he want it?"

"So he could auction it off to the highest bidder among our European rivals. We weren't sure if your mother was alive after Hubbard's Warehouse. We still don't know positively. If she were alive, we wanted to keep her that way. There were many things in play all at once. We wanted to keep all the threads in our hands until the very last moment. When we saw your notice in the paper, we knew the time for action was upon us. I arranged to have your mail opened. Up to that last moment, we wanted to force you to remain imprisoned in those rooms and out of the way. Your trip to the India Office and its results shows how delicately everything was balanced. We wanted to have as few surprises as possible. As it is, the villains have beaten us hands down."

"Henry," Mary put in suddenly, "What about the Home Office getting you reinstated at Oxford? So you can finish your degree?"

Before Lane could answer Henry spoke up, "I cannot go back to Oxford, now, Mary. Surely, after what we have both learned and after...Umrao, you must realize that I can only go to India to hunt down these two jackals. Though, I doubt Khan will return to India. It's too hot for him. But how could I do otherwise?"

She looked down into her own lap, but Henry could see that she was in the grip of strong emotion. He was not surprised. He had expected her to take it badly. She had obviously been hoping that their more cordial relations of the last few days might have changed his mind about many things.

"I am sorry, Mary. I must go."

"As must I," Lane said rising quickly, obviously not wanting to intrude on a personal conversation between Henry and Mary. "If you adhere to your plan, Mr. Booth, and go to India to chase jackals, our paths may cross again. He held out his hand to Henry.

"Do you think you will go to India? It's clear you are not a run of the mill policemen." Henry asked.

"I don't know to a certainty, but if I had to guess, I should say, 'yes.'"

"Then perhaps we shall meet, Inspector," he said opening the door of the drawing room, "for going to India is certainly what I am set on doing. Good day."

"Good day, sir, and good hunting. He dropped his voice. "Watch out for Smythe-White, he is a clever demon and will stick at nothing."

"I shall."

Henry re-entered the drawing room and found Mary where he had left her, but when she looked up at him that was an odd expression on her face. He could never have guessed what she was going to say next.

"Henry," she said, "I, too, shall go to India."

"But, but, I shall be upcountry for months on end, Mary. I may not even go to Calcutta. I shall have to go wherever the hunt takes me."

"But wherever you are, you shall still need cooking and to keep your clothes in order."

"Mary, it pains me to say this so directly, but I doubt that I shall ever marry."

"I understand. But I am still your sister and there is no one in the world dearer to me."

"And what if I do take Smythe-White? One of us must surely die."

She turned very white but answered very clearly, "Henry, I-I looked up to him, spiritually. That was his attraction for me. I can hardly look up to him now, can I? Please say you will have me come out with you— as your sister."

"But your mother..."

"Has many friends and activities to keep her busy."

Henry thought carefully about his next words. "I shall probably live in Lucknow, at least for a time. I can't explain it. I only know I must go back there. But if you come as my sister then I order you to live in Calcutta with Uncle Henry. Under no circumstances will you risk yourself upcountry. Uncle Henry's situation is a comfortable one. He is a confirmed bachelor but would be delighted to have cultured and beautiful young woman in his house who had no expectations of him. I am sure you would be welcome, indefinitely. What do you say?"

She got up from the love seat and walked over to him. There was something mischievous in her eyes. She kissed him on the cheek. "I say, yes," she replied in a very positive tone.

Lucknow 1875

T his seems the only possible place where I can end
this narrative, speaking once more as myself and
not like someone outside the events I chronicle.

I am sitting with my pocket book and fountain
pen in the tall grass which grows around the ruins of
the Residency in Lucknow. From where I sit, I can look
across the Gomti River to the jungle. Of course, it all
looks very different than I remember. It has been transformed not merely by an adult perspective and twelve
years of time, but also by the punitive damage that the
British inflicted on this beautiful place after the siege.
The Residency itself is a broken ruin peppered with
shot. The scarred stones still speak to me of the horrors
that occurred here, and of the heros on both sides of the
conflict.

I have not come here in the more than two years
of being back in India. I only arrived in Lucknow last
night. I had much to do: commercial arrangements to
make with my Uncle, get Mary settled in Calcutta and

of especial importance, put inquiries in hand regarding Khan and Smythe-White. Most of all before coming to Lucknow, I needed time to dull my loss. Now I can think of Umrao here, among the monuments of Lucknow's shattered beauty without breaking down. How strangely everything from this place connected us and drew me to her, my *deradwar tuwaif*, the appellation she bore with such fierce pride.

When I felt ready, I traveled upcountry on the Ganges to Cawnpore, towed on a flat by a steam launch, the same way I had left India as a child. The vivid descriptions from my mother's journal mixed with the present so transparently that I found it dfficult to know if I was seeing through her eyes or my own. The jungle changes little from a human vantage point.

Of course, I stopped at the Memorial Well and paid my respects to the most innocent of the fallen. Here, for long years, I had thought my mother lay with the others, but she had risen from the slaughter as my dream foreshadowed and achieved something remarkable.

From Cawnpore, I traveled the same road my mother had traveled to see Khan before they became lovers, the road between Lucknow and Cawnpore. As soon as I arrived in Lucknow and found myself in the old city, I sought out the beautiful entrance of the Hoosineabad bazar. Once again, I saw the moonlight turn the refined arabesques of the bazaar's gates into a magical passage. They glowed for me under the Indian moon. Here, I got out of my carriage and sent my things on while I walked into the town to find Ahktar Devi's *kotha*. Jasmine still hung in the air.

There are few left of the old narrow streets and buildings which my mother described in her diary. The British destroyed most of these, along with the most beautiful buildings in Asia. I could hear two *tablas* echoing out of some of the buildings near the Hazratganj. In a few places, there were still courtesans smiling down from the carved balconies, in spite of the hypocritical British repression of prostitution in the town.

Much about the *Chowk* seemed still the same as my mother saw it yet, I felt the spirit had gone out of the place. I did succeed in finding Ahktar Devi's *kotha* and stood outside looking at the building. There were no brightly dressed mustachioed doormen. I tried to imagine my mother here on the first night of her adventure, on the night that she, "threw the book in the fire," a young civilian wife, standing in a place where she should never have been. Then I knocked on the door and heard slow footsteps within. A tall, young man, apparently lame, opened the door.

"Is Bismullah here?" I asked.

Why he admitted me, I don't know. Perhaps it was enough that I was English and might threaten them in some way. There was about the whole city a cowed and beaten quality. Even where the streets had been widened and "improved" by army engineers, it was really more of a rape. I stood in the semi-dark hall and waited.

There were smells of delicious food, as my mother had described. At least the *kotha* was not too poor to entertain guests properly. After a while I saw a woman coming toward me out of the dark hall. She was certainly well over fifty, tall, very dignified, with much of the same pride in her face that Umrao had. She made me think of my mother's descriptions of Akhtar Devi, only with features perhaps a little less beautiful.

"Young Englishman, I am Bismullah. Why do you ask for me? I am old enough to be your grandmother."

"Perhaps, but I am told that no one can sing like

Bismullah."

She looked at me sharply. "And do you like Hindustani music?"

"Oh, yes. Very much."

"And who told you my name?"

"Umrao," I said. It was the first time I had spoken her name out loud since I had wakened at the Suttons'. I had written to Bismullah telling her of Umrao's death but that had been over two years ago. I had said nothing about coming to Lucknow.

"You are Henry Booth?" she asked, looking startled.

I nodded. My heart was too full to speak. This woman had been an older sister to Umrao. She was the closest thing to a surviving relative.

"Come, she said, and led the way into the large room my mother had described. There were only two or three men smoking *hukkahs*, hardly a crowd. They had an air of waiting for something. Bismullah barked something at the young man in Urdu, and spoke to her clients. There was a murmur of approval.

"Please sit and enjoy our hospitality," she said to me. "You know what good music is. I shall get the best musicians in Lucknow for you."

And she did. It took about half an hour for the musicians to come but then, Bismullah sang with two *tablas*, and a *sarangi*. They made music for us until the small hours of the morning. The room filled up and there were approving smiles and nodding as the men listened. This was what the *nabob* in London had been trying to recapture.

In between the music, Bismullah stuffed me with wonderful food and watched every smile or happy glance of mine as if I were paying her in gold pieces.

When I began to feel sleepy she made it clear

that I was to stay, free of charge.

"You shall have a girl, a very beautiful flower, not unlike one you have known."

I shook my head in the negative, but when I went to my room there was a very pretty, very young girl in my room, sitting on the edge of my bed. She was about fourteen, a *tuwaif* in the prime of her career. She did remind me of Umrao. I gave her a large tip and tried to make her leave. Her hair was very long and black. She was fine-boned and very pretty.

"You insult me and our house" she said, angrily. "You are my first. I am beautiful, don't you have eyes?" Pride and anger mixed in her voice. "In the old days," she continued in a scolding tone, "I would have been given to a *nawab* for my first night and Bismullah would have gotten a great price. Bismullah will be insulted if you do not have me in your bed. She will beat me." Then she began to cry.

"This is *nakhra*," I thought to myself. "She is going to force me to let her stay." I was too tired to fight with her. So she stayed and slept next to me while I slept. We each got what we wanted. I woke early on the rope bed. The girl was fast asleep. She looked even more like a child than she had last night. I was glad I had not touched her. I left quietly.

It was still early and hardly anyone was in the market when I stepped out of the *kotha*. The goods in the stalls that were open looked very poor, though here and there were some fine embroidered goods which caught my eye as possible exports for my Uncle. I walked rapidly out of the town to the Residency Hill and climbed to this broken, shot-riddled stone which I lean against as I am writing this account of my return to Lucknow. Only now, after time has, to some extent, healed my wounds can I sit and reflect in the very place where Umrao and I said we would plight our troth. There is something about my encounter with the young girl at the *kotha* that has eased the hollow place in my heart. Nothing happened between us, but the fact that someone so young and so like Umrao should live gives me hope for the future.

The sun is rising and I begin to feel its heat on my back. I remember Umrao describing this very scene to me when she began to teach me about her music. As I sit in the grass and squint at the waving fronds, I can almost see a golden haired woman and a little boy playing on the side of the hill. When I look up into the cloudless sky, I see Umrao's sleeping face turned toward me. A heat rises in me like that of the new day. On this day and all others that are left to me, I vow, I shall hunt the killers of my beloved.

The End

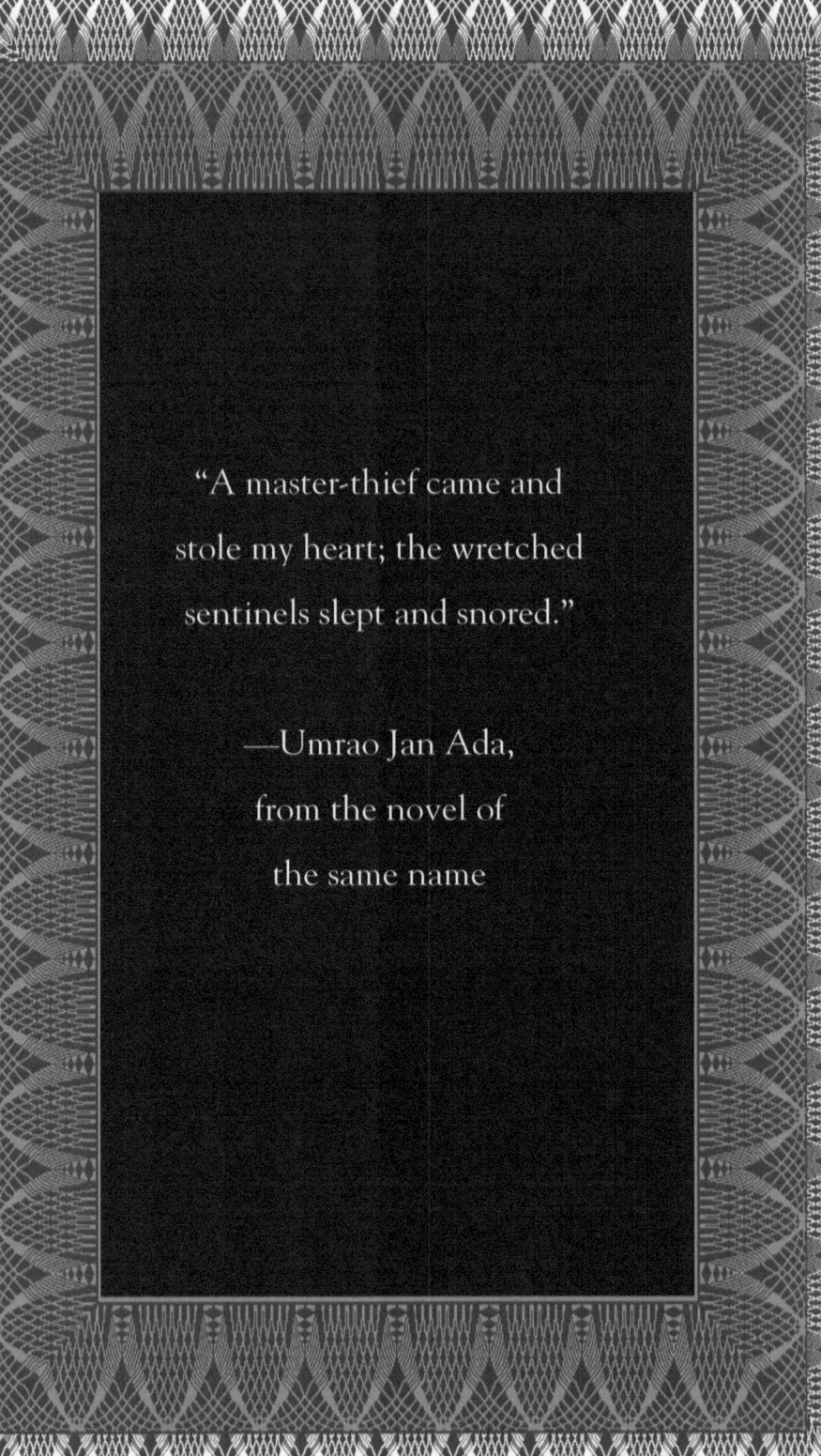

"A master-thief came and
stole my heart; the wretched
sentinels slept and snored."

—Umrao Jan Ada,
from the novel of
the same name

The most sacred site in all of British India

The Memorial Angel at Cawnpore, photographed by Samuel Bourne in 1860

A NOTE ABOUT ALAN MCKEE

Alan lives with his family in Toronto but spends time writing at his second home in Nova Scotia. His special interests are British history and nineteenth century literature. He has been particularly inspired by E.P. Thompson and Eric Hobsbawn, two great British historians.

OTHER TITLES

The Iron Beast
The Minotaur's Children

www.hudsonhousemysteries.com

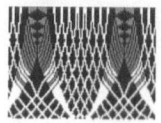